Recoverance
Inc.

Dan Cotton

Recoverance
Inc.

First Published in 2025
Copyright © Philip Mayne

Published by R.Ohm Estate
PO Box 115 Wooroloo
Western Australia 6558
deccotton.writer@gmail.com

Cover design by Philip Mayne
Cover photo – Diana - Pexels.

Our Border Collies Echo and Tika
2010 - 2023

1

Papers cluttered his desk, except for a small area that had become a shrine displaying the last known photo of his daughter. She was pictured sweet and innocent, like any other twelve-year-old kid in her school uniform. Almost three years had passed since Kaitlin disappeared, and though he could not shake the feeling of her being still alive, he'd learned there could be no going back.

Each day that passed gave him hope that she might one-day be returned to him. She was all he had left of his ten-year marriage to a woman who seemed to love him unconditionally despite his myriad of faults. There was no photograph of *her* on his desk. He could no longer bear the memories of Virginia, who caught a bullet from the gun of a cop who was later exonerated. It had nothing to do with her. She'd only been there to remind him it was Kaitlin's birthday, and he should try to be home early for her.

He recalled laughing and brushing off her comments. 'Of course, lovey. I wouldn't miss it for the world,' were the last words she heard him say before the bullet, meant for him, struck her in the heart. The killer, a rogue cop, escaped the consequences, and Clarke Shipton had not forgotten. One day he'd get his revenge, and then it would be, as they said, served chilled.

The door to his office opened slightly.

'Boss?'

'Come in, Kell,' he said.

Kelly Coulson moved cautiously towards his desk and rocked her head in a questioning manner.

'Any news?'

'There're two guys outside. They reckon they've found someone who might be Kaitlin.'

'Where?'

'Bosnia.'

Clark Shipton put his head in his hands and, without looking up, said, 'Brothel?'

Kelly showed no reaction. 'It might not be as bad as it seems.'

He looked up at her, his face creasing with an angry frown, as he snapped, 'How could there be anything worse than that?'

'The embassy will be looking into it. They say if there's proof it's Kaitlin, they'll have her home within a week.'

'Drugs?'

'Serious addiction likely.' She dropped a printout of an email on his desk. 'This has the location and the name she is working under. They say her papers appear genuine for her new surname, and that might stall the embassy effort.' She dropped another piece of paper onto his desk. 'They also gave me this.'

Shipton's expression froze. He looked across at the framed photograph of Kaitlin when she was twelve. In the picture Kelly had just handed him, her once clear bright blue eyes were blackened around the rims, the dimples on her cheeks replaced by sunken hollows. 'It's her. It's definitely her.' He instinctively pressed the new photo against his heart. 'Any ideas?'

Kelly dropped a manilla folder onto his desk. 'They say they're ex-special forces and they specialise in what they call recoverance.'

'What are you waiting for?'

'Pricey, boss, and before you commit, you should meet them and make a value judgement.'

'How long will that take?'

'How long have you got?' Kelly stepped back and pulled the door open to allow entry to a pair of dishevelled strangers with three-day-old beards. 'I give you Bib and Bub.'

'What!'

Bib took a pace forward and dropped into a visitor's chair. Despite his appearance, the man spoke with a cultured English accent and said, 'We don't do things by halves, Mr Shipton, sir, and we have the credentials to prove our success ratio.' He signalled to Bub, who took the seat alongside him. 'My colleague, he's a bit rough around the edges, I'll give you that, but we make an excellent team.'

Shipton turned towards Kelly and mouthed, 'What the fuck?'

'Like I said, boss, they don't come cheap, and you'll need to make your own value judgement.' She left him in the company of Bib and Bub and pulled the door shut behind her.

'Now we're alone, Mr Shipton. Let me introduce the team. Major David Ashton-O'Sullivan, SAS and MI6 retired.' He pointed to himself. 'Yours truly, and we needn't go into the reasons for my early retirement. This is Staff Sergeant Robert Clayton, Ex Australian SAS, and before I go any further, we approached your people, not the other way around. We also know of your history, and your somewhat dubious relationship with the constabulary.'

Bib handed Shipton a proforma account. The top line said, "Recoverance Inc".

'Fuck!'

'Take it or leave it.' Bib said.

They stood as one and were about to leave when Shipton stopped them. 'This is a hell of a lot of money for just a deposit.'

'She's your daughter and, from what we're hearing, it might be a pittance in the longer term.'

Bub spoke, 'My daughter was in a private rehab facility followed by jail. I wasn't there for her as a father, and she fell into the wrong company. Rehab cost the proverbial arm and leg, and then jail. That was free, but she's worth every cent to me, and I'd like her to get her life back for both our sakes.'

Shipton turned to Bib and said, 'If I give you the go ahead for this little excursion, what will I get?'

Bub spoke with a wry smile. 'You think of it as a little excursion?'

Shipton squirmed. 'I didn't mean that exactly…'

'You'll get your daughter back alive and in one piece. How we achieve that will remain commercially in confidence, and the day before you take her in your arms, Mr Shipton, you will pay the balance plus any contingency.' Bub pointed to the total sum at the bottom of the page.

Bib smiled. 'Despite his appearance, Mr Shipton, he really is an old softy, you know.'

'Bib and Bub?'

'You're thinking, who'd employ a pair of ugly nutters who call themselves Bib and Bub?'

The more he fronted these men, the more he began to realise

they had more going for them than a pair of stupid names. Clark Shipton sucked in a deep breath, etched his signature at the bottom of the proforma, and reached for his cheque book.

'Sorry, sir. Cash only and we understand that cash will be difficult to obtain at short notice, but you're the one in a hurry. We have all the time in the world.'

'I'll have the deposit by close of business today.'

Bib extended his hand. 'Pleasure doing business with you, old chap.'

A moment after they left, Kelly burst into the room. 'You've signed them up?'

Shipton's face turned red. 'I've promised them a 50% deposit, up front, by COB today.'

'Shit. The gum nut babies. I hope you know what you are doing, boss.'

Shipton shrugged.

***

Mickey Krakauer stretched out on his settee with his head resting on Jackie Morton's lap. 'Coupla days and we can make proper plans, hey? Jack.'

'I never thought this would happen, Mick.' She tousled his black hair and leaned over to kiss him on the lips. 'Who'd a thought it?'

'We're a weird bunch, aren't we? Five of us signed up to be cops on the same day. One is now the Commissioner of Police. One is a DI, another is dead, and there's me and my ex-cop jailbird lover.'

Jackie screwed his hair in a knot and slapped his cheek. 'Soon to be a fully pardoned ex-cop jailbird, mister. You'd better not forget that.'

Mickey's phone shattered their brief romantic interlude. 'Kell?

What's up?'

…

'Shit, when?'

…

'Is he serious?'

…

'Should I come over?'

…

'Okay, okay, I'll see if I can get a bead on them in the system. I guess if they go under the names of Bib and Bub, it should be easy enough.' The line fell silent, and he rolled his eyes. 'That was Kelly Coulson. Clarkie Shipton has just signed up a couple of reputed ex-SAS blokes to recover his daughter from a brothel in Bosnia.'

'So, what has that got to do with us?'

'There are still a lot of kids missing. If they're successful and the word gets around, there'll be all kinds of incompetent wannabes signing folk up.'

'How do you know the mob Clarkie's signed up are incompetent?'

Mickey shook his head. 'I don't think they are. A while ago, I heard something about a couple of guns for hire. These guys were super clinical and left no forensics worth mentioning.'

'Bib and Bub?'

'Not sure.' He looked at his watch. 'I think I might pop over and have a chat with Clarkie. We've been sorta, "best of mates", ever since we closed down the Gregory mob.'

'Well, don't be late. I'm still all jittery about the pardon, and I'll be needing a cuddle.'

2

Clark Shipton re-read the first line of the proforma, shook his head and looked up. 'Recoverance Inc… Have I done the right thing, Kell?'

'Only time will tell, boss.' She handed him the briefcase containing the promised cash. 'I asked Mickey Krakauer to run them through his system, but I wouldn't hold out much hope of him finding anything.'

'Maybe that's a good thing. His girl is about to receive a pardon, isn't she?'

'Jackie? Yeah, cost her ten inside. They had a thing for years and then Slippery Clitheroe put the mockers on it.'

'I thought you and Krakauer were once connected?'

Kelly frowned. 'It was never to be. Still like the bastard, though. I dunno. If I could live my life again… maybe?'

'You and me both, Kell. I've never asked you, but…'

She cut him off. 'I don't think we're compatible, boss. Anyway, I like my life as it is.'

'Sorry.'

'Don't be. I could never replace Virginia in your eyes, and that would make it difficult for everyone.'

Clarke Shipton had been a career chancer for as long as he could remember, and now, in his later years, he had no one he could trust enough to not cut him off at the knees if the circumstances warranted it. 'Maybe Kaitlin will fill the hole.'

'Jeez, I hope so, boss. I've been getting a bit worried that people are starting to like you. Not everyone dumps cash into remote indigenous communities the way you've been doing it lately.' Kelly lifted the front page of the West Australian. **COR! Clarkie's Outback Revival**. It was a stupid pun, but the smiling faces, pictured at the front of a newly opened health clinic, said it all. 'Good pic of you and the premier, and is that Mickey Krakauer in the background?'

'Who'da thought Clarkie Shipton might one day be seen as a philanthropist?' Shipton said

'Coffee?'

'Nah. Better take this to the guys before I get all excited and give it to another mob.' He lifted the briefcase and headed down to the street.

Bib and Bub were waiting for him, as arranged, in a small bistro a few metres up Beaufort Street.

Bib stood as he entered, shook his hand and, in a quiet cultured voice, said, 'Good to see you, sir.' He indicated that they should both sit. 'As a demonstration of our mutual trust, we will not count the contents now, but we will advise you of any discrepancy when the next payment is due and if any adjustments are needed. The next few days will be somewhat tortuous for all of us, so you must try to be patient. All recoverance comes with significant risk, but we have already scoped out your daughter's location.' He raised his hand and said, 'Three coffees, please.' When the young waiter caught his eye.

'Adjustments?'

'Mr Shipton, sir. You are putting your trust in us, and it would be crass of us to open a case full of money in public. I feel we are on the same plane, and mutual trust works best. Don't you agree?'

'You can be sure that the contents exactly match fifty percent of the figure on your proforma, and I want my daughter back. In one piece.'

The waiter arrived with their drinks, and the conversation relaxed a little.

'We will be on site in two to three days, and we have already arranged transport out of Bosnia.' Bub tapped the briefcase. 'There'll be backhanders and locally purchased supplies. Once they are taken care of, we will make our move. The next thing you will hear is the sound of your daughter's voice. I must warn you, that might not be an easy listen, Mr Shipton.'

Shipton sipped his coffee and closed his eyes. *If Mickey Krakauer and James Carter hadn't brought down the traffickers, I'd still be looking.* He stood. 'Then I won't take up any more of your time, gentlemen. Just find her and bring her home.' Bib seemed about to speak, but Shipton silenced him by walking from the bistro, his shoulders quivering as he struggled to hold his emotions in check.

He mostly had himself under control by the time he reached his office, but recognising his unusual distress, Kelly drew him into a hug and said, 'It's a hug don't take it as anything else.' She felt his shoulders quiver and pushed him away. 'You've made the first move. Now it's up to them, boss.'

'Thanks, Kell.' He turned and walked through the door of his office and closed it behind him.

She picked up her mobile and tapped Mickey's number.

He answered immediately. 'I'm just on my way over. Is he okay?'

'Scared shitless, Mick. He once threatened to kneecap a bloke and he wouldn't have batted an eyelid, but this…'

'There's nothing on record relating to Bib and Bub. I'm thinking that might be a good thing.'

'They reckon if it goes according to plan, she'll be home in a few days.' Kelly looked up as the main door opened. 'You're here already.'

Mickey Krakauer grinned and pointed to Shipton's office.

'Go easy on him. I've never seen him so fragile as this.'

'How the mighty have fallen, hey?'

Kelly frowned and Mickey pushed through the door to see Clark Shipton sit forward at his desk and rest his head on his arms.

He looked up and heeled the moistness from his eyes with the palms of his hands. 'Sit.'

Mickey took the nearest visitor chair and lowered himself onto it. 'Kelly reckons a week, maybe.'

'They reckon she'll be a basket case. The bastards have had her on drugs since they took her.'

'What'll you do?'

'Get her into rehab at the first opportunity.'

'You know what that means?'

'She'll probably hate me, and I'll never be sure she's kicked the shit they've fed her with.'

Jackie has some experience in rehab. I know she'd like to help.'

'I'm not the only one, Mick. What about all the other families who haven't had the resources to find their kids?'

'To be fair, Clarkie, the embassies are probably doing their best, but they're hogtied with red tape.'

'That's why I've hired Bib and Bub.'

'Do you have their real names?'

Shipton showed Mickey the proforma and the other paperwork.

'Maximum confidentiality. If this was army or navy, they'd call it Top Secret. Can I take it you don't know exactly who they are?' Mickey stood. 'Don't do anything stupid, Clarkie. Okay? You have my number. Call me if you need to.' He left the building and tapped a number on his phone.

'Mickey, what can I do for you?'

'Clark Shipton has just engaged a couple of guys to extract his daughter from a brothel in Bosnia.'

'Not my jurisdiction mate, you know that.'

'Just keeping you posted, boss.'

'Thanks for that.'

'You're welcome, sir.'

'Okay, Mickey. What's on your mind?' James Carter asked.

'How many of the trafficked kids have been found? Apart from those we rescued, before they were spirited out of the country.'

'The diplomats have managed to find a couple, but once they hit another country, we're stuffed. Even you should know that.'

'Bib and Bub have found Clarkie's kid.'

'What are you saying?'

'Maybe we should be working with them…'

'Ha, come on mate, we can barely work with our Eastern States colleagues.'

'Shame about that, init.'

'I'll have a word with Arty next time we have a beer.'

'Might be too late. Kelly reckons Clarkie's kid is already a full-on addict. She's been gone almost three years and is lucky to still be alive. She's not yet 16 years old.'

DI James Carter remembered how his own son and daughter were captured as part of a scheme to keep him from progressing an investigation. They were lucky, and he was able to free them before it became a disaster. 'Okay Mickey. I'll call him, but don't expect too much.'

'Thanks, boss.' He pressed end and tapped Jackie's number.

'All good?'

'Who knows? The next few days should see it sorted, one way or the other. See you soon.' Mickey left Shipton's office, walked to his car and felt a hand on his shoulder before he could open the door. He turned to see who it was and felt the barrel of a small pistol press against his stomach.

3

G et in the car and drive.'

Mickey didn't recognise the man who had just hijacked him. 'You understand I'm a cop, I hope.'

'I know exactly who you are, Mickey Krakauer. Just drive. I'll give you directions.'

Mickey looked down at the pistol in the man's hand. It was fitted with a silencer, which made it illegal despite the action he was indulging in. 'Dinky little toy, you got there.'

The man grinned, removed the magazine, and unloaded the weapon. 'Walther PPK. Some call it the James Bond gun. This model is favoured by genuine assassins. It shoots a .22LR, but a .22 in the brain is as deadly as a 20mm cannon. Best thing is, it's almost silent with minimum blood-spatter.'

'You didn't introduce yourself.'

'I didn't. My bad, as they say.'

'You're not from these parts.'

'No. Your friend Clark Shipton has engaged me and my colleague to return his daughter to him.'

'From a brothel in Bosnia?'

'You are a member of the local constabulary, and what my

colleague and I are about to do skirts the edges of legality, Mr Krakauer. Our work requires us to operate in complete secrecy. We will probably be breaking every international law, and we may even be forced to eliminate the occasional bad type.'

'So where are we going?'

'You'll find out sooner if you drive.'

Mickey started the car. 'Let's go then.'

'Take me to the airport. I'll direct you from there.'

'Clarkie says you're ex-SAS.'

'Does he?'

Mickey shrugged.

'If you know too much, you might be a danger to us, Mr Krakauer.' He slipped the magazine into the PPK and racked, 'There are heaps of missing kids.'

'And that is why we require complete secrecy for our operation. If the word gets around that we can do what we say we can, our future work will be made much harder.' The man pointed to a gate at the airport perimeter. 'You can drop me there.'

Mickey did as he was asked, and the man turned to shake his hand.

'Thank you, Mister Krakauer. We *are* honest-ish sorts, and we're only here to help.' He put a finger to his lips and handed Mickey what looked like a blank business card. Then, before hauling himself from the car and making a beeline for the gate, and the small jet beyond. He turned and said, 'There's a number on that card. Find it and use it if you hear of anything we should know about.' He paused, then spoke again. 'Let it ring out and try again three more times. If someone answers you before the fourth attempt, it's because the number's been compromised, and I hope you will know what to do. If not, ring again in exactly one hour. I'll be expecting you.'

Mickey scratched his head as the man left and was about to call James Carter. Then he decided that perhaps he should keep mum about this little sojourn with the wiry, unshaven man, with a plummy voice like a pommy lord. He watched the aircraft roll forward and begin taxiing to the main runway. *Well, Clarkie, I hope you know what you're doing.* He looked down at the card, flipped it over, but could see nothing that resembled a number.

***

'Sorted, boss?'

'He'll be fine. He'll have a word with Shipton about loose lips, and that will be that.'

'Next stop Podgorica.'

'I wish. Stop over for fuel, but we won't be leaving the plane.'

A young flight attendant handed them each a meal and a bottle of wine to share.

'Thank you, but no,' Bib said. 'Iced water will be fine.'

She removed the bottle, and the moment she left, Bub said, 'There's a car waiting, and we'll have around a sixty-k drive to Sarajevo. The border will be no problem, and once we've completed the pickup, I've a light plane arranged to take us to Belgrade, where we'll board a commercial flight to Australia.'

'Well then… that's it then… init,' Bib said. He pulled the lamb cutlet from his small plate with his fingers, chewed the meat off the end and said, 'I think we might need a decent feed in our bellies before we head to Sarajevo.'

'You must be getting old, boss. You always said you fight

better on an empty stomach.'

'It will be a failed mission if we're forced to fight, Bub. I want us in and out with the girl in tow, before anyone notices she's missing.'

Their plan was simple and relatively foolproof. Bub would pose as a client, pay his fee, and take her to her room. Once there, he'd sedate her. Bib would turn up like a raging drunk and demand access to the girls. In the ensuing fracas, Bub would sneak her from the building, drag her into their waiting car and hit the road.

Bib would calm down, pacify the brothel boss with a handful of US dollars, then stagger drunkenly into the night.

Both men were fluent in Croatian and would be discretely armed with a lethal weapon that they had used to great effect. Their ratchet garrottes were made of a fine twine containing *Dyneema*, a polymer fibre 5 times stronger than steel. Invisible to metal detectors, and even in a pat down they'd be hard to find.

Bub was to drive the girl to a predetermined place and await the arrival of Bib. There would be no concession allowed for being late, and then, with or without him, within one hour of the commencement of the operation, Bub would drive to the private aerodrome. 'Easy peasey,' he muttered, and as he reclined in his seat for a doze, he smiled. *The gum nut babies saving kids, who'd a thought it. Thanks, May.*

*****

Mickey arrived home to an enthusiastic welcome from Jackie. He gave her a hug and said, 'Why are you so happy?'

She showed him the email from the Aboriginal Legal Service. 'It's all done. I'm an innocent woman, and I'm so glad that I'd sent out a load of wedding invitations in anticipation of the result.'

'Not that innocent, I hope,' he said, giving her a squeeze.

She took hold of his hands and brought them to her lips. 'I know you're established in the city now, Mick, but have you ever thought of going back to country when we're... you know?'

'Do you miss it?'

'Always will, Mick.'

Mickey's mouth widened into his characteristic grin. 'Just so happens. I spoke to Jimmy Carter last week. He says he'll keep an eye open for a placement.'

Jackie pulled away and opened the fridge to extract a bottle of Australian sparkling. 'Not your actual champers, but then us being dinky die an all that.' She popped the cork, filled two jam jar tumblers, and handed him his.

They chinked, and he'd barely taken a sip when a loud knocking disturbed them.

'Probably nothin.' He stood and walked to the door and saw two shadowy outlines through the glass. *Not Bib and Bub back already?* He opened the door to two men dressed in suits. 'Um... We don't do your God, mate. Thanks anyway.'

The taller of the two flashed an ID that looked official. 'You need to come with us, Mr Krakauer.'

'Who the hell are you?'

'You don't need to know that.' The shorter of the two pulled a Glock from the pocket of his jacket. 'We can do this the easy way or the hard way.'

Guns in pockets? Hardly professional, Mickey thought. 'I'm going nowhere, with anyone, until I know who you are and why you are at my home.'

'Very well, you leave us no choice.'

Before Mickey could respond further, his wrists were bound with a zip tie. Another was pulled over his head and tightened across his mouth so that he could barely emit a cross between a gasp and a squeak. Then they blindfolded him with a black hood over his head.

The tie around his hands was bad enough, but the one around his mouth was painful. He felt himself being hoisted into a van and slid along its metal floor until his head struck a step behind the front seats.

The two men boarded the van, and Mickey felt the driving style go from city roads to country. Eventually, the taller reached around to release the mouth tie. 'Sorry about that. You are now free to tell us everything you know about two men who you are in contact with. We know them as Bib and Bub.'

Mickey spat blood onto the van's deck and spluttered. 'Nothin. I know nothin.'

'Very well, it's such a pity you are making this difficult.' He lifted the hood from his head and held up his mobile phone to display a video of a woman similarly strung.

Mickey recognised Jackie from her eyes. The only part of her face that could define her pleading. 'You hurt her and…'

The taller man laughed. 'And you'll do what?'

4

James Carter checked his emails. There was one from Jackie Morton. She'd forwarded an email from the ALS. He smiled. 'Good for you, Jack, now you can get on with your life.' He jotted a short message in reply, sent it, and decided to pop in on his friends on the way home. 'A decent bottle of something is needed here, methinks.'

It had been a long time coming for Jackie, who was inadvertently caught up in a crooked cop's machinations, and paid the premium penalty, probably because she was a cop and also indigenous. Ten years was longer than most would have got, but she'd received fifteen, was out on parole, and could have been sent back inside for even a minimal infraction. Now, Mickey and she could move on. Mickey had said he wanted to get back to country, and while he'd miss his larrikin ways, he knew it would be best for them both in the longer term.

He picked up a decent champagne from the bottle shop on the way, and when he arrived, he was surprised to find no one at home. 'Jack!' he shouted through the front door. 'Is everything okay?'

It was then that he noticed a smear of recently leaked blood on the door frame. 'Mick! Are you in there?'

There was no reply.

The hair on the back of his neck rose. He followed the perimeter of the house around to its rear and peered in through the sliding door of the family room. It was locked, and the inside was generally tidy, but there were things definitely out of place. Rather than smashing the door, he found a bedroom window and used the champagne bottle as an enforcer.

Once inside, he noticed more blood smears and decided he should call it in. While he awaited backup, he checked the security CCTV, and his questions were answered. Mick had been dragged from the front door to a vehicle parked in the driveway. Sometime later, a different crew had taken Jackie. Her wrists were tied, and she appeared to have some kind of gag across her mouth. One of her assailants was a tall man with a pronounced limp.

'Shit, guys, what did you do to these people?'

There was no answer.

This was now a crime scene, and he needed to be super careful until the forensics people arrived on the scene. He called in his request and soon afterwards a police van arrived with a team who began sealing off the street.

'DI Carter, sir. You were first on the scene?'

'That's right. They are friends who'd just received some good news.' He noticed he still had the champagne bottle in his hand. 'Jackie Morton sent me a copy of the email she'd received from the ALS saying she'd won her appeal. Pretty big thing, don't you think?' He directed them to the security footage. 'I have no idea who these people are, or why they might have targeted Sergeant Krakauer or Jackie Morton.'

The senior sergeant who had led the group said, 'You smashed the window to gain access, sir?'

James held up the bottle, still covered with condensation.

'Any idea why a cop and his girlfriend might have been taken in this way? They are indigenous, aren't they?'

'Are you trying to make something of that, Sergeant?'

The sergeant's face coloured slightly. 'Maybe...'

'Maybe what?'

'I'll have to take over, and you must step away from the investigation, sir.'

James knew why. It was common knowledge that he was close to Mick and Jack, and their recent history had placed them on a small pedestal. 'I'll leave you to it sarge, please keep me posted.'

James had no intention of standing back. He found his car and continued to his home. Stacey might wonder about the champagne, but he was sure he could explain that away.

***

The aircraft touched down, taxied to a halt near a plain brick building on the edge of the Podgorica International Airport, and Bib looked out of the window to see a small group of uniformed officials waiting to assist with their immigration. He unzipped his carry-on bag, removed a wad of US dollars, and jammed them in his back pocket. Bib knew the fee, and he knew the man who would be pocketing his reward. He raised his hand, and the man gave an almost imperceptible nod in reply.

They stood, picked up their bags and headed to the exit ladder, from where they felt the instant shock of the Montenegro winter as they descended to meet the group of officials.

The man who had nodded earlier made the first approach and spoke almost inaudibly over the aircraft's engines. 'You have the agreed?'

'Not here.'

The man turned to lead them into the building. Once inside, the heat was a relief. Then another man entered the room and flipped the relief to tension.

'Major David Ashton-O'Sullivan?' He held out his hands to receive their passports and spoke in English. 'I am Dragomir Kosanović, but you know that. What is the purpose of your visit to Montenegro?'

This wasn't supposed to happen, Bib thought. They were travelling on Israeli passports, using false names provided by Mossad for a previous engagement. 'You must be mistaken, sir,' Bib said, handing him the fakes.

The man laughed, raised a hand, and four men stepped forward to take control of the interlopers and frisk search them.

'Well major, what do we have here?' The man held up the wad of US dollars, turned to Bib's immigration connection and said in Croatian, 'Do you know what is this?'

The man shrugged as if he had no idea.

Kosanović raised his hand again. The four men who were holding Bib and Bub released them. He spoke in Croatian again and dismissed them all. When they'd vacated the room and the door was closed, he said, 'Old friend, you have put me in a very difficult position.' He held up the fake passport. 'We both know who you and your friend are.'

Bib swallowed his shock and said calmly, 'So what do you intend to do?'

Kosanović smirked, opened the passports and stamped them with visas. 'You know me well, David, so you should know I do not tolerate the bribery of public officials.'

Bib nodded towards the money still in Kosanović's hand.

He smirked. 'I will see that this finds a place in a lost children's charity.' Kosanović pocketed the wad, and said, 'You are not armed?'

'We sort of came in peace.'

'Then go in peace, my friend, but watch your back. There are many whose fortunes you might be upending with your plan.'

Bib and Bub left the airport to find their car. It was fuelled up and a quick check of the boot confirmed their equipment was in place.

'What the fuck happened there?' Bub said as he drove into the freezing night.

Bib shook his head. 'Pure luck, old chap. We were at Oxford together and I dragged his drunken stinking carcass home to the digs more often than I'd care to remember.' Bib paused. 'We cannot trust him. He knows who we are, he knows why we're here and for all we know, he might even be involved in the trafficking.'

'The upending of plans?'

'There are only two people who know of our operation, Shipton, and his PA, unless… If the circumstances were different, I'd abort.'

'Should we?'

He shook his head. 'He's given us a heads up but as he said, we'll need to watch our backs.' Bib made a mental note to check out Clark Shipton.

***

The room was pitch black, and it was impossible to make out any shapes, but she could hear her own breathing. Jackie Morton realised her hands were free of ties, and she felt her mouth. The taste of fresh blood was still there from the zip tie used as a gag. 'Mick?' she whispered.

There was no reply.

I must have trodden on someone's toes, big-time. She felt around and realised she seemed to be in a room bare of any comfort. *This is your ultimate black out.*

The room lit up, temporarily blinding her.

A tinny voice over a loudspeaker said, 'We'll interview you soon and if your story stacks up with your boyfriend's, you'll be free to go.'

'Who are you?'

'You don't need to know that.'

'Who says?'

'I do.' The door opened and a tall man limped into the room. There was something about his face that unnerved her. She couldn't put her finger on it, but it was familiar.

'Come with me.'

Jackie felt herself being wrenched to her feet and automatically reacted.

'If you make it harder for us, Ms Morton, we can be even more belligerent.'

She ceased resisting and was dragged to an interview room that could have been in any police station in any Australian town.

'Take a seat.'

She did and watched as her captor flicked a switch on a standard recording device. 'Am I being charged with something?'

'Not yet. That might come after we have interviewed both you and your boyfriend. Your full name for the tape, Ms Morton.'

Jackie obliged, but all she could think about was Mick. *Where have they taken him?*

The man seemed to sense her concerns and said, 'Mr Krakauer will be fine. Shall we begin?'

5

Kelly Coulson popped her head around Shipton's door. 'You have a visitor, boss.'

'Who is it this time?' Shipton replied.

'DI Carter. Remember? He was the one who ended Slippery Clitheroe's career.'

'What does he want?'

'Shall I let him in so you can ask him?'

Shipton automatically cringed at the thought of being fronted by a senior cop, he knew James and stood as he approached him, indicating that he should take a seat.

Before Shipton could say any more, James said, 'Mickey Krakauer and Jackie Morton have been abducted. I'm thinking you might be able to help?'

'Abducted?'

'That's what I said.'

'Who'd do that?'

'I was hoping that you'd be able to tell me.'

'I only spoke to Mickey yesterday. He's a good bloke, but I know nothing about a kidnapping.'

'He said he might look into the backgrounds of the two chancers you hired to find your daughter.'

'That's my business. I didn't ask him to do anything. He's a cop, and you'd know how I feel about that.'

'Well, less than twenty-four hours after you signed up a couple of guns for hire, Mickey and his future wife have disappeared. Their CCTV shows them being dragged off in plastic ties.'

'Do you recognise who did it?'

'I hoped you might be able to tell me who they are.'

'Look, DI Carter, I've come to think of young Mickey as a friend, ever since he blew the whistle on those bastards who were trafficking kids. Why would I want to kidnap him? I don't even know his future wife.'

'I think you do, Mr Shipton, but that's beside the point. Two of my people are missing and you were the last person to see them.'

'I'd like to help, but you know how it is.'

James handed him his card, stood, and turned to leave. 'If you hear anything…?'

'You'll be the first to know.'

On the way out, Kelly touched his arm as she closed the door. 'He doesn't know anything, Jim. It was me who asked Mick to run a check on the men. He said he'd try but was of the opinion there'd be nothing to find. Clarkie doesn't know that we had a break in last night. Nothing appears to have been taken, so I didn't want to bother him. I don't suppose it's related to Mickey and Jackie?'

If you hear anything?' James said

'You-betcha. Mickey and I were once… well, a long time ago and I'm glad he's found some happiness.'

James looked hard at Kelly and knew he was judging her authenticity from the simple elegance of her attire and almost bare makeup, which seemed to contrast with her position as the Girl Friday of a well-known wheeler dealer. She could have been the PA of a CEO in the oil industry and there was nothing in her eyes that indicated she might be lying. 'Thanks.'

'I hope you find them.' She glanced down at a white square envelope.

James noticed and said, 'Something else?'

Kelly nodded to the door of Shipton's office. 'He doesn't know it yet, but Clarkie and I have been invited to their wedding.'

James smiled. He hadn't seen any mail, maybe his would be waiting at home. He found his car and headed back to the office, his mind heavy with concerns for his friends and his isolation from their plight.

When he arrived at the office, he made his way to the cyber division where the black curly mop of Mandy Stephenson was bobbing to a tune as she tapped on her keyboard. 'Hey?'

She jumped with fright and yanked out her buds. 'You could have warned me.'

'Sorry. There is some CCTV video coming in from Mickey Krakauer's place. Can you get me a copy? It's important.'

'Mickey? What's he done?'

'Got himself abducted, along with Jack.'

'You realise that I might not be in line to see it when it arrives?'

'Just do your best. All I need is the clips of the people who took them. I've already seen them, so they should be logged as evidence.'

Mandy tapped a few keystrokes and a fuzzy video appeared. 'Not the best resolution, but that's often the case.'

'You already have them?'

She pointed to a date. 'Looks like they were logged a few minutes ago.' She tapped on her keyboard. 'I've just made copies and shifted them to my computer.'

'Can you sharpen them up?'

'I'll do my best.' She glanced at her watch. 'Will tomorrow be soon enough?'

'As quick as you can.'

***

'You have been seen attending the offices of a known criminal who has links to money laundering operations.'

Mickey looked around at the ancient structure they had brought him to, shrugged and said, 'I'm a cop. I visit dens of iniquity every day, as a matter of course.'

'Your friend Clark Shipton seems to enjoy a charmed life. Is it his police connections, perhaps?'

'Am I going to be provided with a lawyer for this interview?'

The man smirked. 'This interview is beyond the common law, Mr Krakauer.' He tossed a sheaf of papers across the desk. 'These are documents we retrieved from your friend's office. There are also extracts of our surveillance notes. You may like to read them before you respond.'

Mickey flipped through the papers and stopped at the copy of an email from the Bosnian Embassy detailing the location of Clarkie's daughter. He tried to suppress his swallow when he saw the series of photographs.

The man noticed his discomfort and smiled. 'Great gimmick, that second barrel, Mick. Did you really think you'd get away with it?'

That was the point at which Mickey recognised his captor. 'Knee still giving you trouble, is it?'

The man scowled.

'Is this what all this is about?'

'You fired your service weapon at my knee.'

'Perhaps you should have been more polite.'

'You then swapped the barrel.' He pointed to a photograph of Mickey's glove box and the unwrapped item.

'And you planted it there.'

'Sadly, Mr Krakauer, that won't work. We know you are involved with criminals, and we know your future wife is currently on parole after serving ten years of a fifteen-year sentence. Don't worry about her. Very soon she'll be back inside a nice warm cell with three meals a day provided courtesy of the government.'

This time, it was Mickey's turn to smirk. 'I'll say no more until I have a lawyer present.'

'Sorry, Mr Krakauer, that won't be possible. Your dealings with Shipton have seen to it that this matter is now a national security issue, and you are being held under the terrorism act of 2005. I'll get you a copy if you like. You'll have plenty of time to familiarise yourself with it.' He signalled to his colleague, who escorted Mickey back to a cell.

***

They crossed the border with ease, their papers having already been authorised by Kosanović meant they were in effect legal.

Bub breathed out the air he'd been holding in his lungs and said, 'I'm glad we're through, boss.'

Bib said, 'I'll drop you off near the location and send you a text when I'm ready.'

'No worries. Let's hope it's plain sailing from here on in.'

Bib said, 'Remember, the minute we pick up the girl, we will be on the wrong side of the law. She's underage and we are planning to take her to another country. In Bosnia that is considered trafficking, and they will throw the book at us if we're caught.'

'Well, we can't be caught then, can we, boss?'

Bib said nothing. He'd been around long enough to know that even the best laid plans could come unstuck. 'It's on Obala Kulina Bana. I'll drop you a hundred metres from the location. Look for the graffiti on the walls outside?' He handed Bub a photo of the building he would be entering and pointed to a downward leading set of steps. 'There's a door entry system. Say Olga sent you. If they query that, just shrug and walk away. They shouldn't, but best to be safe. If there's a problem, we'll apply Plan B.'

'Which is?'

'I haven't decided yet. You know what to do once you're inside.'

Bub opened up the latest picture of Kaitlin on his phone.

'They have a half decent bar, but I don't need to tell you to take it easy. Check around until you see her. Then make your move.'

'What if she isn't there?'

'Then we'll go and come until she is. You might even become a regular. Don't worry, I know she is at this location, and I also know there is a large contingent of those who prefer their girls young. Kaitlin is about to leave that category and when she does, we're likely to lose her to a bullet in the head.'

6

They'd shoved him into a cell like something out of a fifty's movie. It even had a vertical row of steel bars mounted across a small window near the top of the wall above the slab of thick timber that served as a bed. Mickey slumped onto the skinny unpadded bunk and wondered if Jackie knew what had happened. There were no sounds coming from other cells, but he could hear the purring of a small engine, and the floor was dirty with a thick covering of dust that must have accumulated over years of disuse.

'Where the hell am I?' he muttered.

There was no reply.

'Jack!'

Nothing. Not even the sound of an occasional passing vehicle.

He stood on the bunk and attempted to see what was outside, but all he could see was a sheet of rusty corrugated iron that had been propped against the wall, maybe to minimise his visibility.

The window had a glazed panel on the other side of the bars, with an old-fashioned pane of wire reinforced glass, and he'd need something heavy if he were to smash it enough to be useful. He looked around. There was nothing in the cell that could help him. His captors had removed his belt, his shoelaces, and his wallet. As a matter of habit, he reached for his phone. It wasn't there.

Mickey had been in some tight spots during his younger life, and his dad had made sure that he had a good survival skill on country, but this was different. For the first time in his life, he felt helpless.

What made things worse was that he had no idea where he was or even why they had arrested him under the antiterrorism laws. 'Hey!' he yelled at the loudest level he could muster.

Nothing.

How long might they keep me here? He wondered, and again yelled, 'Jack!' just in case she was also there.

Nothing.

***

Bub stepped out of the car, put on a jacket that carried a whiff of stale whisky, and started walking towards the four-storey building that Bib had described. As he walked, he watched their car disappear into the night, and then he was there. A faint sound of music was wafting from the entrance, along with an aroma of something garlic flavoured.

He hadn't eaten for several hours and felt his stomach growl as he sucked in a deep breath and stepped down the stairs towards the door. Next to its jamb was the door entry system mentioned by Bib. It had a video feature, and the moment he pressed the button. An overhead light bathed him in its glow.

A voice spoke in Croat and said, 'State your business.'

Bub replied in the same language. 'I'm a visitor to Sarajevo and last night, I met a woman called Olga. She said this was a fun place where I might meet some interesting young ladies.'

'Olga again,' the voice grunted, and the door opened into a dimly lit lounge in far better shape than the exterior of the building. A man in his thirties held out his hand and said, 'Papers?'

Bub handed him his fake passport.

The man shone a torch on the pages and then on Bub's face, before handing it back and leading him to a bar area.

'You may like to enjoy a drink and then perhaps you make a choice from the menu.'

Menu? He felt hopeful. No one said anything about food.

The man handed him a clip board with two laminated sheets of paper. 'These are the ladies we have available tonight. When you are ready, speak to Maria.' He nodded towards a woman in her forties who was serving drinks to the mostly middle-aged clientele.

Bub found the photo of Kaitlin on the second page near the bottom, and he wondered if that was in order of ranking or customer preference. He ordered a cold beer and nearly choked when she told him the price. Then he leaned back against the bar to take in the general ambience.

There were at least twelve scantily clad, almost childish looking girls draping themselves over potential customers. Bub couldn't see anyone he recognised as Kaitlin but immediately recognised three faces among the customers. He imagined he'd seen them on TV recently but couldn't remember where or when. Taking a sip of his beer, he waited.

After a few minutes, Maria approached him. 'Your beer, okay? You not drink much?'

Bub emptied his glass and ordered a second.

Maria smiled knowingly. 'This your first time here. Not to worry, you will find all our girls loving, and most of all, clean.'

Bub smiled, pointed at the picture of Kaitlin, and waved his hand around the room. 'I like the look of *her*, but I don't see her.'

Maria scowled. 'She is here, but she is bad mannered and is not allowed into the bar area. We have to cater to all fetishes here.' Maria gestured him to follow her and led him into a smaller but similarly decorated room, where three teenage girls in lingerie huddled together on a couch. When they saw him enter the room behind Maria, they hunkered down and tried to ignore him.

Maria grabbed Kaitlin by the arm and dragged her forcibly towards Bub.

He smiled.

Kaitlin scowled and spat in his face.

Maria smirked and let her eyes wash over Bub's taut physique. 'She needs a good beating. You might be the one to deliver it. In many ways.' She pointed to a closed door and held out her hand. 'Short time, five-hundred US dollar. In advance.'

Bub played the dumb tourist and openly counted the cash from the wad he'd jammed into his wallet. 'We won't be disturbed?'

Maria's eyes lit at the sight of the cash. She laughed. 'Better not kill her or it will be another five-hundred.'

While this was happening, Bub noticed Kaitlin's face was growing angrier. Then he saw the darkly coloured track marks on her arm as she wrenched her hand free from his grip, strutted to a door and flung it open.

***

James left Mandy and glanced at his watch. He still had time for one more visit before he headed home to Stacey and the kids. They'd agreed that he'd at least try to be home most evenings so they could all have dinner together and he was struggling to keep up his side of the bargain.

He headed back to Beaufort Street and turned into a tiny side road that had several private dwellings converted to offices along its length. Some had been tastefully renovated, but the one he was seeking had an almost derelict appearance with a small but similarly unkempt front garden. There were no parking bays free nearby, so he continued to a loading bay that he knew would be empty. He parked in the bay, placed a small, laminated sign that said POLICE BUSINESS, on the dash, and then headed to his sister's office.

Six months earlier, Angela's top end legal firm had decreed her SNLR (services no longer required). She was paid out and started working for a pittance, with a small group that provided free legal services to the down and out.

James pushed in through the door and tapped his finger on the small bell on the reception counter.

A woman in her late fifties appeared. She was wearing a name tag that said she was Gloria, and she was carrying a tray laden with cups of tea and some muffins on a plate. 'Sorry, we'll be closed for at least two hours.'

James glanced at his watch. Two hours would take him way past his home time. He flashed his police ID. 'I need to speak to Angela Carter. She's, my sister.'

'Oh. One moment.'

He heard voices and the tray clattering as it was placed on the table on the other side of the part-open door.

The door then opened fully, and a gaunt-looking woman with close cropped greying hair, and wearing a flannel shirt, over ripped jeans, came out.

He barely recognised her. 'Ange?'

She ignored his shock at her appearance and pointed to the reception settee. 'We're about to have a major policy discussion, so you'll need to be quick.'

He sat, and she sat beside him. 'Sorry to interrupt,' he said.

'Did you not see the closed sign on the door?'

Her voice seemed terse and far from how he last remembered her. He shook his head. 'I recall you choosing a bad time to ask me for help once.'

'What is it, Jim? I hardly hear from you for months and then you're suddenly barging into my office and dragging me from an important meeting.'

'Did you get an invitation to Mickey and Jack's wedding?'

'There was something in the post this morning I haven't had a chance to look at my personal mail yet. Is that what all this is about?'

'No. They're both missing. They were taken by some heavies earlier today. The video from their security camera looks bad.' He turned his head towards her but couldn't hold back the emotion.

'Is it because...?'

'It has all to do with the past and, plain and simple, I think I'm about to be sidelined again because of my connections to them, and...' he swallowed hard. 'I've a bad feeling about this, Ange.'

She reached out to put her arm around his shoulders.

Her gentle touch shattered his chances of holding things in, and his head fell to her chest like a little boy who'd just lost his favourite toy.

'I never thought I'd see you like this, big bro. What can *I* do? I've got nothing left in me, since...'

'They don't deserve this shit, Ange. Mickey's never been anything other than a straight down the line officer and Jack was jailed for something she didn't do. They've just received word that her pardon has been granted. They've sent out their wedding invitations, and now this.'

'You say they were taken by heavies. Shipton's mob?'

'No, he's as shocked as I was. Whoever it is, they have some clout and I'm getting the feeling that the level of attention from our mob to their disappearance might be conveniently minimal.'

'Arty?'

'Too early to involve him.'

'Okay. As you know, my fortunes have slipped somewhat, but the denizens of my current deep hear and see things. I'll drop a couple of sneaky questions and see what comes up.' She stood and nodded towards the room she came from. 'Sorry, bro, this meeting really is important.' She dragged him into a hug and said, 'Give my love to Stace and the kids?'

He headed back to his car and removed the laminated sign from his dash, the parking ticket from his windscreen, and muttered, 'Bastard,' before heading for home.

His phone rang as soon as he started his engine. It was his immediate boss, who had stayed in the role after being invited in to suppress activity and find no evidence in the trafficking case.

'Carter. Two of our people are missing. Where are you?'

'Heading home.'

'You can forget that. Get your arse back in here we need all hands to the pumps.'

James tapped end, and then Stacy's mobile number.

'All good?'

'No, Jackie and Mick have been abducted. I'll have to go back in. I'll call...'

The line went dead.

7

The small engine fell silent, and the tiny armoured well-glass light fitting blinked off, but at least there was a skerrick of ambient through the small window. He hadn't heard voices, and certainly not Jackie's. *I hope she's okay.* 'Hello!'

There was no reply.

He hadn't eaten for hours and the place he was being kept in seemed derelict, with probably no facility for catering. It reminded him of the time his dad had sneaked off in the night, after settling him down to sleep, and then leaving him alone in a cave shelter.

Mickey remembered waking up and calling for his dad, to no avail. He'd wandered out and found the almost invisible track they'd used to find the cave. He'd called out again, but there was no reply.

They'd mentioned Jack's parole, so they can't yet know she's been pardoned. There's hope yet. When I don't come home, she'll have Jim Carter on the case and then all hell will be let loose. He lay back on the bunk and rejoined his dad on their outback mystery tour.

He could hear his father's laughter. 'You good bloke, Mickey. I knew you fina way. No worries.'

It was early dawn when his eyes opened after a gust of wind blew the tin. It scraped along the wall and clattered to the ground to wake him. 'Dad?'

There was no reply.

He looked around the cell and then stood on the bunk for a squiz through the small window. There was nothing but scrappy bushland as far as his eyes could see. Then he noticed that white ants had been working on the timber surround of the glazing. He reached up and gave it a shove. It moved, but not quite enough. He grabbed the bars and shook them. The frame came loose easily and showered his bunk with dust and debris.

He heard voices outside. *Will they notice my handiwork?* He shoved the bars back into place, swiped the fragments from his bed, and lay back with his head resting on his hands.

The door screeched open on its rusting hinges, and a stranger handed him a can of warm coke and a barely warm takeaway meal of some kind.

'Bon appetite.'

The door screeched shut, and he was once again in complete silence until, as day approached, the purring of the small engine began again.

***

The door closed behind Bub, and he heard a lock turn. *Shit, didn't expect that.*

Maria's muffled voice answered his silent question through the door. 'You have thirty minutes, then we unlock the door. Enjoy.'

He turned to Kaitlin and spoke softly in Croatian. 'I know who you are and I'm here to help you.'

Kaitlin stripped off her skimpy outfit to lie naked and spreadeagled on the bed.

'That's not what I'm here for.' He reached into his bag, pulled out a loaded hypodermic, and covered with her with the sweater and a pair of trackie daks that he'd brought with him. 'Sorry, a fashion statement I aint got. Give me your arm.'

Kaitlin's face took on a look of puzzlement.

Bub then spoke quietly, in English, 'I'm working for your father. Follow my instructions exactly and you will be at home with your family in less than one week.'

'My dad?'

'Clark Shipton?'

She spoke in English. 'Him? He's a fucking criminal. I want nothing to do with him.' She looked at the hypodermic and smiled. 'You got me a fix?'

'Not quite.' Bub grabbed her arm and turned it to show the tracks. 'The people who did this to you are the real criminals.' He jammed the needle into her upper arm and pressed hard on the plunger.

She pulled away, and the needle came out.

Bub looked at how much she'd taken. 'Not a full dose let's just hope it's enough to work.'

'*They* give me what I need.'

'And what must you do to receive your payment?'

This time, she snarled her reply in Croat. 'It is nothing.'

He tapped Bib's number on his phone and when he heard the ring tone, pressed end. 'I've just sedated you. We haven't much time now. My colleague will be here soon to create a disturbance so that I can get you out of here. We have a plane and papers to take you home, but you will need to cooperate.'

Kaitlin scowled. 'What about the other girls?'

'They are not on my list, and we don't have the resources on this op.'

'I go nowhere without Agnetha and Bronwyn.'

'Were they…'

She nodded towards the door. 'They are my only friends.'

This wasn't supposed to happen. Kaitlin was supposed to walk out meekly while Bib was harassing the management. Carrying her out kicking and screaming would not work, so he tapped a quick text to Bib.

> We have a problem, boss. Three girls
> and one won't go without the others.

Despite Bib's casual disposition, Bub knew in the back of his mind there would always be a fallback. Planning operations like this involved human nature, which always defied logic, and Bib had come from a world that had its own distinctive methodology.

> I'll be there in five. Get them ready.

> I'm locked in with the subject. The
> others are outside.

> Easy lock?

> I've seen worse.

> Can you get to the others without
> alerting?

> Back room, it might be possible.

> Do it and text a thumb up when done.

Bub noticed Kaitlin staring at him. 'We're changing the plan. You will need to convince your friends to come. If you can't. Say so now.'

'I can.'

'Good girl. I'm about to pick this lock. Will there be anyone on the other side?'

'They don't come near us unless a weirdo wants our bodies. A weirdo like you, I guess.'

For the first time Bub thought he noticed a twinkle in the girl's drug dulled eyes. 'My partner's brought enough stuff to get *you* home. We weren't expecting three.'

'I will manage and share.'

Bub pulled out his lock kit and dropped to one knee beside the door lock.

A knuckle rapped. 'Five minutes.'

He gestured to Kaitlin to hide the travel clothes, while he put away his lock device and stood, before dropping his trousers and throwing them on the bed. 'I'll take another thirty minutes.'

Kaitlin leapt forward and flung her arms around him just as the door opened and Maria entered with her hand held out for more dollars. 'You must be some special kind of weirdo. One-thousand dollar US.'

'You said five-hundred.'

'Inflation and weirdo tax. One-thousand. Take it or leave it.'

Bub was now in a spot of bother. He had only a little over five-hundred left. He stepped back from the door and pulled out his wallet. 'Okay.' He reached into a pocket on its side and palmed a small coil of yellow string with leather loops. He handed his five-hundred to Kaitlin and Maria reached out to grab and count it. It was enough of a deflection, and the last sound Maria heard was the squeak of the ratchet as the garrotte tightened around her neck, almost to the point of severing her head.

Of all the horrors Kaitlin had seen in her young life, her captor struggling to live while falling to the floor was the most horrific. She gasped and almost fainted.

Bub shook her by the shoulders and said, 'Where are the others?'

She pointed a quivering hand to the room outside.

'Speak to them. We don't have much time.'

Maria's leg gave a final twitch, and Kaitlin gasped again.

'Now!'

Kaitlin tottered outside, and Bub dragged Maria's body to the side of the bed that would make it invisible from the door. He then released the ratchet of the garrotte, removed it from her neck, and re-coiled it into the pocket of his wallet.

The next thing he heard was a drunk singing an ancient Croatian love song and swearing at the man who had let him in. He looked into the main room and saw the chaos of clients scrambling for cover, in case the phone the man was waving around might lead to photographs. He grabbed Kaitlin's hand and dragged her towards the door.

She, in turn, towed her two friends.

The doorman yelled, 'Maria!'

There was no response, and Bib silenced him with a single strike from an empty fake champagne bottle.

All five rushed up the stairs to their waiting car and clambered in.

Bib started the engine and gunned it in the direction of the airport. 'We have a major problem, guy, and galls.'

'I am sorry. It is my fault.' Kaitlin slurred in Croatian. The sedative had kicked in, and her eyes had begun to droop.

'You can speak English now, missy.'

'Yes, thank you.' She began scratching at her face.

'They'll all need a fix soon, Bib.'

'They'll have to wait until we're on the plane.'

Bub looked at Kaitlin.

Her eyes were rolling, wide, and staring. 'Soon please,' she whimpered.

8

DCI Callum Birchmore scowled as James Carter entered his office. He pointed to a chair and said, 'Sit, DI Carter.'

James followed orders and sat.

'We've never seen eye to eye, have we, Carter?'

'It's been difficult, sir. Perhaps we just got off to a bad start.'

'They say you're close to the commissioner.'

'We joined the Police Academy on the same day. He's a senior officer. I respect him, and I follow his orders.'

'Word also has it that he might be up for replacement.'

'I'm sorry, sir. I thought I was called in to help find Sergeant Krakauer and his fiancé?'

'That is not a priority, DI Carter.' Birchmore dropped an A4 sheet onto the desk in front of James.

'What?'

'Serious stuff, terrorism, particularly in view of the failure of the voice referendum.'

'Mickey? Mickey fucking Krakauer? Mickey Krakauer, a fucking terrorist?'

Birchmore smirked. 'They say he was also in the same intake as the commissioner: yourself, Jaclyn Morton, and your deceased girlfriend, DS Jennifer Crawford. I could say a few things about that piece of work, but I won't. Quite the little gang, aren't you?'

James knew Birchmore was trying it on. He also knew he was in danger of losing his cool. He suppressed his anger and deflected the comment. 'Mickey and his fiancé are not, in any way, terrorists.'

'Have you read the complete docket or just that word?'

James picked up the sheet and slowly read it. When he finished reading, he said, 'This is total bullshit, and you know it.'

'I understand the Federal Police have arrested him and his girlfriend, and they are holding them at separate but secret locations. I have held them off from picking you up, but I'm not sure how much longer I can do that.' He dropped a series of photographs on to the desk beside the paper. 'Recognise anything?'

'It's me. I was visiting my sister's office.'

'Angela Carter. Failed big-time lawyer, and now helper of those supposedly less fortunate.' He dropped another photograph of Arthur Bertram and Angela at a table for two in an intimate restaurant setting. 'This is her, all cozied up with the commish. Bit cozy with him, yourself, I understand.'

James smiled. 'Fuck me, sir, so I have a respect for my overall boss and... is that a picture of two mature and consenting adults enjoying a dinner together?'

'Don't get smart with me, DI Carter. You know very well what is going on there.'

James shook his head in resignation. He felt nothing but despair. 'What do you want me to do, sir?'

'I want you to find out what is happening and keep me informed so that I can inform our colleagues in the Federal Police.' He dropped another set of photographs.

'A plastic bag in a glove compartment?'

'Containing a Glock barrel used to kneecap an officer during a traffic stop?'

'So?'

'So, that glove compartment is in Mickey Krakauer's vehicle. He shot a fellow officer in the knee. At the time, he was accompanied by his fiancé.'

James remembered the limp on the man who he'd seen on the security video. 'I'll look into it, sir.'

'Good. Thank you. You are dismissed.'

James found his car and drove home. Stacey hadn't started dinner, and she threw her arms around his neck the moment he walked in through the door.

'I thought you'd forgotten again. They are beautiful. Thank you so much.'

It was only then that he noticed the vase jammed full of long-stemmed red roses adorned with a ribbon saying, "Happy Anniversary Darling". *Shit.*

Andria and Jack ran out of the dining room shouting, 'Happy anniversary, Mum and Dad.'

James struggled with the bizarreness of the situation, but he took his seat at the table and thought. *Who the hell sent those? I wish I had.*

***

Twilight had begun to descend on Mickey's prison. The purring of the generator had stopped again, and the light in his cell had flickered out. He reached up and removed the bars from the window hole and pushed against the framed glazing. It moved, but not as easy as he hoped it would. He dropped his pants and rolled them around his fist. Then he punched the window as hard as he could.

It fell with a clatter to the ground outside and he replaced the bars and his pants, just in time.

The door screeched open, and another takeaway meal with a warm can of coke was placed on his bed.

'Bon appetite.' The man said and pulled the door shut.

Mickey heard the lock grate as his guard turned the key in its ancient lock.

He muttered, 'That's it until morning,' and opened the bag that contained his meal. It was fish and chips and reasonably fresh. He cracked the can, slaked his thirst, and began to ponder his next move. 'Of course, it *would* help to know where I am. Can't be too far from civilisation if I'm eating fish and chips.'

He finished his meal and removed the bars from the window. His next move would be a struggle, but he took a run, used the bunk to give him a lift, and half dived to squeeze through the window hole. Mickey's broad shoulders provided the greatest obstacle to his escape, but he could now see the outside and, with a bit of a wriggle, he knew he'd be there soon.

He squeezed through to his waist, but his next dilemma was finding a way to land without breaking his neck. There was no room to twist around, and he'd need to catch his full weight on his arms. The ground was bone dry and probably as hard as rock. One false move and he might be dead or in a wheelchair for life.

He continued to wriggle through and squashed his feet together to spread his legs and provide a degree of grip on the window hole. The drop was about one-point-two-metres from the tips of his fingers, and it gave him no margin for error.

Gradually he edged further out and was soon held only by the spread of his knees. 'Here goes nothing,' he said, and swung himself to the side as he closed his legs to release his body. The momentum carried him, and he landed flat on his back.

Mickey lay for a while. The fall had hurt, and he wondered what damage he might have done. He did a quick check around and nothing seemed to be broken. He tried to sit, then he rolled to one side and lifted himself to his feet. *I've done it, and I'm alive. Over to you, dad.*

***

Clark Shipton called Kelly into his office and said, 'Any news, Kel?'

She shook her head. 'They said they'd be on locally purchased burners and won't be talking until they're back on Aussie soil. Sorry boss, I wish I could give you more.'

Shipton leaned back in his chair. 'Have I done the wrong thing, Kell?'

'Only time will tell, but we won't hear anything until they're home, hopefully with your daughter in tow.' She paused. 'Can I get you something? You look totally knackered.'

Shipton shook his head, then he scoured the proforma with his eyes. 'They said a couple of days.'

'You know how things are, and these guys have some serious cred.'

Shipton turned his phone screen towards Kelly. 'Thursday, they should be done and dusted by tomorrow according to this.' He tapped the tip of his finger on the copy of the proforma.

'They also said the operation had an elevated risk. Just sit tight, boss, and wait for them to make contact.'

'Scotch. Neat. Join me?'

Kelly found a bottle and two glasses. She filled his, three fingers, and covered the bottom of hers with a splash.

'How long have you worked with me, Kell?'

'Fifteen years.'

'I'll bet you remember the day you started.'

'Yeah. You were a complete arsehole. Nothing much has changed.'

Shipton grinned. 'Fifteen years, and you've put up with this arsehole all that time.'

Kelly stood to leave.

'Stay, Kell. I need you around more than ever right now.'

She sat and poured a decent measure into her glass.

'Thanks. I didn't have many friends. Then Mickey Krakauer came along and now he's been disappeared by someone. Can we do anything there?'

Kelly looked towards the ceiling. 'There is something. I didn't want to bother you with it. We had an intruder. There was nothing stolen and no damage, but things were moved and...'

Shipton reached into the draw of his desk. He pulled out the proforma. 'This?'

Kelly shrugged.

'So, this intruder might now know what I'm doing?'

9

'Why are our lives so complicated, Jim?' Angela mumbled. The alarm clock was still a way off, screaming at her to get up and she'd tossed and turned all night. Having mentioned Jim's problem to one of her clients, she'd received an answer she'd rather not have heard. Apparently, there was a group of disgruntled ex-cops putting it about that they were feds. She'd made a few calls and had come up with a vague solution.

She'd never seen her brother so low, and she remembered how she'd felt when she believed she'd failed Tom Gregory.

Immediately, dark thoughts filled her mind, and she tried to push them aside, but they weren't going anywhere. She dressed in her jogging rig, picked up her phone and buds, and set off for an earlier than usual run. The music helped take away some of the sting and she ran much longer than usual before she returned to her home and checked on Oliver. He was completely away with the fairies, and she'd need to drag him out of bed to get him ready for school.

She looked down at his innocent face and felt warm inside. *Time for a shower and an early brekkie.*

The walk to her office was relatively uneventful until she tripped over a sleeping homeless person as she approached.

He swore a string of obscenities and pulled his crocheted rug up over his head.

She was first in today, and she filled the kettle for the stragglers. When it boiled, she made herself a cup of instant and as she settled down to make a start on her emails, she noticed something glinting outside her window. She saw the homeless man, and the glint was coming from under the edge of his rug. It was a camera lens, and it was pointing directly at her. She stood, returned to the kitchenette, and picked up the full kettle. Then she walked outside, tipped the boiling water over the man, and kicked his camera into the bushes when he screamed in pain.

'Arsehole!' she yelled, found the camera, and removed its memory card. 'Sue me.' She yelled and stomped back into her office to call her brother.

'You're up and about early.'

'I've just given short shrift to a surveillance monkey disguised as a homeless person. He was lying in wait outside my offices. I stole his camera card. Are you interested?'

'I'll drop by on the way to work.'

'No. I'm scared. I'll come there.'

Twenty minutes later, Angela flashed her legal creds at the receptionist and asked for Detective Inspector Carter.

The woman flashed back a strange look, pressed a button on her console and said, 'She's in reception now, sir.'

...

The woman looked up from her desk. 'What is it in connection with?'

'It's a private matter.'

'She says it's a private matter.'

...

'He's not here at the moment can I get him to call you?'

'Forget it,' she said, and as she turned to leave, a man introduced himself as DCI Callum Birchmore. She knew who he was, and she knew how he'd managed to inveigle himself into the local force. 'Should I know you?' she said.

'Maybe not, but I know you. Please come this way.' He led her to a lift and pressed the up button. When the door closed, he said, 'Your brother is a bit of a loose cannon, Ms Carter, but no matter. Now I have you here. I'd like to ask you a few questions.'

Angela pressed the record button on the digital voice recorder she always carried in her pocket. 'Are you arresting me for something you regard as nefarious, DCI Birchmore?'.

'That remains to be seen, Ms Carter.'

The door opened onto a bland corridor, and Birchmore indicated she should turn right.

'Far enough, Ms Carter. My office.' He pointed to an open door and when they were both inside, he closed it and said, 'Think you're smart, don't you?'

'I beg your pardon.'

'Quite the little team, aren't you?'

'Team? What are you talking about?'

Birchmore laughed. 'Your big brother, The Police Commissioner, an ex-con and her beau the blackfella cop from the bush.'

Angela was gobsmacked by his tone. 'Excuse me. I was happy to answer your questions, but you'll need to subpoena me if you need any more.' She stood and walked out, made straight for the lift, and pressed down.

She was still shaking from the bullying tactics of Birchmore as she sat in the driving seat of her car, turned on her engine and pulled out into the traffic to head for her office.

A car pulled out immediately after hers and stuck steadfastly to her tail. 'I see,' she said, and turned on to a servo forecourt to fill her tank.

The car continued with no indication that she might be of interest.

***

Mickey wandered cautiously around the small crumbling stone and iron building. It looked like it might be the remnants of an early country town. 'That would account for the lock up,' he muttered.

Most of the buildings were derelict, or in the process of falling into anonymous piles of bricks. Then he saw the generator. It was a red Honda, and it had an extension cord leading into the dilapidated building. He now knew exactly where he was, but he followed the lead and found the door to his cell. It was a heavy timber door with black cast iron hinges like an ancient dungeon. He smirked.

The only sound he could hear were birds, and he recognised most of their trills. Youndegin was a police outpost dating back to a time when his people were regarded as little more than wild animals and Mickey could almost hear his father's voice telling him the stories, in his soft and mellifluous way. They'd stayed here for several days, while his dad performed smoking ceremonies to send away the bad things that lurked there.

Though it wasn't home, for a short while it felt like it and he knew he'd need to move on before his jailers returned. The nearest major town was Cunderdin, and he could follow the track or go bush. There was no contest and three hours later he felt his father's breath on his neck, as he stepped onto the Great Eastern Highway, only a few kilometres east of the town.

Mickey's dishevelled appearance meant he had little hope of picking up a ride, so he began his walk into town, where he hoped he might have better luck. At least once there, he could make a telephone call and let Jackie know he was safe.

The hiss of brakes snapped him from his thoughts of Jack and how worried she might be. He climbed the small steps up to the cab window and saw the driver's grinning face.

The man yelled over the noise of the engine. 'Where ya goin, cuz?'

Mickey was about to say Cunderdin. 'Perth or somewhere near?'

'No worries, cuz. I'm heading down to Freo, but I can drop ya.'

Mickey couldn't believe his luck, and when he slumped on to the seat, the driver shoved a pack of sandwiches across. Then he reached over his shoulder and handed him an ice-cold can of coke.

'She makes me healthy stuff, but...'

Mickey saw the man's large gut, grinned, grabbed the sandwiches and began eating like there'd be no tomorrow.

*****

James Carter's phone tooted. It was a text from a number he didn't recognise:

> Hey Boss. In a truck
> headintoperth.
> Need to talk.
> Mick.

The last few days had singed James's sense of trust, and he decided not to answer. For all he knew, it might be a troll with a malicious streak. Instead, he called Angela and asked why she hadn't dropped over the camera card as promised.

'You'd better ask that of that a'hole, Birchmore. He stopped me dead at reception and called me into his office to start giving me a serve. I walked out.'

'You didn't mention the camera card to him?'

'Absolutely not!'

'Where are you now?'

'I'm heading to Oli's school and then home. I've had a gutful today.'

'I'd really like to see what's on that card.'

'Well, you know where I live. Thanks, bro. Sorry, I was a bit short. It's been a shit day.'

The call ended.

10

'When was the last time you had a fix?'

All three shook their heads.

'Five hours? Ten hours?'

Kaitlin said, 'They usually give us a needle at the start of the day.'

'That's good. You'll be almost at the end of its run. Have any of you used Suboxone film?'

Their heads shook in unison.

'Well, this is what I'm going to do.' Bib tapped Bub's shoulder and indicated he should pull over and stop. It was dark, and he switched on the cabin light. 'I have enough to tide you over, but not for the entire journey. It is only a substitute for the shit you are on, and you might not like the results. Problems?'

All three shook their heads.

'They say there's a risk with this but, hey? I'll give you each a piece of film. Pop it under your tongue and let it dissolve. I'm told it tastes bad, so you'll need to put up with that. It'll take between five and ten minutes. Do not swallow it.' Bib removed some paper sachets that resembled sticking plasters from his bag and handed one to each of the girls. 'They say you'll get about eight hours' relief from withdrawal. Okay?'

All three nodded and kept their mouths shut as they waited for the strips to work.

Bub turned off the cabin light and pulled out on to the road.

It wasn't long before the girls' withdrawal fractiousness ended, and they relaxed enough to doze off. Bib said, 'I found out about that stuff just before we left. The last thing we needed was to be pulled up for dope smuggling. Now all we need to worry about is their clients talking to the cops.'

'Somehow, Bib, I think they'll be keeping their heads real low for a while. That place is as secure as anything, and I'm certain the only way in is via the door we used.'

'The aircraft to Belgrade won't be a problem, but we only have tickets and papers for one child, from there to Australia.'

'They'll need some clothes too, Bib. They're not exactly dressed for travel.'

Bib turned around to look at their sleeping passengers. Kaitlin was wearing the trackie that Bub had provided, but the other two were in filmy lingerie that barely covered their intimate parts. 'I didn't want to involve the embassy.'

'Maybe it's time to bite the bullet,' Bub said.

'No, I have a few connections. Before we go any deeper, I'll try them first. Remember, we are well outside of the law on this job, and the embassy might chuck a fit of the wobblies. Once the girls are in Australia, they'll be safe-ish and if we can get some media coverage...'

'Won't that expose our methodology?'

'Not the media I intend exploiting.'

***

James drove his car into a public carpark in Hay Street, parked it, walked to a taxi rank, and gave the driver Angela's address. On the way, he called Mandy and asked if she'd drop over to look at some pictures.

'I'm being watched like a hawk, Jim. There is a touch of nervousness abounding at this nick.'

'Okay, I'll take a look first and if there is anything, I'm sure I'll need your help.'

'Call me.'

The taxi arrived at his sister's house the moment the call ended. He paid the driver, looked around, then headed to her repaired and newly painted door to give his best policeman's knock.

Oliver answered the door and shouted, 'Uncle Jim's here, Mum!'

James patted him on the back and said, 'Kitchen?'

Oliver disappeared into the study.

Angela was in the process of preparing a meal. It looked like something with chicken, and she was loading it into a heavy cast iron frying pan. 'Chicken cacciatore. Never made it before.'

'A weird thing happened yesterday. My wife got all excited about a huge bunch of roses.'

'I'm sorry. I knew you'd forget and…' She lidded the heavy pan, hoisted it into the oven and closed the door, before clapping her hands like a baker who'd just finished kneading his bread.

'Thanks,' James said and raised his eyebrows questioningly.

'I can cook, you know.'

'No, the um…'

'Ah. Yes. Do you have your lap top handy? Oli's using mine to do his homework.'

'I'll get it.' He stepped outside and remembered his car was in Perth. 'Sorry!' he called as he returned to the kitchen to find Angela standing with a gun to her head.

The man holding the gun had blisters on his face, and an angry expression. 'Camera card or…'

'Where is it, sis?'

'In my handbag in the bedroom.'

'Better let the man have it then.' He raised his hands, stepped aside, and nodded towards her room.

The man changed his aim to James and moved closer.

Without warning, Angela opened the oven, grabbed the iron pan and swung it in the direction of the man's head. It made a sound like a dull thud and his pistol fired, sending a bullet ricocheting from the tiled floor. The chicken cacciatore splattered around the kitchen and the man fell to the ground.

James yelled, 'He's fucking shot me,' and joined the man on the floor.

It was hard to tell which was blood and which was the cacciatore, but Angela dragged James away from the mess, and quickly realised he'd only been clipped by the ricochet. She helped him sit up against the kitchen cupboards just as Oliver came through to see what was going on.

'Phone for an ambulance, Oli.'

He retreated to the study, and she heard him speaking calmly on the phone.

James struggled to his feet and shook his head while clutching his bleeding arm. 'That cacciatore was gonna take a while.'

'No cook recipe.' And then she lost it to hysterical laughter.

***

There had been no reply from James, and Mickey was feeling worried when he found a bench in the Midland Gate shopping centre. At least no one dared sit near him. His appearance ensured that. Then he saw a little girl looking up at him.

'Are you poor?'

He looked up and couldn't help but smile. 'No, I'm the

luckiest man alive at the moment.'

'You don't look lucky.'

'Well, it's all relative. You see, I'm actually a policeman and I'm about to be married to the loveliest woman in the world.'

The little girl smiled and then ran into the shop where her mother was paying for her purchases.

A few moments later, the little girl returned, dragging her mother by the hand. 'He says he's the luckiest man in the world, but he smells awful.'

Embarrassed, the woman dragged her kid away, and it was not long before the security guards arrived.

'Come on mate, you can't hang around in here.'

Mickey stood and headed compliantly for the entrance.

The guards stayed a few metres behind until he left the building.

Then he turned to confront them. 'Call DI James Carter. Tell him Mickey Krakauer is here.'

One guard sneered.

The other had an epiphany. 'Aren't you the bloke who got involved with those missing kids?'

'Sergeant Mickey Krakauer. I can't identify myself, but Jim Carter will.' He held out his hand. 'Give me your phone I'll call him myself.'

The demeanour of both guards suddenly changed. The first stepped back, the second held up his phone. 'Number?'

Mickey spelled it out.

'Busy. Sorry mate.' He pointed to a pay phone. 'They're free now. Stay out here until you're ready to go to wherever your home is.'

Mickey sat on a low wall. It had been a bad couple of days, and fatigue was washing over him. He looked up at the payphone cubicle, stood and walked over.

The cable had been wrenched free of the box, and as he stood staring at the damaged handset, a paddy wagon tooted its siren. He turned to look, put the phone back on its hook, and waited for the inevitable.

'Sergeant Mickey Krakauer,' he said when the officer approached him.

'Oh yeah. Pull the other one.' He then arrested Mickey for damaging public property, cuffed him and was about to shove him unceremoniously into the cage when the wagon radio blurted.

The address of the incident sounded like Angela Carter's home. It seemed there'd been an altercation and a senior police officer had been shot. The cop undid Mickey's cuffs and said, 'It's your lucky day. Beat it.' The cop jumped back in the vehicle, and it sped off with its siren blaring.

Great, Mickey thought. *This is getting me nowhere.* He wandered around looking for a working payphone and when he found one, he called Jim's number again.

There was no reply, so he tried Angela.

She picked up instantly. 'Who is this?'

'Mickey Krakauer. I've been trying to raise Jim.'

There was silence at the other end.

'Hello?'

'Shit, is that really you, Mickey or…?'

'It's really me, Angela. Who was shot?'

'Jim. It's only a flesh wound. He's here.'

Mickey heard the scuffling sound of a phone being passed over.

'Did you text me?'

'Yup. You didn't respond.'

'I didn't recognise the number. Mick, there is some bad shit happening. Can you lie low and keep your head down?'

'Sir, I have no money, no ID. I've escaped imprisonment from a ghost town near Cunderdin, and I look and smell like I've been dragged through the stinkiest part of the local tip. Can you let Jack know I'm okay and ask her to pick me up? I'm at Midland Gate?'

There was a long silence before James spoke. 'Sorry, Mick, Jack was taken on the same day you were. We have no idea where she is, and it seems the feds are involved.'

'Claiming we're terrorists?'

'That's what they say.'

'It's what they told me too, but they aint feds. I know one of the blokes who took me. He was a WA cop a year ago.'

'The one you kneecapped.'

'You know about that?'

'Puts me in a bad position, Mick. Please find somewhere to keep your head down as best you can.'

The call ended and Mickey called Clark Shipton.

Kelly answered.

'It's Mickey, can someone pick me up at Midland Gate?'

'Be there in a flash, Hun.'

11

The girls were still fast asleep when they arrived at Sarajevo Airport. Bib drove around the perimeter until he turned into a stub road leading to a gate. He clambered out of the car and tapped on the combination lock. When he was done, it slid open. He returned to the car to drive through and watched it close behind him. In the distance was the glistening outline of a single-engine aircraft and, as he drew close, he could see it was the Beechcraft Bonanza they'd ordered.

He found a set of keys taped under the wing, opened up the plane, entered the cabin, and made his way to the pilot's seat. He then switched on the static power and the gauges lit, showing fuel was as expected. He returned to the car and told Bub to help the girls aboard, then he dipped each of the tanks. He never trusted an unfamiliar weapon, either. He'd been caught before, and only his wits had saved him.

Bub gathered their bags from the boot and hustled the sleepy girls on to the plane.

Bib then excused himself and jogged across to a brick building. The keyring he was holding allowed him access, and he found a locker room. A few minutes later, he was back on board the plane with a couple of one-piece flight suits. 'Sorry girlies, these will have to do.'

Kaitlin smirked as her friend's dressed in the gormless, way too big, outfits. 'Better than running around in your knickers.'

They both grizzled.

Bub made sure they fastened their seat belts, and they sat back to await the next part of their adventure.

Bub remained in the rear, while Bib ran through the checks and eventually fired the engine. In a few minutes, they were taxiing to the main runway, with Bib conversing with the tower. 'They've given us the go ahead, so we'll soon be airborne. There should be some snacks in an Eski behind the rear seats. Enjoy.'

The take-off was flawless, and they had broken the hump of the op. The next problem would be the trip to Australia, and papers wise, now entirely up in the air.

When they'd levelled off, Bub unhitched his seatbelt and opened the large Eski.

It was packed with ice blocks, packs of sandwiches, one shot fruit juice containers and several cans of soft drinks.

He was about to ask for preferences when Bib yelled, 'Pack of anything and a coke, Bub?'

Bub picked up the first sandwich pack and a can of what looked like cola with Cyrillic writing on it and passed it down the plane.

The girls weren't hungry, and they hunkered down with sullen expressions on their faces.

'Tomorrow we should be in Australia,' Bub said.

Their expressions remained the same.

He looked at each of them in turn and thought, *this has been all too easy*.

***

Mickey found the low wall again and sat hunched forward. He

had no idea how long he'd have to wait before Kelly arrived, and there was every possibility the cops would return to pick him up. *That wouldn't be so bad*, he thought. At least he would be with his own kind, and it wouldn't take too long before someone might recognise him.

As it happened, he didn't have to wait that long. He felt a hand on his shoulder, flinched, and offered his hands for cuffing.

'Hey stinky. Come on, we can go back to mine, and you can have a shower.'

He looked up and saw her face. She'd changed so much over the years and today she looked even more beautiful than the day he first met her on a foot patrol down a side street in Northbridge. 'Kell,' he smiled. 'Am I glad to see you?'

She reached out and ignored the stares of passersby as she took his hand and hauled him to his feet. 'You've had a bit of a rough trot, then?'

He followed meekly to the underground car park and Shipton's Ferrari. 'Does he know you have that, Kel?'

She smiled, 'Clarkie's a new man, Mick. I think if I asked him for it to keep, he'd write out the papers there and then and even pay the transfer.' She opened the passenger door and said, 'Beware, it's a lo-ong way down.'

Mickey lowered himself gingerly to the seat that seemed to be only a few millimetres from the tarmac and shuffled into place. 'You sure it still has its wheels?'

Kelly laughed, flopped gracefully into the driver's seat, and pressed the start button. The engine growled into life and soon the red car was on the road, attracting the attention of everyone, as it purred its way to the city. 'I thought it best to leave the top up. Okay?'

Mick didn't care. His dulled senses were being purged by the scent of a lovely woman, and he was so relaxed, he dozed off to be rudely awakened when she turned the car into the carpark of her apartment, and it clattered over a ramp designed for a more sedate vehicle.

'Here we are, my friend.' She stepped out, helped him to his feet, and escorted him to the lift. 'It's not the Arete, but it's clean.' The lift arrived at her floor, and she led him to her apartment.

Mickey took in the relatively opulent ambience of Kelly's home and said, 'Clarkie certainly looks after you.'

'Mostly just me, Mick. I live a simple life these days and my home is my escape.' She showed him the bathroom and handed him a fresh towel. 'Give me a shout when you are nearly ready, and I'll pass you in some temporary togs.'

Mickey stripped his filthy kit and dropped it to the floor, then he stepped into the steaming shower and half wished Kelly had offered to wash his back. The thought sent his nether regions into turmoil and then guilt burned through as he remembered Jack had also been taken. 'Done, Kel!' he yelled.

The door opened a crack, and an arm reached in with clean trackie pants and a tee-shirt. 'He was as big as you, so they should fit.'

Mickey dried off and stepped into the tracksuit pants. They were top quality, and the tee-shirt had some writing on the front that he couldn't read.

'Wow! That looks better. What do you want me to do with your old togs?'

'Bin them, Kell, or whatever, but first I need to start looking for Jack.'

Kelly's expression slumped, but she handed him a coffee. 'Relax, mate. Clarkie and me have the feelers out. If anyone can find her, it won't be your mob.'

Since the new DCI had come aboard it was all about a quiet life and maintaining the status quo than the policing he was used to.

'Any news of Clarkie's kid?'

Kelly's face lit up. 'They have her and she's on her way home.'

'Fantastic. He must be real happy.'

'I think he's secretly dreading it. The guys said she'd need a long rehab and a strong will from him. Then, of course, there are the two stragglers they weren't expecting.'

'Stragglers?'

'Don't know too much, but Kaitlin refused to cooperate unless they brought her mates.'

Mickey raised his eyebrows.

'More coffee?'

He shook his head.

'Okay, now you're all caffeinated, spiffy and fragrant, let's be off to the office and a heads up from Clarkie.'

***

Jackie Morton rubbed her eyes. She had no idea how long she'd been held captive in the windowless room. She'd heard sounds outside but couldn't distinguish them other than vague murmurings and the occasional shout. Her bodily functions had told her it was at least three days, during which they'd fed her takeaway food and cans of cola for drinking, and the debris was piling up in the corner. The room had a basic ensuite bathroom, meaning she could attend to her personal hygiene. Other than that, she might as well have vanished off the face of the Earth.

Mickey had answered the door and never returned. Soon afterwards, she was assaulted by two men. She touched her face, still sore from the cable tie they'd strained across her mouth.

The bastards had seemed professional in a cruel way. In fact, their cruelty told her they were not of an Australian police force, despite their claims of being federal cops. She'd never seen a single ID even when she was hauled in for their stupid terrorism related questioning. 'Mickey!' she yelled.

She knew he couldn't hear her, but a sixth sense from somewhere deep inside told her he knew where she was, and he'd be there to free her at any moment.

'Stop dragging your feet, Mickey, and please hurry up,' she muttered.

12

Bib spoke over the intercom. 'We'll be landing at Belgrade in an hour. I had us on Qatar with a couple of flight changes to Australia, but things have become complicated with the extra passengers. Luckily, I have some connections on the ground, but I'll need some time to pacify them. I can't do anything until we are there, and I'll have to leave you ladies in the capable hands of Mr Bub.'

The girls shrugged as one, and Bub squeezed through to join Bib in the co-pilot's seat.

'What do you reckon, boss?'

Bib indicated he should put on his headphones and then he spoke quietly over the restricted channel, 'Touch and go. I haven't seen my connections for years. They might even be dead for all I know.'

'Great.'

'Have I ever let you down?'

'Nah, but there's always a first time.'

'Oh, ye of little faith, Mr Bub.'

'How long will you need?'

'One hour at best, then everything will be up for grabs.'

Bub swallowed hard. They'd been in some sticky situations

before, but now they were technically guilty of the very thing they were trying to stamp out. If Bib couldn't fix up their dilemma, they'd be in the frame for trafficking people without papers across international borders. People smugglers at best, human traffickers at worst, add to that, their three passengers were under aged drug addicts.

The one thing he'd learned since working with Bib was that his boss always underestimated the chance of success, and his connections were likely at the deep state level. That meant serious business and if anything was to go wrong… It didn't bear thinking about. He opened his sandwich pack and bit into his egg curry butty. 'That's a stroke of luck, my favourite,' he said, washing it down with a mouthful of coke and trying to relax.

He could see the geometric shapes of the runway light formations in the distance and felt the plane begin to lose altitude more quickly.

'Hang on to your hats, chaps,' Bib said as the wheels struck the tarmac, and he slowed down to taxi to the private area. He'd filed a flight plan, and he'd communicated with the tower. So far, they were legal. That might change if the immigration authorities discovered two additional undisclosed and undocumented teenage passengers.

The aircraft came to a halt near a bland-looking building with a wall of glass doors and minimal internal lights. Bib told everyone to stay on board until he sorted immigration out. There was no reason for them to make a physical check, but it was the dead of night, and anything could happen. He stuffed a wad of dollars into his hip pocket, left the cabin lights off, lowered the steps and, with logbooks in hand, strode confidently to the building.

***

For Mickey, the drive to Clark Shipton's office was almost a surreal experience. He was sitting in the bucket seat of a high-end sports car with a beautiful woman. He watched her face as she drove and felt tickled by her little girl expressions of frustration and joy as she skirted obstacles.

He saw her face turn towards him and her eyes blinked. 'I haven't shown Clarkie the invite yet,' she said.

'Jackie is organising everything, but I know that if you're on the list, it is because she wants you there.'

'I would hope so.'

'No. I don't mean it like that. We are only inviting a select few. It will be a small affair, and we don't want a big fuss.'

'I know how she feels. Even if Clarkie won't come, you won't mind if I come alone?'

'Do you think he'll be a party pooper?'

'I dunno. He's been real funny since Virginia died, and then Kaitlin's disappearance didn't help.' Kelly drove into the secure parking area around the back of Shipton's office. 'Need a hand, big fella?' She grinned as Mickey struggled aggressively to extract himself from the car.

'I'm a four-wheel-drive bloke, Kell. We step down, not up.' He followed her up the back stairs to the offices and observed that the rear seemed far more upmarket than the front. 'Bit flash?'

'Clarkie likes to keep a low profile with the public.' She tapped a code into the door lock and held it open for him. Then she pointed to a coffee machine. 'Help yourself and grab a seat. I'll tell him you're here.'

Mickey ignored her offer of coffee and instead of sitting, he leaned against the wall and slid to the floor. *Where the hell are you, Jack?*

He could see her face wreathed in darkness, but she seemed

resolute and defiant. Then the man with the limp pushed open the door to her place of captivity and Mickey remembered the stories his dad had told him. He followed the procedure for closing down his consciousness and entering the state he called his dreaming.

***

Jackie flinched as the key turned in the lock of the windowless room they were keeping her in.

The tall man with the limp entered and said, 'Your man declined to cooperate with us and he's...'

Jackie waited for him to continue.

He didn't. He turned, walked out and re locked the door. A few seconds later, the light went out.

She was becoming used to the dark, but the man had said something that might lead to several inferences. The first was that they had killed him. She couldn't bring herself to believe the man she thought of as some kind of superhero could possibly be dead. He was far too young for that.

Perhaps he's badly injured, and they want me to help them resuscitate him or something? If that's the case, why am I still here?

'They'll be playing with your mind, Jackie.'

She didn't hear the voice. It was Mickey's alright, but via her a channel to her mind that he said his dad had once mentioned. Mickey's dad had lived bush for most of his life, and he'd taught Mickey many forgotten ways. One of them was the ability to communicate without sound, over vast distances. Few knew of it or were capable of accessing it, and it was difficult to master because of the need for a total shut down of the conscious mind.

If Mickey has shut down... The thought didn't bear thinking about. She had to keep *her* mind alive and defy the bastards who had taken her. She listened hard for sounds from outside, but it was as though she'd been trapped in an acoustic bubble. She lay back on the bunk, closed her eyes, and tried to imagine him arriving on a snow-white horse to rescue her. It was the stupidest thought she could think, but it reminded her of the stories her mother had read to her as a child.

She'd almost forgotten about the white woman who'd birthed her, and who lost her way in alcohol soon afterwards. Despite her problems, her mother was a woman who'd always done the best she could for her daughter, given her circumstances.

Jackie remembered the day there was a big fuss made of her and the head teacher called her to his office. She never saw her mother again, and no one knew the whereabouts of her father. Since that day, she'd vowed to do the right thing by everyone and when the opportunity to become a police officer arrived, she grabbed it with both hands and made many lifelong friends.

Mickey Krakauer was the first and only man she'd truly loved. She yelled out, 'Where are you, Mick?'

There was no response.

13

'M ajor O'Sullivan. You made it.'

The sound of Dragomir Kosanović's chortling voice unnerved him slightly as the man himself pushed through the glass doors of the building and marched past him towards the aircraft.

'Fancy meeting you again so soon.' Bib said with a grin. 'You certainly get around.'

Kosanovich stopped and turned around to face him. 'Da. International people smuggling is such a problem these days. You found your girl? You have her with you?'

Bib shrugged.

Kosanović about turned and walked towards the aircraft before turning to face him again. 'This girl. She is pretty. No?'

Bib shrugged again.

'Da,' Kosanović said. 'Of course she is.' He put his foot on the bottom step of the ladder and Kaitlin fell forward through the door to throw her arms around his neck and twirl him back to face Bib.

'Uncle Draggy, you came for me.'

Bib was confused. 'Uncle Draggy?'

Kosanović laughed. 'I was her best customer. How are you,

my sweet?'

'I need my special lollies, Uncle Draggy.'

'Of course you do, and Uncle Dragomir will see to it.'

Bib felt the cold steel of a gun barrel press against his neck, and he attempted to turn. The attempt was halted by a painful clout from the wooden butt of an AK47.

'My friend can get a little touchy when there are girlies around, Major O'Sullivan.' He turned to the man and said, 'He is a friend, Vladimir. Treat him well.'

Vladimir shoved Bib towards the building, with the muzzle of the rifle pressed into the small of his back.

If this is well, Bib thought, *I'd hate to see what's not.* Then he saw the reflection, in the entrance door, Kosanović was climbing the steps into the aircraft, and he knew their number was up. There were thousands of US Dollars in a couple of bags on the plane, plus the other two girls, and Bub.

He was in the building before anything else happened and a few minutes later Kosanović followed him with Kaitlin.

'What happened to your colleague, Major? Did you leave him behind?' Kosanović dropped the two grips to the floor. 'His bag is still here?'

Bib said nothing. The first rule of a fuck up was to keep mum until you had no other option.

'Very well. My friend, Vladimir, will take you to meet your connection at the international terminal, and you will be free to continue your journey. There will of course be the statutory fee. Cash is fine, US dollars are preferred.' Kosanović smiled and Bib pulled the wad of notes from his hip pocket.

Vladimir lowered his gun and watched intently as Kosanović counted the dollars. 'Good. That is good,' He gestured to Vladimir, and said in Croat. 'Take him to the main terminal and make sure he boards his aircraft.'

Vladimir hesitated and raised the muzzle of his AK to the level of Kosanović's gut. He replied in Croat. 'My share or I take it all.'

Kosanović smirked. 'I don't think so, Vladimir. Do as ordered or face the consequences.'

Bib couldn't believe his luck, but the last thing he needed was a fire fight. That would attract all the wrong people. 'Excuse me.' He dropped to one knee, removed a wad of cash from Bub's bag, and handed it to Vladimir. 'See. Everyone gets their share.'

Vladimir grinned. He could see that he had the upper hand, he was now on a winner and could double his money in an instant.

Bib saw his finger move towards the trigger of his weapon and acted quicker. The garrotte, stored neatly in the key fob pocket of his jeans, was deployed in an instant. The man's trigger finger never had its day and, as he fell to the ground, the dull thud of his head striking the hard floor was the only sound he'd ever make again.

Sweat began beading on Kosanović's forehead as he witnessed his own life passing before him.

Another violent death had Kaitlin swoon to join Vladimir, in a heap on the floor.

'Time for playing games is over Uncle Draggy.' Bib had rescued the AK from the falling man, before he hit the ground, and aimed it at the stomach of Kosanović.

'You know if you fire that you are gone, big-time, Major.'

'And so are you, my friend, and you know I will, if I need to.'

Kosanović said, 'You have twelve hours to leave the country. After that you are fair game.'

Bib held out his hand and Kosanović handed back his bundle of notes. Then, while keeping the barrel aimed, he removed the wad from Vladimir's dead hand and released the ratchet of the garrotte. 'We're done Uncle Draggy. Now I need a vehicle to take me to the terminal.'

Kosanović handed him a set of keys.

'Thank you, now pick up your little girlfriend, and take her to the car.'

Kosanović lifted the feather light body of Kaitlin and led the way to the car park. As he fed her into the rear of the cabin, he muttered something about it being the last time he'd be helpful, and the butt of the AK silenced any further dissent he might have.

There'd be some explaining to do when he recovered consciousness but by then, Bib and Bub would be out of the country. Next, he needed to find Bub and the girls, and he needed to find a way to bypass immigration to leave Serbia. These ops were never easy.

***

Mickey felt a hand on his shoulder. He blinked open his eyes and said, 'Where the fuck…?'

Kelly took his hand and helped him to his feet. 'Clarkie wants to see you.'

Mickey followed her to the office.

Shipton was in his usual place and his face seemed more relaxed than last time. 'Had a text on my burner, Mick. Bib and Bub are about to start their journey to Australia.'

'Meanwhile, no one knows where Jackie is and…'

'We do, Mick. Your mob don't have a clue.'

He stared Shipton in the eyes and said, 'Where?'

'Not that far away from here. They're keeping her in an old disused recording studio. It's totally soundproofed, so her screams can't be heard.'

Mickey's jaw clamped tight, and he pushed back the chair to rise to his feet.

'Only joking about the screams, mate. So far, she hasn't been harmed, but the place is well guarded by an armed mob of ex-cops who believe they are the saviours of the world.'

'Locals?'

'Mix of feds and locals.'

'You say armed?'

'Like ready for a full-scale war.'

'Shit.'

'You got away.'

'Yeah, but I have skills that Jack doesn't. I was also in a place of isolation and left alone at night.'

'I can't be seen to help you rescue your fiancé, Mick. You know why.'

'Give me the address and I'll scope it out.'

Shipton handed him a sheet of paper, with an address in Bayswater. 'Armed like they're ready for war, Mick.' He paused. 'If it hadn't been for you, I wouldn't be this close to seeing Kaitlin again.' He showed him the screen of his burner. 'Bib sent me this from Belgrade.' It was a picture of a gaunt teen girl whose once pretty features were damaged by her addiction. 'It's definitely her.' He swallowed hard. 'I can't thank you enough Mickey Krakauer. Take care, my friend.'

He felt Kelly's hand on his shoulder again and stood.

As he left Clarkie's office, Kelly handed him a wad of cash and a burner phone. 'You'll be needing these.' Then she pulled him into a hug and said, 'Go gettem big fella, and bring her back safe.'

Mickey noticed the tear that had escaped from one of her eyelids and he kissed it away. 'Thanks, Kell.' He felt he'd added six inches to his height as he danced down the rear stairs to the carpark and almost skipped into Beaufort Street.

When he eventually stabilised, he hailed a taxi, gave the driver Angela Carter's address, and as the cab moved off, she answered his call.

'Hello?'

'It's Mickey. Don't hang up, I need to speak to James.'

'He's not here they've just taken him in for questioning about the shooting… there are a couple more officers, and I've been charged with the grievous bodily harm of the man with the gun who was threatening me.'

'I know where Jackie is being held.'

'Well don't tell anyone…' the phone went silent.

14

With Valdimir and Kosanović out of the way, Bib returned to the Beechcraft. He turned the key, opened the door and lowered the integral steps, then he stepped up to enter the cabin. 'Bub?'

There was no reply.

He checked between the seats and the small storage area at the rear of the cabin. There was no sign of anyone having been there. 'Bub,' he called again, and felt the aircraft lurch slightly. He turned to see his partner standing on the steps.

'She's a goodun, boss. Kaitlin recognised the bloke you were talking to. She said he was an a-hole who regularly used the brothel. I asked her what she wanted to do, and she suggested what happened next.'

'Uncle Draggy, eh?'

Agnetha and Bronwyn were behind him on the ladder; their sullen expressions exchanged for smiles as they flopped into the aircraft seats.

'Where is Katie?' Bronwyn asked.

'She's okay, she passed out, but she's in the car that we'll use to take us to the international terminal.'

'Kosanović?' Bub asked.

'Temporarily indisposed. His mate, Vladimir, is permanently out of circulation.'

'Shall we go then?'

Bub turned and gently encouraged the girls down the few steps to the tarmac.

Bib followed, locked up the aircraft, then overtook them to hug the building's walls and lead them to the car. Kosanović was still away with the fairies when Agnetha and Bronwyn stepped over him to squeeze into the back with the reviving Kaitlin.

'Okay, this is the plan,' Bib said. 'I'm going to drive you to the main terminal, where I'm going to leave you while I make some arrangements. Only Kaitlin has papers, so I'll need you to remain calm and behave as though everything is tickety-boo. Understand?'

Kaitlin was still stunned by her experience, Agnetha nodded her head enthusiastically, but Bronwyn remained sullen.

'Good. Bub will look after you and I have every confidence in his ability.' He handed Bub a business card. 'If anything happens to me keep on to Mumbai. Call him, and he might be able to help out.'

'General Verma Rajput? What's his role?'

'Chief of defence.'

'How will he be of help with an immigration, slash trafficking problem?'

'Connections Bub, just mention my name and see what happens.'

'Hopefully it won't be necessary. All good, girls?'

They nodded again.

Bib drove into the drop off area and Bub, with his charges, made their way into the terminal. It was late at night so there were few people around.

Bub found a coffee lounge operating with a lone barista and ushered the girls into a corner booth that would provide a degree of seclusion. 'Hungry?'

They all nodded.

He noticed the place did burgers at various levels and pointed to the menu.

Kaitlin said, 'Can I have scrambled eggs?'

The other two became instantly animated.

'Scrambled eggs it is, then.' He headed to the counter, gave his order, and hurried back to the booth. 'He reckons he can do that.' So many things had gone wrong the last thing he needed was something else.

The three grinning faces beamed back at him, and he remembered the first day that his daughter broke through her malaise. Their scrambled eggs arrived. They looked appalling and tasted as bad, but they tucked in like a family at a picnic. Then, for the first time since their pickup, the girls began talking and trying to recall things about their homes.

Bub needed to ensure they knew that things might still get tough. He said, 'Kaitlin has papers. You two don't. we won't be able to leave until Mr Bib resolves the next move. Understand?'

They nodded.

He looked at Kaitlin. 'We weren't expecting three.'

'I couldn't leave without...' her eyes began to fill with tears.

Bub patted her hand and spoke softly. 'We know that, and Mr Bib will sort it out. I know he will.' He rolled his eyes at his massive display of tentative confidence. 'Eat up. It might be some time before we get another chance.'

A TV screen was displaying a Croatian news channel and bub recognised two of the three faces he'd seen at the brothel. They were standing behind the third, who was giving a speech translated into Croat. The English-language version was toned down to the minimum and he couldn't make it out, but he knew instantly who they were.

***

Mickey tapped the taxi driver on his shoulder and pointed to the address on the paper Clarkie had given him. 'Sorry, mate, change of plan, can you chuck a uey?'

The driver made a U-turn.

'Keep going for a bit and drop me at the end of the street.' Mickey looked at the meter and handed the man a generous tip, along with the fare.

The man swore under his breath. 'Not enough.' He pointed to a barely readable laminated card on the dash.

'Yeah, I'm a black fella, and I'm also a cop. Wanna make something of it?' Mickey opened the door, stepped out, slammed it shut, and the cab's wheels squealed as the driver put space between him and his passenger.

Mickey grinned and began his walk to the recording studio. As he drew close, he could see that Clarkie was right. While there were no firearms on display, there were far too many muscle-bound characters hanging around for something as simple as a disused building.

He was about to enter the yard to suss out the premises when a man nudged past him on his way through the gate.

'Careful, mate.' Mickey said.

The man pulled aside his jacket to show Mickey the automatic pistol he had jammed down his trousers.

Mickey turned away, to hide his smirk, as he continued his walk towards the building. *Defo amateurs*, he thought. I'll bet they'll all be down the pub, after dark, bragging about their accomplishments and embellishing their roles. 'Perfect.' He turned around and headed back to the gate.

The makings of a plan had begun fomenting in his brain. All he needed to do was pull it off, and he'd save his girl. Mickey sucked in a deep breath. He was feeling hungry, and to think creatively he needed to eat.

He headed to a lunch bar he'd noticed at the end of the road, pushed through the coloured tape fly curtain, and was greeted by the smiling face of a kid who looked no older than fifteen.

Mickey pondered the items in the glazed display case and made his selection.

The kid took his money and said, 'You new around here?'

'Busy, is it?'

'That new mob that just arrived has me rushed off my feet. You with them?'

Mickey shook his head, 'No.' He pulled a coke from the chiller and sat at a table.

'I'm glad. They're all arseholes.'

'Why would you say that?'

'They never ask for anything nicely.' She suddenly stepped away from the counter and moved to the corner as a large man blustered in through the fly screen.

'Burger and chips and it better be better than the shit you served up last time. Who the fuck are you looking at?' He said in the direction of Mickey.

Mickey said nothing and picked up the free newspaper he'd found on the table.

'Hey, I'm talking to you.'

Mickey ignored him. He wanted no confrontation. Not yet anyway.

'Hey, cuz. How are ya?' A third man, wearing motorbike leathers, had entered the lunch bar, and he seemed to be speaking to no one in particular.

The heavy shoved him aside to make way for him to leave just as another leather clad individual walked in.

Mickey now had a serious reason to be worried. He'd been caught in a similar situation once before. Back then he was on duty and even though he had his Glock and his Taser to hand, they gave him no time to react, and he'd copped a severe beating from the three who set on him. He remembered awakening to find he still had his weapons. He put his head down and waited for the onslaught. It didn't come and as he turned to see what was going on, he saw the heavy lying on his back, with the second set of leathers dragging him out by the feet.

Mickey closed his eyes. This was not the way he expected things to turn out. He opened them again to see the first man crawling away and the two new ones sitting at his table.

'If you're Mickey Krakauer, Kelly sent us.'

Mickey said nothing.

'She said you were very capable, but a bit of help wouldn't go amiss.' The man handed him a business card.

He looked at the card and was immediately struck by a large blue crucifix to the side of the man's name. 'Pastor Jedidiah Morton? What the...'

'Fuck?' The pastor finished Mickey's sentence with a wide grin. 'Kelly and I have been good friends for years, and you must be Mickey Krakauer?'

Mickey said, 'How did you guess?'

Pastor Jedediah laughed. 'Black fella being harassed by a white fella. Not hard to work that one out.'

'But how did you know...?'

'Kell said you'd be down here sussing things out and ready to take on the world. Jackie Morton, she's your woman in she?'

Suddenly the name meant something to Mickey. He raised an eyebrow and couldn't help but tilt his head.

Jedediah smirked. 'She my cousin. Her dad were my uncle. We've never met, but it's been on my mind for a few years. When Kelly mentioned you, she told me about you and Jackie.'

Mickey grinned. Now there were three. He nodded towards the other man.

'Half bro — say hello, Kevin.'

'Hello, Mr Krakauer.'

'So where do we go from here, Jedidiah?'

'Call me Jed. Everyone else does. I was hoping *you'd* tell me, cuz.'

Mickey's initial elation began to deflate like an old party balloon on a gate post. 'I wasn't planning for a team effort.'

'Yeah, that's what Kelly said.'

15

The light went on in her room, the hinges squeaked, and the door opened. The man who entered was unfamiliar to her, but he was carrying a bottle of *Jack Daniels*, two cans of coke and a pair of tumblers.

'Hey, babe. There's just you and me now. The others have all gone for a quick drink and I didn't think it was fair to you to be on your own.' He set the bottle, cans, and glasses on the small table that she'd used for her meals.

'No thank you,' Jackie said.

The man poured some bourbon into each of the glasses and followed it with coke before handing her a glass.

Jackie shook her head and soon realised he would not be taking no for an answer.

He put the glass down and reached out to grab her by the wrist and pull her to him.

She screamed.

He laughed and grabbed at her crotch while his other hand grasped her around the neck. 'No one will hear us. Why do you think we chose this place?'

Jackie knew she was well and truly out gunned. He was a large man, and though it was mostly blubber, she said, 'If I say yes?'

The man released her and handed her a drink. 'Then we'll make sweet music together, baby.'

Jackie felt her stomach churn, but she needed to play him along. If he was the only one guarding her, her chances of escape had just increased by the power of ten. She smiled sweetly and watched in disbelieving amusement as he suddenly began a slow descent to the ground, only to be replaced by another grinning man in bikie leathers and wearing a silver crucifix.

'Cousin, Jaqueline,' the new man said. 'I hear congratulations are in order.'

Jackie's puzzlement turned into abject fear when another man in leathers arrived and said, 'All clear, boss.'

They changed to elation when she saw Mickey in the background. 'Mick?' she squeaked.

He pushed between the leather works, took her in his arms, kissed her on the lips and said, 'Time to go home. You've got a wedding to plan.'

The enormity of the moment was too much, and his grip tightened as she felt herself slithering to the floor.

***

'Sorry, boss. I couldn't let Mickey go it alone.'

'No worries, Kell. Those two are so far away from me to have little effect on the business. I didn't know Jed was Jackie's cousin, though.'

'Neither did I, but they sorted it, and Mick and Jack can at least cuddle up in their own bed tonight. You, okay?'

'It's been a long time since I experienced such pleasure.'

Kelly reached for the scotch and a couple of glasses, poured three fingers each and walked around his desk to put down his glass and kiss him on his bald spot. She was about to return when she felt his arm snake around her waist and reached for his hand to remove it.

She was too late. He'd risen to his feet and taken her in his arms.

Suddenly, compliant she melted against him. 'Clarkie?' she murmured

He mumbled something she couldn't catch.

'We shouldn't be doing this.' Then her lips found his, and all options flew out of the window.

Clark Shipton awakened in his own bed, to a smiling face whose owner's lips reached out to his. 'Katie's on her way home,' he said.

'What will she think of her gang boss dad sleeping with his newfound moll?' Kelly replied.

Shipton's mouth formed into a tight smile. 'I'm giving it all away, Kell. That Jed bloke said if I repent, everything will be okay.'

Kelly's smile changed to a look of fear. 'You've gone and got religion?'

Shipton grinned. 'Nah. I just want to be a proper dad. I've made enough legit over the years, and since young Mickey came on the scene, I've given most of the dirty money to places where it might do some good. I'm not poor, Kell, but I'm startin to feel a little honest, and I'd like Katie to be proud of me.'

Kelly kissed him deeply on the lips again before they made slow and instinctive love.

***

Almost two hours had passed, and Bub was becoming worried. The Airport terminal had begun filling with people and there was still no sign of Bib. He checked his burner. Not even a text. The girls were starting to get edgy. They needed their fix and if they didn't get it soon, he'd have a major problem on his hands.

It was Bib's bag that held the Suboxone, and they were already showing signs of withdrawal. He began making plans in his head. The embassy might be his best call, but that might also lead to consequences that no one was prepared for. 'Coffee, guys?'

They shook their heads as one.

Kaitlin said, 'We need stuff, Mr Bub.'

Bub said, 'Bib will be here soon and…' He smiled with relief as he saw him push through the terminal doors and walk quickly to where they were sitting.

'Move it. Don't ask, just walk naturally, and follow me.' He turned.

They followed him to the doors and through to the car they'd arrived in.

As soon as they were mobile, Bib spoke. 'Serious problem. There'll be no papers for anyone except Kaitlin. I've blotted my copybook in a few places, but I thought we were good here. '

'What next?'

Bib handed the girls their *Suboxone* films. 'Remember, under the tongue, don't swallow them.'

They grabbed them hungrily and followed his instructions.

'Freight.'

'Freight?' Bub said.

'I've tracked down an old mate who's outside of the system. It might not work, but at this stage of the game we've got nothing to lose.' He continued driving around the perimeter road until he saw what he was looking for. The tail of a dark blue 737 was protruding from an open hangar and scissor lifts were trundling back and forth while a ground crew loaded it with flight containers.

Bib drove through the gate and walked to the tacky glass

partition door of a small office. On the window were the initials FFS In gold leaf. He pushed through the door without knocking and without letting his friends know how long he might be.

Kaitlin, Agnetha, and Bronwyn had dozed off on the back seat. Their little fix had given them some relief, but there was no relief for Bub, and when a man in uniform tapped on the window and spoke to him in Serbian, he almost swallowed his tongue.

He wound the window down and replied, 'I'm waiting for a colleague.' He pointed to the window with the FFS initials.

The man grabbed the handle of the door and opened it.

'Come with me. All of you come with me.' This time he spoke in English and this time his tone was forceful.

Bub leaned back and tried to awaken the girls, but they were well and truly away in fairyland.

'Quickly, we don't have much time,' the man said. 'Move it!'

Bub clambered from the car and began dragging the girls out, one by one, to prop them up against the car.

Uniform grabbed Kaitlin, Bub reached out for Agnetha and Bib appeared to take charge of Bronwyn. Between them they dragged their charges into the hangar, sat them on a bench and, Uniform, handed out water bottles to each of the blankly staring girls.

'Okay, guys.' Bib said. 'This is what's going to happen.' He pointed to the man in uniform. 'This is my friend, Frank. He has agreed to help, but I'm afraid it won't be that comfortable.' He gestured to the huge blue aircraft glistening in the hangar lights. It had the gold FFS logo emblazoned on its tail fin and the words, in tiny white print along the fuselage.

FRANK'S FREIGHT SERVICES

'We are going to post you home. You'll stop at a couple of

places en route, and your final destination will be Perth Airport. Sorry, I don't have an itinerary. It's not one of those trips.'

Frank stood and pointed to a flight container. 'You'll be going in that.' He gestured to a pile of cushions by the side of its opening. 'Grab as many as you need and pack yourselves tight. You can come out once we're airborne, but you'll need to return to the container on my say so. Understand?'

Agnetha and Bronwyn nodded.

Kaitlin backed up. 'I thought I had papers?'

'This is the only way we might have a chance of getting you all home in one piece.' Bib said.

She grabbed a cushion and threw it through the door in a huff.

Agnetha and Bronwyn complied fully and eventually Kaitlin's mood eased.

'I suppose it'll be a bit of a hoot coming home in a box. Dad once said that's what I'd be doing if I carried on the way I was.' Then her face screwed up and tears flooded from her eyes. 'I'm so sorry, Daddy.'

Her friends hugged her, and something vaguely resembling peace, descended.

16

Clark Shipton pushed away his breakfast plate, checked his phone, and said, 'Nothing.'

'Give them time, Clarkie. They said it wouldn't be easy.'

'Nothing ever is,' he said.

Kelly checked *her* messages. 'Jackie and Mick have made it home.' She turned her screen towards him to show him the text she'd received in the night.

'Do we know who was involved?'

'Jed reckons it was a bunch of disgruntled ex-cops who were trying to get a lead on Bib and Bub. He thinks they might be hoping to get a cut of the action.'

'You said, were? Does that mean they're no longer in the game?'

'There's big money at stake; not all the missing girls came from poor families and there are some who would be prepared to fork out big bucks up front to get their kids back.' She looked directly at Shipton and blinked her eyes. 'If their plan works and they can get a slice of Bib and Bub...'

'It seemed to me more of a grudge match between Mickey and that bloke with the limp. If, as you say, they were once cops, I reckon something might have happened between them back in the day. How squeaky clean is Mickey Krakauer, Kell?'

'I'll ask Jed next time I see him. he seems to have a handle on just about everything.'

'Is this Jed really a god botherer?'

Kelly smirked. 'Jed is whatever he thinks is best for Jed.'

'Find out about this grudge thingo. We might be able to use it.'

She began loading the dishwasher and knew she couldn't be a part of anything likely to hurt Mickey.

'Leave that, Mrs What's it'll fix it.'

'Is that what you call her?'

'Virginia hired her years ago. I don't think I ever learned her name.'

Kelly slammed the door of the machine shut and said, 'I'm going home. You've got Mrs What's it. You don't need me.' She heard him say something, but it was too late his door had closed behind her.

Instead of returning to her own apartment, Kelly called in on Mickey and Jackie.

Mickey answered the door, his look of surprise epic.

'Sorry to bother you, Mick… Is everything okay?' she saw Jackie appear behind him. 'You must be Jackie. Congratulations, and thanks so much for the invite.'

Jackie stepped around Mickey and said, 'Will you be coming?'

'First, I need to talk to the both of you, about something I've heard.'

Mickey stepped aside, 'Welcome.'

Kelly followed him, and Jackie followed her, to their small lounge. 'Take a seat. Kelly, isn't it? You two go back a way, I believe.'

Kelly wasn't sure what to say but said, 'It was nothing serious we just met one night when he was on duty and… It didn't last long.' She side-eyed Mickey and continued. 'I got the feeling there was someone else, and I got on with my life.'

'So why are you here, Kel?' Mickey asked.

'Clarkie said something that struck a nerve, and I think you need to know.'

'Wasn't it Clarkie's involvement that helped get Jackie released?'

Kelly shook her head. 'No. Jed did that. Jed is an acquaintance of mine who owed me a favour, but I didn't know he was related to you, Jackie.'

'I didn't know either,' Jackie said.'

She focussed her attention on Mickey. 'Well anyway, that's beside the point. Clarkie thinks there's animosity between you and the bloke with the limp.'

Mickey laughed. 'You remember him, Jack?'

Her face went blank, and she shook her head.

'That day, on the way back from Warakurna. When those cops followed us and then pulled us over. I knew they were a part of Clitheroe's mob from his early days, but they didn't know I knew. His limp came from a bullet that I put in his knee.'

Jackies face filled with an expression that matched her epiphany. 'Now I remember, I was totally bombed on that trip. Then you switched the barrel of your Glock.'

'And they've been trying to dredge up evidence since. They claim to have found the other barrel, in my glove box, and tried to use it to get me to give up the goods on Bib and Bub. It wouldn't have made any difference, I know nothing about those two, other than what Clarkie told me.'

Kelly's eyes widened. 'So, they have something on you, that they might be able to use?'

'All they have is a photo of a Glock barrel wrapped in plastic, which isn't the one from my service issue weapon, which is in its rightful place. Until about six of months ago, the dodgy barrel was still in my glove box. They were probably waiting for an opportunity to search my car.'

'Aren't you worried?' Jackie said.

Mickey grinned. 'I'd already disposed of the original and the photo they showed me was a fake.'

'But they could try to use it?'

Mickey grinned. 'Let them.'

'Does Jim Carter know about this Mick?'

'I've never mentioned it and the bloke I shot never raised the matter. I don't even know his name. I just knew who he worked for.'

'So, if Clarkie and Limpy get together…'

'From my meeting with the man, I think he uses the name Bib. He's more likely to cure Limpy's knee through the medium of a bullet in the noggin.'

'I thought you said you'd never met him?'

'A man I think might be Bib, hijacked me and my car. I drove him to the airport but before that, he wanted to make sure that their mission was a complete secret. He was armed and he could have maintained his secrecy by shooting me there and then, but my impression of him is, is that he's a man of integrity. Albeit it a killer if necessary.'

'So, what if Clarkie has an agenda of his own? He's paid a small fortune up front as a deposit. What if he thinks, that with a little help from Limpy and his mates, he can save a large chunk of the final payment?'

'Then Limpy will cease to be relevant, and maybe Clarkie might just have wasted his money.'

'You think Bib and Bub would kill the girl?'

'I didn't get that impression. Like I said he could have easily killed me, and he didn't even try.'

'There are three girls.'

'Three?'

'Kaitlin is Clarkie's daughter. There are two others Agnetha and Bronwen. Apparently, Kaitlin wouldn't leave without her friends.'

'How was that going to work?' Mickey asked.

Jackie stood. 'I'll make us all a cuppa.'

'It isn't. They had fake papers for Kaitlin, but the other two are effectively stateless.'

'So how are they going to get them into Australia?'

'That's were Bib and Bub's connections come in. If someone else turns up on the scene. The whole operation could be blown to smithereens.' He patted his pocket. 'My phone, my wallet?'

Jackie returned with their tea. 'You lost summat?'

'My wallet.'

'You had nothing remember. You said they cleaned you out of everything at the ghost town.'

Mickey said, 'Shit. I'm gonna have to go back there… Now.' He grabbed the keys to his car before remembering he'd dropped Bib's card into his centre console. He returned from his car, grinning from ear to ear, and clutching the small white card. He handed it to Jackie. 'He said there were a number on it somewhere?'

Jackie shook her head, flipped it over and shook her head again before handing it to Kelly.

'I know Bib and Bub are what you might call spooks, but would they use invisible ink in this day and age?' Kelly said.

'UV, maybe. Clarkie has a scanner. He's been done a few times with counterfeit stuff and…'

'Jim Carter will have access. I'll call him and… No. Better not. Can you check this card with Clarkie's thing?'

Kelly acknowledged with a nod.

'Whatever happens, Clarkie must not gain access to this number. If he has another agenda, we'll need to be several steps ahead of him.'

'I knew there was a reason I needed to come here today. Don't worry, I'll be at your wedding, Jackie. I wouldn't miss it for the world.' She opened her arms and drew Jackie into a warm and genuine hug.

17

Kelly wanted to be in the office before Shipton, but she knew her stop off at Mickey's would have made that more difficult. Nevertheless, she breathed out with relief when she saw his car was not in the car park, ran up the back stairs and turned her key in the lock. Once inside, she headed for her office, turned on her computer, and turned around to see him rummaging through her handbag.

'I beg your pardon, Mr Shipton. What do you think you are doing?'

He said nothing, just upended her bag and emptied its contents on to her desk.

'Hey. What the hell is going on?'

'Just checking. I've been hearing bad things about you, Kelly.'

'From whom?'

'None of your business. Do you have a contact number for Bib and Bub?'

'Why would I have any number for them? I have had nothing to do with them. Isn't there one on the proforma?'

Shipton turned and headed for his office. He then pulled the file from the cabinet, tipped its contents onto his own desk and snapped, 'Shit!'

'Would a coffee help?' Kelly began tidying things back into her handbag. 'If you'd asked…'

'Sorry Kel, after you stormed off this morning…'

'My impression of your two mercenary chappies was that they went black when on ops.'

Shipton said, 'Me too, but I'm hearing that they've left a get out of jail card with someone.'

'Well, don't look at me. I want your daughter back almost as much as you do, and if I knew anything that might be helpful, I'd be the first to tell you.'

'Where did you go when you left me this morning?'

'I went home and had a shower. I was angry. I don't want to be a Mrs whatsit in your life. You can call it buyer remorse if you like.'

Shipton's angry expression switched to hangdog, and he reached out.

Kelly pushed him away. 'You'll need to try harder, boss.'

'I think you went to Mickey Krakauer's place.'

Kelly felt her face flush.

'I knew it.'

'You had me followed?'

'For your own protection. I had Virginia followed as well. She eventually got used to it.'

'Didn't stop her collecting a bullet, did it?' Kelly immediately realised she'd stepped over the mark. 'Gosh… I shouldn't have said that. That isn't me.'

'I'll be out for the rest of the morning. Don't be here when I get back and don't bother coming in tomorrow.'

She'd been summarily fired and given the under-the-counter way that Clarkie paid his staff, it meant she was effectively broke. She waited until he left the building, found his UV scanner, lit up the number on the card and snapped a pic with her smartphone. She immediately texted the pic to Mickey and realised her mistake when her eye caught the slight movement of the tiny office surveillance camera, as it came to rest.

***

Bib's burner buzzed with an incoming call. He looked down at the screen. No number was showing only the words International Call. He showed the screen to Bub.

'You expectin a call, boss?'

'There's only one person who has this number, and that's a cop named Mickey Krakauer.'

'What are you going to do?'

Let it ring out.

The phone stopped buzzing and Bib waited.

It buzzed again.

He let it ring and again waited.

It buzzed again and again.

Bib set the timer on his watch for one hour and waited.

The hour came and went with no further calls. Whomever had tried to make contact had given up and only time would tell if Mickey had remembered the procedure he'd mentioned.

Frank arrived to advise them of the next part of the plan. 'We will be taking off in one hour and expect to land in Mumbai on schedule. Getting there isn't a problem but if the people on the ground decide to do a routine customs check...'

Bib thanked him. 'We've had closer calls, Frank. We'll play it by ear and, if necessary, the ladies will need to stay in their little cabin.' He raised his eyebrows towards the girls, who were squashed in among a pile of cushions in the open flight container.

They nodded back at him with three individual "not-our-fault" expressions.

It had been about eight hours since they arrived at the FFS hangar. Their substitute drug was starting to wear off, and they were becoming edgy.

Bib had noticed their distress and said, 'It won't be long now, and it will be all worth it in the end.'

'We need some stuff, Mr Bib.'

'I'll have enough to get you to Mumbai from here or Perth from Mumbai. Can you try to hang on?'

They all scowled and slunk back into their cushioned hideaway.

***

Clark Shipton returned to his office the following morning. Kelly was not at her desk, and he remembered he'd fired her. He was disappointed. *I'll have to work on that*, he thought. Kelly had become a major asset but, more than that, he'd developed a fondness for her that he never considered possible after Virginia.

He heard a sound out in the reception area. 'Kel?'

There was no reply.

Shipton rose from his desk, looked outside, and saw a tall man in a suit with one of its jacket pockets hanging out of shape, because of the weighty item it was concealing. 'Who are you?'

The man turned to face at him. 'Clark Shipton?'

'Who wants to know?'

'I don't take kindly to being set up by criminals like you, Shipton. Where's the woman?'

'Woman?' Shipton knew who he was referring to but decided to play along.

'Be aware that I don't play games. Where is she?' The man took a step forward and slid his hand into his distorted pocket.

Shipton noticed his action and his limp and smirked. 'If you're referring to my PA, she no longer works here.'

The man frowned. 'Good, you appear to be on your own, so no witnesses.' His hand appeared to lock in a grip on the item in his pocket.

Shipton grinned. 'Mickey Krakauer said you were an unprofessional mob.'

The tall man began to pull the item from his jacket.

He didn't allow for Shipton's foot, which might have been punting a Sherrin, but he got two for the price of one, and the man fired the weapon aimed directly at his own foot. Blood spurted from the leather as he fell to his knees from the double whammy assault on his person.

Shipton had been a street fighter in his youth and wasn't one to miss an opportunity. He swung his knee into the man's face as he fell. His moaning was silenced as blood gushed from the region of his freshly deviated septum.

Shipton picked up his phone and tapped a number.

'What!?'

'I'm sorry.'

'You're wasting your time. Find yourself a whatsit bimbo.'

'I've had a bit of an altercation in the office.'

'So!'

'The bloke with the limp is languishing on my floor with a broken nose and a bullet through his foot.'

'So, you won't be going along with them, then?'

'Can you get Mickey to come over?'

'I can ask him, but I think he believes you and Limpy are getting it together to squeeze out Bib and Bub.'

'I know, that thought once crossed my mind, but it's long since left the building.'

18

Kelly Coulson hung up on her boss and tapped Mickey's number.

A voice she didn't recognise answered, 'Hello, Kelly Coulson.'

Kelly quickly realised her mistake and remembered that Mick probably had her name in his contacts list. So, her name, maybe even her face, would have appeared on his screen. She ended the call and ran to her car. After what Clarkie had just said about Limpy, the chances where, he'd be getting another visit soon.

She turned the key, found the street, and floored the accelerator while keeping one eye on the rear vision mirror. So far, Limpy and his cronies had been on the front foot. They had a lot to gain if they could reduce Bib and Bub's rewards for their own benefit, and she took a roundabout route to throw off anyone who might be following her.

Mickey answered his door. He'd showered and changed into his work clothes, and Jackie was behind him in the hall. She was holding his service Glock, clearly capable, and ready to use it if necessary.

'Kel? Come in.' He held the door open, and she followed him down the short hall.

'Clarkie's office was broken into, by one of the men who took you and Jack. He might look like a quasi-office type these days, but Clarkie's no slouch when it comes to a fight.'

'I thought you said Clarkie was warming to them dollar signs, etc.'

'Look. I'll make no excuses for him. Clarkie's a crook. His brain's wired differently to normal people, but he does have a code. If someone tries to cross him, they'd better watch out.'

'Are you saying the deals are off?'

'I'm not saying anything, Mick, but right now I think he needs your help and quickly.'

Mickey glanced at Jackie.

She reached to wrap her arms around the one nearest to her. 'You're going nowhere without me, Mickey Krakauer.'

'Jeb, and his mob?' Mickey said.

Kelly replied, 'I don't think you can rely on them, Mick. They're small-time heavies who like a good punch up, but they've served their purpose.'

Mickey turned to his fiancé. 'You have wedding stuff to plan, Jack. You've done enough.'

Jackie pointed the Glock at Kelly and said, 'What's the deal?'

'Clarkie needs help with the disposal of a lump of raw meat on the floor of his office.'

'He's dead?' Mickey said, taking his gun from her and holstering it.

'Not quite, but he's expecting a team follow-up visit.'

'I've a lot at stake and I'm not sure I'm the man for the job.'

'You're the only man for the job, Mick... Please.'

'I don't have a phone. All my stuff was nicked when they took me, even my police ID and driver's licence.'

Kelly handed him a phone. 'It's a burner.' She reached into her handbag, pulled out a wad of cash, and handed it to Jackie. 'I know, he's a cop, and trust me, this is not a bribe.' She held up her phone and showed the number she'd called. 'I rang you by mistake. If you can track the location of your phone, I think you might find the man who has your stuff.'

Mickey found his laptop, logged in, and within a few seconds, his phone location was displayed on the map. 'It's in the same place they kept Jack.'

Kelly smiled. 'Not such a big mistake, after all.'

***

Bib and Bub had settled in, to wait for their departure, and were relaxing in the row of five courier seats provided directly behind the walled off flight deck.

'Drink or sommat to eat?' Bub said.

'Thank you, but no,' Bib replied.

'Mind if I do?' There was no reply, so he looked in on the girls, who were sleeping. He didn't bother wakening them and made his way to the small galley to grab a sandwich and a can of coke from the fridge. When he returned, he said, 'We've known each other for a while now and I'm probably one of the few who knows your real name.'

Bib said, 'Best we keep it that way. The fewer people know about us, the better.'

'I was Aussie SAS, and you were in the pommy mob, but when you were speaking to Shipton, you let slip a couple of things.'

'My bad, Bub.'

'Six and the SAS do have a connection, though.'

Bib smiled wryly, put a finger to his lips and said, 'Hush.'

'So why are you here?'

'Bureaucracy, Bub… and the fact that I offended a bureaucratic prick, in a suit, who was assigned the job of administering my team.'

'Ah… that sort of makes sense, but your skills, time served, and connections would have surely swamped a bit of argy-bargy.'

'Not as simple as that.'

'But they threw you out?'

'Not quite. I was sent to the naughty corner to cool off, but the command chain was broken, and I could never work with him again.'

'So, you retired?'

'No one retires from the business I was in, Bub. Too many secrets, too many lies, and plausible deniability means just that. Thankfully, my superior's superior considered my skills worth keeping, so I'm in a sort of casual reserve status. Apparently, senior management, loosely known as the British Government, considers me a loose cannon. As it happened, my entire team was wiped out when my replacement took over and followed the bureaucratic prick-in-a-suit's orders to march into a setup. Then the prick-in-the-suit left the building, and he hasn't been seen or heard of since. Plausible deniability works both ways. And there you have my potted history, for what it's worth. What about you, my friend?'

'I was in it for the long haul. My marriage wasn't, and when my daughter became addicted, I needed to put her first.'

'Mrs Clayton?'

'Mrs Clayton was killed in a traffic accident. It's not something I want to talk about.'

'Did that affect your daughter's relationship with you?'

'She thinks her mother left us. She's in a serious place right now, Bib, and when she gets out, whatever it costs, she'll be in rehab until I'm satisfied that she can remain clean. She hates me right now, but maybe when she's over the hump we can talk about our ongoing relationship. Were you ever in a relationship, Bib?'

Bib laughed. 'I once thought I might like a long-term gig, indeed I came very close to one lady, but maintaining it was another matter. Our business does not make allowances for families. When I left without warning, in the small hours, and didn't return for 7 months, the yellowing goodbye note, waiting on my return, said it all. Eventually, I gave up on relationships and learned to make do with the occasional one-night stand.' He stretched. 'Maybe one day?'

'These kids?' Bub nodded towards the container.

'They could have been my daughters if she'd have been prepared to stay. She's married to a diplomat now. I've bumped into her occasionally. She seems happy enough. These people traffickers and the kind of slavery they bond these children with, must be eliminated at all costs, Bub. Your daughter?'

'I don't think she fitted their demographic. She was well past their age preference when it started to go wrong, but she'd become a rebel and would have been easy meat during her earlier times. This might seem like a silly question, but apart from that general, do you have any other contacts in Mumbai?'

Before bib could answer, Frank approached them and said, 'We'll be ready to taxi soon. Take-off in about thirty minutes. Better make sure the girls are okay and secure.'

***

The questioning was being deliberately dragged out. With James in one room and Angela in another. DCI Callum Birchmore was in his finest smirky element as he viewed the proceedings via video. He had provided a list of questions for each set of interrogators. Between them, he was sure they would come up with a mismatch, and that would be enough to hang James Carter with his own petard.

It turned out that the man with the camera and scalded head was a contractor, allegedly employed by the AFP, but he had no identification papers. This, he'd said, was because of the confidential nature of his work. The hit with the cast iron chicken cacciatore pan had fractured his skull, so he was unable to answer any but the basic questions that the officers had put to him.

In effect, he'd called around to collect his camera card that had been misplaced during an earlier skirmish with the woman who'd panned him, and he was accusing Angela Carter of assault and aggravated theft.

Angela didn't deny taking the card and, during her interview, said she'd downloaded the data relevant to her, to her computer. She offered the interviewing officer the empty card plus a thumb drive containing the items, which were of no concern. She then advised the files that were of concern had been transferred to her lawyer, who nodded in agreement.

James Carter had responded similarly in his interview and pointed out that it could have been much worse as the chicken cacciatore had not yet been cooked and the man had not suffered more burns.

After several hours of questioning, it was becoming apparent that the hit with the chicken cacciatore vessel could be considered as nothing more than a bold and obvious act of self-defence against a person making threats with a firearm.

They were given a break and James called Stacey to let her know they'd been taken in for questioning and that she might like to look in on Oliver because of his mum's absence.

'How long for?' she asked.

'I can't say. For as long as they can stretch it out. Don't worry, it's just another fuck up. If you can contact Mickey for me and tell him what's going on. That would be great.' He heard her huff at the other end and said, 'Sorry. This should have been fixed up earlier, but….'

19

The 737 began its taxi to the main runway, where it waited for clearance. Over their headphones, they could hear a heavily accented voice in communications with the tower. When at last they were airborne, and relatively free of the rules and regs, Bub opened the container and invited the girls to join them.

All three were now in early withdrawal. Their agitation was worsening, and Bub looked at Bib.

He shook his head. 'We don't have enough and I'd rather they were good for our eventual arrival in Perth.'

'Please!' Kaitlin whined.

'Not yet. The longer we leave it, the better you'll be. Hey, I'm a soldier, not a doctor, and you'll just have to put up with my decision. Right or wrong.'

Kaitlin scowled.

'Scowl all you like, madam. We were only expecting one of you. We've taken a huge risk in bringing your friends and you need to start thinking about them.'

'When *can* I have something?' she whined

'I was planning to keep you on ice until we leave Mumbai. Then you'll get your dose and be feeling better when you arrive in Perth.'

Kaitlin sniffed and wiped snot from her nose with the back of her hand. Agnetha and Bronwyn seemed less anxious, but Bub's experience told him that it wouldn't be long before they too were in full withdrawal, with all the problems that engendered. He tapped Bib on the arm.

Bib knew what he was going to say and replied in advance, 'Nope. We can't take the risk of them being raving loonies when we get to Perth.'

'What if we give them a reduced dose halfway to Mumbai and another halfway to Perth?'

Bib shook his head.

Bub looked at the three girls with an *I tried* shrug.

Bronwyn, who had barely spoken until now, said, 'Thank you for what you're trying to do, Mr Bib. Thank you for helping me escape.'

'Do you have your parents contact details?'

She shook her head and tears spilled down her face as she looked away. 'I'll take half if it helps me get somewhere safe,' she sobbed.

Agnetha said, 'Me too. I can't remember much about my life before I was in a heroin high, having rough sex with grossly overweight men in suits. They stank of drink and drooled all over me.' She retched when the thought crossed her mind, and she put her arms around Kaitlin.

Kaitlin was shaking, her face dripping with sweat. She pushed her away and glowered at Bib. 'It's my dad who's paying your wages.'

'What's that got to do with anything?' Agnetha said.

Bib rankled and turned to Bub. 'Advice?'

'We let them get real bad, then administer a split dose. I estimate it'll be a couple of hours after take-off before they'll be hanging out big-time. Half a dose might just settle them till we get through Mumbai. Then we drag it out until nearer home and give them what's left.' He looked at all three girls in turn. 'Best I can offer right now.'

Kaitlin scowled her usual look in his direction. None of them had as yet suffered the full withdrawal symptoms and in their captivity, they were too valuable to be slowed by sickness. 'I'm so sorry, Mr Bib, I can't help this.' She'd witnessed both men kill in cold blood, and they done it for her. They were hard and focussed, but on her side. 'Thank you for all you've done.'

Bub headed to the galley and brought them back some sandwiches and ice-cold cokes. 'Better try to keep your strength up it won't be an easy ride.'

'How would you know!?' Agnetha snapped, her eyes now red from rubbing and her nose becoming snottier.

'I have a daughter who is going through exactly what you are experiencing. Trust me. It will be worth putting up with some grief if it means being back with your family.'

'Ha! My dad's a fucking criminal.' Kaitlin threw her open coke across the cabin, followed up with her sandwich and began weeping and scratching furiously.

There was nothing Bib and Bub could do. The operation had already exceeded its anticipated share of screw ups and while it might make life easier, it wasn't practical to pull out the garrottes.

'Let's hope Mumbai passes without a problem. I don't need any more right now,' Bib said.

***

'There is nothing to be gained by this, DCI Birchmore. Kindly free my client and his sister so he can be with his family, and she can be with her child.'

DCI Callum Birchmore showed his frustration by thumping

the interview table and threatening James with instant dismissal. 'We cannot have the relatives of our police officers bashing up civilians.'

James struggled to hold back a smirk. He looked at the aging, cigarette tarnished woman who had been assigned to him as his lawyer for the purpose of the interview.

'You know the rules.' She stood and moved to open the door. 'Mr Carter. You are free to leave. If there are police disciplinary matters pending in your capacity as a Detective Inspector, they are nothing to do with me.'

James stood and looked directly into the eyes of his immediate superior.

Birchmore snarled. 'Get out of my sight, Carter, and take that half-arsed lawyer of a sister with you.'

James felt his ire growing, and the more he saw the blubbery face of Birchmore, the more he wanted to release it via a fist.

His lawyer was quick to stay his arm. 'Not worth it, Mr Carter. Ask your sister. If you want my two penneth, she's a better lawyer than he thinks. Isn't she, DCI Birchmore?'

Birchmore stood and walked out.

James collected Angela and called a taxi. 'Let's get you home,' he grinned, 'via my place, and maybe a takeaway joint.'

When they arrived at James' home, they heard the shrieks before the door was answered. A frazzled Stacey opened the door and said, 'Thank God you're here.'

James's face froze. 'What's happened?'

His question was answered when three kids roared into the house from the back yard.

'Daaad!' Andria's red face yelled.

'What's happened?' he repeated.

The two boys appeared. They were filthy, soaking wet and

grinning like idiots.

'Ah. I see. Sorry, Stace, I thought…'

'It started as a bit of fun with hoses, but as usual it got out of hand. You and Oli staying for dinner? You must be starving?'

Angela put her hands up in a no thanks gesture.

James said, 'I insist. It was your chicken cacciatore that saved our bacon.' He grabbed the two boys by their collars before they could scurry away. 'And these two need a bath.'

The matter was settled and, with everyone scrubbed up and sitting at the table, they were a family again.

'So, the bloke shot you in the arm, Uncle Jim?'

'It was only a scratch, Oli. A couple of stitches, a good-sized sticking plaster, and I'm all good.'

'Chicken cacciatore?' Stacey said.

'I'd just put it in the oven,' Angela replied.

James said nothing.

Angela couldn't help herself, but she kept a straight face and said, 'I was trying out the "no cook" recipe.' She wiggled her fingers in the air around the words, no cook.

Stacey frowned. 'No cook?'

'Yeah, it gives you a head start when you're being attacked by an intruder.'

James was trying his hardest to keep his eyes off his sister.

Then she snorted, and they both lost it.

'I'm confused. Chicken cacciatore, no cook recipe? How do you make that?' Stacey's serious expression sent them off them into further paroxysms of laughter until eventually its contagion took over.

When they'd all simmered down, Stacey said, 'Seriously, though?'

Angela pursed her lips into a tight smile. 'I'd forgotten to put the oven on.'

A look of revelation washed over Stacey's face, and she covered her mouth with her hand. 'So, this questioning you were called in for?'

'Just Birchmore trying it on,' James said. 'He had no case, but he's after my blood and I can't afford to give him another chance.'

'Will it go any further?'

'Right now, let's eat, then we'll worry about what happens next.' He felt his phone buzz in his pocket and ignored it.

A few minutes later Stacey's phone began tooting in another room.

20

Mickey Krakauer ended the call when James Carter didn't pick up. Mandy, in the cyber division, was his last resort.

'Hi, Mickey.'

'I tried to call Jim Carter, but he's not answering.'

'He's probably switched off his phone. Birchmore chucked a wobbly, but they had no case to answer, and he had to release them.'

'So, they're no longer there?'

'That's what I heard.'

'I need to speak to him urgently. I know where the geezers who took me and Jack are, and I'm planning to go after them. I'd rather it was sanctioned by the department, but…'

'Leave it with me. I have Stacey's number. I'll give her a try.'

The line went silent.

Several minutes later, Mickey's burner rang.

'Mick?'

'Sorry to bother you, boss, but I have a lead on the people who took Jack and me. They're pretend cops, but worse, they're a disgruntled mob from way back who might be trying to muscle in on Clarkie Shipton's deal with the two blokes who are bringing his daughter home.'

'What can I do?'

'As cops, they approached Clarkie. Kelly immediately saw through them, and it's her belief that they want to shoehorn themselves into Bib & Bub's operation, maybe stop his daughter from talking and perhaps leverage future deals. I believe we need to raid the place and round them up. There might even be some benefit intelligence wise.'

'Wait, what are you saying?'

'They are a gang who are claiming to be federal cops with fake ID papers to match, and I wouldn't be surprised if they weren't in league with some of the genuine local cops over here. They seem to have no worries about formality and discipline, and they are sloppy with their weapons, which makes them even more dangerous.'

'Where do they hang out?'

'There's a disused recording studio. It's where they kept Jack until a couple of Kelly's mates freed her. My phone was stolen when I was taken, and I've tracked it to the same place.'

'I'm in the position of general dog's body at the moment, Mick, and I have little say about what happens.'

'Shit.'

'Not entirely shit. As you know, I have a few friends in the force who are actually on the right side of the law, and they might be interested in an unofficial raid.'

'What happens if something goes wrong?'

'We can't let it. I'll muster a reliable group, and we can go through the possibilities. I don't need to tell you that if it gets back to the hierarchy before we complete the operation, we'll all be out on our ears before you can say not guilty.'

'Okay, boss.' Mickey pressed end, turned to Kelly and said, 'We have a thumbs up, but it won't be easy. We'll all be off grid and that means we'll be unprotected. Now, about this lump of meat in Clarkie's office?'

Jackie grinned, handed Mickey his gun, and picked up the car keys.

'Where are you going?'

'You are not getting out of my sight until this is over, lover boy.'

***

The approach to Mumbai had begun and Bib was secretly happy he'd taken Bub's advice. They'd suffered the anguish of the girls that, with a fractional dose of *Suboxone*, had eased.

They were secured into the container during the descent, and a seal was applied to make it look real. Now all that needed to happen was a more lightweight than usual inspection team who would skim over papers and wave them on.

Frank had called through a generic order of food and drink for their arrival, and, other than fuel and mechanical checks, they would only be staying until that work was complete. He switched his coms to internal only and said, 'I hope that will keep the immigration people off our backs, and once the inspection is completed, we can be on our way.'

The 737 wheels hit the tarmac and the rumble of the landing gear vibrated through the aircraft.

Bib tapped on the container and said, 'We've just landed at Mumbai. Total silence if you please, ladies.'

There was no reply.

He hoped that meant they were taking him seriously.

The aircraft taxied to the hard stand and came to a halt. Just like the previous places, a welcoming committee stood waiting on the tarmac.

Once the shutdown routine was completed, Frank walked aft and opened the hatch to the outside. Hot and humid air rushed into the cabin, and it was stifling within minutes.

A ladder was rolled into place, and the ground crew ascended to complete their security checks.

Frank handed the leader a manifest and waved to the row of containers. 'All sealed, but you are free to unseal and check any or all the containers.'

The leader waved him aside and walked down the row. 'This one.'

One of his assistants clipped the wire seal and opened the door.

The leader with the manifest began ticking off the items and when he had finished, he slapped Frank on the back. 'All jolly good old chap. When are you scheduled to leave?'

'As soon as we've refuelled, and our flight checks are complete.'

'So, we won't be indulging ourselves this time?'

'Sorry, Jay. We have some medical supplies that need expediting.'

The look on the leader's face froze. 'Medical supplies? You are meaning drugs, my friend? Show me, please.'

Bib had been observing the discussion and the facial expressions coupled with body language that had suddenly gone south. He approached the official.

'Jay, is it?'

The leader said, 'Who are you?'

Bib stepped forward, grasped the man by the arm, and led him through the door and down to the tarmac. 'Sorry, old chap. I can't say anything, but if the manifest is examined in too much detail, it might have serious repercussions for General Rajput...' He followed with a knowing nod.

Jay's face froze at the mention of the armed forces commander.

'The General must not be involved, but I am a personal friend of his and you may confirm this by telephone while we wait.' It was true, Bib was, in fact, a past combat buddy of the general, so he had no problem with Jay confirming his friendship. He asked for a piece of paper, wrote down the general's personal number, and handed it back to him.

Jay gave a know-it-all smirk. Reached for his phone and tapped in the number.

Bib listened to the barely audible tinny ringtone, and it was his turn to smirk when the phone was answered by a sleepy voice.

Jay quickly ended the call, looked down at his watch and said, 'It seems you are as you seem, sir.' He waved to his team, and they left the plane to continue on its way.

When Bib returned to the cabin, Frank's nervousness was manifesting itself. 'What the fuck…?'

Bib held up his phone to show a Mumbai time of 0200. 'Not a good idea to call your boss at two am.'

'You know his boss?' Frank asked.

'He's an old buddy of mine who would have been dead meat if we hadn't saved his bacon last year. I helped close off an assassination attempt and General Verma Rajput owes me big-time, but I still wouldn't want to explain our cargo to him.'

Frank seemed relieved. 'I'll get the checks over with, and we can be on our way.' He turned and disappeared onto the flight deck.

'What about the girls?' Bub said.

'They stay in their box until we're airborne.'

'Is that wise, boss? There can't be much air left in there.'

'Then they'd better breathe easy for a while.' He placed his ear against the container's thin walls and listened. 'I'd say they were asleep. Ask Frank how long before departure.'

'Hey, Bib,' Bub said. 'Did you notice anything familiar about the faces at the brothel?'

Bib grinned. 'Took a load of random pics with my phone. Bit fuzzy in places, but mostly recognisable.'

'I saw some of them on the telly while we were at Sarajevo.'

'The brothel punters?'

'Three of them. If I'm not mistaken, they're Australian officials on a trade mission. I think one might be a minor government minister the other two are possibly public servants.' He held his hand out. 'Got your phone handy.'

Bib activated his burner, switched to the pictures app and handed it to Bub, who began scrolling through.

'Ha! Take a look at this, Bib.'

Bib expanded the picture to show the dimly lit faces of the teen decorated customers.

Bub pointed at the screen. 'Blakely. Minister assisting the minister for Foreign Affairs. The other two are his chief of staff and a PR hack. I know the hack's face, but I can't put a name to it.'

Bib leaned towards the skin of the container and said, 'Kaitlin. I think we might have the key to unlocking our paper's problem.'

She didn't reply.

Bib turned to Bub. 'You can open the box but keep them secure. I need to make a short excursion. When I return, we'll continue our flight. Okay with you Frank?'

Frank grinned and said, 'Oops, sorry chaps, there's been an unfortunate delay in our flight plan.' He smirked at Bib, tapped him on the shoulder and said, 'I guess we'll see you when we see you then.'

Bib picked up his bag and, without further ado, walked down the ladder from the aircraft and disappeared into the night.

21

The man with the limp was still in a heap on Clark Shipton's office floor when Mickey, Jackie and Kelly burst in.

'Oh dear,' Mickey said, 'I think we might be needing a wheelbarrow.'

Shipton laughed. 'He'll be a dead weight, but with the two of us, we should be able to shift him without much trouble?'

'It won't be a good look if we're seen dragging a flaccid body across your carpark,' Mickey said.

Shipton said, 'Yeah, s'pose you're right and I've never felt comfortable hauling bodies around in rolled-up carpets, either.'

Mickey dropped to one knee and checked the man's vital signs. 'He's out cold, but do you think he might be trouble if we revive him?'

'Not if we gag him and cuff him.' Shipton said.

'Do you happen to have a set of cuffs handy?'

Shipton shook his head.

Kelly beamed and cleared her throat.

They both turned to face her with quizzical expressions.

She left the office and returned with an ancient leather bag, unclipped the tarnished brass fastener, and reached in to remove a cluster of what looked like implements of bondage. 'Bet you've forgotten all about this stuff. Hey, Clarkie.' She sorted out, from the cluster, several sets of velvet covered handcuffs and various other items that might be found in a sadomasochist's closet.

Clarkie laughed. 'I thought Vera had taken all that stuff when she left.' He picked up two sets of cuffs that were separated by a longer than normal chain and had pink feathers attached. 'These.' He smirked. 'We'll strip the bastard down to his undies and leave him where someone'll find him. He can do his own explainin when the time comes.'

Mickey stood back. 'What you do is up to you, Clarkie, but you know I can't be involved.'

Clark Shipton sucked in a deep breath. 'No worries, get yourself home, Mick. Kel and me'll fix it.'

Kelly disappeared again and returned with a bag trolley. 'If we lash him to this and wheel him down the back stairs with a cover over him... the carpark isn't overlooked, so we should be able to get him into a car without too much trouble.'

Mickey knew that, regardless of what happened next, he could not be a potential witness to an unlawful detention and assault. He turned to Jackie, who was trying to not laugh at the antics of the pair, and nodded towards the door. As she followed him out, he struggled to not picture Kelly and Clarkie bumping the trolley down the back stairs, one step at a time.

***

Frank unsealed the freight container to give the girls a much-needed breather. Bib had given him no indication of the time he'd require, to fix up the papers he seemed confident of securing, and all three were unconscious and verging of suffocation. 'Bub!'

'This doesn't look good.'

'It wasn't my idea to become part of a murder plot, Mr Bub.'

'They'll be okay once we get them some air and as long as we don't receive any official visitors, they'll be okay in the cabin.' He lifted each of the girls, carried them out of the container, and lay them on the deck behind the seats. The movement seemed to revive them, and as they began to breathe normally, they awakened to exhibit more of their earlier behaviour.

'I hope Dave returns soon,' Frank said. 'I've delayed our departure, but for how long…?'

Bub raised an eyebrow at the partial use of Bib's real name. 'I know you're a mate of his, Frank, but we have a strict protocol on ops. It's protecting everyone, including you, and we can never be sure who might be listening.'

Frank said, 'Sorry, but you understand my point?'

'How long can you delay?'

'Thirty-six hours max, then we'll be hit with penalties, and maybe more inspections. Not good, if you get my drift.'

'He's never let me down in the past and I'm sure he understands your problem.' He glanced at his watch. 'We still have twenty-three hours before we must leave. A lot can happen in that time.' He looked down at the girls, who were showing increasing signs of distress. He tried to comfort them and said, 'Not long now and we'll be on our way.'

'Do you have their medication?' Frank asked.

Bub shook his head.

'I might be able to lay my hands on something, but it won't be the prescription stuff you guys have.'

'How long will that take you?'

'I'll need to speak to Jay, and I don't want to see him on this plane again.'

Bub said, 'twenty-three hours is a long time for these kids to wait.'

'Want me to give it a go?'

Bub reached for the burner and checked for messages. He sent a code to Bib and waited. 'I'll see what he has to say.'

Bub's phone tweeted.

> They need at least twelve more hours for the production of emergency papers. What is the problem?

> Frank has to leave in twenty-three hours or be subject to penalties and more inspections. The girls are withdrawing badly, and I have no stuff.

> Frank says he might be able to get stuff, but it will not be the real McCoy.

> I'll try to speed things up. Hold fast and await further orders.

Bub showed Frank the message.

'Well, they'll be climbing up the walls soon. When that happens, I might have to bail out. My business revolves around my integrity, and I can't be implicated in a scandal, least of all one involving drugs. I'll give you twelve hours and then you are off the plane and fending for yourselves. Sorry, I have no choice.'

As he spoke, the door to the forward cabin behind the flight deck opened and a blonde-haired woman, dressed in a captain's uniform, appeared. She said, 'Fronk?' in a heavily accented voice. 'Vat is goink on?'

Frank said, 'Hello dear. This is Mr Bub.'

'Ver iss ze ozzer von?'

Bub was about to speak when Frank answered his question before it passed his lips. 'My wife and co-pilot, Magda. She boarded just before you. You were sorting out the girls.' He pointed to the forward cabin. 'Bit like a small caravan in there, we lost a bit of space for cargo, and we installed extra seating because sometimes we need extra help, but we have everything we need for a long haul. Magda's been sleeping. She'll be piloting the next leg, and it doesn't do to be fatigued.'

'I'll start preflight, darlink, time you got some rest,' Magda said.

'No rush, dear. Take-off's been delayed a few hours.'

Kaitlin began whining and calling for Bub. 'I need my stuff, Mr Bub.' She stood up from behind the seats and saw Magda. 'Have you brought it?'

Frank winced.

Magda frowned. 'Vat iss this stuff you speak of?'

Bub noticed Frank shrink from his wife's question. 'Does she know, Frank?'

Frank rocked his head. 'It's a long story, Magda…'

'Then it had better be a good von, my love.' Magda looked across to Kaitlin. 'You are?'

Kaitlin shook her head, confused, as her friends stood and wrapped their arms around her.

'Mr Bib and Mr Bub are taking us back to our families,' Agnetha said, scratching and shaking as she spoke.

'Vat is wrong viss you?'

Bronwyn held out her arms for inspection.

'Vat iss your age?'

'I don't know. They…' she pointed at Bub, 'say we are all fifteen, going sixteen years.'

'Jesus Christus, Fronk. Vat iss goink on behind my back.'

Bub stepped forward and said, 'I'm sorry, ma'am. My colleague and I were under the impression that everyone involved in this flight was aware of our reason for being here.'

'Zen be explaining, please.'

Bub ran through the basic reasons for the operation, while leaving out specific details such as the killing of Maria and the braining of the doorman. 'We were given no choice but to bring all three, rather than just Kaitlin. They have been subjected to drug use as a part of their servitude, and the poor blighters are experiencing withdrawal. Sadly, we didn't have enough drugs to pacify all three of them, and two of the girls also need papers.'

Magda's face hardened into a gaunt mask, and she strutted towards the three kids.

Frank squirmed. He had no idea what she would do. She'd been warned of a special cargo, but not its details.

'Bastards,' Magda said. 'My poor babies. Come.' She held open her arms for the girls who weren't sure of what to do. Then her nose wrinkled. 'Fronk, diese kinder are filzzy. Zey are needing a good bath and clean clothes.'

Frank nodded and shrugged, gormlessly.

'Right, von at a time. You will use our shower. Unterstant?'

All three nodded.

'Then come. You, Fronk, vil stay out here until ve are ready to leaf.'

'Yes dear.' He shot a glance at Bub.

'Sorry, mate, I didn't even know you had a wife.'

22

On the way to the car Mickey said, 'You up for a bit of biffo, Jack?'

'The bastards that locked us up?'

Mickey raised his eyebrows.

'Hold my beer,' she said, and dropped into the passenger seat.

Mickey fired the engine and eased out of Shipton's private carpark. He handed her his burner, showing the location of his actual phone. 'This is where they are. There'll be no help for us or backup available until tomorrow, maybe.'

Jackie sucked in a deep breath. 'Doesn't feel quite so bad now I've had my pardon confirmed.'

Mickey drove to the recording studio and parked one-hundred meters away. He looked at the dash clock and said, 'It'll be dark in a couple of hours. This is where they held you, and I don't know what their armoury is like.' He checked his Glock and then he called James Carter.

'Mick?'

'I can't wait for a possible—slash—maybe, backup. Jackie and I are going in as soon as the time is right.' He ended the call there, knowing his friend and boss would be on a spot, and turned to Jackie. 'We'll let it get dark, then we'll take out the stragglers who haven't gone to the pub. When we know which one they're at, we can work out our next plan of action. I need to make a call to Bib and Bub, so bear with me.'

Jackie waited patiently as he tapped in the number he'd found on the card that Bib had given him.

He had strict instructions on how to make the call. And he knew he'd need a clear hour for the actual connection. Each time the phone at the other end connected, he disconnected. He did it four times and set his timer for one hour. He would make his final call then and hope that Bib was able to answer.

'What's the plan, Mick?' Jackie said.

'If it's anything like last time, they'll leave a couple of stragglers to hold the fort, who'll have orders to call if anything untoward happens.'

'Then we render the stragglers safe and lie in wait for the drunks to return?'

'About sums it up. Lack of knowledge of their weapons means we'll need to be quick and dirty. Fortunately, the place is soundproofed no one will hear what we're doing.'

'That it, then?'

'I'd like to see if they have any paperwork that might be compromising. If we can find that, we can officially close them down.' He looked in the rear-view mirror and saw a dark-coloured car pull up close behind him. A second or two later, another pulled in front and backed him in. 'Shit!' he blurted

'Now what do we do?'

'We wait, as if nothing has happened.'

No one disembarked from either vehicle.

Mickey held Jackie's hand and sat tight as his phone timer ticked to an hour. Its quiet beeping triggered his final call to Bib.

'Mickey. Did you try to call a while ago?'

'No. I was otherwise detained, but I need you to know that there have been a group of fake cops sniffing around Shipton's offices. I'm sorry, I think Kelly might have inadvertently given away your number when she black lit it, on Clarkie's scanner.'

'Ah, makes sense. They didn't follow through. So?'

'So, they know what you are up to, and they know about Clarkie's contract. We're thinking they might want to silence Kaitlin.'

Mickey heard a chuckle at the other end.

'I didn't think it was that funny.'

'I did. You can let Clarkie know that all is good, and his girl is on the last leg of her journey home, but we've had a few hiccups.'

'Hiccups?'

'I can't say over the phone, but there is likely to be a bit of a… Mr Colins?' His voice lowered to a whisper. 'Sorry, old chap, have to go. See you soon.'

The line fell silent, and Mickey smiled as he turned to Jackie. 'Clarkie's girl is on her way home.'

'Fantastic.' Her eyes widened as she pointed to the other side of the car. 'I think someone wants to speak with you.'

Mickey swung around to face his window. A hand was tapping the business end of a Glock against his window. He pressed the down button and waited for the blast in his face. At least Jack might have a chance if he was in the way.

'Sergeant Mickey Krakauer?'

'Who wants him?'

The face behind the smile said, 'DI Carter sent us. He said we were to follow your instructions.'

'Doesn't tell me who you are?'

'We're off grid Mick, best keep it that way.'

Mickey felt a surge of adrenalin. 'Get in the back.'

The man stowed his gun and did as he was requested. 'We understand there is a cadre of fake cops holed up...' he pointed to the recording studio just as a small group noisily exited the building.

'They'll soon be heading to the pub,' Mickey said. 'They'll leave a couple behind to hold the fort, and that is what we've been waiting for.'

The man in the back seat said, 'We'll get ready and lead.' He opened his jacket to display his body armour. 'Jim Carter said there might be some action, so we came dressed for the party. As soon as we've made it secure, we'll give you a hoy and you can do whatever it is you need to do.'

Mickey felt a huge wave of relief. Having an armed response group on hand changed the entire dynamic. 'Who authorised this?'

The man in the back seat spoked, 'Like I said, we are off grid, so you'd better hope nothing goes too wrong.' His face widened into a smile. 'If we win, we'll all be heroes. If we lose, we'll be sweeping the car park for the next whatever.'

The man stepped out and within a few seconds his group were furtively making their way towards the recording studio.

'What the hell happened there?' Jackie said.

'You tell me. I don't have a clue other than Jim Carter has drawn on some sneaky resources. Come on, let's see what they're hiding.' He pushed open his door and stood.

By the time they were close enough to the studio, the ARG had dispersed around the building. It was dark and their black uniforms effectively rendered them invisible.

Mickey heard a loud voice and felt Jackie grab his arm. He waited until he heard another voice shout all clear before moving quickly to enter the studio. The lights were all on and two men were cuffed on the floor in a corner of the first room.

The man from the back seat returned and said, 'Interesting set up. Notice anything?'

Mickey looked around and realised that he was standing in a replica of a typical police station. 'Gone to a bit of trouble, haven't they?'

Back seat spoke again. 'Well, that's us done, Sergeant.'

Mickey stared in disbelief. Then Jackie and he jammed their hands into nitrile gloves.

Within minutes, they had the lanyards and the fake IDs belonging to so-called federal officers. There were also several files full of papers that might be useful down the track, but most of all there was a copy of the proforma signed by Clark Shipton and photographs of his daughter. Several other photographs also surfaced. They might have been girls in similar circumstances, but that was for another time.

23

Major David Ashton-O'Sullivan put his phone in his pocket and waited patiently until the time arrived and he could shake the hand of the Australian Consul General. 'Thank you for seeing me, sir. May I assume you've been informed…?'

The man moved to take a seat behind his ornate desk and said, 'Please be seated, Major.' He pointed to a chair.

Bib sat and waited while the Consul gathered his thoughts.

Eventually, he spoke. 'This is disturbing, to say the least. We've checked out your story and if we provide you with special papers for these young women, we might be considered complicit…' He tailed off and shuffled through a file in the desk. 'The Bosnian authorities have confirmed the finding of two bodies in a room, surrounded by several traumatised and underage girls. Would that be anything to do with you or your expedition?'

'I simply facilitated the extraction of three young ladies when we had only intended freeing one.' He showed a phone scan of the contract signed by Clarke Shipton. 'His daughter was taken three years ago by an international trafficking gang, who sold her on to a specialised brothel in Sarajevo.'

Colins said, 'Kaitlin Shipton. She was reported missing by her father, but the police could find nothing. He, of course, has a chequered past.'

'And she, of course, is an innocent party,' Bib said.

Colins winced. 'These affairs are deeply concerning, major. Hundreds of children vanish without trace each year and there seems to be no remedy.'

Bib noticed the Consul's eyes flicker. 'Something else?'

He shook his head. 'Sounds too much like a coincidence, but one of my colleagues lost his daughter in similar circumstances. She was attending a local international school, here in Mumbai, and then one day she and her friend were gone. We still don't know whether they went together or if they're alive or dead. The Indian authorities were in charge of the search, but they found nothing.'

'I'm sorry, I can't be of help. These recovery ops take a lot of research and…'

'Maybe…?' he reached out and handed Bib a photo mounted in a cheap locally made frame. 'This was her. We found it in her father's office after he returned to Australia.'

'We can always discuss this later, sir, but right now, my colleague and I are in a bit of a jam.'

'And I am not sure I can be of assistance to you. There are too many questions, and too many people would be implicated if I were to authorise a clean set of papers for each of the girls.' Colins stood. 'Now, I must apologise. I have members of an Australian trade mission waiting to meet with me.'

Bib pulled his phone from his pocket and found the video of the incident in the brothel. 'Would that be these chaps, sir?'

Colins' face paled, and his brow furrowed with a frown when he scanned the low light blurry images in the video. Then his face froze. He said, 'Oh my God… Oh my God. Stay right where you are, Major.' He stood and strode from the room. A moment later, Bib's phone rang.

***

Jackie opened a cupboard in the corner of an undoctored room. She stopped and sucked in a deep breath before calling Mickey.

'I think you've struck gold, Jack,' he said.

'What do you reckon?'

'Until it's tested, we won't know for certain, but I reckon it might be crystal meth.'

'How much?'

'Twennie packs at about a kilo each… anything from $2,500 to $120,000+ per kilo, depending on its quality. Let's say, at worst case, a street value of $2.5M.'

Jackie whistled through her teeth. 'So, these guys are serious?'

'And a lot worse than Clarkie, and at least he doesn't pretend he's something more than he is.' Mickey found the man from the back seat and led him to their find. 'Enough to carry off a formal raid?'

The man laughed. 'You got what you were looking for?'

'Enough I think.'

'Well then, our anonymous tip off has more than paid off. We'll stay here until their friends return from their drinkies, but you two can head for home if you like. It's a win-win, I think.'

'I think we should stay to see this through,' Mickey noticed the pained expression on back seat's face. He tapped James Carter's number on his phone.

'Mick? Everything okay?'

'Jack found 20kg of methamphetamine in 1 kilo bags. Somehow, I can't imagine it's legally the property of the federal police.'

'You'll need to take possession of it as evidence.'

135

'I don't have a warrant, and what about the blokes you sent?'

'What blokes? Stay right there and make the arrests. I'll sort things out with a warrant, even if I have to go over Birchmore's head.'

Mickey turned to the back seat man and said, 'You know who *I* am. Perhaps you might like to identify yourself?'

'Don't make this difficult, Sergeant Krakauer.'

Mickey noticed the man's hand move towards his Glock. 'I've called it in. My boss is about to action the next move and if you don't take your hand off that weapon, I'll arrest you for going armed with the intent to strike fear.'

The hand moved back.

'Thank you. Now, the next move will be to take possession of the evidence and make some arrests. You can stay if you choose, but if you do, you will be acting under the orders of DI Carter. Identification, please.'

The man pulled out his Police ID.

Mickey grinned. 'Does DCI Birchmore know you and your men are moonlighting, PC Mason?'

Mason flinched.

'I take it he doesn't. So, I am taking possession of all the evidence, including the drugs…'

'You can't do that. You don't have a warrant.'

'Who says I don't?'

'DCI…' Mason stopped speaking.

'So, he does know you're moonlighting and doing it without official authorisation.'

Mason's hand moved towards his Glock again just as Micky's phone beeped.

He checked his messages and said, 'But you see, I do.' He held up his phone to show the message attachment.

Mason's face coloured when he saw the signature on the document. He called his men together, and they left in relative silence.

'What was all that about, Mick?'

'Arty's come up trumps and obtained an emergency warrant.' He handed her his keys. 'Bring the car over and we'll load it up. Jim's message said there's a team heading over.'

'No wonder the first mob left in a hurry.' Jackie said.

'We've plenty of time. The pub won't shut for hours, so what say we do some more poking around?'

'Will I need to cancel my date with Tom Cruise?'

'Possibly. Let's see what else we can find. You take that side, and I'll start over here.' Mickey returned to the room where the two men were secured and said, 'Where do your bosses keep their paperwork?'

Though both were conscious, neither spoke.

Mickey began rifling through drawers and filing cabinets. *These people have gone to a lot of trouble to look real, and yet?* Most of the stuff was copies of old cases, so someone, at some time, must have had intimate connections with the AFP. He rummaged further and found a thick file with Clark Shipton's name on it, and a second file with the name Callum Birchmore on its cover.

Interesting.

He pulled it from the cabinet, opened it out flat on the table, and whistled through his teeth when he saw its contents. The documents in both files dated back to long before Mickey was even a cop. It seemed that Birchmore had been involved with several suspect convictions and there was mention of his possible involvement in the murder of a gang member's wife. Mickey was more interested in Clark Shipton's file that inferred he had a finger in almost everything at one time or another, including human trafficking. His daughter Kaitlin had gone missing towards the end of that exposure. 'The plot thickens,' he murmured.

Though Clarkie's money laundering activities featured in the file, he was by no means big-time, but he seemed to know exactly what he was doing. He'd set up an import export company from a shell and used it to syphon off profits via a second shell company based in the Cayman Islands. This company would order items from a supplier and resell them to the Australian entity at a massive profit. Even with their huge mark up, the items he imported — priced in cents — were resold for multiple dollars. Significant returns landed safely in his offshore account, and he still made enough of a profit in Australia to pay a marginal tax and keep the wolves at bay.

Clark Shipton was into everything from kitchen utensils to underwear. The file detailed his websites, which featured catalogues with direct purchasing sections. In effect, Clarkie would barely need to lift a finger to make a continuous and almost tax-free killing.

So why did they take his daughter? What did he do? He put the file under his arm and went looking for Jackie.

24

Bub's jaw dropped when the girls returned from their freshening up. It seems Magda had given them items of her own clothing, and they looked almost respectable.

'Vat iss ze matter, Herr Bub, you look as if zomeone has given you eine electric shock.'

'Sorry, Magda, it's the first time I've seen them properly dressed.'

'Ya, they much better now.' She turned to Frank, who had just returned from his excursion into the world outside the aircraft. 'Ver haff you been, Fronk?'

Frank mumbled, 'Getting something for the girls. They'll be in trouble soon if they don't get something.'

Magda said, 'Ya, okay.' She took the small bag he offered, whispered to each of the girls, followed them into the flight container, and pulled the door shut.

***

Bib waited patiently for Steven Colins to return. He'd learned from bitter experience that it was best to handle his ilk carefully. However, his patience was coming close to failing him and he knew he was in danger of acting recklessly. He began a controlled breathing regime he'd practiced for years.

At last, Colins returned and took a seat on the other side of the desk. 'Major. We have a significant problem.'

'I agree. Very soon, I will need to be taking my charges away on a plane.'

'That is not the problem I am referring to.'

'Oh?'

He handed Bib his phone with the screen lit up on the picture of the brothel punters. 'That photograph constitutes a significant problem.'

'Well, that isn't my fault. I have no control over your trade missions wherever they may be.'

Colins pointed his finger to another face in the picture. 'I believe that young lady is the daughter of the senior Indian official, who went missing around the time of my colleague's daughter.'

'Well, at least he will now know where she is.'

'He has connections to the top end of Indian society.'

'So, they should be able to raise the funds for another mission. They won't even need to do the groundwork. I and my colleague have done it all for them. Might they even be able to go through government channels?'

'I'm not sure about that. The girl might be considered defiled. Her family might even reject her.'

'Listen, Stephen. All I need is papers for Agnetha and Bronwyn. As for the trade mission and the others, they are not a part of my task, but I must warn you that it won't be beneath me to use them as leverage if needed.'

Colins thought for a moment. 'Are all the girls Australian Citizens?'

'I don't know. They have little memory of their past lives, have no papers, and the only one I can vouch for is Kaitlin Shipton.'

He stood. 'Thanks for your help. I need to be moving my bottom, and the girls will be needing their medication.'

'Wait.' Colins sat and pulled out a printed pad of forms. 'How old are they?'

'All under sixteen.'

Colins gestured that he should sit. 'because of their age, I'm prepared to stick out my neck and see that all three are issued with official emergency passports. These are temporary and will expire in twelve months. When that happens, they might be liable for deportation.'

Bib held back the smile, forcing itself onto his lips.

'This medication?'

'They have been forced into heroin addiction by their keepers. I have been eking out some Suboxone as a temporary measure, but I had only provisioned for one girl.'

Consul Colins picked up his desk phone and spoke quietly. When he finished, he returned to his conversation with Bib. 'This is a local doctor who will supply that item.' He wrote a name and address on a post-it-note and stuck it on the back of Bib's hand. 'We're done here, Major.'

A soft knock on the office door drew Bib's attention.

'That'll be Dorothy. She'll fix up the EPs. Shouldn't take too long. Perhaps, for obvious reasons, could I ask you to keep our meeting in the strictest confidence?'

Bib stood and shook the consul's hand before following Dorothy down the corridor to her office.

***

Mickey heard a squeal before he saw Jackie struggling in the arms of a large man who was holding a pistol to her neck.

'Stay where you are, Krakauer. Make a wrong move and she's meat.'

'Who the fuck are you?'

The man grinned. 'You think we'd leave this place without a fallback plan?'

Mickey felt cold steel press against the back of *his* head.

'Kill him,' the man holding Jackie ordered.

Mickey was as good as dead. No *one could survive a bullet to the head at this range.* He heard a metallic sound like the movement of a trigger being squeezed. He instinctively rocked his head and felt the burn of the blast as it took away a part of his ear. *Think clearly, Mickey,* he thought. *Slow down, to panic now will be fatal for both of us.* He dropped to the ground as if dead, then rolled before kicking out at the weapon in the hand of the man gripping Jackie. It flew across the room and clattered into a corner the moment a second bullet from his attacker ripped into his bicep. He knew there was no surviving this, but he felt no pain — *that will come later* — He reached out for the leg of Jackie's man and pulled his knee forward. The man struggled to retain his hold on to Jackie as he skidded on blood and lurched to one side.

Jackie used the opportunity to make a grab for the weapon he'd lost control of and gripped it in a two-handed aim before turning it on Mickey's shooter.

The man laughed and, with one hand, swung his pistol towards her, pulled the trigger and missed.

A split second later, the bullet from Jackie's gun smacked into his chest to the left of his sternum.

Mickey caught the man's weapon as it fell and fired a single shot into the head of Jackie's attacker, before collapsing in the pool of his own blood.

Then slow motion switched to breakneck speed. Everything went black, and the last thing Mickey heard was the reassuring sound of Jackie's voice.

***

Bub's burner squawked. He answered it. 'How are you going? Frank's becoming intense?'

'I'm right this minute sitting across the desk of a lady called Dorothy and attempting to remain patient. She'll need a photograph of each of the girls for their temporary passports. Can you arrange that?'

'They are with Magda. Frank was able to get hold of some stuff and she's seeing to them.'

'The photos are needed immediately if we are to get temporary passports. Tell Magda to stop whatever she's doing and get those pics. Then text them to me. We don't have much time, and I can't afford a bureaucratic change of mind.'

Bub heard the silence of the ended call and banged on the door of the flight deck cabin. There was no reply, no sound from within at all. He called Frank. 'Hey, Frank, can you make contact with the missus?'

Frank put down his book, joined him, and listened at the door. 'I have a key, but if she's decided to be alone, she can bolt it from the inside.'

'Give it a try.'

Frank inserted a key in the lock and turned it. The door wouldn't open. 'Shit… Magda!' he shouted.

Nothing.

'We'll have to break it down.'

'You'll be lucky. We stop at some strange places, Bub. That door is reinforced you'd need a tank to blow a hole in it.'

'I need photos of the girls for their temporary passports. Bib is waiting as we speak, and he can't wait much longer.'

Frank tried calling Magda on her mobile phone, but it was switching to voicemail. 'She's not contactable.'

'So, now what?'

'The Copilot's window is an escape hatch that can be opened from the outside. The external release is under a small spring-loaded flap, but I'd need to get on top of the aircraft, and we don't have a cherry picker to get up there.'

Bub ran to the exit and down the stairs to the ground. He looked around and checked out the hangar roof.

Frank followed him out of curiosity.

Bib said, 'Show me where it is.'

Frank led him around the aircraft and pointed up to the Window.

'If I can get on top of this thing, how easy is it to open?'

'It's designed for emergency services. You simply pull a small lever, and the window drops into the cabin.'

'I need some rope. Can you find me some?'

'There is a locker on board with some coils of rope to be used in the event of a cargo slippage. I've always doubted they would be much use and, so far, so good, we've never needed them.'

'Will there be enough to help me rappel to the top of the plane?' He pointed to the roof trusses.

'Can you do that?'

'If I have enough rope, I can. Show me where it is, and move it, Frank. We have no idea what is happening in there.'

Frank heeded the warning and ran back up the ladder to the rope stowage. He flipped the catch and lifted the lid. There was only one coil of rope. 'Shit!' he exclaimed. 'This should be full.'

'Great news, Frank. We'll need to check around and see if there's anything lying around the hangar.' Bub judged the length to be enough to reach down long enough for a short drop to the fuselage. *If I have to, I will,* he thought. He turned to speak to Frank, but he was running around the hangar looking for something, presumably rope.

When Frank returned, he was hangdog. 'Sorry, mate, there's nothing.'

'All we need is a photo of each of the girls and this is turning into a nightmare.' He ran back to the cabin door and began banging. 'Magda! Whatever you're doing, we need you to stop and get out here.' He placed his ear against the door and heard a soft moaning sound. 'Magda!'

The next thing was the sound of a bolt sliding and a vague face appeared. 'I tried to help, but they insisted I prove it was okay.'

'Who?'

'The girls. I did not like what Fronk got, but I keep a stock of Valium for my own use, and I thought zat might help with their withdrawal. Zey didn't trust me and insisted I take a dose before zey did.'

'Where are they?'

Magda opened the door and pointed to the three slumped bodies.

'Christ, have you killed them?'

'I do not think so, but I have not tried to revive zem yet.'

'Well let's start trying… NOW!'

25

Jackie Morton's frantic voice galvanised James Carter into action. 'Have you called the ambos?'

'Sorry, Jim, I haven't. I don't know how many of the bastards are still hanging around and might come in shooting. I've put a temporary tourniquet on Mick's arm, but I'll need fighting help, and I'm scared out of my fucking wits.'

'I'm on my way. Do you have any weapons?'

'The one I grabbed from the one who grabbed me, plus another pistol that Mickey was able to take control of.'

'Okay, so you'll at least have a chance. I'm calling in the paramedics and I'll be there with anyone I can inveigle. Hold fast, and, Jack, you've come this far. Let's not lose it all at the last jump.'

The call ended and Jackie felt her heart breaking. Mickey was relying on *her* first aid skills when he should be in a hospital bed with a specialist surgeon attending him. She sucked in a deep and quivering breath and said, 'Don't you fucking die on me, Krakauer.' The words released a flood of salty tears, and she rested her head on his chest.

She could hear no heartbeat and knew he'd need urgent CPR. Her training kicked in and she began the chest compressions.

'Hurry up, Jim.'

After a few minutes, she had no idea how many she heard activity outside. She reached for the gun and held it two-handed, aiming at the door. A short while later, she heard a siren and hoped it was an ambulance. Then she heard a muffled voice, followed by a shot.

'We are in so much trouble here, Mick.'

She thought she heard his voice mumble something incoherent. Then the door flew open, and James Carter entered, followed by two paramedics. 'The shot?'

James said nothing. He simply lifted her to a standing position and held her in a hug while the ambos did their thing. Then he spoke. 'Mickey's a tough old chook, Jack. It'll take a lot more than this to knock him over.'

The ambos left with Mickey on a stretcher while James escorted Jackie to the ambulance and helped her aboard. 'I'll be right behind. Just work that magic of yours.'

Magic, she thought. She looked down at the man she loved and saw condensation forming under the oxygen mask.

'You did a great job, ma'am. Probably saved his life the with your CPR and that tourniquet. It looks like he might have lost a lot of blood, but this'll help.' He hooked up a bottle of fluid and set the drip. 'Copper, too. They'll give him the best chance, so don't you worry.'

Jackie felt herself going cold, and she began to shiver, as the Paramedic slipped a silver blanket over her shoulders.

'You're in shock, but we won't be long, and we've told them to look at you, too.'

The sounds in the Ambulance seemed vague and surreal. One minute Mickey was full of life and vibrant, now he was nothing but a fading shell. 'Stay with me, Mick. You can't leave me now.'

She took his hand and felt sure he squeezed hers back.

***

Several hours had passed since he called Bub, and Bib had switched his concentration to sniper mode, a forced calmness that took many years of field practice to achieve. He studied Dorothy as she went about her admin tasks and barely flinched when her voice cut through his fixation.

'Everything's done, Major. All I am waiting for is the photographs.' She glanced at her watch. 'The passport section will be closing soon, sir, and tomorrow's Friday. It's usually a busy day and you might not get what you want before next Tuesday, at the earliest.'

'It must be today. There are people's lives at stake here.'

'That's as maybe, but I'm limited in what I can do with what you've given me.'

Bib called Bub. 'What's the problem?'

Frank's voice answered, 'That you David?'

'Frank? Where's Bub?'

'He's in the process of reviving the girls. Magda gave them some Valium to help with their withdrawal and knocked herself out before locking them all in the cabin.'

'Valium?'

'She uses it occasionally.'

'How much longer?'

Bub appeared, snatched the phone from Frank's hand, and ran back to the cabin. 'I'm about to send them. Sorry they won't be studio standard, but they're the best we can hope for.' He snapped off several portrait shots of each of the girls and attached them to separate texts, along with text of their names. 'Pick the best of this lot.' He pressed send to dispatch the last.

***

DCI Birchmore responded negatively when he heard the news that James Carter had initiated a response to the recording studio matter. 'Who gave him that authority,' he blustered to the young PC, who had just dropped some papers for his signature.

The PC made no comment before leaving.

Birchmore picked up his phone and bashed his finger hard against its screen. He waited, but there was no response. After a few minutes of anxious finger drumming, he rose to his feet, headed for his car, and pointed it in the direction of the recording studio.

When he arrived, he was taken aback by the number of officers already stationed around the building, and ambulances leaving with the injured parties.

'Where is DI Carter?' he asked a uniformed constable who was stretching more crime scene tape around the premises.

The man pointed to the building. 'Apparently he arrived in the nick of time, sir.'

'Did he?' Birchmore shoved the man aside, lifted up the tape, and ducked under before marching directly to the main entrance and almost walking headlong into James.

'Oops,' James said. 'Almost on a collision course there, sir.'

'I want a full report of what went on here today and it had better be good, because I think you might be getting a call from internal affairs.'

'Oh, don't you worry about that, sir,' James said. 'It'll be good. I understand they know you quite well, too.'

'What do you mean by that?'

'It'll all be in my report. Sorry, sir, we are a man down, who is fighting for his life, so he must be my priority. If you'll excuse me.' James sidestepped and allowed Birchmore access to the entrance, where a sergeant greeted him and ushered him inside.

'What the hell happened here, Sergeant?'

'Mickey Krakauer had a bit of a contretemps with a man and a gun. His girlfriend came to his aid and managed to shoot one of them with the man's own gun. Mickey had already lost a lot of blood from the gunshot wound, but he got off a shot at another attacker with the first man's pistol. They were bloody lucky, if you're asking, sir.'

Birchmore grunted. 'As of now, I'll be taking over this investigation, sergeant. I want all the evidence bagging and made available for my perusal. Got that?'

'Yes, sir.'

****

The ambulance screeched onto the ED ramp of Fiona Stanley Hospital and the paramedics extracted the stretcher, complete with what seemed like a barely alive Mickey Krakauer. A blood smeared Jackie followed them as far as she could but was stopped at the doors to the triage.

'Are you next of kin?' a kindly voice asked.

'I'm his fiancé. This wasn't supposed to happen. They said I could stay with him.' Jackie covered her face with her bloodstained hands. 'They were shooting at us, and we had no choice but to fight back.'

The person who spoke ushered Jackie to a seat and said, 'No worries, love. You might be in shock yourself, so I'll triage you right here and now.' She waved for someone to bring her a piece of equipment on a trolley and as she rolled up Jackies's sleeve to check her blood pressure, she noticed the amateurish green-black prison tatts on her arm. Though she completed the triage, her attitude had changed dramatically. 'You will remain seated until you're called. Have you used any drugs in the last twenty-four hours?'

Jackie was horrified by the question and shook her head.

'Hmm,' the woman said. 'Alcohol?'

Jackie shook her head again. 'I just want to know that Mickey's okay.'

'Is he the man you came in with?'

'Yes, he's a police officer, Sergeant Krakauer. Can you ask for me?'

'They'll tell you when there is any news. Right now, you should remain seated until called. Understand?'

Jackie settled in for the long wait before she heard her name called.

'Jacklyn Morton?'

She looked up at the face that had spoken. 'That's me.' her watch said it had been almost four hours since they'd arrived.

'Follow me.'

She followed the man through the doors into the ED, and he led her on a circuitous route to a bed.

'Mick?'

'He's heavily sedated, but everything went well, and he should make a full recovery. He's a lucky man to have you on his side.'

Jackie said, 'How long before he'll be able to talk?'

'We're not rushing him. He lost a lot of blood…' He raised his finger to a nurse who had followed them. 'Help this lady get cleaned up and find out why she was made to sit in the triage room while displaying obvious symptoms of shock. When you've done that, call me.'

'Yes, Doctor,' the nurse replied.

Jackie slumped on to the chair beside the bed and felt the tears welling as she took his hand. 'We've had a long wait, Mick. I can wait a bit longer.'

'Miss?'

'Yes…?'

'Come with me I'll help you get rid of that blood.'

'I'd rather stay here, if you don't mind.'

The woman left, returned with a small trolley, and began softening the dried blood on Jackie's face and hands. When she finished, she handed her a hospital gown and said, 'If you'd like to change into this, you can remove those stained clothes. I can guarantee you'll feel a lot better when they're gone.'

Jackie slipped the gown over her shoulders before dropping her trousers and removing her top. 'Thanks. I'll need to put them on to go home.'

'Sorry, Miss Morton, the doctor says he'll be keeping you in overnight.'

26

Bib forwarded the photographs to Dorothy's email address and watched her face as she reviewed them.

'They all look half cut,' Dorothy said.

'They probably are,' Bib replied.

She turned her screen around to face him and said, 'Can you pick the best of the bunch? I can't?'

Bib tapped a picture for each of the girls and said, 'They're better than the mugshot I have in my passport.' He didn't mention that he had several under different aliases.

Dorothy smirked. It was the first time she had shown any humour. 'Mine too,' she said. 'I hate my passport pic. It makes me look like a junkie.'

'You and me both, Dorothy. I'm always surprised when immigration people recognise me from it,' he said, rolling his eyes.

She completed the process and forwarded the files to the department handling emergency passports. 'All done,' she said. 'Now we wait.'

'How long?'

'Until the passport department has finished with them. It's been given priority job status by Stephen Colins, so hopefully not too long.' While she was talking, the laser printer began chuffing out some documents and she said, 'Looks like there is someone in Stephen's office who would like to speak with you.'

Bib pulled back his craned neck and said, 'What about?'

Dorothy stood to retrieve the documents, and her face dropped when she saw their content.

'Something wrong?'

She shook her head but made no eye contact with Bib. 'He's waiting for you, and this might take about one hour.'

'Do your very best. I have less than six hours to get an aircraft into the air and I still have a few other things to do,' Bib said, as she left the room clutching the papers. His phone beeped. 'Hello?'

'It's Bub. Frank's getting anxious, and he suspects the authorities are planning some kind of operation.'

Bib's professional calmness began shifting towards a professional aggression, and he felt the hackles rise on his neck. 'Put him on.' He heard the scuffling sound of the phone being transferred from hand to hand.

'David, I'm in a real spot here. This was supposed to be a simple lift and shift with no further problems. There are now some people walking around my aircraft. They are carrying out some sort of inspection, and the last time I saw anything like this was during a suspected terrorist attack.'

'How long have we got?'

'Depends upon the stability of the security watch officer. If he gets nervous, we might be converted to instant cactus.'

'Keep your cool. Everything is going according to plan, and the passports should be in my grasp within the hour.'

'Might be too late. Someone is climbing the stairs to the cabin.' Frank's voice was giving away his fears. The aircraft was his living. Any problems that diminished that were, for him, a nightmare.

The call ended.

Bib made his way to the consul's office and knocked on the door. 'Come in, David.'

The Consul was sitting at a meeting table with a well-dressed Indian gentleman at his side.

'This is Sachin Shukla, he's here about those images you obtained in Bosnia?'

***

James Carter left the hospital when he knew Mickey was heading for surgery. He cast his eye over the people waiting in the triage and saw Jackie slumped in a chair. There would be little he could do, even if he asserted his police status. As soon as he arrived at the station, he headed to Mandy's desk.

'I've heard the news she said. Will Mick be alright?'

'They reckon so, but they found these, and I don't want them to get into the wrong hands.' He dropped the files onto her desk and pointed to the one with Birchmore's name on it.

Mandy rolled her eyes. 'Why am I smelling that sweet stink of dynamite?'

'It seems we have a Trojan horse in our midst. The mob out at the recording studio all have police accreditation, but none of them are serving members. I fully expect a response from DCI Birchmore to my role in the raid and I am of the opinion he is the Trojan, if that makes sense.'

'Why would he risk everything to protect those scum, Jim?'

'I don't think he has much choice. He was brought in to quash the people trafficking case and, when he couldn't, he was retained to keep the lid on any deeper investigations. Mickey's relationship with Clark Shipton has raised the pressure. You will note that Shipton once had a connection, albeit tenuous, with the traffickers.'

'But his daughter was taken.'

'That's when he realised the mess he'd got himself into.'

'I thought this was more about a gang wanting to insert themselves and benefit from the recovery of trafficked kids.'

'Me too, but all that has changed. It's possible that Kaitlin was punishment for his inactivity. Once she's back and can be interviewed, she might be able to answer questions that some folk might prefer weren't answered.'

'You're scaring me, DI Carter. If anyone finds out I have this stuff…'

'Can you feed it all through a scanner?'

'I'll have to do it when no one is around.'

'Then do it when you can. As soon as you're ready, I'll ring the bell. After that, I am certain these papers will vanish like so many more before them. So, when you've finished, I'll take control of the originals, and we'll find a way of circulating snippets of the copies.'

'Just a first glance throws up a whole lot of prominent names.'

'And they are across the nation. When this breaks, there will be hell on earth.' James patted her on the shoulder. 'Might be the worse IED you've ever disarmed.'

'Thanks for nothing.'

James left her to do her work and noticed her slipping the files into her briefcase as he turned to leave. He passed his desk en route to his vehicle and saw a sheet of white paper square in the centre of his blotter. He grinned, *I'll see you in the morning, boss.* He dropped into his car and made a call on his mobile. When Arthur Bertram answered his call, he briefed him on the day's activity.

'Glad you're on top of it, Jim. Make sure you keep me posted.'

The call ended, and he headed home via the hospital and a quick look in on Mickey.

27

Okay, sitrep. The passport fairy has fixed up the problem and reckons an hour of overtime should see them done. I've squared her off with a wad of cash, and I'm heading to see a doctor who can dispense *Suboxone*. By the time I get back, the papers should be ready, and we can be on our way. That ought to please Frank and Magda.' He ended the call and called up the address on Google maps. He knew Mumbai well and it was no more than ten minutes away on foot. By the time he'd arranged a lift, he'd be on his way back.

The doctor's surgery resembled an old English country house, but there was no shingle indicating that a medic was practicing. Bib pressed the tarnished brass doorbell button and heard a *ding* from somewhere inside.

After a while, a short round gentleman opened the door.

'Good evening, doctor, I am given to understand you may be able to help me with a small problem,' Bib said.

'I am sorry, sir, but I am not the doctor. I am Mr Vishwananda, her practice manager. She is not here, but I am expecting her to be coming back at any time.'

Bib showed the man the note he had been given by the Consul. 'This is the correct address?'

'Yes, sir. If you would like to take a seat, I am sure she will not be long.' He led Bib to a small wood-panelled waiting room with three chairs surrounded by aspidistras and other plants in pots.

'I take it the doctor doesn't see many patients?'

'The Memsaab has many patients, but rarely attends them here, sir. Please make yourself comfortable and wait until she returns.'

'With the greatest respect, Mr Vishwananda, I'm short of time, and I need a supply of a drug that I understand the doctor can provide. I have been recommended to her by Mr Colins of the Australian Consul General.'

The man's head rocked from side to side. 'Then it is perhaps better that you go and come when she is here.'

Bib had promised Dorothy he'd be back to collect the documents within the hour, and he well knew how elastic time could be in some parts of Asia. 'Does she have a number I can call?'

The man wrote a mobile number on a piece of paper and handed it to him. 'She might not answer if she is dealing with a patient or does not recognise the calling number.'

'Could you call her for me? This *is* of an urgent nature, and I would not trouble her otherwise.'

'Please, sir, take a seat and wait.' He disappeared through the door and Bib did as he requested.

After half an hour passed, Bib dialled the number of the Australian Consulate. He was answered by a robot message advising the Consulate was closed and would not reopen for general business before Monday. He sucked in a deep breath and settled in for an indeterminate wait for the arrival of the doctor. While he waited, he called Bub.

'I think we're still okay for time, though Magda and Frank are getting a bit fractious.'

'I'm stuck in the doctor's surgery, waiting for her to return and hand over the *Suboxone* films. As soon as I get them, I'll head back to the consulate and pick up the papers. Hopefully, I won't be too late.'

'That'll be a relief for Frank. I think we're getting close to using up our brownie points.'

'He'll be okay, and I'll be in touch if there are any further developments. What effect did Magda's Valium have on the girls?'

'All three have been very quiet, but I can't say how long that'll last.'

Bib had no sooner pressed end and settled in for his extended wait when the door to the waiting room opened and she entered.

'David, isn't it? I am so sorry you have been kept waiting. Steven Colins called me and told me what you were doing. I am so sorry, but I have to say that I cannot prescribe the drug you require until I have had the opportunity to examine the patients. You will understand the fragility of my position. If something were to go wrong…?'

Bib looked up at the dark-haired beauty who had appeared in his line of sight and felt sure his heart skipped a beat. Although she spoke English with a subtle Indian accent, she was pale skinned and almost the spit of the woman he might once have married.

'Are you alright, David?'

'Yes… Yes. I'm sorry, it's nothing.'

'Doctor Amrita Devi, David, but you may call me Amrita. So, when may I see these ladies?'

'If it's okay with you, we can go via the embassy, pick up their papers, and then head straight to the airport.'

'Good, then I'll just pop out back and get a few things together.' Amrita pulled the door shut behind her.

After a while, he became concerned and listened at the door. It seemed silent beyond. He turned the knob, pulled open the door and saw the small round man's body down the corridor, on the floor. His wrists and ankles were secured with plastic ties, and beyond, he could hear angrily whispered voices. He headed towards the sound and saw two men and Amrita. One was holding her; the other was roughly attempting to secure her wrists with similar ties. 'Hello, chaps,' Bib said. 'Having a spot of bother, are we?'

Both men turned to face him, and one removed a small pistol from behind his back.

Bib wasn't carrying a weapon other than his garrotte. He hooked his finger through the leather loop and considered his approach.

Amrita's eyes were wide with fear.

There was one obvious gun, and he could not be sure if the other man was armed or not.

One spoke in Hindi, of which Bib had the barest of smatterings, 'Keep out of this, it is none of your business.'

Amrita countered with, 'They want drugs. Someone tipped them off that I had some here.' Her voice sounded stressed, but she continued making a fair fist of the struggle.

'Where are they, doctor? Perhaps I can help?'

The man with the gun spoke. 'Get back in your room. This has nothing to do with you.'

'I think you might be wrong, old chap. You see, I'm here for drugs too. If we work together, we can both be on our way without further ado.'

'Vee vill not be dealing with you,' the other man said, this time in English, and this time he flashed an official looking badge.

'Well, that might be a problem for you, rather than me. Amrita, tell me where the drugs are kept.'

Her face drained and a look of horror replaced the colour. 'I thought you were a good man. They can kill me before I will do what they want.'

'Okay, chaps. I think I can find what we're looking for.' Bib unhooked his thumb from the garrotte, raised his hands in a standard defensive posture and slowly edged towards the two men. They seemed nonplussed by his action, but one pulled Amrita aside as he approached.

'Do nothing foolish, sir, or we will kill the woman,' the armed man said, holding his gun towards Bib in a single-handed aim.

To Bib, it was immediately obvious the man had little experience. He hooked his thumb in the garrotte, and as he drew close, he slumped between the man's arms, while looping the garrotte around his neck in a smooth and practiced manner. Soon after the squeak of its ratchet, the man's life ended neatly and much less bloody than if he'd been shot.

'One down and one to go,' Bib said, as he swivelled to bring his elbow up under the chin of the now startled man holding Amrita. She pushed herself free and Bib heard the man's teeth break as his jaw clamped shut before he followed up with a right hook that finished the job.

'I must attend to Mr Vishu,' a trembling Amrita said.

Bib calmly released the ratchet, and returned the garrotte to his pocket

She fell to her knees beside her associate and went through the motions of checking his vital signs. 'I think he will be fine. Though there is some blood from a superficial head wound.' She held out her hand to Bib. 'Please, help me to my feet.'

He took her hand and raised her, then lifted the man and carried him to an examination table.

Vishwananda uttered nothing other than a moan as his head fell back on the pillow.

'Mr Vishwananda has been my practice manager for many years. he is very good with the books but not so good with terrorists.' Her smile sent a tingling shiver down Bib's spine. 'Thank you for helping me.'

'Now I need *your* help.'

Amrita sashayed out and crossed the corridor to another room. She returned a few moments later with an overnight bag and a small package. 'I will drive you to your aircraft and then, Mr Vishu and I, must find a way to leave the country. The people you just dealt with are not drug dealers, as they claimed. They are agents of the IB, that is the Indian Intelligence Bureau, and I have been in their sights for some time. Now they have tracked me down I'm as good as dead.'

'Then let's get Vishwananda into your car, and you can take me to the Australian Consulate.'

28

Mickey was sitting up in bed when James walked in on him. 'Hey, Mick, you're looking pretty good for someone who almost bled out.'

He responded with a smirk. 'Bastards won't kill Mickey Krakauer that easy.'

'How's Jack?'

'Dunno. I haven't heard a thing.'

'If you're okay for a moment or two, I'll go and check on her. I'm sure they said they were keeping her in for observation.'

'Thanks, boss. She saved my bacon. If she hadn't shot the bastard, I'd be on a slab in the morgue. Instead of lying in bed, living it up on the slop, they pass off as food.'

'Birchmore has it in for us, Mick, so you'll need to keep your head down.'

Mickey grinned. 'I'm onto it.' He rested his head on the pillow and pressed the button on the controller to lower the back of his bed.

James headed out to the reception area and asked for Jaclyn Morton. He was given directions and told to speak to the nurse on the ward. The receptionist then said, 'It might be better to wait a while. She has a number of people in with her at the moment.'

'No probs. Thanks.' Instead of waiting around like a lemon, James made his way to the ward and was shocked at what he saw.

A police guard was stationed outside a private room. He showed his credentials, and the officer said, 'No one is to enter without DCI Birchmore's permission, sir.'

'Is she under arrest?'

'I'm not permitted to say, sir.'

The door opened and Birchmore appeared with what looked like a retinue of plainclothes officers. 'What are *you* doing here, Carter?'

'Checking on the health and welfare of an old friend.'

'I'd be careful how you describe your relationship with Ms Morton. She's breached her parole conditions within your cognisance and is about to head back to the slammer.'

'Are you aware she's been pardoned?'

Birchmore smirked and slithered away along the polished floor of the corridor, his retinue clinging like ticks to a bobtailed goanna.

When they were out of sight, James said, 'I'm DI Carter. I'd like to see my friend, please.'

The young officer on guard duty wilted. He stepped aside and held the door open for James.

Jackie's face was hidden by the sheet, but he could tell she was in distress. 'Hey, I've just seen Mickey. He's looking good.'

Jackie pulled the sheet down from her face. 'Jim, thank God it's you. They're looking for any way they can to lock me up again.'

'Give me the name of your lawyer. I'll have a word if I can.'

'Just when everything was going so well.'

'As far as I can see, nothing has changed, but information is about to come to light that might alter everything.' He handed her a pen and his notebook. 'Write down your lawyer's name.'

*****

Mandy Stephenson made three printed copies of every document in both files. She then methodically clipped them into new folders and moved the scanned files to an encrypted directory on her private cloud. She smiled and licked her lips. It had been a big job, but worth the effort.

It was hard not to notice the many references to Birchmore, in particular the emails from several ministerial departments. These made blatant reference to the required delays, the general obfuscation expected, and the risks if the obligations weren't met. They went back well beyond the time of the previous police minister, who had not been seen or heard of since his hurried resignation for "family reasons."

From what she'd seen, there was a conspiracy to defeat the rule of law at several levels of politics, and she was convinced that there was enough to prove Birchmore had been deliberately shunted in to ensure that the necessary disruption occurred.

She switched her attention to Clark Shipton's file, and her stomach churned over some of the things he was alleged to be involved with. The most striking thing about both files was the number of crossovers and coincidences. But, while Clark Shipton had been a bad lad in his time, there was also a note that confirmed him as a registered police informant.

Mandy had assumed Shipton's minder was Mickey Krakauer, but *his* name appeared in neither file. 'What's going on Mick?' she murmured.

She placed the originals and two printed copies of both files in her briefcase, then turned to head for the lift, and then her car for home. As she opened the door to exit the deserted cyber division offices,

Callum Birchmore blocked her way. 'Excuse me, sir,' she said, moving to the side to pass him.

'Open your briefcase, Sergeant.'

'I beg your pardon, sir.'

'Do as I say. You're not in the bomb squad now, girly.'

'Can I see your warrant to conduct a search on my person, sir?'

Birchmore flinched. He was expecting his weight of rank to be more than sufficient to overwhelm her.

'I see. Thank you, sir. Now, if you'll please excuse me?' Mandy stepped around him and walked calmly to the lift.

Birchmore didn't follow, and she resumed her intended trip to her home. Her partner was in bed and fast asleep when she arrived. Their daughter, Josie, was asleep in her cot, so Mandy walked out into the small garden and made a call to James Carter.

His slumber befuddled voice said, 'Are you still at work?'

'No, I've just arrived home. Sir, these files are either beautiful fakes or seriously dangerous documents that could see a number of people behind bars in double quick time.'

'Birchmore?'

'He seems to be the linchpin in the whole shemozzle. We need to talk and spend some time going through them in detail. I think you should involve your sister, if she'll consent.'

'Does Birchmore know what you have?'

'I think he has an inkling. He tried to do a "stop and search" on me as I was leaving. When I asked him for his warrant, he backed off quick-smart. It stinks, Jim. According to the files, Birchmore is deeply involved with the mob at the recording studio. Those who almost killed Mickey and Jackie.'

'Okay, where are the files now?'

'I have the originals and a couple of copies in my briefcase. I've moved a complete set to my personal encrypted cloud directory, and there is a copy in the drawer of my desk.'

'I'll bet he has those in his sticky little hand as we speak.'

'My thoughts exactly. He'll know what we have, but he won't know that we have the originals complete with original signatures and notations.'

'Should be interesting, when we get in tomorrow…'

'Someone's in my back yard…'

'Hide the files and dial 000. I'll be there as soon as I can.'

***

The brief interlude with Amrita had almost knocked Bib off kilter. She'd brought back the memory of pain in a distant time. A time when his duty forced him to step aside from his desires when he knew, deep down, he should have stayed. The proximity and fragrance of her body tormented him as she drove him through the Mumbai streets to the Australian Consulate. When they arrived, the building was in darkness, but a video intercom allowed him to alert anyone still there to his presence.

A robotic voice answered, 'We are closed for business. Please return on Monday, when we will be open as usual.'

'Wait!' He was too late. He pressed the intercom button again, but the AI generated voice had returned to its cupboard, and he knew he had failed. *At least I can give the girls some relief from their withdrawal symptoms.* He tapped Bub's number and waited while it rang out. He tried it again with no luck. *I think those men must have followed me to Amrita's place. Could others have taken over Frank's plane?*

Uncharacteristically panicky, Bib bashed the button on the intercom again.

Nothing.

He'd turned to leave, when he heard the tiny voice calling in the distance.

'Mr Bib. I have your papers. Please don't go.'

Bib peered into the gloom and saw a diminutive figure pop out of a side door and approach him. It was Dorothy, and she looked so much smaller, away from her desk and her position of power.

'I waited as long as I could, major. I was about to leave for the night when I heard the intercom. It is very loud when the place is empty.' She handed him a package. 'These should get them home safe.' She smiled. 'Thank you for the gift. Goodbye, major.' A car arrived, Dorothy stepped in to its rear, and she was gone.

29

Frank said, 'About time. These costs will be to be added to your…' He stopped speaking when he saw Amrita and Vishwananda. 'Who are these people?'

'Sorry Frank, I have a couple more passengers for you. I promise they'll be no trouble.' Bib turned to Amrita and felt a massive surge of something that resembled an adrenalin hit.

She smiled in response. No words were necessary.

When everyone was settled, Bib began typing up a message to Shipton and attached a copy of their proforma with a list of additional expenses. He noticed Amrita glance in his direction… His concentration drifted and he was glad he'd sent the paperwork off.

***

Birchmore arrived back at his office and called his trusted people around him. 'If we can't get this situation under control and quickly, a few of you might be joining the Centrelink queue. Got that?'

Heads nodded, and two officers raised their hands.

One said, 'We have things to attend to, sir. May we be excused?'

Birchmore glared at them, looked around at those in his office as if assessing the numbers and said, 'Remember what I said, so do what you have to do and then get straight back on this investigation.'

The pair turned and almost fled the room.

When he'd finished his briefing and the others had left, Birchmore took his seat behind his desk, pulled the burner phone from his drawer and tapped a number from a list.

'Under control?'

'Not quite, but I'm getting there. I need a warrant to turn over all of Clark Shipton's premises. If we can get some hard evidence regarding his police connections, the rest will fall into place.'

'Fishing trips are frowned upon these days, Callum, but you know that.'

'I have evidence that the Police Commissioner is working in cahoots with him on a number of potentially serious…' A knock at the door distracted him. 'What is it?'

'We've intercepted a communication from a company called Recoverance Inc.'

'Wait. Sorry, sir, I'll have to get back to you.' He ended the call and said, 'What on earth are you going on about?'

The man handed him a copy of a text message.

Birchmore read the document and said, 'Next couple of days, then?'

'They will be stopping for fuel in Myanmar and a delivery of cargo. Then it's non-stop to Perth.'

'But only if Shipton makes the final payment.' Birchmore smirked and pointed to the line that said, "Unless the amount is paid in full before our departure from Yangon International Airport, our freight will be offloaded and will become your responsibility." 'Sounds to me that Shipton will be expected to make a payment anytime in the next couple of days.'

The man spoke. 'The cyber division has been monitoring his financial activities. As soon as they get a fix on the payments, we'll be able to track his account transactions. Then we will see exactly what he is up to.'

'Good. Get on with it.' The man left, and Birchmore renewed his call to the Attorney General. 'We might have evidence of possible illegitimate cash transactions within two days, sir. Then we will hit him with the warrants.'

'It had better be good, Detective Chief Inspector. There is a lot riding on this.' The call ended.

><

'They'll be refuelling in Myanmar and then non-stop to Perth. That's good, isn't it?' Kelly passed the printout of the text message, and its attachment, back across the desk.

'They are asking for an additional US$250,000 to cover contingencies. I've already bunged them a quarter of a mill with the same to pay on completion…'

'What is she worth to you, boss?'

Shipton put his head in his hands. 'The money's nothing, Kell. I have the balance ready for transfer from legal account to legal account, but the additional amount will need to come from a different source, and I know the cops are sniffing around everything I do.'

'They always have, boss.'

'They've been trying to get something on me for years.'

'Can you get the extra amount without, you know…?'

'It is possible but getting it out of the country without raising a red flag might be a problem.'

'What about your PRC import export mob? They do it all the time, all legit, and your name won't appear anywhere in the transaction record.'

Shipton stood, walked around his desk and said, 'I don't know what I would do without you, Kell.'

'Don't start that crap again, boss. Just use your freakin nous and get your daughter back. Then we can maybe talk about other things.'

Shipton's back straightened, and he seemed to grow three inches in height. He sucked in a deep breath and said, 'Let's do it.'

***

It was late when James Carter arrived at his sister's house. He raised his eyebrows, when he noticed she was in night attire and there was an empty champagne bottle with two glasses. 'Sorry, I didn't realise you had a visitor, but I needed to alert you. Birchmore laid this on me earlier.' James showed Angela the photograph of the intimate dining experience she had shared with the police commissioner.

Angela's face beamed with glee. 'We've been dating each other for years, Jim. You know, of course, that he is a single man of a certain age. I am a middle-aged single parent of a similar age, but what you might not know is that I have just accepted a certain proposal.'

'Arty… and you?'

'Why not? You have even said you like the man.'

'We were classmates in the Police Academy. We got along well, and everyone knew Arty was to be fast tracked, but...'

'Well, there you are, and now, who knows…?'

'Everything alright, Ange?'

James turned his head towards the sound of the voice.

'DI Carter. What a pleasant surprise.' Arthur Bertram emerged from the bedroom and cinched up the tie of his bath robe. 'Has she told you of our news?'

James felt his face colouring, in the compromised presence of the state's most senior police officer. Knowing he was soon to become his brother-in-law didn't help. He sucked in a deep breath, and said, 'Congratulations, sir… and you Ange.'

'Arty at home, Jim. We've been mates for years and I am so glad you could be here at this particular moment.'

'Well, I guess I'll leave you lovebirds alone then.'

'Stay. There is something I need to discuss with you.' Arthur indicated he should sit.

Angela said, 'I'll make us all a cuppa.'

'There's bad shit happening, Jim. That new bloke. The one my predecessor hired to slow things down has enabled a whole stratum of crime to go untreated. It's like white ants in the foundations and if we don't eradicate it, the whole shebang will come tumbling down.'

'I know and I believe Birchmore has been playing along with a bunch of fake feds. We, that is mostly Mickey Krakauer and Jackie Morton, were like foxes in the chicken coop. Mick's now in hospital recovering from a severe injury and Jackie is a few rooms away, being hounded by Birchmore's goons.'

Arthur said. 'Throw in Clark Shipton and I sense a time bomb is about to go off.' He stood, walked into the hall, and returned with a leather satchel. His hand reached inside, and he withdrew a wad of papers. 'A few weeks ago, I inserted a couple of officers into Birchmore's department. They have been steadily building a dossier of evidence, and they believe he is about to do something underhand, and most likely illegal. Their evidence already lists illegal phone taps and dubious internet activity.'

Angela returned with their tea. 'Very cosy.'

James ignored her and scanned the documents that Arthur had provided. 'This is quite serious. It goes up as far as the AG.'

'Now, Clark Shipton. I've known Clarkie for years, and sure he has a rep as a bad lad, but he's more your old-style spiv and he has fingers in more pies than I care to think about, but Clark Shipton has never physically hurt anyone. Nor has he paid others to do it.'

'So human trafficking is okay in your view?'

'No, and I know he became involved back in the day, but it was only on the fringe. Once the reality of what was happening dawned, he backed out, and when his daughter was taken, he knew it was revenge. Straight out revenge.'

'So, these two characters who are bringing her back to him will be tweaking the noses of a hard-core mob who are maybe protected from above?'

'She might also have information about her captors, Jim, and you know what that could lead to.'

'Her life will be in danger from the moment she sets foot on Australian soil.'

'Got it in one, Jim. I thought we'd sorted this lot out, but they're like a cancer and keep popping up in the strangest of places.'

'Mickey Krakauer has become close to Shipton in a benign way. He's temporarily out of circulation, but I also have a working relationship with Shipton, so I'll see what I can do… If I need your help?'

'At the drop of a hat, Jim.'

'Then I'd better get home to my family before the divorce papers hit the court.' He leaned over and kissed his sister on the cheek. 'Looks like a year of full-on bloody weddings.'

'Well, it's time Stacey had something new to wear.' She stuck out her tongue and it reminded him of their childhood.

30

As expected, Stacey was in no mood for polite conversation, she closed her book, turned out her reading light and pulled the bedclothes up tight.

'Got some good news tonight.'

'Oh?'

'It's part of the reason I'm late.'

Stacey rolled on to her back, sighed and said, 'Okay, what is it?'

'Angela's getting married.'

'Oh, I am glad.' She sat up. 'Anyone we know?'

'Arthur Bertram.'

Stacey's face took on a confused expression. 'I know that name.'

'So you should. He's my boss.'

Stacey's hand flew to her gaping mouth. '*The* Arthur Bertram? The Police Commissioner?'

'The very same.'

'She never mentioned anything.'

'She says they've been dating for years on and off.'

'Well good for her.'

James slipped into bed alongside his wife and kissed her on

the cheek. 'I am trying to wind things down, Stace, but there is a lot happening and the next few days are likely to be intense.'

'There's always something.'

'But things are starting to move.'

'So, what happens now?'

'Tomorrow I'll be meeting with Clark Shipton. How that will go is anyone's guess, but I believe he has some connections that might help us bring down a major conspiracy.'

'How are Mickey and Jack?'

'Going well but Jack has been put under pressure by Birchmore. He seems to think she should be back in jail despite her pardon.'

'And he's looking for something to facilitate that?'

'Probably, but they are out of circulation for the moment, and I have no intention of bringing Mickey back in until they're both well again.'

'We RSVP'd an invitation to their wedding so I suppose I should get something suitable?'

'Better look for two things then because it looks like we'll be going to Angela and Arty's too.'

She reached up, put her arms around his neck and drew him down to her.

It had been a long time since she'd kissed him that way, and he had no intention of letting her mood go to waste.

***

'Hey, DI Carter. What brings you here?' Kelly Coulson was in her customary, PA to the CEO of a major blue-chip company, persona and regalia.

'I need to speak to Mr Shipton.'

'Clarkie's out at the moment, is it something I can help you with?'

James stalled.

'If it's about his daughter. There really is nothing I don't know.'

'When is she due back?'

'The recoverance company have told us their aircraft will be refuelling in Myanmar shortly. They have asked for increased funds to meet their costs, and Clarkie is arranging that now. Before you say anything. It's all legit. He knows your colleague is conducting surveillance on his accounts and they've been tapping our phones.'

'May I?' James pointed to a chair.

'Please. How is Mickey and his fiancé?'

'Coming good.'

'Good. James isn't it, or do you prefer Jim?'

He remembered last night's conversation with Arty and said, 'I guess Jim, is okay.'

Kelly reached into a drawer on her desk and removed a file. 'This is the proforma Clarkie signed. He expected more than they estimated but US$250,000 was a bit more than a few readies.'

James opened the file and saw the two photographs of Kaitlin. The first as an innocent teenaged girl in her school uniform the second as a haggard old woman not yet sixteen. 'Bastards.'

'There are two more girls coming with them. Kaitlin wouldn't leave without them. They will all need to go into rehab immediately.'

'Do you think Mr Shipton would be up for a sting?'

Kelly's eyes tightened. 'I can't speak for him on that, but he knows they took her from him out of revenge, so he might be willing to give karma a nudge. For your answer, you'll need to communicate directly with him.'

James handed her his card. 'It has my unregistered private

mobile number on it. If he uses a burner, there will be no bugging and it will be between me and him if he calls.'

'I hope Mickey recovers well. If you see him, will you pass on my kindest wishes?'

James stood. 'Of course. Make sure your boss calls me. It's important.'

***

'It's me. I've just had DI Carter in and I'm calling on a burner. He wants to talk to you. Would you call him on this number, it's also a burner and I have one here for you. He knows they are tapping our lines, and he wants to set something up.'

'What do you think of Carter?'

'He's always seemed straight down the line to me, boss. The cash?'

'All good. You were right on the ball there, Kell. The cash is in their bank already.'

'I confess I'm getting just a little exited, boss. Think she'll remember me.'

'We'll be lucky if she remembers anything, Kel. I'll give Jim Carter a call. He was once Mickey's boss but they're also friends.'

***

Bib heard a beep from his phone just as Frank began his taxi to the hard stand, for refuelling. He looked out of the small windows and saw a reception committee gathering on the tarmac. They weren't quite what he had expected. A small contingent of troops had fallen in, and an officer appeared, who seemed to be giving them instructions. Bib approached the flight cabin and knocked.

'Come in. Everything's okay,' Frank reassured him.

'What about that mob?' he pointed to the tarmac.

'It's Burma, Bib. It'll be okay.'

The aircraft halted forward movement and Frank left Magda in control as he opened the door to receive the ladder. While the ladder moved into place, a fuel truck cruised into line, followed by a scissor lift to receive the container with the consignment of goods Frank was dropping off.

He descended the ladder and held out a wad of papers to the man in command of the soldiers.

The man scrutinised the paperwork and watched as the scissor lift lowered the container. As soon as it was down, he issued a command and checked off each item as the troops cleared its contents, piece by piece, hand to hand, directly into a blue panel van. When it was done, he scribbled on the paperwork and handed it back to Frank. The troops then reformed and left, marching behind the van.

'That was efficient, Frank,' Bib said.

'Private consignment. Say no more, nudge-nudge, wink-wink.' As he was speaking, they heard the clunk of the fuel nozzle locking into place and he ran down the steps to check on the progress.

Bib looked at the text message. It said:

Funds transferred, check account.

Bib checked into his banking service and smiled. The balance of the account plus a separate US250,000 had been deposited and cleared. 'All good,' he murmured.

Frank returned from the fuel tanker. 'We'll be here for a few hours then straight to Perth, non-stop.'

Bib turned to look at the consignment *he* was handling. The girls were asleep. The Suboxone was doing its job, Amrita and Mr Vishu were awake but looking nervous. They'd been ripped from their home and taken to a plane for a destination country they knew little about. He walked over and caught Amrita's attention. 'He's looking a bit better.'

'Mr Vishu always heals quickly.'

'But you're looking a little stressed, doctor.'

'I do not know what is happening to me. One minute I was running a successful medical practice in Mumbai and now I am a refugee.'

'I'm sure it's only temporary, and once we're landed things can be straightened out.'

'I hope you are correct, Mr Bib.'

31

'Mr Shipton, you got my message.'

'Kaitlin's return is close at hand?'

'I think you might know that there is still a cohort of the traffickers, who took your daughter, at large. We rounded most of them up a year ago, but a few scraped through the net and are trying to recover their network and protection.'

'The fake cops?'

'Small part of it, but the disease goes right through to the top.'

'What next?'

'Your daughter is on a plane heading to Perth. Hopefully she should arrive sometime tomorrow, which doesn't give us much time.'

'I'm not in my office right now. Can we meet somewhere?'

'I could pick you up if you give me your location.'

'I'll finish my coffee and begin walking up Beaufort Street in the direction of Bulwer, keep an eye open near the crosswalk.'

The call ended and James pulled out of his parking space. From this moment, everything needed to be hidden from general view. He'd already formulated a plan, but Clark Shipton would need to be completely out of it.

Traffic was light as he turned onto Beaufort and drove

sedately. True to his word Clark Shipton was waiting. He appeared to be making a call on a mobile phone and James swallowed hard before pulling to the side and lowering his window.

Shipton stuck the phone in his pocket and dropped in beside him without a word.

'Calling someone?'

Shipton laughed and showed James his switched off burner. 'Worked then? Kelly got it for me on your instructions.'

James re-entered the traffic, turned left into Vincent Street and headed to Lake Monger, where he found a parking space and indicated they were as far as they were going. The walk trail was within easy reach and James said, 'Fancy a stroll.'

Shipton smirked.

As soon as they were clear of the street noise James said. 'Kaitlin will almost certainly know something, and her two friends will only add to that kitty of knowledge.'

'You intend involving my daughter.' Shipton stopped dead in his tracks. 'Don't you think she has had enough of this shit.'

'She will be in great danger Mr Shipton...'

'Clarkie... If we're to be working together call me Clarkie.'

'We know they are listening in on everything you say on the phone or in your emails. I'd like you to feed them. They know Kaitlin is due back any time. Only we will know exactly when.'

'So, I'm to tell them when she's arriving via their phone tap?'

'Exactly.'

'How will we know the exact time?'

'Mickey Krakauer has a contact number. It's better you stay as far away from the airport as possible.'

Shipton shrugged.

'You want your daughter back in one piece. I want these

bastards locked up. It's a quid pro quo, Clarkie.' James fell silent for a while to allow Shipton to process his thoughts. Then he spoke again, 'I was talking to Arty Bertram yesterday.'

Shipton laughed. 'Arty and me had a few ups and downs in the early days but…'

'Yeah. He said.'

'Is Arty in on this?'

'No, but he's given me carte blanche, and it's best we keep him out of the loop until we're certain we can pull it off.'

'We've become strange bedfellows Arty and me. Virginia liked him a lot. She was right when she said he'd go far.'

'Okay, so now you know.'

'How much does Kelly know?'

'Nothing, it's better she's an innocent party, and it might lend some authenticity to the disinformation. 'Mickey's in contact with Bib and Bub and from there it's down to us. Meanwhile you go about your normal business as if nothing has happened.'

They returned to the car and James dropped him back at the pickup point. From there he headed to the hospital and Mickey.

***

Mandy Stephenson heard a hushed conversation from one of the cubes. A few seconds later the officer stood and headed from the room in a hurry. 'Someone's in a tearing rush,' she said to no one in particular.

'Just got a lead on a big undercover case,' a voice replied.

'Anything I should know about?'

'Something Birchmore's dealing with. He'll be a happy little chappy when he gets the news.'

'News?'

'Something about that trafficking business. They reckon their closing in.'

'That'll be good,' she called back.

'Yeah, anyway you didn't hear it from me.'

Mandy entered a text into her burner phone and pressed send.

***

Magda circulated the cabin with a tray of coffees. 'I could have been an air hostess you know. Instead, I traipse around ze vorld viz my husband, as his co-pilot.'

No one responded. Other than with a thank you for their drink.

Bib caught Amrita looking in his direction again. He carried his coffee and sat in the seat next to her. 'I'd ask if you were enjoying the flight, but you would probably pour your coffee over me.'

Amrita smiled. 'I think you are much to blame for my circumstances, David, but I know I should be thanking you. Your friend from the consulate said there was a warrant out for the arrest of me and Mr Vishu. Black market drugs, apparently, and that we should leave immediately.'

Bib was about to respond when his burner buzzed. He let the call drop out and waited. A few seconds later it rang again. He allowed it to run for two more times before he picked up.

'Mr Bib, it's Micky Krakauer. Things are happening and I need to forewarn you.'

'Of what Mickey? We are still in Myanmar, but we should be leaving in the next hour or so.'

'I'll hand the phone to DI Carter. He'll explain better than I can.'

'Mr Bib. I'm DI Carter. I was involved in the original trafficking investigation.'

'I saw your name in the paperwork. You did well.'

'Thanks. Not well enough. There are some remnants who are

aiming to make life difficult. At first, we thought they were trying to cash in on your success, when in fact they want to scupper everything.'

'Go on?'

'Kaitlin and her friends are likely to have information relating to those who trafficked them. I believe it is the traffickers' intention to use their, not inconsiderable, power to eliminate any possibility of a breach of their confidentiality.'

'And?'

'We are setting up a sting. For it to work we will need your cooperation.'

'What do you need from me, DI Carter?'

'The exact time of your arrival so that we can ensure you are safely away from the airport before the others arrive.'

'How will I know you are the good guys?'

'You won't, but you trusted Mickey Krakauer and so far, he hasn't let you down.'

'How will this sting work?'

'Soon after your aircraft lands we will provide a team and a vehicle to extract everyone but the crew. You — slash — they, will be taken to a safe place from where we can continue our discussions out of sight and earshot of those who would do you harm.'

'This all sounds a bit Mickey Mouse to me, DI Carter.'

'It will make more sense when we close in on those who are trying to screw this operation up. I would like to make it quite clear that I am not acting on any higher orders. Sadly, it's they who are pushing for the elimination of the witnesses.'

'The airport comes under the jurisdiction of the Federal Government, as I understand it.'

'Yes, and the people we are dealing with are connected, in

some dubious kind of way, to the AFP. They are somehow protected, and we need to show them up for what they are.'

'Mr Shipton is aware of this?'

'He is actively involved. He knows his communications and data are all under surveillance and though he doesn't know it, he will be feeding the listeners with misinformation. This is why we need your actual arrival time, so that we can throw a spanner in their works. None of the surveillance on Clarkie's offices has been officially sanctioned, but we have been conducting our own internal monitoring and have discovered evidence of dodgy high-level police involvement.'

'How will I contact you?'

'Just text a time to this phone, it's a burner, and we'll take it from there.'

'Then wait for my text. Goodbye DI Carter.' He ended the call and turned to Amrita. She'd fallen asleep with her head resting against his shoulder. He eased her aside without waking her, kissed her cheek and said, 'Forgive me, but I couldn't help myself.' He took her empty cup and made his way back to the galley where Frank was doing the washing up. 'Magda?'

'Having a lie down.'

'Can you give me a precise time of arrival in Perth?'

'As soon as we are away from here. It will be plus or minus a few minutes unless we hit weather.'

'Thanks.'

32

'Hey, lazybones, and Jim.' Jackie was looking in much better health than the last time he'd seen her. 'What's new?'

'You know something, Ms Morton. Your bloke knows it all and I'm heading for home before Stacey sends out a search party.' He kissed Jackie on the cheek. 'I'm sure you both have lots to talk about. Can I drop you?'

Mickey slipped out of bed and said, 'Just give me a minute to get dressed.'

James found his car and noticed another vehicle pull out behind him. He grinned, *that didn't take long.* He headed to the home of Mickey and Jackie and dropped into the office before making his way to his own home. His brief discussion with Mandy confirmed that their misinformation was getting out.

She pulled up a screen and pointed to a display of an audio signal. 'This activity has increased dramatically since a call came in earlier. I think something might be in the offing, Jim.'

'I guessed that when I received your text.'

***

One hour later, Kaitlin, Agnetha, and Bronwyn had pulled up the armrests between their seats and were huddled together as if they were unborn triplets in their mother's womb. Bub was sitting cross-legged on the deck jotting notes into his pocket diary, while Mr Vishu and Amrita still seemed away with the fairies in the two remaining seats. He could sympathise. The stress of their sudden change of circumstances had probably left them wiped out. At least the dressing on Vishwananda's head was gone, his wound having healed miraculously. Bib wandered over to Bub and gestured.

Bub stood quietly, joined him, and they both squeezed through the small access door into the cargo hold. The gap between the smaller container, used by the girls, and the fuselage was an ideal place to chat in private.

Bib spoke in an almost unintelligible whisper, 'I've had a call from Jim Carter, he's a DI with the WA police. There's intelligence of a planned raid on the aircraft when we arrive in Perth. They are currently disseminating misinformation in the hope that we can get on the ground and away from the plane before these people are aware we have arrived.'

'Seems like a good idea to me,' Bub murmured.

'We can't afford to take any risks. We've achieved all of our operational goals, and I'm not prepared to allow some half-arsed wannabes wreck our mission.'

'That too, seems fair to me.'

'Just thought I'd give you a heads up. They'll be armed and, as you know, our weapons are of a somewhat personal nature and not suitable for a major confrontation.'

'So, what are Carter's intentions?'

'He is signalling that our arrival will be much later than the fact. He says he will have a team ready to assist us on arrival and will be in a position to make arrests when the dodgy mob arrive to kick arse and take names. Frank will have a good idea of our arrival time soon after we leave here. I'll let Carter know, and then we'll sit back and enjoy the trip.'

'What about customs and immigration?'

'Same as we would have had before this other mob came on the scene. We might have to modify our plans nearer the time, but my intention is to disappear at the first opportunity. I have an idea that I'll broach with them once we're on the move.' He glanced at his watch. 'The girls will be needing their medication soon. They'll need to be compos mentos when we land, the last thing we'll be needing is three withdrawing junkies making squealy noises.'

'Amrita has checked them over and they're responding well to the *Suboxone*.'

'I'm suggesting we use the container from the start of the girl's trip. We should all be able to squeeze in without too much trouble, and I'll let Carter know so he can arrange transport immediately or as soon after we land as possible.'

'Will other containers need offloading before we can move theirs to the hatch?'

'Frank has it in hand. He's done this before.'

They returned to the cabin where Frank was speaking softly to Amrita.

'Where are the girls, Frank?'

'I thought they were with you.'

'Shit! Bub...?'

'On to it.' Bub took the ladder three steps at a time and began scouring the area around the plane.

Bib's phone tooted with a message.

> You'll get the passengers back
> when you agree to our terms.

He ran to the door and called Bub. 'Just got a text message. Get back on board.'

When Bub arrived back in the cabin, all faces turned towards him. 'What the fuck happened?'

Frank answered, 'They were just sitting there with Mr Vishu in a sort of huddle. I heard someone call Kaitlin's name. She got up and walked to the door. When she came back, Vishwananda and the three of them left together. I wasn't aware they were being kept prisoner.'

'They weren't but someone got to them, and I've just received a text to the effect we'll need to agree to some terms before they'll be returned.' Bib turned to Bub and indicated he should follow him, and they both descended the ladder to the tarmac. 'They can't have got far.'

'If this mob have connections in Myanmar, then we're royally screwed,' Bub said.

Bib smirked. 'I need you to stay with Frank and the plane. We don't have much time and I'm guessing Frank wants to be out of here ASAP. I don't care what you tell him but make it something along the lines of, I have it in hand and I'll be back shortly.'

Bub returned to the aircraft, while Bib disappeared into the shadows and tapped a text to James Carter.

> Minor glitch. Will be in touch
> soon.

***

James showed the text to Mandy. 'Looks like things aren't going as smoothly as we hoped.'

'I get the feeling these blokes have been in worse situations, sir. I'm sure they have a backup plan. Let's face it they've chopped and changed a few things since their mission started.'

'I hope you're right. We'll lose everything we've worked for if the bastards win.' He sucked in a deep breath and said, 'How much can you track with your tech?'

'*My* tech doesn't belong to the police department. If we are to use mine, we can't do it here.'

'I'll call Stacey and tell her I'll be late.'

'And I'll let Jean know there'll be another place for dinner.' Mandy made her call, picked up the files and followed James from the room. 'Let's hope my car doesn't blow up,' she quipped as they hurried across the carpark. It didn't and within thirty minutes they were sat facing Mandy's home computer.

She tapped a few characters on her keyboard, and a map of the world appeared. 'This is something of my own invention, sir, so I'm not sure it will be judicially safe. Just saying, because anything we find here will be outside of the police system. Understand?'

'Something has happened in Myanmar and Bib and Bub will need all the help we can give them.'

Mandy entered *Myanmar* and waited. The screen zoomed to the small Asian country. She keyed in the number Mickey had given her. It was Bib's burner, and a small flashing blue dot appeared near the Yangon International Airport. 'Well, there you are Bib appears to be outside the airport. What he's doing is anyone's guess?'

'That is the only communications device they have or at least they have told us of. So, knowing where he is? How does it help?'

'They are delayed, he, or they, are off the plane and at large in Myanmar. That means anything can happen. It is considered a rogue state, and the Military have virtual carte blanche.' Mandy pulled a phone from a drawer in her desk. She turned the screen away from James, tapped in a short text, then slipped the phone into her pants pocket. 'Let's see where that gets us.'

While they were waiting Jean summoned them for dinner, the

meal was based on a vegan recipe, and the food was served with chilled water in a carafe.

James recalled the time when Stacey went completely vegan, it only lasted for a short while and when she fell pregnant with their first child, Jack, she got back into meat big-time. He smiled.

'What's so funny?' Mandy said.

James related the story with a slightly humorous twist and both women found his struggle wry.

'Sorry, Jim. Vegan it is. I went completely over the top.' Jean shot a glance at Mandy.

'I got used to it,' Mandy said and reached down for her phone. 'Got an answer. Let's see.' She'd received a reply to her text and smiled. 'Good onya, Gerry.'

'Good news or bad.'

'The good news is, he's an old contact from my army days and is in Myanmar and he has some top-level connections, the bad news is, there'll be little they can do legitimately.'

'Can you ask him for help?'

'Better than that, he's just offered. He'd actually heard rumours about ex-soldiers who have been rescuing young females from bad people.' She looked down at her phone just as another message came in. 'He's received intelligence about a 737 freighter carrying passengers at the Yangon airport. A member of the regime had a delivery that appears to have been collected. We also heard there is a local group who facilitate the trafficking of children internationally, and that they may be connected.'

Mandy tapped on her phone. A few seconds later what she saw astounded her.

33

Bib moved quickly and silently through the dimly lit streets of the city that surrounded the airport. He was heading towards the embassy precinct, where he hoped to meet up with an old friend. As he drew closer, he texted:

Have 4b2 need dowels.

He wondered if his old call sign still carried weight. Only time would tell. An obvious problem might be the several days growth of beard. Beards weren't common in Myanmar and if someone thought he might be acting suspiciously, he could be pounced upon and carted off to the nearest Myanmar nick, where he would undoubtably be interrogated at their leisure.

Interrogation wasn't Bib's main concern, he knew the ropes, but it would delay their progress, and progress was money that they needed to continue their work.

A black sedan drew alongside him and continued at a walking pace. Bib gave no sign that he had noticed anything unusual and kept his steady stride. After a few metres the car picked up speed and disappeared into the traffic. He now knew the regime were on to him and that he could expect further trouble to eventuate, but he continued until he saw the Australian Embassy building in the distance. Though Bib was a British citizen, he was acting on behalf of his Australian charges and his links to MI6 gave him tenuous connections in most embassies.

Another black car drew alongside. This time the rear passenger door flew open, and he was hauled bodily into the vehicle.

***

We have him.

The message was brief and to the point. Mandy's contact had acted promptly. The blue dot on her computer that signified Bib was now heading through the Australian embassy gates.

She showed the message to James.

'So now what?'

'So now we wait.' Mandy replied.

James returned to the table and thanked Jean for the meal. He sipped at his iced water and looked around the room. On the farthest wall was a framed photograph of a young man in uniform. Beneath the photo was a set of court mounted medals. There was something about the collage and Mandy noticed his gaze.

'He was a colleague.'

'Was he…?'

'The one on my desk?'

James nodded towards the picture and the medals. 'Not just fruit salad then?'

'He was a good friend who didn't make it home. He might now be our best hope.'

'So how will he be of help?'

'He won't but his brother will, he's my contact on attachment to the Myanmar Embassy.'

They returned to the computer just as the blue dot representing Bib disappeared.

'What happened there?'

Mandy pointed to the building. 'Aussie Embassy. He's probably inside.'

***

Frank began pacing up and down in the small passenger cabin. 'We can't hold off much longer. Every minute we're on the ground beyond our assigned time; invites scrutiny we don't need.'

'I thought you had a good connection with the regime?' Bib said.

'It only goes so far, and they are past masters of deniability.'

'What does that mean?'

'It means the delivery has already been taken to a secure hiding place. During the unloading all CCTV was shut down in the area of the plane, so there will be no evidence other than the paperwork which will be denied or claimed as a fraudulent transaction.'

'What are Bib's chances of doing a fix up to get the girls back in a short time.'

'Probably zip.'

'So, what's your prognosis, Frank?'

'If we're not back on track within six hours, I leave without him. There is only so long I can delay things and every minute of delay costs money that I can't recover.'

'Do you have a cell phone, Frank?'

He shook his head.

'Magda?'

'Better ask her. Most of my coms are via radio with the tower. I prefer it that way.'

'Where is she?'

'Probably getting her beauty sleep or reading or something.'

Bub knocked on the flight cabin door. 'Magda?'

The door opened. Magda looked out over bub's shoulder. 'Ven are ve leafing, Fronk.'

'Soon, dear, just waiting for Bib.'

'Zis vould have to be ze vorst flight we have ever done, Fronk.'

'He'll be back soon, I'm sure of it. If not, in six hours we leave without him.'

Bub swallowed hard. This was the first mission he'd been on that had the potential to end in ignominy, but Bib's uncanny knack of keeping things on track had never failed and he knew he had to trust in his colleague's ability. He looked out of the cabin door and could see only the twinkling lights of the airport and its surrounds. *Come on Bib, let's get this show on the road.*

***

The black car slowed to a halt and the Australian driver said, 'End of the road mate.' He opened the rear door and pointed to the lift. 'Third floor, they're expecting you.'

Bib thanked him and pressed up on the call pad. When the lift arrived at the floor, the door opened onto a bland wall. He stepped out and looked both ways. There was nothing to indicate he was in an embassy, and then a door to the right opened.

'Major Ashton-O'Sullivan? Follow me, if you please?'

Bib did as bidden, and the man led him into an area comprising offices as equally bland as the corridor outside. On the way through the man signalled to a young woman, who stood and left them to continue. He opened a door and said, 'Grab a seat mate, she won't be long with some tea and bickies.'

Bib raised an eyebrow.

'That's what you Pommy types like, isn't it?'

Bib tried to not roll his eyes.

'While we're waiting, perhaps you'd like to give me a summary of why you're here.'

'I'm hoping you might be able to help me find a young lady I've been helping to reunite with her parents.'

'You've lost her. Here. In Myanmar?'

'I've actually lost three, here, in Myanmar.'

'That's a bit of a bugger init.'

'You might say that.'

The door opened and the young woman arrived carrying a tray with a teapot, two cups, milk and sugar and a plate of chocolate biscuits. 'Anything else, sir?'

'She'll be right, Shiela.'

The door closed behind her, and the man introduced himself as Gerry Biggins. 'I got a message from an old friend who has, more or less, filled me in.' He smiled. 'As it happens, we keep an eye on the movements at the airport, and we think we might know where your people are.'

Bib suppressed the surge adrenalin that followed Biggins' comment. 'I need to get them back on the aircraft soon or it might be impossible to get them out of Myanmar.'

Biggins said, 'Sadly, it seems the Australian Federal Police are involved with their arrest and that puts me on a bit of a spot, old chum.' He pointed to the Australian flag hanging limply from a pole against the wall behind him.

'Would it be possible to make a call to Australia?'

Biggins lifted the handset from his desk phone and handed it over.

Bib tapped in the mobile number for Clark Shipton and waited. The call connected him to a voicemail. 'Shit. Mr Shipton, I need to speak with you urgently. I will try again in fifteen minutes.' He handed the phone back to Biggins.

Biggins gave a tight smile and tapped a number into the phone. 'Mands? great to speak with you again.' He pressed a loudspeaker option on the phone. 'I have a gentleman in my office; you might like to fill him in on what you told me.'

'Mr Bib?'

'Yes?'

'Sergeant Mandy Stephenson, West Australian Police. I know you are in the process of extracting some children from a place in Bosnia.'

'This is a private matter and I'm not sure this is of any interest to the WA Police.'

'Trust me Mr Bib. It is. Those girls are the tip of an iceberg, and certain people want them out of circulation because of what they might know. I'm handing you over to DI James Carter who will be able to give you some more information.'

'G'day Major. Yep, I know your name too,' James said.

'What is going on DI Carter?'

'I'm going to send you a copy of a message we received not long ago. I think you'll find it says it all.'

Bib's burner beeped with a text message. He extracted the attachment and opened it. 'Shit.'

'Problem?' Biggins said.

Bib turned the phone around so that he could read the document.

'Oh dear. Now we do have a problem and I'm not sure how we get out of this one.'

'You're the man on the spot here in Myanmar, Biggins.'

'My brother's ex-colleague, Mandy Stephenson, contacted the man you are with, and uses the name, Bub? She'd heard you were having some difficulties, and your charges had gone astray.'

'He would be right. Our mission has been compromised from day one.'

Carter said, 'And now we've received a ransom demand.'

'And we don't know where they are...'

Biggins cut in. 'We do.'

'What?'

'We know exactly where they are.'

Bib frowned. 'So why didn't you say?'

'Because there was Buckley's chance of doing anything, if the Australian Federal Police were on the case.'

Carter's voice broke through. 'Those you are referring to as the Federal Police are a gang using the AFP as a cover. They do have some high-level protection, but they are simply crooks who want to get to the girls before they can spill the beans about those who trafficked them.'

'I'd need more than that DI Carter.'

'Well Mr Biggins that's the best you are going to get, so we need to make a decision about this ransom. They say they will give us twenty-four hours to raise 250k US Dollars for each of the girls. After twenty-four hours it will double. Then they will kill a girl for each day the ransom is not paid.'

'I'll get back to you.' Biggins pressed end and turned towards Bib. 'This is where they are.' He brought up a map on his computer. 'This building is in a high-density part of the city. It's heavily controlled by the regime, and the current rules make is impossible for me, as a diplomat, to act. The Australian Government has strict guidelines regarding ransom payments. They don't pay.'

'Even though at least one is an Australian citizen.'

'Prove it. None of them are carrying ID papers.'

'That's because they are all on the plane they were removed from.'

Biggins leaned back in his chair. 'Sergeant Mandy Stephenson was close with my brother. They served together in Afghanistan, and she did her best to save his life, regrettably, my brother didn't come home.'

'I'm sorry about that, I also had many friends who didn't return,' Bib said.

'The building the girls are being kept in is only lightly guarded but trying to get in and extract your charges will most likely stir up an unfavourable response.'

'What do you propose?'

'Something I was going to get to before we heard of the ransom demand.' Biggins kicked a heavy sports bag out from under his desk. 'Ex-regime weapons. They lose them all the time so their deniability will be maximum.' He handed Bib a sketch plan of the premises. 'Best I can do. This is an old part of town, but it is where they are being kept.'

Bib unzipped the bag containing two Kalashnikovs, fitted with suppressors, and a box of ammunition. Two Russian made pistols and several magazines, along with some grenades and the Chinese equivalent of a Claymore. 'There's enough to start a small war in here,' Bib said.

Biggins smirked, 'As long as it is a deniable war, Major.'

Bib stood and hefted the bag, concerned it might be heavy enough to draw attention to him if he was walking along the streets that surrounded Yangon International Airport. He thanked Biggins and said, 'Don't wish me luck, I'll need more than that.' They shook hands and Bib stepped into the lift.

34

Birchmore slammed down his phone and yelled to those in the outer office. 'Ashton-C'Sullivan's at the Australian Embassy in Myanmar and he knows of the ransom demand. What have we got on him that we can use?'

Everyone responded with shaking heads.

Birchmore tapped in another number into his phone. He waited patiently while the ringtone cycled several times and was about to hang up when a sleepy disgruntled voice answered.

'What is it? Whatever it is had better be good at this time of night.'

'DCI Birchmore, Sir. Perth.'

'Well?'

'We have a slight problem.'

'No, Birchmore, you have a slight problem,' the Attorney General replied.

'The prodigal is in our Embassy in Myanmar.'

'Well have him arrested. You must be able to find something to charge the fellow with.'

'It's a federal jurisdiction, sir.'

'Isn't there a team over there in WA?'

'Which team, sir. There seem to be two groups each acting

independently of the other.'

'Well then, you'd better see to it that the right one is given the correct information.'

Birchmore winced as the line went dead. He had good reason to be stressed. He'd been shoehorned into this job to slow down or sideline any further investigations into human trafficking. With the big money end of town involved, he would need to tread carefully or be sucked into the mire. He tapped DI Carter's mobile number into his phone but got the voice mail. 'DCI Birchmore. My office, now!' He then called the land line that Mickey Krakauer was supposed to be available at.

Jackie answered. 'Hello?'

'DCI Birchmore. I need to speak to Sergeant Krakauer.'

'He gone away,' Jackie said, trying to restrain the chuckle in her voice.

'When will he be back, it's important that I speak to him?'

'Dunno, mista, he gone away.' The call ended.

***

'Who was that,' Mickey said. 'No one calls us on the landline anymore.'

'Birchmore. Says he needs to speak to you and it's very important.'

'Ah.'

'That's what I thought.' She pointed to the clock on the bedside cabinet. 'Ten pm. He's certainly burning the midnight oil.'

'Good for him. He can wait.' He tapped Clarke Shipton's name on the burner's screen.

'Yeah?'

'Clarkie, it's Mickey.'

'Can't you sleep. Hey, heard you've had a bit of a rough time of things.'

'Yeah, but I'm good now. Just had Birchmore chasing me. I'm guessing it's to do with your daughter.'

'That twat can fucking wait. You've seen his file. He's as involved with the trafficking as anyone else. Just to update you, I've had a message to say they've stopped at Myanmar to make a delivery and refuel. Next stop, Perth. Kell's already organising a party to welcome her home.'

'Hmmm. Isn't Myanmar a bit dodgy?'

'I get the impression it's just a pit stop, then they'll be on their way.'

'If you say so. It's late but I'll give James Carter a call he might know something more.' Mickey ended the call and tried James.

He picked up immediately. 'Mick?'

'Sorry, boss. Birchmore's chasing me. I thought…'

'Me too. I'm not in any hurry to interact with him and I have some news for Shipton. His daughter and her two friends have gone missing and now their captors have issued a ransom demand. Mandy Stephenson has an ex-army contact in the embassy and he's, supposedly, helping out.'

'That's not exactly good news for Clarkie; he's expecting them home any time with no mention of a ransom.'

'Well, there's rules about ransoms, meanwhile get some rest. There's nothing we can do until Bib and Bub come up with the goods. Whatever happens they still have to get here and I'm still working on the sting. As soon as we get news, I'll set it in motion.'

Mickey decided that it might be best if Clarkie didn't know his daughter was missing, or the ransom, whatever that was. He ended the call and turned to face Jackie. 'The girls have gone walkabout in Myanmar and now there's a ransom demand.'

'Great.'

'Better get some sleep. We might need all the help we can get in the next few hours.' He kissed her on the lips and then sleep became the last thing on his mind.

***

Bib slung the sports bag over his shoulder and waited while the lift descended to the embassy car park. The door opened and a man of Asian appearance reached out to shake his hand.

'I am Robert Chan, sir. Mr Biggins said you'll be needing a lift.' He pointed to the rusting hulk of an ancient white Mercedes blowing rank diesel fumes into the already foul air behind him. 'Said you might want to blend in on your drive back to the airport.'

Bib grinned and shook his hand. 'That will do very nicely.' He threw the bag in the boot and slipped in alongside Chan. 'How much do you know?'

'Enough. I will pick up your friend and I'll drop you near the place where the young ladies are being held. Then, sir, I'm afraid you will be on your own until the job is done.'

Bib sat back to take in the sights of the town while he tapped a text to Bub.

Bub replied:

Got it. Will do.

Bib had spent SAS time in Myanmar as a young soldier, back in the days when it was called Burma. The city streets of the old capital Yangon hadn't changed appreciably, though he knew enough to realise the release of the girls might cause them to close like a steel trap if they got it wrong.

Chan's driving was erratic, just like a local, and he grinned like an idiot for most of the trip. His expression only changed briefly when someone on a motorbike cut him up. Then he wound down his window and launched into an angry tirade of abuse.

The motorcyclist gave him the bird and carried on, regardless.

Bib raised his eyebrows.

Chan grinned. 'It is expected, Mr Bib. Never do the unexpected if you wish to hide in Myanmar.'

His comment brought Bib back down to earth. His mind had been in turmoil as he tried to work out the best way to approach the next part of the operation. Although the ransom gave a twenty-four-hour deadline, he needed to end the stalemate within five hours, or Frank's flight plan would be in jeopardy. This meant he wouldn't have the usual time to suss out the location, but Chan knew his way around the regime and the way of life in Yangon. 'When we finish what we need to do, how will we get back to the Airport?'

Chan's grin switched to a serious expression. 'I will collect you. I am told you are very good at your job, so there will be no problems.'

'I wish I had your confidence.'

Chan's expression slipped back into a grin before he hung a left and floored the accelerator before hanging a wheel squealing right. 'Nearly there.'

Bib turned around to look through the rear window and saw the single headlight of a motorcycle. 'A tail?'

Chan said, 'Not for long.'

'But it means they are on to us.'

Chan's grin returned. 'This is an embassy car. They always try it on. It is a game for them. They have so little else to do.' He chucked another right, and the motorcycle flew past. 'There is a well-known brothel up this street. They will now think I am taking an embassy visitor for an exotic evening of erotic pleasure.' He laughed aloud. 'I love the English language, don't you?' and then his face turned serious. 'Would *you* like to stop for a bit, Mr Bib?'

Bib sensed the car's lurch to the left.

'We are here,' Chan said

The gate near Frank's plane was slightly open and Chan stopped outside. A moment later Bub appeared at the head of the ladder and joined them in the car.

'What's next, Bib.'

Bib turned to Chan and said, 'Can you give us a few moments?'

They stepped out of the car and Bib handed Bub the drawings of the building they needed to infiltrate.

'Straight forward enough,' Bub said. 'It says there is no CCTV, but we can't take that for granted.'

Bib pointed to the room that the girls were being kept in. 'No idea how secure it is.'

Bub said, 'I can't imagine it would be to prison standards.'

'Then let's assume it is. Any sign of Vishwananda?'

'He apparently left with the girls. Amrita seems as confused as me.'

They pondered their situation and soon afterwards Bib tapped on the window.

Chan said, 'Ready, sir?'

Bib said, 'Let's get it over with.'

He clambered in, slammed the ancient door, the car lurched forward, and his grin reappeared. 'You know what to do?'

35

James turned to Mandy and said, 'They've hung up. Let's hope they have a plan.'

'My guess is that Bib already knows exactly what to do. He'll have handled many similar operations over his career. The mob holding the girls will not be expecting a physical attack. If they are anything like those who took Mickey and Jack, they'll probably be on the grog awaiting the bank to tell them the cash has arrived. Then they'll kill the girls and do a runner to Thailand.'

'Great.' James said.

'Yeah, well they gave twenty-four hours to pay up the first amount and Bib won't wait that long. He knows the government will stall, and he has nothing to gain by waiting for them to come to an agreement.'

'So, there is nothing we can do but wait.'

'About sums it up, sir.'

'Assuming they eventually get here, it makes the sting on arrival even more important. We need to stop this dead in the water and this time there will be no sympathetic attitude towards those on the fringe. We go for everyone.'

Mandy's partner, Jean appeared holding a tray with coffee

and biscuits. 'Are you two getting somewhere?'

'Thanks for the coffee, babe. Might be a long night,' Mandy said. 'I'm going to create a neat little trap that will capture everything they do.'

'How?'

'You'll see.' She reached into a small black case beside her desk and extracted an identical laptop to the one they were using. 'Mine,' she pointed to the one on her desk. 'That's the police issue unit from my work desk. Most of the data, on that, is on the network servers but I can access it from anywhere.' She opened a drawer and pulled out a small plastic case. 'When I've finished here, we'll have a window on their world, and they won't even know it.' She breathed out took a sip of her coffee, and said, 'Go home to your wife, Jim. You don't need to know what I'm doing, and it's probably best that you don't.'

***

The journey to the building where they suspected the girls were being held took them through some of the seamier parts of the old town. Chan slowed to a halt and said, 'The place you seek is in the next street. I suggest you take a walk and familiarise yourself with it.' He opened a map that had two locations marked. 'We are here. They are there.'

Bib studied the location and handed the map to Bub. 'Whadya think?'

Bub thought for a couple of minutes while comparing the map with the building's sketch plan. 'No sweat.' He pointed to a narrow alleyway that extended down the side and allowed his finger to move towards a rear entrance. 'My guess is that they won't be expecting trouble this soon, so the chances are it won't be secured.' His finger moved over the plan to the first-floor section that had been circled. 'We go in at the rear and take the stairs. Do it right and we might get away with garrottes, the AKs will bring down the whole neighbourhood if shooting starts.'

'Set the AKs to semi auto and hope we don't need more. The suppressors won't help that much and the last thing we need is a firefight.'

'Okay, Bib. Shall we take a walk and check this place out?'

Bib opened the door and began walking quietly down the street, clinging close into the shadows of the buildings. Bub went the opposite direction. Their plan being to meet at their destination.

Chan switched off his engine and relaxed to wait in the dark. He looked at his watch, its ancient illuminous hands telling him it was four o'clock. He grinned, *perfect.*

***

Birchmore was becoming more agitated by the minute. No one had mentioned a ransom. The girls were supposed to have been eliminated far away from prying eyes. Now everyone would know of the operation and how long before the press got the message was intangible. He called the AG again.

'Some good news I hope.'

'Someone has initiated a ransom demand…'

The silence at the other end was such that it could be only cut with a stout pair of garden shears.

Birchmore listened. 'Sir?'

'You had better have a good explanation for this, Birchmore.'

'It didn't come from us.'

'Who did it come from?'

'I'm still trying to find out. My operator in the cyber division is scanning various options.'

'If this gets into the media…'

'I'm well aware of what might happen, sir.'

'Get on top of it and get this operation back under control. You have a lot to lose, Birchmore.'

Birchmore ended the call and muttered, 'And you, the biggest, will fall the hardest.' He made his way around to the cyber division. It was deserted. He looked at his watch. *Midmorning, where are they all?* He'd lied about his cyber officer's progress and now the man was nowhere to be seen. He was about to leave when the door opened, and Mandy Stephenson appeared.

She ignored him, went directly for her desk, pulled her laptop from its case and began tapping on the keyboard.

'Sergeant Stephenson.'

'Yes, sir?'

'What are you working on?'

She turned her screen towards him. 'Not the nicest job this, Sir, but then you'd understand, wouldn't you?'

Birchmore stared at the screen. It contained a list of email addresses. Most meant nothing but one of them had stood out as if it had been highlighted. It was a private address used by the AG. He knew it because he had used it himself for private communications. 'What are those?'

'Just random addresses that seem to turnup when we start tracking paedophilia sites. Sometimes we get lucky and can track the user, but many are setup as anonymous.' She tapped a couple of keys, and a bar chart appeared. She pointed at the screen. 'There's a lot of activity at the moment. Mostly to do with those missing girls. It seems they were trafficked by George Gregory's little cohort. But then you'd be aware of the work done by DI Carter in closing that down.' Mandy had been observing his body language and knew she was pressing buttons. She tapped on her keyboard slammed the lid of her computer shut, dropped it into its carry case and stood. 'Sorry sir I have an appointment.'

Birchmore barred her way. 'I want to see everything on your computer Sergeant Stephenson.'

She handed him the laptop and walked away.

'Password?'

She spelled out the word D-0-n-k-e-y-b-r-a-!-n-s. 'Enjoy.'

***

Mandy didn't dare to turn around, lest he saw her struggling to hide her smirk. The computer was her regular police owned device, but the hard disk had been replaced. Its data configured to send anyone who used it on a tortuous trip to the reconstructed plans for the arrival of the girls, and how they would be extricated from the plane at the airport. She had also set up a remote access facility that would enable her to watch his fumbling, and every keystroke would be logged. She called James. 'Good morning, sir. I hope you slept well.'

'With you on the job, Mandy, I feel a lot better.'

'Birchmore thinks I have an appointment, but I'll be at home. I don't know how long it will take him to find my little sting scenario on his own, but I'll be there help him stumble on to it if necessary. Any news of the girls?'

'Not yet the bloke in Myanmar sent me a text to say that Bib and Bub are working on their extraction. From now on everything is fluid. Of course, if they fail, we might be back to square one with a vengeance.'

***

Mickey tapped on the door of Birchmore's office.

'Come.'

He pushed open the door and in a deep voice said, 'You rang.'

Birchmore didn't register the Lurch reference, and he continued.

'You rang, *sir.*'

'You rang, sir,' Mickey said.

Birchmore grunted and pointed to the laptop on his desk. 'What do you know about computers?'

'Not a lot, *sir.*'

Birchmore looked up.

perhaps you should back off a bit mate.

'I want you to go through this and report back to me with everything you find.' He paused. 'This is straight between you and me. If anything gets out, I'll know you are the one to blame. Get it?'

Mickey nodded.

36

Bib approached the building cautiously and he could see Bub heading down the road towards him. He removed a small device from his pocket and activated it in silent mode before holding it out in front of him.

'Cameras, Bib?' Bub murmured.

Bib pointed to the visible items mounted on the walls of the building. 'Oddly, none of them are active, and there are no wireless devices.'

'Think they've deliberately switched them off to lure us into a trap?'

Bib shook his head and pointed to the nearest device. 'Looks like something's chewed through the wiring. Probably rats.' He led Bub down the narrow alley between the buildings. At its end was a barred steel gate. 'Let's hope it doesn't squeak.' He lifted the crude latch, pushed it silently open and sniffed the air.

'You thinking what I'm thinking?'

Bib said, 'It's meth.'

'Shit.'

Bib went through the gate and around to the rear of the building. Then he froze and raised his hand to stop Bub. On the floor outside the rear entrance was a man clutching a meth pipe.

His back was to the wall and though he was breathing he was far away in fairyland.

Bub made a garrotting action with his hands.

Bib shook his head. 'He's going nowhere for a while. Looks like he's been mixing his drinks.' Bib gave the man a shove, and he fell over. 'I'd say he's hit on an opioid and followed up with an opportunistic meth high.' He carefully opened the door and walked into the passageway shown on the drawings. At the end of the passage was a staircase. He pointed up and stepped aside to let Bub take the lead while he covered him with his AK.

Bub ascended the staircase hoping there were no creekers. There were none, it had probably been built at a time when quality was more important than cost. As soon as he reached the short landing, he beckoned Bib.

There were a number of doors, all closed, and the building seemed permeated by the sickly-sweet scent of meth. Bib tried the first door. The room was packed wall to wall with bags filled with crystal. He tried the next one. It was the same. He turned to Bub and said, 'This is a meth warehouse.'

Bub followed him along the landing with each door opening onto a meth consignment.

Bib opened the last door and gagged. The three girls were unconscious, hogtied, and lying in their own excrement. There was no sign of Vishwananda, and his automatic reaction was to cock his AK but there was no need. Whoever was demanding the ransom had probably already videoed the girls and expected them to die. The ransom was a chancer's try on and Bib needed to get them back to the car and a medical facility as soon as possible. That meant risking the flight to Australia and hoping they survived. He sent a thumb up emoji to Chan and signalled to Bub that he needed help to get them down the stairs.

Bub picked up two of the girls and held one under each arm as he moved rapidly to the exit.

Bib threw the other over his shoulder in a fireman's lift and followed.

Chan's car arrived as they appeared from the alley way, and he leapt out to open the rear doors for Bib and bub to throw in the girls. The old-fashioned bench seat in the front, allowed room for both men, and Chan at a squeeze, and he slammed the car into gear.

'Wait!' Bib leapt from the car, ran to the boot, reached in and removed the claymore from the bag. Next, he ran down the alley and placed it inside the rear entrance with its trip wire connected to the doorknob. He armed it and ran like hell to the Mercedes. 'Go!' he yelled.

Chan ignoring his call to action, moved off in a sedate manner, as though nothing had happened, and drove in his usual erratic way to the airport.

⋇✳✳

James Carter answered his phone to the unknown number half expecting it to be a scam call.

'DI Carter. Ashton-O'Sullivan, Bib. Three girls are on the plane, and we are taxiing for take-off. As soon as I have an ETA, I'll message you. Then it is up to you.'

'Thanks for that. We can now start getting things in motion.'

'We still have a slight problem. Hopefully everything will be okay by the time we get there.'

'Well, it's good to know they are on their way.'

The call ended with no further comments.

Carter sucked in a deep breath and called Mandy. 'They are on the plane and on their way.'

'Fantastic news, sir. Any idea when?'

'Direct flight, about twelve hours. Bib reckons there is still a problem, but he hopes it will be sorted by their arrival.'

'I'll call Mickey and get him started on the plan.'

***

Bib looked at the three filthy children lying apart on the cabin floor. his nose wrinkled at the stench of theirs and his, clothing, and he noticed Bub was acting similarly. He grinned.

Bub grinned back. They'd both been through this before, though carrying wounded men with their guts hanging out was a little different. 'They'll scrub up okay.'

Amrita did her best to clean them up and make them comfortable, then she'd astounded everyone by producing a phial of naltrexone from her doctor's bag. 'It won't help with the meth, but it might reverse some of the effects of opioid in their systems. I am sorry, Mr Bib, there is no guarantee they will survive, but it's all we have.'

The sun had barely risen as the aircraft lifted off and Bib and Bub peered through a window to try to spot where the building was. It didn't matter, nothing was going to happen to the kidnappers, of that they were certain.

'Hey, look.' Bub pointed to a pall of bluish white smoke arising from a back street. 'You don't think?'

'Someone probably set their breakfast on fire,' Bib grinned. 'On the subject of breakfast.' He knocked on the door of the flight cabin and opened the door.

Magda turned from her co-piloting and responded. 'Do not come in here in that disgusting state. Vat do you vant?'

'We're all hungry, ma'am.'

'Zen you vill have to vait. Zis isn't a scheduled airline you know.'

'You are so kind, ma'am, of course.' He closed the door and said, 'Ve vill haff to vait.' He then mumbled, 'No wonder they lost the bloody war.' He stepped into the small toilet, stripped off his clothing and did the best he could to rinse away the shit in the small sink.

When he finished scrubbing, he wrung them out as tight as he could, and put it all back on again and said, 'That feels better.' He poked his head out and said, 'Your turn, Bub.'

***

The awaited text arrived, and James Carter smiled.

ETA 1800 Perth time

He called Mandy, Angela, and Mickey on their respective burners. 'Genuine ETA 1800. Time to kick off our plans.' He lay back on the bed and kissed Stacey. 'Busy day today. Might be late. But then it will all be over.'

She nuzzled his neck. 'Let's hope so.'

Another message came in as she spoke.

The girls have papers but might also
need legal assistance. Please arrange

He called Angela and repeated the text.

'I'm so glad, Jim. Of course I'll make myself available, and as you might expect, it just so happens that one of my team has extensive immigration experience.'

He could almost feel the excitement in her voice, but he tried his best to temper it, 'Might be a long haul and they'll still be at considerable risk. There are some who think they know a lot more than they have admitted to so far.'

'I'm not the innocent twit I was when I took on Tom Gregory's case, big brother, but thanks for the heads up. Does the commissioner know?'

'I've kept him away from this for as much as I could. He'll be needed when the shit really hits the proverbial and you can bet that Birchmore will be firing with both barrels.'

'Any idea how far up it goes?'

'If you recall we were generous with our hold-off on some who seemed to have minimal connections. I believe this time there'll be a much harder stance. I haven't mentioned anything to Shipton. He'll be getting his daughter back, albeit in pieces, but he'll have plenty of questions to answer about his own past connections. He won't be told of her confirmed arrival time until after we have closed in on the Birchmore mob. Get prepared and I'll keep you posted.'

37

Angela showered and put on her best head kicking lawyer suit. The flannel shirt and jeans could wait for another day and for the first time in years, she was feeling exalted. Her blood effervesced through her veins just like it did on the day she learned she'd won the appeal for Tom Gregory. Then, as if someone had pulled out her plug, she remembered what happened and her excitement crashed. She took a deep breath put the past behind her and attempted to focus her mind on the matters ahead.

An iciness swarmed over her psyche as she drove through the streets to her little run-down office suite in Northbridge. There was no one outside under a crocheted rug, and when she walked in all eyes turned towards her.

Gloria's, fifties plus, eyes popped, and she said, 'My, we've gone up in the world haven't we.'

A titter of laughter that followed was cut short when Angela spoke. 'We're going to have a long day and I'm counting on you all to give of your best.'

'What's happening?' Gloria said.

'I can't give you the full details just yet but your experience of immigration and such, is going to be invaluable. My friends have managed to rescue some trafficked souls who have been under a forced heroin addiction for around three years. At least one is known to be Australian, and she will be arriving with what might be considered creative paperwork. The origins of the others will need to be determined, and they will all need to be placed in rehab, in a secure establishment...'

'Prison?' Gloria interrupted.

'I sincerely hope not. They are all not yet sixteen and have been subjected to years of sexual assault. They will almost certainly be broken. I'm hoping, not beyond repair.'

As though someone had flicked a switch, the mood changed in the office. Gloria left in silence and began to clear her desk. She called to her clerk who joined her.

Brian Carpenter, who had some degree of success with several drug misdirected kids, said, 'It'll be hard yakka, Ange.'

'Tell me about it. One thing for certain, I do not intend to fail again.'

Knowing what was in her mind, Brian headed to his office and began rearranging his own appointments.

She called after him, 'We might appear to be a tin pot little office, Brian, but that is all about to change.'

***

Birchmore summoned Mickey Krakauer to his office. 'Okay what have you found on that laptop?'

'Not a lot, boss, but then I'm not sure what I'm looking for. I'm a copper not a nerd.' He handed him an envelope.

'What's this?'

'As you might know, sir, ex-Sergeant Jaclyn Morton has been exonerated on appeal, and we are getting married in a couple of weeks. This is a request for transfer to a country station where I can maybe do some real good.'

Birchmore opened the envelope pulled out the two sheets of paper, read the top one and sniggered. 'I'll decide who goes bush and who stays here.' He tore the papers in half and dropped them into the waste bin beside his desk.

Mickey hoisted the laptop and placed it on Birchmore's pristine blotter. 'Maybe the cyber division will have more luck, boss.'

'Get out of my office, you waste of fucking space.'

'Certainly, sir.' He turned and headed to his car. Mickey had bigger fish to fry today, but he wondered if Birchmore might re-read his letter including the second page. He'd registered a copy on file, and he smirked. *Well, I told you so.* He sent a text from the burner and James Carter answered it immediately.

> Well-done, Mick, now we wait.

***

James sent a text to Arthur Bertram:

> Sir, we have three trafficked girls
> arriving at Perth Airport ETA 1800.
> I need to speak with you urgently.
>
> DI James Carter.

He'd no sooner tapped send when his burner rang.

'Jim, what's happening.'

James described the recent events and how he was planning a sting type operation to winkle out the dodgy cops. 'The plan is to get the girls away and safely ensconced. That's all taken care of, but I'll be needing backup when our friends hit the airport.'

The Police Commissioner fell silent.

James felt a chill shiver pass through his body. 'I'm sorry, sir, I...'

'This is the first time I've heard of this, Carter and now you're expecting me to jump to it, at your request.'

'Secrecy was the most important part of our plan, sir. We know who the leaders are, and I've put my neck on the line. If necessary, I'll carry on without your support.'

Another long silence, permeated with the sound of shuffling papers. 'Thank you Marrianne. That will be all.'

James heard a door close and more paper shuffling.

'Okay, I'm alone at last. You now have my ear. What the fuck are you planning?'

James relayed a more detailed outline of the operation. How the girls would be extracted from the plane and taken into protective custody. Once completed the team arriving to arrest the people smugglers would find nothing. 'We have been distributing faux intelligence and we know they are acting on it. A complete squad of fake federal police have been weighing in with the locals and their objective, we believe, is to move in and prevent the girls from communicating any of the horrors they've been put through.'

'Think you can pull it off?'

'If not, there isn't much more I can do.'

'Names?'

'DCI Birchmore. I have a file that is not very favourable. It lists high-level connections that will be affected by this operation. He has several acolytes who see the benefit of hanging on to his shirt tails and they've had a cushy number since he was brought in to ward off investigations.'

'By high-level?'

'The federal AG is the highest we know of. There is no evidence yet of his physical implication, but if DCI Birchmore's file is anything to go on, you can at least expect the sky to fall.'

'Shit.'

'The aircraft arrives at 1800. They and their rescuers will be unloaded in a flight container and taken directly to a safe place. Birchmore thinks the aircraft is arriving at 2000. That gives us two hours clear and once they close in, we'll have the whole shebang neatly contained in one place.'

'And you want me to authorise a mob to round them up?'

'If it's possible. There are enough of us, who still believe in what we're doing, to give it a go.'

'You realise that as soon as I make a move to assist it will go around the place via Wi-Fi and might compromise everything you have done to keep it quiet.'

'Mandy Stephenson has digitised and hidden the contents of the file, and she has been largely responsible for the misinformation campaign. I'll get her to send you a copy of what we have then you can better decide what is needed.'

'I'll look forward to seeing this file of yours. I'm still getting my head around some of the strange goings on in the department that occurred before I was promoted.'

'Thank you, sir.'

The call was ended at the commissioner's end and James began having doubts about the conversation they had just had. He now had no choice but to proceed and hoped that he'd pressed all the buttons in the correct order.

***

'Kell, It's Mickey.'

'Hey, good lookin, what ya got cookin?'

'Huh?'

'Yeah, okay, before your time. What's new?'

'The girls are arriving tonight. Jim Carter's sting is all set up…'

'Should I be telling Clarkie about this?'

'The fewer who learn of it the better and I don't want him getting all excited and turning up at the airport. He'll have the same info as Birchmore's mob. Once the girls are safe, he'll be the first to know.'

'Are they okay?'

'Bib and Bub have been medicating them with anti-withdrawal drugs, but I believe they're quite frail.'

'Shit. I think Clarkie was expecting to be taking his daughter out for dinner and being all daddy-like with her.'

'That might have to wait.'

'Corrupt cops? Are these the ones who took Jackie?'

'A bunch of locals are working with them, and we believe DCI Birchmore might be leading the pack.'

'Birchmore, I've heard that name. Wasn't he the one who was brought in to catch the traffickers in the first place?'

'More to slow down and obfuscate the investigation. It was Jim Carter who did most of that work.'

'Yeah, but you helped bring it to the boil. Clarkie has never forgotten what you did. That publicity you sorted attracted Bib and Bub, Soon Kaitlin'll be home, and Clarkie will be over the moon.'

'Okay, Jim Carter is setting up a sting that will draw in Birchmore and his cronies. They're putting it about they are shutting down a people smuggling enterprise. In fact, by the time they arrive to do their policey stuff, the girls will be long gone, and Jim Carter will move in to arrest the whole shebang.'

'Bit risky, isn't it? Cops versus cops.'

'Jim has the backing of the commissioner.'

'You realise that if something is in the offing Clarkie's eyes and ears on the street will be reporting back?'

'That's why I'm taking a big risk and telling you. We don't

want Clarkie anywhere near the airport until the girls are safe. If he comes up with anything stall him as long as you can.'

Kelly glanced over at the half full bottle of scotch on the credenza. She smiled. 'Might have to use my girly wiles, you reckon.'

'Too much information, Kel. Let's get Kaitlin back and into a safe place before he goes on any rampages.'

38

Bib looked at his watch and nibbled on one of the sandwiches that Magda had reluctantly made for them before taking over the role of pilot. 'Three hours to touchdown. That fit with your estimation Frank?'

'Magda is rarely wrong. She has an instinct for these things.'

Bib glanced across at Amrita.

Amrita caught his eye and smiled. She'd set fire to something in his soul, and he smiled back, wishing things could be different. He picked up his bag and signalled to Frank and Bub.

They followed him through to the space beside the girls' flight container. 'All good?' He nodded towards the cabin area.

'So far, the poor blighters seem to be recovering quite well from their experience. Three hours to go and they'll be under proper medical supervision.'

'I meant Amrita. Something going between you?'

Bib shook his head, 'Not possible.'

'She's done a brilliant job so far, Bib.'

'She's a doctor that's what they're trained to do. Shipton's cash is in the bank, so we'll have no reason to hang around. Same exit as last time only it will be from a freighter not a passenger jet.'

Bub had already worked that part out. 'It'd be good to have a doctor available on future missions. This one has been a nightmare with two types of drugs and the general health of the subjects.'

'Are you suggesting we become a threesome?'

Bub shrugged.

'She's not attuned to our style old chap. She might become a liability and that is the last thing we need.'

'I was thinking more along the lines of a mission consultant who we could call on at the drop of a hat.'

Bib shrugged changed the subject. 'It would be nice to see the face of Kaitlin's dad when he sees his daughter for the first time in three years.'

'Sadly, Bib, that's a reward we can't afford.'

'Frank knows what we need to do. Right, Frank?'

Something was bothering Frank.

'Spit it out Frank,' Bib said.

Frank looked up and around the aircraft interior. 'This is all I have, Dave. I could lose it at the drop of a hat.'

Bib pulled his burner from his pocket and tapped in a number. 'The contents of this text will hand you a major get out of jail card if you use it wisely.'

Frank's phone bleeped. 'Shit.'

'Australian trade mission, complete with the flagrante delicto under minister. Like I said, Frank, use it if you must. It makes no difference to me.'

Frank closed the message.

'Sometime soon we'll need to get those babes into the container and make them comfortable for the rest of their journey.'

'Where are they going after we get to Perth?'

Bib showed him a text message he'd received from a lawyer.

'I believe she is Jim Carter's sister, and she's made the arrangements for them to be taken to a secure private clinic, run by an old pal of mine. From that moment on they will be no longer of our concern and the rehab centre will assist with their rehabilitation and any immigration problems.'

'Are you envisaging any?'

'Just playing safe.'

'What about Clark Shipton?'

'He knows nothing about the imminence of their arrival. He will be advised as soon as they've been moved. By then we'll be long gone on a scheduled flight to Singapore.' He reached into his bag and produced a new proforma. 'This is our next job.'

Bib peered at the text. 'We're going back to Bosnia?'

'Via Mumbai. One of the kids, in those photos I took, was the daughter of a high ranking Indian official. I've doubled the fee and added a large contingency. He didn't bat an eyelid.'

'She might be lost in the field by now.'

'We've had worse.'

***

Mickey's burner tooted it was a text from Jim Carter.

My place in ten minutes.

'Sorry, Kel. I have to go.'

She reached out and dragged him into a hug, 'Take care Mick.'

He pushed her away and skittered down the back stairs just as Clark Shipton's Lamborghini rumbled into the car park.

Its window lowered, 'Hey, Mick?'

'Sorry Clarkie, gotta go. Catch ya later.' Mickey climbed into his vehicle and left.

'That, Mickey, seemed in an almighty hurry, Kel.'

'He has things to do and places to go, boss.'

'Any news of Katy?'

Kelly felt her face colour. 'Not yet, but I don't think it will be much longer.'

Shipton's face stiffened. 'You wouldn't be lying to me Kel?'

Kelly shrugged.

'Because I'm hearing there is a special plane arriving at around eight o'clock tonight. Big police presence expected. Why are the cops interested? It's only my daughter for chrissake and they haven't been able to help so far.'

Kelly shrugged again.

'Kel… Is that why Mickey was here? Do you know something I don't?'

'Mickey said that a DCI Birchmore might be bringing a squad to deal with things. He didn't say what.'

Shipton's face froze. 'Did you say Birchmore?'

'That's what Mickey said.' She felt her body language was beginning to give her away, and she attempted to recover. 'Nothing to do with Kaitlin.'

Shipton pushed through the door to his office and unlocked his safe.

Kelly caught a glimpse of a semiautomatic pistol. 'What are you planning, boss?'

'Nothing you need to know about, Kel.' He walked to the carpark entrance and headed down to his car.

Kelly heard the engine start, and she texted Mickey.

***

James Carter had set his games room up as an incident control centre and was busily pinning photographs to a board mounted on the wall. He smiled when Mickey arrived and pointed to an urn with a sign that said "coffee". Mandy Stephenson had a laptop computer connected to a large screen, and she was busying herself writing scripts that would cut down the time wasting later.

'Mickey, nice to see you again, is Jackie coming along?' Angela said.

'She wouldn't miss this for the world, and we'll need someone back at base to keep things tidy when the shit… Well, you know.'

Angela introduced her colleagues, Gloria and Brian Carpenter. 'Gloria's expertise is immigration, and Brian has a long connection with drug problems.'

Mickey shook their hands but said nothing.

Angela puffed out her chest and said, 'Mickey helped expose the trafficking racket that led to the situation that these poor wretches find themselves in.'

He smiled and headed to the coffee urn where he was met by James.

'So far they seem to have taken the bait and are gearing up for action at around eight o'clock.'

'Clarkie might not agree, boss. Kelly said he was packing a loaded automatic and heading for his car.'

'Shit. How much does he know?'

'He knows everything.'

'We'll need to be prepared for them arriving on time. Can you contact B&B?'

Mickey tapped a message into the burner Bib had given him. There was no point phoning and waiting for an hour.

A reply came back almost immediately.

> Thanks Mickey. We'll expect the
> worst.

***

Bib turned off his phone and made his way through to the cabin area. He walked over to Amrita and sat beside her.

She smiled. 'You must either be a very brave man, or stupid to help these children, Mr Bib.'

'No, Amrita, I'm angry. These are kids who have been taken away from their families to satisfy the pigs who choose to prey on the underage. I want to thank you for all that you have done to keep them at least a little bit safer.'

She placed her hand on his and said, 'I'm glad I have been some small help.'

Her touch sent micro-shocks through his nervous system, and when he tried to respond all that came out was stuttered gibberish. He switched to battle control mode, took a deep breath and said, 'You will not see me again after we land. We have another project that cannot wait. I'm told there will be a legal team on hand to assist everyone who needs it. They have expertise in drug rehabilitation and immigration requirements.' He cleared his throat. 'Think you'll be seeing Mr Vishwananda again?'

'I don't know.'

'We'll be on the ground in less than one hour.'

Amrita gripped his hand, pulled it towards her lips, and kissed it. 'When I first saw you, something happened to me. Thank you for being there, even for such a brief moment in time.'

Bib pulled his hand away, stood, and looked towards the girls. 'We need you in your box, girlies. Sorry.'

The three stood as one and separated to hug both Bib and Bub tightly before stepping into the container.

'Amrita?'

she followed the girls.

'Soon after we land this container will be unloaded and placed on a truck that will take you to a safe place. People will then deal with those who want you out of the way. Once that has been attended to, they will be contacting your families. Kaitlin, your father will soon learn of your arrival. Your extraction has cost him a lot of money, and you might find he's a bit different from when you last saw him. Try to be nice.'

Kaitlin scowled. 'I need stuff.'

'Soon.'

39

James signalled to his team, and they assembled outside to begin their journey to the airport. They were lightly armed, but their backup support was prepared for a small war.

The three black vans drove in convoy and turned into the gate to the freight terminal where they were parked while the troops disembarked and were then driven to a place out of sight from the road. Next, they took up their positions to wait for the arrival of the aircraft.

While they were waiting a small truck arrived and the driver approached James.

'Load to pick up?'

'Soon. They are on their approach.' He pointed to the blue aircraft readying to land.

A mobile scissor lift arrived next and stationed itself next to the truck. Everything was in place and now all they needed was to get the girls free and allow the aircraft's genuine cargo to be unloaded.

The time from landing to taxiing seemed to be getting longer by the second and James heard the sound of the cocking lever of a semi-automatic rifle. 'No shooting please. Let's see what we have to work with first.'

There was no reply.

***

The Boeing 737 at last lumbered into position and a few minutes later its engines began to wind down. A large hatch on the side of the aircraft swung open, and a scissor lift moved in to take the first container. It rolled off easily and was lowered to the height of the truck's tray. A few seconds later it slid onto the tray and the truck moved away.

James looked at Mickey, Micky looked at Angela.

'I thought it was a half size container…' James stopped speaking when a convoy of police vehicles with flashing lights, and sirens whooping, drew to a halt beside the plane.

The door to the first vehicle opened and DCI Birchmore stepped down from the cab. He was beaming from ear to ear. 'Arrest this lot. If anyone puts up a resistance, you have my permission to shoot them.'

Birchmore's group began rounding up the men that James had recruited. He called Jackie at base and said, 'We were rumbled. Birchmore is here with a fucking SWAT squad.'

'Is Mickey, okay?'

'Everyone is okay, so, far but…'

Birchmore stepped into his face, snatched the phone, and stamped on it. 'Unload this fucking plane then search all containers and arrest anyone you find in them.'

He hadn't noticed an airport security contingent heading at full speed in his direction.

Mickey smirked. 'This should be interesting.'

The leader of the group stepped out of his vehicle and yelled, 'Who's in charge here.'

Birchmore raised his hand.

'Identify yourself.'

Birchmore held out his police ID.

The leader of the security group laughed. 'This is federal property clear the area, or you will be placed under arrest.' He paused and raised his eyebrows when he saw a man wearing an AFP uniform. 'What's this? You. Come here.'

The man moved forward with a sullen expression on his face.

'Show me your ID.'

The man looked at Birchmore then back at the leader. 'Sorry sir, Left it at home.'

The leader stepped into the group and said, 'You, you, you, and you. IDs please.'

One by one they shook their heads, and the leader issued an order. His men raised their weapons.

James signalled to his group to fade away if they could.

Another scissor lift arrived to take another container.

The leader of the security group yelled, 'Halt. I am impounding this aircraft until further notice. No cargo is to be moved until I give the word.'

The standoff between Birchmore's team and the real AFP had become intense. James looked at Mickey and whispered, 'I think we have a problem.'

'The best laid plans, hey, boss?'

As they were murmuring to each other, they, along with the rescue group were gradually distancing themselves from the plane and the standoff.

'What happens now, boss,' Mickey said.

'Your guess is as good as mine. When they find those girls, all hell will break loose.'

Mickey was about to reply when a gunshot rang out and the AFP leader was spun around by the impact.

The genuine AFP mob moved to close in on Birchmore's crew and more shooting began. This time Birchmore fell, and his group immediately succumbed with their hands in the air. It was over.

James saw a man he didn't recognise. He was peering out from the illuminated hatch of the aircraft his arms raised in a WTF shrug. A woman appeared alongside him and yelled at the AFP Leader.

'Vat are you do-ink. Ve haff a cargo to unload.' She turned to the unknown man and yelled, 'Fronk, you must fix this.'

A mobile ladder arrived and rolled to the hatch. As soon as it made contact, several uniformed men boarded the plane.

By then James and his group had silently left the area. When he slumped into the driver's seat of his car, he put his head in his hands and said, to no one in particular. 'What a complete fuck up.'

The others boarded and their small convoy moved away from the airport.

***

Kelly was drumming her fingers nervously on her desk as she looked around at the general unruliness of the office. *Except for his desk, Clarkie's office is usually pristine,* she thought. *I must find out how to contact Mrs Whatsit, she seems to be in charge of cleaning everywhere, judging by the accounts. Pity it's always Clarkie who does the contacting.*

Her mobile phone squawked and scared the crap out of her, 'Fuck's sake, Clarkie, what's going on? The office is becoming a shit hole, hardly somewhere nice to bring your daughter when she gets here.'

He replied, 'Should have known better. The airport was a complete fuck up. the feds have arrested everyone, and the only good thing is that Birchmore copped it.'

'How do you know that?'

'I was there. They didn't even get the container off the plane before it was surrounded by AFP.'

'What happened to Birchmore?'

'He collected a random 45 from somewhere. That's all you need to know.'

'What about Kaitlin?'

'I don't know. Only one container was unloaded, and I never saw any passengers.'

'Oh, Clarkie, I'm so sorry.'

'Yeah, well it was probably a stupid idea, anyway.'

'So how do I contact Mrs Whatsit? She seems to have given up on the offices.'

'She asked for some time off, not long after Bib and Bub came on the scene. When I get a minute, I'll track her down and tell her to get back to work.'

***

Mickey sent a group text to Bib and Angela Carter.

> Sorry. Looks like we stuffed up big-
> time.

A second later a "Tears of laughter" emoji arrived from Bib with a brief text.

> Head to the safe house.

He showed it to James, 'What does that mean?'

'I think it means we need to regroup, but away from the city.' James put the car in drive and turned towards the east. 'The safe house is a Buddhist run rehab centre east of Perth. Given everyone and their dog will be out looking for us, it seems as good a place as any.' He flicked the car radio on just as an announcer was saying "Breaking News".

'In a shock announcement, just moments ago, the Australian Attorney General, Mr Robin Pettirosso has declared he will immediately step down from the coveted role and move overseas for a short break. He has quoted mental health problems, family pressures, and has apologised to the Prime Minister and Cabinet for the short notice. We are awaiting a response from the PM and will bring that to you as soon as we can.'

'Bit of a turn up, boss.'

'Interesting, I wonder who'll pick up that ball and run with it.'

Mickey had just participated in the worst operational screw up of his entire police career and the last thing concerning him was a politician jumping ship. 'This Buddhist thingo. Is that where they were going to take the girls?'

'Apparently, they have an amazing reputation for success in drug rehab and they're highly selective who they take.'

'By selective, do you mean "Monetised Clients".'

James didn't reply. 'Better call Angela and let her know we won't be needing her services. Then, can you text Stacey and tell her I'll probably be late again?'

Mickey tapped Angela's number and waited for a response.

There was none.

'He texted Stacey with Jim's message.' Her reply puzzled him.

Great job, guys, take your time.

He showed her response to James.

'Shit, I just can't win.'

****

Angela and her team could barely contain their dismay as their car passed through the gates of the rehab centre. Both sides of the meandering driveway were abutted by tall trees with wildflower clusters around the bases of their trunks, but the beauty and peacefulness of the place was lost to the intensity of their personal gloom.

Today was supposed to be the triumphant return of three innocent young girls, who for years had been ruthlessly exploited by a gang of money-grubbing scumbags. They would have spent the next few months winding back the evil and clearing their systems of the foul drugs they'd been forced to imbibe. Then they would be returned to their families to, maybe, recover their lost lives.

She'd never forget the text from Mickey and Bib's almost instantaneous reply. All that time and effort wasted in an incompetent stuff up. Angela turned the final corner of the drive and saw the pristine white temple-like building, fronted by an expanse of perfectly manicured lawn.

There were no human beings to be seen, but a pair of black gloved wallabies, munching on the short grass, looked up as if to welcome them.

If you have to go through the experience of rehab, this seems like an idyllic place, Angela thought, as she continued around the grassed area and parked in front of the temple.

As soon as her car came to a halt a tall, bone-thin, monk in a saffron robe glided to the car to greet her. He bowed pressed his palms together in front of his chest and said, 'Hello... Ms Angela Carter?'

Angela hoisted herself from the car and said, 'Yes.'

'Please follow me and please bring your friends.'

The monk led them through the entrance to a small garden area at the rear. He held the door for them and said, 'Please join us for tea.'

In the centre of the lawn was a round table set with crockery.

'Tea?' Angela said.

'They will be here soon please be allowing the serenity of our home to permeate your consciousness. The tea is to sip on while you wait,' The monk excused himself and glid back into the building.

'What the hell,' Gloria said. 'A complete screw up and they offer us a freakin cup of tea.'

Brian poured tea into each of their cups and selected what appeared to be a small cake from the accompanying plate. He bit into it and said, 'Hmm, not bad. Who will be here soon?'

Angela replied, 'Well, I guess it will be James and his team, if they were given the same instructions as us. I feel so bad that it went so horribly wrong, even to the extent of police officers being shot.'

The door to the temple building opened again and three small figures dressed in simple white shifts appeared. They followed the monk to the table and sullenly waited.

Angela's jaw dropped.

The monk said, 'This is Kaitlin Shipton, he turned to the two other girls. These are Agnetha and Bronwyn. They have been registered with us for the duration of their recoverance.'

'Recoverance?'

'It is an archaic English word that signifies the act of regaining something lost or the process of healing and restoration.'

Angela barely took in his explanation. A few moments earlier she believed that the entire operation had been a failure. 'Kaitlin? How are you feeling?'

The girl scowled. 'I need some stuff.' She side-eyed her friends. 'Them too.'

By then the monk had vanished back into the building and Angela offered the girls a seat at the table. 'You've had a long journey. You must be very tired.'

None of them spoke.

The door to the temple opened again, and several armed men wearing masks pushed through.

40

The sight of the group caused those around the table to freeze. Then one of the armed men pulled down his face covering and said, 'Ange?'

'Jim,' she squeaked. 'How…?'

'I have not the slightest idea. We were expecting the girls to arrive in a container which would be brought here. Birchmore's mob arrived early, then the real feds turned up, and it was on for one and all. I thought…' He looked across to the three girls. 'I thought we'd blown it.'

The tall monk arrived, bowed to the group and held out his hands. 'Now may you please relinquish your weapons of war.'

James signalled to the team and handed his own weapons to the monk, who placed them in a canvas bag.

'You make take them with you when you leave.' He bowed and said, 'Namaste.'

Once the clattering of the weapons ceased, Angela said, 'Does Clarkie know his daughter is safe?'

James shrugged.

'I texted him to say it was a stuff up boss, and that we would be here.'

All faces turned to the door of the temple which was, once

again, opened by the tall monk.

A scowling Clark Shipton barged through, trailed by Kelly Coulson who tottered on her high heels, across the grass.

'Hi Mick,' she said.

Shipton ignored everyone and strode directly to the girls sat at the table in the middle of the garden.

Kaitlin flinched with fear.

He suddenly stopped, reached for the pocket handkerchief in his suit and fell to his knees to begin bleating how sorry he was, and dabbing at the copious tears that had begun flooding from his eyes.

Kaitlin stood and approached him. 'Daddy?' she said, as she drew level and reached out with her right hand to swing it until it struck him with full force across his face. She then crumpled to her knees, and he helped her up and into a hug.

'I guess you reckon I deserved that and you're probably right. If I'd been a better dad, this might not have happened.' He turned to Agnetha and Bronwyn. 'These are your friends, the ones that you wouldn't leave behind?' He felt her head fall against his chest and the wetness of her tears soak into his shirt. He called them to him and pulled all three into a hug. 'They say you'll be going through some shit for a while, but I promise you I'll never let you down again.'

Kelly wiped her nose with a tissue, sidled close to Mickey and whispered, 'Fuck, Mick… is that *the* Clark Shipton we're lookin at?'

***

Bib read Mickey's text and grinned as he showed it to Bub. 'Oh, ye of little faith, eh.' He raised his hand to wave off the truck and texted Mickey to tell him that they should head to the safe house. He didn't say he'd be there, because by the time the truck arrived with its contents, he'd likely be sitting in the business class cabin of a jet and sipping Champagne, his first alcoholic drink since the beginning of the operation. 'We've done our bit, Bub, it's time to go.'

'Can I assume we'll be grabbing a bit of R&R in Singers before we head to Mumbai to get a signature on that proforma?'

'You might be right, my friend, let's pick up our things and get spruced up.' He reached into his bag and produced two lanyards, pulled one over his head and handed the other to Bub. 'These'll take us anywhere in the airport that we need to go.' He turned to Amrita and said, 'Are you sure about this?'

The smile that first won him, lit up her face. 'I have never been so certain of anything in my life, David.'

They escorted Amrita like a prisoner into the public area and once clear of the doors, Bib grabbed her by her hand to tug her to a row of shops. He handed her a credit card and said, 'You can't be travelling in what you're wearing. Don't worry it doesn't need a pin, so grab something nice and comfortable and we'll maybe do better in Singers. Bub and I must excuse ourselves briefly, we have to pick up our kit from storage and we'll be back in a short while.' He pointed to the screen with the flight schedules. 'Number five on the list. That's ours. We'll meet you in the club lounge.' He grinned. A text had just arrived from Mickey Krakauer.

> All safe and in the hands of the
> monks. How did you pull that off?

He texted back.

> Sorry, old chap, trade secret.

***

Mickey read the text before deleting all references to Recoverance Inc, *and that's the way it will stay, mate. Great knowing you.*

'Who was that, Mick,' Kelly asked.

'Spam text. Gettem all the time.'

'Me too.'

'This is very nice and all that, but I think we now have some serious work to do.' James leaned towards Angela and kissed her on the cheek. 'Over to you now, sis.' He was about to head for the temple exit when the tall monk appeared.

Angela waved goodbye to her brother and signalled to the monk. He approached, and she said, 'How can we work here, there is much to be done. Kaitlin is Australian and has papers to match. The others?'

'They have temporary papers, Ms Carter. We will be happy to work with you, to find out who they really are.'

She observed the motley bunch. A father attempting to reconnect with his long-lost daughter and her two proxy sisters like innocents, lost in a strange world. Mickey was standing close to Shipton's PA they were whispering in an almost intimate way. 'Mickey?'

He ended his discussion. 'Angela?'

She took the few steps closer and introduced herself to Kelly.

'You're the one who defended Tom Gregory, aren't you?'

'Screwed that one up big-time.'

Kelly smiled. 'We've all been there, sister.'

'Mr Shipton?'

'He's in shock. If it hadn't been for your fighting for Tom Gregory's freedom no one would have known what was going on.' She clasped Angela's hand gently and said, 'Thank you so much.'

'I heard Kaitlin's mother died. Such a shame.'

Kelly smiled, 'You never know, some good may eventually come of it.'

Weird comment, Angela thought as she followed the monk into the temple.

He showed her to a small room with a table and two chairs. 'This will be yours to use for the duration of their recoverance. The children will need a few days to settle, and all we ask is that you respect our privacy and serenity.'

'I haven't seen any other monks.'

'They are engaged in the process of recoverance, mmm, it is a long and sometimes tender procedure.' He waved to the bush that surrounded the temple. 'You will soon learn of our other occupants and where they live.'

'Thank you.'

The monk bowed and left.

Angela sat at the small table and as the silence overwhelmed her, she remembered Tom Gregory's text and wished she could go back twelve years to start all over again. Tears welled and as she dabbed them away, she shook herself, stood, and re-joined her team in the garden. Kelly Coulson seemed to be struggling to draw Clark Shipton away from his broken child who was the only thing he had left of Virginia, the one love of his life.

Kelly put her arm around his shoulders and said, 'You need to break away and leave them now, Clarkie. These people know exactly what they are doing and the sooner they can start the better.'

Shipton politely excused himself and clung to Kelly's arm as they walked to the temple. He looked around and spoke to Angela, 'You might have mucked up the Gregory trial but, thanks.'

Angela gathered her small team together, and said, 'The boss monk says we need to give them a few days before we start our work.'

'Anyone fancy a beer?' Brian said.

Gloria responded, 'You can have a beer laddie, I'll be downing a few G&Ts.'

'Make mine an SSB,' Angela said, knowing the work would soon be starting in earnest.

41

James stopped off at the police headquarters and asked to speak with the Police Commissioner. 'It's quite urgent.'

The receptionist smirked. 'You'll be lucky, sir. All hell's breaking loose.'

'Tell me about it.'

She smiled, 'I'll give him a call.'

James paced up and down while he waited for a response. It came a few minutes later.

'You may go up, sir.'

He pressed the call button at the lift and waited. A few moments later the door opened, and James stood back to allow the passengers to exit. He said nothing and pressed the button for the commissioner's floor.

The door to the anteroom adjacent the commissioner's office was open, but he knocked before entering.

'Ah yes he's expecting you, please take a seat and I'll let him know you're here.'

The commissioner's PA spoke quietly into a handset and before James' backside had touched the seat, Arthur Bertram's door opened.

'Good to see you, Jim. Come in and take a seat.'

James was expecting a solo meeting, and he was shocked to see several senior officers sitting around the meeting table.

Arthur Bertram pointed to a vacant chair and said, 'This is DCI Birchmore's replacement. DCI Carter will be in charge of the new division that will focus solely on human trafficking and cybercrime.' He noticed James flinch at the use of the wrong rank. 'Time is of the essence DCI Carter, and you have been doing the job with a flair when others were somewhat worse than lacklustre.'

'Thank you, sir. I wasn't…'

Bertram cut him short. 'Everyone around this table is behind you. Am I right gentlemen?'

They all nodded enthusiastically, and James sat as ordered.

'We've been through the list, ranked in order of involvement, by Sergeant Stephenson, and we have initiated a number of search warrants which are currently being executed.' Commissioner Bertram then said, 'There will be no holding back and anyone who has involved themselves in any way with this despicable gang will suffer the full weight of the law. Your job will be to make the charges stick.'

'Big job, sir.'

'We're confident you can do it, and you'll have the full support of my team.'

****

Clark Shipton was sitting at his desk, surrounded by the people who had unintentionally become his closest and most trusted friends. He turned to Angela and said, 'I understand your practice looks after those who are somewhat distressed, and you must realise that my daughter now has the full benefit of my wealth.'

'Our charter allows for us to charge as we think fit, Mr Shipton. Our philosophy is to do our best for our clients.'

Shipton smiled. 'I will expect to pay top dollar for your services, Ms Carter, so I will expect nothing less than your best.'

'What about Agnetha and Bronwyn?'

'Until we find their families they are my family too. It's been a long time, Ms Carter.'

'He means every word, Angela. I've never seen the old bugger so charged up,' Kelly said.

Shipton harrumphed. 'And it took a black fella to make the difference.'

Gloria and Brian's face froze at his vernacular.

'No need to look like that. When I first knew Mickey Krakauer was on the job. I thought here goes the usual crack. Send the bottom of the barrel to shut this waster up. Let me tell you, right now, I'd rather have Mickey and his people on my side than almost anyone else in this town.'

Angela said, 'We have another day up our sleeve before the rehab will allow us to interview the girls. The police must be involved because we need to close down the current operations of the trafficking cabal.'

'And my daughter was brought up to never snitch, right? I've contacted the rehab and that skinny monk, Siddhartha, said, that as Kaitlin's parent, I can spend some time with her before you begin. I will be encouraging her to tell all, even the bad stuff she knows about me. I was involved in the trafficking, more by accident than design, and as soon as I knew what was going on, I walked away. That's when she disappeared. You have the file I gave Mickey?'

'We have a complete copy, and Mickey has hidden the original. He was concerned it might fall into the wrong hands.' She held up her phone to show the text message she'd just received from her brother.

Birchmore dead. More to come.
Keep an eye on the news media
and watch your back.

Shipton grinned. 'Not mucking about then?'

***

Bib had arranged to be seated next to Amrita on the aircraft.

Bub knew he had much to learn about her and though his friend had already allowed his emotions to become tangled, he knew he would also fight to control any further slippage. He was in the seat across the aisle and felt happy that his colleague had at last found someone that he might one day share his life with. He was also confident that their adopted career might make that difficult. *Only time will tell,* he mused as he watched their heads bob in intense conversation. He sipped on the flute of champagne and breathed in a sigh as he thought of his daughter and her travails with her own recoverance. *As soon as this job is out of the way I'll talk to Bib. Maybe I'll stop for a short break and spend some time with her.*

Amrita barely had wet her lips on her champagne when she turned to Bib and said, 'You have been very kind to me, David, but I am most worried about Mr Vishu.'

'As far as I know he is still in Myanmar, somewhere.'

'He has no family in India. That is why I gave him a room in my house, and a job as my clerk. Poor Mr Vishu. In other countries, some might refer to him as an incel.'

'I think we should leave it there.'

Amrita replied, 'I understand. The other girl, the one back in Bosnia?'

'That might be a bit of a problem op. We knew where Kaitlin was, but the chances are that the remaining girls, if they haven't already been murdered, will have scattered to the four winds.'

'Murdered?' Amrita said.

'I'm sorry, it's the way it is. These creatures, I prefer not to dignify them with a human term and would rather call them scum, regard the girls as disposable assets. When they reach a certain age, they're taken for a drive. Their valuable organs are then harvested and packaged for sale to the highest bidder. Kaitlin and her friends were close to their disposal dates, and we got to them just in time.'

Amrita drew back a gulp of her champagne. 'The girls from India?'

'One is Australian, the other is an Indian national.'

'I have heard stories about the children of wealthy parents being taken for ransom purposes. Is it possible that…?'

'It was never mentioned that the Indian girl and the other were friends. The Consul had noticed the Indian girl in some random photos that I took in the Bosnian brothel. There was no sign of his colleague's daughter in those photographs, but that doesn't mean she wasn't there but occupied at the time.'

'And now they might be dead?'

'Or on the run from their captors. Problem is if they're on the run, they'll need their fixes, and that means…'

'Back to square one?'

'Or worse.' Bib reached out and placed his hand on Amrita's.

She grabbed it and held it to her cheek. 'David. We must find them. What can I do to help?'

Bub lost the thread of the conversation when he found himself chatting intently with a flight attendant whose adoring visage said he might be in the process of winning himself a night of transient comfort. Bib approached and excused himself to the attendant who headed for the galley.

'Sorry to be a party pooper, Bob. We need to have a chat about the new mission.'

Bob Clayton unclipped his seat belt and followed Ashton-O'Sullivan to his seat, then took up position with his back to the bulkhead and slid to the deck to face Bib and Amrita.

'We know the Indian girl was at the same brothel as Shipton's daughter and maybe even the Aussie kid, but there is a strong possibility they'll have done a runner. That will make it particularly dangerous for us as we might have to put ourselves about in the city.'

'And we won't have the benefit of surprise. Your old mate Kosanović will be on to us like a ferret, and he has a big axe to grind.'

'Exactly, so we'll need to think outside the box.' Bib's phone vibrated, and he reached for it. It was a voicemail, and he held the device to his ear for privacy and to minimise the background noise of the aircraft.

42

Siddhartha gathered the girls together in his spartan office. They sat at his order, and he spoke. 'My name is Siddhartha. It is my sacred duty to assist you to become yourselves again. This will not be easy and though the recoverance team of whom you are familiar, have provided you with some support medications, here you will learn meditation techniques that will give you additional strength to overcome your forced addiction.'

'Are you saying we won't get our stuff?' Kaitlin blurted.

'What we give you will serve you far better than any stuff, Ms Shipton.'

'Does my dad know we're gonna do this meditation thing?'

Siddhartha flinched as the door to his office flew open and three armed men appeared.

Two took up position guarding the door while the other marched in and sat on the corner of Siddhartha's basic wooden desk. He pulled back the cocking lever on his rifle and said, 'We'll take care of these little beauties now, Mr Monk.'

Siddhartha said nothing. He raised his hand to gesture that the girls should leave.

The man on the desk smirked. 'See that wasn't too hard was it. Come on, girlies, we'll get you some nice stuff.'

The girls stood and prepared to follow the man out when his colleagues reached in to grab them.

Bad move. In a whirl of flashing saffron, Siddhartha easily exploited a flailing nunchaku to remove the consciousness from the outside men and finished off man number one with a similar flourish. He then ordered the girls to sit and rang a small bell.

Several monks arrived to confiscate the arms and drag away the attackers.

As they were finishing, he said, 'In future, please respect our serenity.' He closed his door. 'I am here to protect you and to help in your recoverance. Those men were here to take you to hell and prevent you from speaking about your experiences.'

Kaitlin began scratching at her arms and whining, 'I need stuff. You know that.'

'And your friends?' Siddhartha asked. 'What about them?'

Kaitlin stared at the two girls she'd travelled with almost as if they were strangers. 'They are not my friends.'

Agnetha and Bronwyn shrank back on their chairs.

Agnetha said, 'Then why did you make those men bring us here?'

Kaitlin wiped her nose with the back of her hand. 'My Dad's paying, and I need my stuff.'

'I want you to help me, Mr Siddhartha,' Agnetha said. 'If she wants to make a fuss, let her. I don't care.'

Siddhartha rang his bell again, this time three times, and a girl about two years older than Kaitlin opened the door.

'Kaitlin says she needs her "Stuff", Marianne. Please explain to her what we do here.'

Marianne took Kaitlin by the hand and said, 'Like this.' She showed her how to sit cross-legged on the floor, then took her hand and drew her down. She then gestured to the others to do the same, closed her eyes and began to hum softly.

Siddhartha saw that the other two were copying Marianne, but Kaitlin was still resistant. He caught her eye smiled and said, 'At least give it a try.'

She closed her eyes and before long all four seemed to be locked in a trance.

Siddhartha let the humming proceed for a short while and then touched Marianne on the shoulder.

She opened her eyes, let the three girls continue for a few minutes longer, then one by one, she touched them as Siddhartha had.

They opened their eyes and looked around as though in a daze.

'Show Agnetha and Bronwyn to their accommodation Marianne. I will spend a little more time with Kaitlin.' When they left, he spoke softly, 'You did well my little one. Marianne is only a good teacher because she has been through what you have experienced. I frown on using drugs to reduce the addiction of drugs, but I am permitted to supply medication in the initial stages of your recoverance.'

'I will try Mr Siddhartha, I really will, but...'

'I know. It will be hard, and I might seem unforgiving, but it is only because I want you to escape from the hell you have had the misfortune to have lived in.' He raised his sparse eyebrows.

Kaitlin stood. The door opened and Marianne arrived. 'Come,' she said taking Kaitlin's hand and leading her away.

Siddhartha reached into the drawer in his desk took out a mobile phone and tapped in a number. The phone went to a message bank and Siddhartha left a few words.

Geoff Castle, Major. Had a visit
but rendered them safe. This

time we were lucky. Thanks.

***

It was time to take the fight to the enemy and James Carter knew who that was. He texted Mickey, Angela, Mandy and others who he could trust.

> I want you in my office in one
> hour. Birchmore is gone, but he's
> only the tip of the iceberg and
> we'll need to move swiftly if we
> are to close this mob down.

Mickey was the first to respond.

> On my way, boss.

Mandy Stephenson arrived with her laptop at the ready and a sheaf of printed reports. 'I've knocked out the list you asked for. There are some big noises on it, who will put up a big fight once they know we're after them.'

'Yeah, we let them go in the first cull. We hoped they'd received a shock and awe warning, but their connections are still leading them to believe they're immune.'

'It's gonna come as a big shock then,' Mandy said.

Soon after Mandy arrived, there was a commotion outside James' office. It died down when he opened the door and welcomed the Police Commissioner.

Mandy almost curtseyed but restrained her urge.

'Sergeant Stephenson, I hear you have done much to help us get to where we are.'

She blushed, 'Just doing my job, sir.'

'I understand a few of our soldiers are still here because you did your job, too.' Arthur Bertram pointed to the Medal for Gallantry ribbon on her uniform shirt, held out his hand and grinned. 'I'm so glad you are on our side.'

Mickey Krakauer arrived just in time to water down Mandy's embarrassment.

'And the famous Sergeant Krakauer, I'm in very salubrious company today. Good to see you sergeant.'

'Sir,' Mickey responded without a hint of emotion.

'You might all be wondering why *I'm* here.'

A subtle group shrug followed.

'DCI Carter has been appointed to lead a team whose job will be to close down the trafficking cartel and root out those who would still like to profit from modern day slavery. Jim?'

Carter fanned out the papers that Mandy had printed. 'These are where we will begin. I must emphasise the importance of evidence gathering procedure. The people we are after are well resourced and will not hesitate to use their high-powered legal teams to rip us to shreds if we make a mistake.' He was disturbed by the door opening and the entry of his sister. 'Glad you could make it.'

'Glad to be here.' She nodded towards the commissioner with a tight smile on her lips.

'My sister, Angela, will be working with us to ensure we are right up to speed legally, before we commit to actioning any evidence that we uncover.'

Arthur Bertram entered the conversation and said, 'So there are no misunderstandings, Ms Carter and I have been in a relationship for some time. She understands that this will in no way influence any overarching decisions I may be required to make.' He breathed out with relief. 'Well, at least that's got that out of the way.'

James's relief at Arty's own outing showed on his face. 'You all know Clark Shipton and his PA Kelly Coulson. They have both given me a declaration that they will be crown witnesses if required.'

Mickey held up the file Clark Shipton had given him. 'This is crammed full of information and evidence that might not be acceptable to a court, but it might give you all a better understanding of what has been going on.' He handed a copy to each in attendance. 'As the DCI said. We must be one-hundred percent sure of ourselves before we take any action. If in doubt do nowt until you've discussed it with either me or the DCI.'

'I think we've covered everything,' The Police Commissioner said. 'Over to you DCI Carter.' He turned and walked from the office to a tangible silence outside. 'Don't mind me officers, please continue,' he murmured. No one noticed the grin on his face as he headed to the lift that would take him to his own office.

43

Bib killed the voicemail and focussed on Bub. 'That was Siddhartha. It seems we still have a mole in our system. Three armed men arrived to take the girls from the rehab. Siddhartha dealt with them, but they were supposedly taken there in secret.'

'Still compromised then. It's been happening right from the start,' Bub said.

'I'll tip off Mickey Krakauer. That fellow has a networking team like you'd never believe.' Bib jotted a text and pressed send. 'Now we wait.' He rested back in his seat and took a sip of his champagne. 'I still have a few useful connections in Bosnia, so I'll call on them for assistance if necessary.'

'What if they won't help?'

Bib laughed, 'Routine procedure, my friend. They are only connected because I have them by the balls.' He took another sip of his champagne.

Amrita joined the conversation. 'You'll have the same problems you had with the previous girls. They'll have fake papers.'

'Maybe we'll get lucky.'

Bub said, 'Am I to assume we'll be looking for both girls?'

'I'll be happy with one but if we can find both, we'll be on a roll, a bank roll. As soon as we get to Mumbai, you can contact the Indian public servant, and I'll deal with the Aussie consul. We'll need photos and birthmarks and any other positive ID information. If there are any available papers, those too. The chances these traffickers got their passports when they captured them are remote. The problem we had with the last batch was that they didn't have documents. Agnetha and Bronwyn still haven't connected with their parents.'

'Will the rehab be able to help?' Amrita said.

'Sid's pretty switched on but there is not much more we can do. We were saddled with those two and we needed to make a spot decision. Bring all three or none.'

'You will still have the problem of the Indian family rejecting their daughter because she is sullied,' Amrita said.

'They have told the Consul, they want us to find her, and that's good enough for me.' He paused before speaking again. 'We have very little to go on this time. With Kaitlin we had everything in place. Our only problem was the Aussie mole who must have tipped off the locals.'

Bub smirked, 'I hope your mate Kosanović's headache has gone.'

'Don't worry, unless he gets a message from someone, we probably won't see him again.'

***

'Mrs Whatsit, Clarkie. If she can't get in here, we'll need someone pro-tem. I can't work like this.'

Shipton handed her a slip of paper. 'I found this when I was going through my desk. She's always been paid in folding money so there are no tax records or super or anything official.'

Kelly rolled her eyes. 'Like me, you mean.'

'You know I'll look after you, Kel.'

'I'd be nicer to know I was being officially looked after, if you know what I mean.' She stared at the name on the paper. 'Karla Kosanovich. Where's that name from?'

'Wouldn't have a clue, Virginia said she was from Croatia but she had barely any accent so she must have been here since she was a kid. She does my cleaning. Who cares?'

'I care, Clarkie. It's just that Mickey thinks there is a mole, and that's why we're having strange things happen. Bib and Bub were very strong on confidentiality and if she was able to get hold of their information and send it to the wrong people, we might have compromised the very people we were relying on to get your daughter back on her feet.'

Shipton's face coloured. 'Shit,' he spluttered.

'Exactly. How long has she been incommunicado?'

Shipton blushed again. 'As soon as I knew Kaitlin was at the rehab, she asked for time off.'

'Have you heard from her since?'

He shook his head.

'Soon after that, three goons turned up to threaten the monks. They want to silence any future comments from the girls. How much has she given out about you, slash, our little operation here?' Kelly tapped Mickey's number on her phone.

'Hey, Kell, how's things?'

'Clarkie's cleaner. I reckon she's been talking out of turn.'

'Shit. I just had a message from Bib. Someone has been feeding information to the wrong people. Do you have a name?'

'Karla Kosanovich.'

'I'll text Bib, he might know something. It might take a while though; they're in the air at the moment.'

'Is there any way you can track her down? If she's blabbing to all and sundry…'

'Leave it with me.' He pressed end and tapped James Carter's number. When James answered, he said, 'We need to track down someone called Karla Kosanovich. She's Clark Shipton's cleaner. Bib and Bub reckon their operation has been compromised and Kelly Coulson asked me if we could find her.'

'I'll get someone on to it. If Shipton can get hold of her tax records, that might help.'

'I'll ask.' Mickie sent a text to Bib, at least he'd have a heads up even if there was nothing in it.

***

'Ha!' Bib said. 'There you have it, the mole is Shipton's cleaner, Karla Kosanovich. She has to be, anything else would be too much of a coincidence.' He showed the text to Bub.

'Think we'll be rubbing shoulders with her namesake again soon?'

'I hope not, Bub. If we do, it'd better be terminal.'

'This Kosanović person, is he likely to find his way to Mumbai?' Amrita said.

'Kosanović is a man of numerous talents, Amrita. I have run up against him many times in various countries. He's what you might call my opposite number in the SOA OBA otherwise known as the Security and Intelligence Agency of Bosnia and Herzegovina.'

'So, what you are saying is that he may well turn up and get mixed up with our plans?'

'If he does, it will be because of top end involvement with trafficking. Probably the same reason there were Australian officials receiving unofficial entertainment at the Bosnian brothel. No one at that level chooses exposure and they will use everything in their power to prevent it happening.'

'The three men at the Rehab?' Amrita said.

'That, and our task will be complicated by the fact that we will need to seek out the missing girl under the alerted eyes of the SOA OBA.' Bib turned to Bub. 'You once told me you liked a bit of "biffo", I think that's what you called it.'

'I'd prefer to get in and out without.'

'Me too, and that will be our plan. I think it's time to turn the tables on Uncle Draggy. So, as soon as we hit the ground in Mumbai, I'll contact Mickey Krakauer. Let's see if we can't generate some fake news for the consumption of Dragomir Kosanović.'

The dinner service began, and Bub resumed his own seat, while the flight attendants pushed their trollies up and down the aisles. The young woman who'd spent an inordinate amount of time with him earlier, stopped and offered him a glass of wine. 'Thanks,' he said and focussed his eyes on her name tag. 'Thanks, Fiona.'

Fiona fluttered her eyelids, smiled back at him and continued her service.

Perhaps there's hope, he thought, and chowed down on his meal. He checked his watch, *only 8 hours to go.* He craned his neck to look across at Bib and Amrita and struggled to suppress a smile. They were holding hands and deep in a cheery conversation with neither paying much attention to their meals. *Let's hope the next mission is as successful as the last.*

Bub finished his food and jotted some notes in the log he always kept of their missions. This would be their fourth, and the last one could easily have ended in disaster had it not been for Bib's coolness and his global connections. He knew the next part of their trip would be fraught with the kind of danger he thrived on but, with a mole in the works, the risks had increased exponentially.

Since The Croatian War of Independence, the entire area had become a hotbed of spying and intrigue, and no one could be trusted to be who they were or said they were. Yet Recoverance Inc was about to leap into the deep end.

He resumed his glance at his friend and partner. He'd never seen him so happily involved with anyone before. Usually composed and efficient, David Ashton O'Sullivan was exhibiting all the hallmarks of a man in love. A major distraction of this nature would be the last thing they needed at this part of the mission.

A few hours after they left Mumbai they would be on the streets of Bosnia, hopefully with eyes wide open for a glimpse of at least one of the missing girls. To catch this glimpse, they would need to insert themselves deep into the addict community. Bub recalled the time he was searching for his daughter and how she was caught up in a mess of distrust with the added trauma of withdrawal. When she couldn't get even the dodgiest of hits, she would have easily killed for anything that served the purpose.

Ultimately, he was forced to go along with her addiction and mortgaged his home in order to effectively become her dealer. When he was finally able to win enough of her trust, he dragged her kicking and screaming, away from the crowd she had surrounded herself with.

Beatrice hated him for it, claiming the drugs were doing her no harm and that he had no right to isolate her, but she couldn't stop him from having her sectioned and delivered to a secure rehab centre.

Apparently, from the reports he'd received, she was progressing positively and had begun to respond favourably to the detox treatments, then she was caught in a drug scam and ended up in jail.

At least his background was now useful, and he could tell himself that he was helping other families, if not his own. He glanced at his friend again. They were dozing and Amrita's head was resting on Bib's shoulder. He was about to sit back and do a bit of dozing himself, when the friendly flight attendant dropped to a squat alongside.

'I thought there was something about you that rang a bell, Mr Clayton. Do you remember me?' she asked.

He dredged into the deepest recesses of his mind, but nothing came to light. He shook his head and said, 'Sorry.'

'I used to be Fiona Hartley until...' she pointed at her name badge. 'You're Beattie Clayton's dad; you'd have to be.'

'You know my daughter?'

'We went to school together and we were best friends, then she one day she just disappeared. Is she okay?'

Beatrice's school days occurred during his longest overseas assignments and, as such, were areas of great vagueness to him. 'You have me at a disadvantage; I was away a lot back then.'

'I know, Beattie was always going on about her soldier hero dad. She was so proud of you.'

Bub didn't want to tell his daughter's best friend that she hated him and was in jail for drug dealing.

Fiona must have noticed his seeming reticence to talk and said, 'Sorry, I shouldn't have said anything. It's none of my business but when you see her again, please tell her I asked after her.' She touched the corner of her eye with a finger and sniffed. 'Sorry.'

Bub followed her with his eyes as she sashayed down the aisle and felt a huge surge of guilt when he realised, he'd almost contemplated crawling into bed with a woman who was his daughter's age, and worse, her friend, and he'd been unwittingly introduced to a part of Beatrice's life that he never knew. He pressed the call button.

Another flight attendant arrived at his seat, 'Mr Clayton?'

'Is Fiona available.'

'I'll ask her.'

A few moments later Fiona arrived and spoke softly.

'I'm sorry, I might have seemed a little abrupt. Beattie's not been well, and…'

Fiona squatted. 'Drugs?'

'How do you know?'

'She got in with a bad crowd and I could see it going belly up. I'm so sorry, Mr Clayton. If there is anything I can do, please don't hesitate to contact me.' She wrote her name on a blank business card and handed it to him. 'I'd love to chat more if I get a free moment.'

'Me too.'

'I'll speak to the cabin manager.' She stood and left him to his own devices.

44

The departure of the Police commissioner triggered an outpouring quickly brought under control by James Carter. 'Let's not get carried away. The next few days will be a hard slog and we can't afford for anyone to go off half cocked.' He gave them each their assignments and asked Angela to stay back after they all left.

'I hear congrats are in order, *DCI* Carter.'

'They called it dead men's shoes when I was growing up.'

'Well, whatever, you deserve it big brother.'

'I'm going to be relying on you as a trusted source of advice. There are too many of your profession featuring in those lists, and once they become aware of the depth of our investigation, the whole town will probably clam up.'

'Fortunately, our little outfit is as far removed from mainstream as you can get.'

'Mickey reckons there is a mole lurking in the system. He seems to think it is Shipton's clearing lady which means she has a direct connection with the main operators. Bib and Bub are aware, but they seem capable of taking things in their stride.'

'They come from a background that makes thinking outside of the box a life saver. Perhaps we need to develop similar skills. I'll keep you posted with anything I hear and let me know if you need advice before you go jumping any guns.' Angela picked up her things and headed down to her car. Given the recent events, she double checked everything before she started her engine. She had no sooner closed the front door to her offices than heads popped out into the tiny corridor. She raised her hand in a wave towards the meeting room.

The mixed bag of AC and Associates followed her and took their seats.

'Well, as you know, I've been asked by the local constabulary to provide confidential advice. By confidential I mean that nothing said within these walls must be repeated outside, to anyone.'

Gloria raised her hand. 'What if we receive information from our clients that possibly links them with the people the police are watching?' she looked down at her notes. 'What about the three girls we are now being asked to help?'

'They are in the custody of an independent and secure rehab unit and will be of no interest to us until they are able to communicate. Two of the girls have lost almost all memory of their origins and we will be looking to get them visas as a temporary measure. They arrived with temporary papers, issued by the Australian Consulate in Mumbai, which will expire in twelve months, so they should be okay for a while and as they will be out of sight and out of mind, I expect nothing much to happen.'

Angela looked at the faces around the room.

'For once we have an upper hand. We are a small and independent team that can work flexibly without the complexity of the behemoths you all know of. We don't have the huge, vested interests that could stymy a police investigation and that's the way it must stay.'

Brian Carpenter raised his hand. 'The place in the hills is not a registered rehab centre, and I hear they employ unorthodox methods to achieve their goals.'

'Sounds just the right place for kids, who have been used as sex slaves, to recover out of the public eye. Already someone has been talking out of turn and some strangers began ferreting around. Fortunately, the head honcho keeps a tight ship, and I doubt there'll be much slippage from that part of the world.'

She paused while they took in her words. Then she said, 'Any information you receive from our clients, that you believe might be helpful should be passed directly to me. The last thing you need is someone heavy breathing down your neck. Does everyone understand?'

They all nodded.

***

Mickey Krakauer headed directly to Clarke Shipton's office, his intention being to confront Clarkie, about his cleaner's activities and to work out how they might use Karla Kosanovich to their advantage.

Kelly beamed when he pushed open the back door. 'Clarkie's in, if you want to speak to him.'

He waved for her to follow. 'Both of you, Kell, things are hotting up.'

'I'd better put the kettle on, then.' Kelly smiled. And a few seconds later joined her friend who was sat opposite her boss/lover.

'Now that Kelly's here, I'll cut to the chase, Clarkie. Jim Carter, who you know, has been promoted into the vacant place DCI Birchmore once owned. Jim has been tasked to close down the traffickers once and for all. This time there will be no privileged few.'

Shipton shot a glance at Kelly.

'Yep, I know you were in it at the start but as I understand it you are now Crown witnesses.'

'So where to from here?'

'Firstly, there is the problem of Mrs Kosanovich. It seems she's been passing information to the wrong people.' He grinned. 'What we need to do is turn the tables and start passing adjusted info. This is where you come in.'

Shipton looked up at the ceiling. 'Me?'

'Track her down and get her back to work as if nothing has happened. Then you can leave the rest to me.' He turned to Kelly, 'I'm sure between us we can come up with some interesting alternative facts.'

Kelly puffed out her chest. 'I can't wait.' She focussed her attention on Shipton and said, 'Would you like me to write her a grovelling letter saying how much you have missed her and ask her to come back soon?' While he processed her comment, she left and returned with a tray of tea and biscuits. 'Sorry, Mick, there are no chocolate bickies, if I put them out, he scoffs the lot in one hit. Anyone would think he owns the place.'

***

James Carter asked Mandy Stephenson to stay when the other's left. He pointed to her laptop.

She opened it and set it on the desk so they could both have a good view of the screen, 'Think there's a chance we can fix these bastards once and for all, boss?'

'I wish I knew. The problem we have is that some of the names on the list are almost untouchable. Even trying to get them into court would cost the state's budget in legal fees.'

'Maybe we need Mickey's connections. He knows most of the Press by their first names.'

'But then we'd be up against their masters, who'd be shitting themselves with the risk of the civil backlash.'

'If you remember it was Mickey who turned the tables the first time around. I'll speak to him quietly. Let's see what sweet music his

Didgeridoo can make when he works it.' She scrolled down the list of suspects. They were still coded with degrees of involvement and two names stood out. Both were positioned at the highest level in the state's hierarchy, without being in government, but with as much control of state affairs as the Premier.

'We'll need to be very careful with those two and there are a few more like them.'

Mandy said, 'Unless we can get them to trip themselves up, publicly, over a fact or two.'

'That would require a degree of almost espionage-like investigatory work that we aren't budgeted for,' James said

'Ever heard of bots?'

DCI James Carter raised his eyebrows.

'There will be a communication somewhere. These folk are always contriving the ability to hold someone else responsible for their, shall we call them, peccadillos.'

'Are you proposing we "bug" their computers?' James waggled his fingers in the air as he said the word bug.

'Who me?' Mandy pursed her lips.

'Anything we find would be thrown out of court if it wasn't discovered under warrant.'

'All we need is reasonable suspicion, sir.' She pointed at the names on the list. 'They wouldn't be there if there was no connection with the trafficking even a spurious connection. You okay with me talking to Mickey about this?'

'I guess I have to be if we are to move on. Make sure you keep it to the highest level of discrete.'

45

It wasn't long before Fiona found her way back to Bub's seat. She lightly touched him on the shoulder, pointed to a pair of vacant seats at the rear of the cabin and said quietly, 'Boss chook say's it's okay, but I'll have to leave if we get busy.'

Bub followed her to the vacant seats and Fiona stepped back to allow him access. 'Thanks,' he said and slumped into the furthest seat.

Fiona sat next to him and immediately opened a small wallet that she'd removed from her pocket. 'This was us when we were kids.'

Bub stared down at the aging photograph of his laughing daughter, wearing a school uniform alongside a girl who appeared from her bearing to be a best friend.

'We had so much fun back then, Mr Clayton.' Fiona dabbed a tear from her eyes. 'She was a real live-wire and always had me in fits of laughter…' She turned towards him. 'If there is anything I can do to help, please, you mustn't hesitate to ask.'

'You know… I can barely remember that time. Back then there was so much going on that I can't even talk about.'

Fiona flipped out another photo. 'Remember this.'

The picture was of him and a group of giggling girls at what appeared to be a birthday party. Beatrice was sitting astride a bike looking extraordinarily smug. 'I bought her that bike.'

'And she was so proud of you.'

'So you said… Didn't help, did it?'

'Where is she, now?'

'Jail.'

'I thought you said she was in rehab.'

'That's what I tell anyone who knows her. She's due out soon and…'

'You want to be there for her.'

'It isn't that simple.'

'What's more important, jetting around the world in business class or your daughter?'

Bub stood. 'Thanks for your interest. I'll pass it on. I'm sure she'd love to see you again one day.' He wrote her name and the prison location on the card Fiona had given him and handed it back to her before squeezing past her to take his place in his prescribed seat. The memories Fiona had stirred were almost unbearable, and although he knew when Beatrice was freed from her sentence the chances of him being there for her were at the best slim. *You are so right, Bib, this business makes no allowances for relationships.*

***

Mickey Krakauer seemed surprised when Mandy Stephenson appeared on his doorstep in the middle of the evening. 'Come in,' he said and led her to his small kitchen. 'Can I get you anything?'

She shook her head. 'Is Jackie around?'

'She's having a long soak in a hot bath.'

'So, we won't be disturbed for a while?'

'Okay, Mandy. Spit it out.'

'We might need some of your particular skills. I have been, sort of, given permission to do a bit of rooting around in a few computer systems. I'm hoping I'll turn up some interesting evidence that might ultimately lead to high-level search warrants.' She opened her laptop and showed him the names.

'Shit… Hope your life insurance is up to date.'

Mandy grinned. 'I understand you have a certain way with members of the press.'

'Yeah, but at that level most of the people I know would run a mile.'

'That's more or less what DCI Carter said.'

Mickey said, 'Jimmy Carter, I should have guessed.'

'He believes in you, Mick.'

'Yeah, but do I believe in my own ability?'

The door opened and Jackie walked in draped in a bathrobe. 'I thought I heard voices.'

'You know Sergeant Stephenson, Jack?'

Jackie nodded. 'Things are hotting up then?'

'We hope so, but in a nice kind of way,' Mandy said. 'He was just saying he wasn't sure he believed in his own capabilities.'

'That from someone who was dumped alone in the outback as a child of ten years old and found his way home in one piece…' Jackie reached out and wrapped her arm around her man. 'You can do anything big fella.'

'That's what we're hoping.' Mandy patted Jackie on the arm. 'And with you behind him he'll be invincible.'

When the door closed behind Mandy, Jackie turned to Mickey. 'What are they expecting of you?'

'Work the press when they find something. I think the idea is to cause a couple of big noises to out themselves.' He mentioned two of the names.

Jackie's jaw dropped. 'There'll be repercussions.'

'Tell me about it.'

'Think you can pull it off?'

'It wasn't just whitefella kids who were trafficked, Jack, but Bib and Bub have only found three white girls, and one is a crim's daughter, Kaitlin Shipton. If Mandy can turn up some evidence that matches disappearances on country, I think I'll find a few people who'll be happy to risk their necks. First thing in the morning I'll start reviewing the cases of missing kids who would otherwise not receive attention. After I do a bit of police work in relation to a certain Mrs Kosanovich.'

***

Siddhartha squinted through the small unidirectional viewing pane in the door of the room being used to help the three girls in their early steps towards recoverance. He couldn't help but smile when he saw that all three were in a relaxed state of meditation. They had been through a major trauma in their young lives and had earlier been administered Suboxone to minimise the symptoms of their withdrawal. He was about to leave when Kaitlin opened her eyes and focussed a wide-eyed stare in his direction. He stopped and she continued to stare even though she couldn't see him.

He murmured, 'What is it my child?'

'I have remembered something.' She mouthed, her eyes flickered shut and she was back in her trance.

Siddhartha knew better than to fracture the moment. He closed the viewing pane silently and returned to his cell like office. Once there, he found his phone and texted Bib:

Good things are happening my friend

The legal aspects of the girl's incarceration were of little concern to him, but she was a minor and he knew he had a duty to keep her father in the loop. He would do nothing about that until she was in a normal state of consciousness and, by then, the others might also be finding lost memories that would quantify Kaitlin's.

He was still concerned about the earlier attack on the premises and though the men had been arrested by the police, there was nothing reported in any of the media. It was as though they had simply disappeared into the system.

Despite his chosen separation from the world, Siddhartha was aware of the trafficking that had led the girls to his establishment. He knew the police were investigating and he was naturally resistant to broadcasting any hint of success. He didn't need size fourteen boots clomping around and, most of all, he didn't need them demanding answers to the questions he didn't have, particularly if it became known that memories were stirring.

He was also aware that someone had been talking out of turn, and he knew that might mean further intrusions by the people who made their living from the suffering of innocents. He had begun writing notes and building a timeline of events, that the girls would need to pass through before he would consider them to be ready for the world, when he saw a shadowy movement outside his window.

Siddhartha stood and faced the door to his office.

Someone knocked.

He opened the door to see the police officer known as Krakauer. 'Yes,' he said.

'Mickey Krakauer, reverend, I'm not sure what title I should use for you, but I hope that shows I come in peace.'

Siddhartha offered Mickey a chair. 'How can I be of help to

you?'

'There's someone leaking information about the girls and how they arrived here.'

'I am aware of that, but how can you be of help. Your other officers are aware of the event that occurred recently, and to my knowledge nothing has been done.'

'That is the problem we all have. This trafficking business is controlled at a level way above regular blokes on the street.' He showed the press release that featured the resignation of the AG. 'You can read whatever you like into that, but I'm reading cold feet.'

'What can I do, my role is to help people to recover from their addictions and move back into a normal life.'

'I might need your assistance. We need to find out who is leaking the information that keeps setting us on the back foot.'

'How can I help with that?'

Mickey handed the monk a card with his mobile number written on it. 'We are attempting to track down a woman by the name of Karla Kosanovich. We believe she is the one who has been tipping off the traffickers.'

Siddhartha's face stiffened. He tapped a code into his phone and another monk arrived within a few minutes. 'Mr Krakauer, please tell him what you have just enlightened me with.'

Mickey repeated his statement about Karla.

The new monk shook his head in what seemed to be disbelief, 'Madam Kosanovich has worked here since the facility's inception, Mr Krakauer. She could not possibly be the person you are referring to.'

'Where is she now?'

He shook his head again. 'We understand she is taking a short holiday.' He looked up at Siddhartha, who seemed unflappable.

'Can we find her for, Sergeant Krakauer?'

The new monk hesitated.

Mickey said, 'The people she is leaking to, are no better than modern day slave traders, so your help will be appreciated.'

The monk turned towards Siddhartha, held his hand out for a pen and wrote down an address. 'I think she still lives there.' He bowed. 'And that is all I can tell you.'

Mickey thanked both monks and turned to leave.

'Please, Sergeant Krakauer,' Siddhartha said. 'We seek only peace and tranquillity.'

I'll do my best, reverends, but there're no guarantees, he thought, as he headed for his car.

46

The resignation of Adrian Courtney, Australia's Attorney General, had caused a stir in the corridors of power. One of the country's most senior politicians, the press was having what they liked to call a field day. No one in government seemed prepared to discuss the reasons for his departure, short of his stated health and family concerns.

None of that rang true. Politically, he'd been flying on a high of polling results and had been considered by many the next in line for PM.

Angela Carter began a search of his background. There were questions that needed answering and he would have been at the apex of any high-level trafficking enquiry, now he was, gone, just when they were about to see a possible result. She called her brother who was as perplexed as she.

'When the big fish leap out of the river and onto the bank, Ange, it says a lot for the condition of the water.'

'Very profound, Bro.'

'Yeah, but true, Ange. Mickey managed to get an address for Mrs Kosanovich. She's been working as a cleaner in the rehab place since it was established.'

'You are joking.'

'Nope. Her job with Clark Shipton was probably moonlighting.'

'When Mickey told Bib, Bib said he'd had a run in with a man called Dragomir Kosanović in Bosnia. Bib knows him well, apparently. They've had altercations in the past, and given they were heading back there to rescue another girl…'

'The last thing Bib wants is someone tipping him off to things she might have heard here.'

'Got it in one. All the missing girls' lives are now at risk.'

'Where's Mickey now?'

'Heading to the address given by the boss monk at the Rehab centre.'

'If he manages to find her, what then?'

'Well, to my knowledge she's not broken any laws.'

'So how will he stop her from carrying on?'

'I guess we'll need to leave that up to Mickey.'

'While I've got your ear, I've had my people doing the rounds of international missing persons within the age range of Agnetha and Bronwyn. We're thinking Bronwyn—not her real name— might be an Aussie, but it looks like Agnetha, which is her real name, is an English national of mixed parentage. A thirteen-year-old girl, fitting her description, disappeared while on holiday in Stockholm where she was visiting her Swedish father. I have Brian looking into that further. Don't hold your breath, it might be a red herring. Nothing else on Bronwyn yet, but he's working on it.'

'Worth setting up a meet with the boss cocky of the Rehab?'

'Siddhartha says they are at a critical time, and he would rather we let them have some peace. He has promised to contact me when he believes they are ready.'

***

They were lining up at the immigration gate at Chhatrapati Shivaji Maharaj International Airport when Mickey's text reached Bib's phone. 'It's from Mickey Krakauer.' He read the text. 'They know who the mole is. He reckons it's a woman by the name of Karla Kosanovich. Where have I heard that name before?'

'Great.' Bub said. 'So, we'll be on the back foot before we even get to Bosnia.'

'Maybe not, he says she went off grid when she knew the girls had arrived safely.'

'So where to from here?'

'Carry on as usual. If Uncle Draggy rears his ugly head, we'll deal with it at the time.'

Immigration passed without a hitch, and they boarded a pre-booked limousine for their hotel. When they arrived, they were greeted like heads of state which wasn't Bub's preference. He would have preferred to slink off to his room without fanfare. Unfortunately, the civil servant, whose daughter they were there to rescue, had a different idea.

The beaming man introduced himself to Bib, 'Sachin Shukla, at your most humble service, Major. Thank you for considering our daughter's worthiness of the significant risk you have agreed to submit to on our behalf.'

'Mr Shukla, with the greatest respect, we'd prefer to work with minimal fuss...' He gestured to the bouquets and the fawning hotel employees.

'Ah, yes. I do understand Mr Bib, I think.' He spoke in rapid fire Tamil, glanced at Amrita, then turned back to Bib and said, 'You are invited to my home, where you will meet the rest of my family and, I hope, enjoy a meal with us.'

Bib looked to his colleagues for their approval and said, 'It's been a long flight may we have some time to recuperate?'

Shukla wobbled his head effusively and said, 'I will send a car around, in two hours.'

Bub said nothing. He wasn't someone who enjoyed the social life, but he knew it would be something to be endured and over relatively quickly. Then they could get on with the job they came to do.

For reasons of simple propriety Bib and Amrita had taken separate rooms. Bub knew there was something afoot, but he wasn't prepared to destroy his partner's chances of brief happiness. What did concern him was the diversion she might present. Bib was a cool and effective operator when that trait was required. Mix it with a love interest and the distraction might become a serious weakness. From now on, he knew to tread carefully.

The three exited the lift and headed to their separate rooms for a short break and a refreshing shower before heading out to join Mr Shukla's family.

They always travelled light when on a quest and there would be no formality of dress. Simple shirt and pants for the males and a lightweight summer dress or a sari, for Amrita.

Bub revelled in the pressurised water of his shower, and when finished, he lay on the bed for a while. He almost dozed off when his regular phone buzzed. It was a text from his daughter, and he sat up in a hurry.

> I'm now out of that stinking joint. I waited for
> you but as usual you weren't there. I'm taking
> my life back. Don't bother to call.
> B

Beatrice had never communicated in this way, and he was unsure of how to deal with her perfunctory comment. There was little he could do, from where he was, but to call the number he had for the Jail.

'Ms Clayton is no longer of our concern.'

'I thought you might have contact details for her.'

'Sorry. No.' The call ended, and Bub felt his world had ended with it. *She was supposed to be safer inside. There has to be more to it than this.* He felt reluctant to interrupt Bib. The last thing he wanted was to disturb the amorous moments that might surely be happening. Suddenly he began having doubts. *How long before she's back on H or worse.* He texted Bib.

> Beatrice has been released. I feel like a shag on
> a rock.
> Hope I haven't interrupted anything.

Bub's phone rang immediately.

'You okay, old chap?' Bib's voice sounded with a genuine angst.

'I thought she might be safer in there.'

'I have a few connections. I'll see what I can do. Oh, and you didn't interrupt anything, but I think it will be just you and me. Amrita's called off she says she has an appalling migraine.'

Bub heard Bib's room phone ring to interrupt their conversation.

'Looks like our car has arrived, old chap, so I suppose we'd better get on with it.' Bib said.

Bub ended the call, and as he slipped his wallet into his pocket, he sensed the almost invisible bulge of the garrotte through the fabric. *Let's hope I won't be needing you tonight.*

***

Mickey's trip to the address of Karla Kosanovic had proved to be a red herring and regardless, according to the WA police records she had no prior convictions, but that didn't mean there might something in another jurisdiction. Mickey held off from making a connection with his Eastern State's colleagues. After his experience with Birchmore the last thing he wanted was tip off others that he might be onto something. Instead, he found his way to Mandy Stephenson's section and told her what he hadn't discovered.

'I could… but I wouldn't dare, Mick.'

'But you could if necessary?'

'There are better ways to skin a rabbit than hacking other jurisdictions systems. Leave it with me I'll see what I can come up with.'

Mickey felt a sense of relief when he left her and returned to his desk. That relief was shattered when he saw the letter. It was from the internal investigations division, and it referenced Limpy's knee. He'd been asked to show due cause, and he wasn't in the mood to waste time on it. He folded the letter and slipped it into his hip pocket before ringing Angela Carter.

'I can't find much about Mrs Kosanovich she isn't anywhere in our system. Has she popped up in anything you've seen?'

He sensed her head shake as she answered. 'The name should stand out, but it doesn't. There is some good news, though. Brian has tracked down Agnetha's father in Sweden. The bad news is the local cops are holding him on a murder charge.'

'Shit!'

'Apparently a man came to his house, enquiring about his daughter. The man wasn't happy when he told them he hadn't seen or heard of her for three years. He then shot him.'

'You don't think…?'

'I don't know what to think, Mick. I've asked for more information but…'

'He's in Sweden, his daughter is in a secure rehab centre in Australia, and suddenly, after three years, he gets a visit out of the blue from a stranger who he shoots… and we can't even find Karla Kosanovich.'

'Somehow I think we'll need to try harder, Mick.'

Mickey ended the call and headed directly for Clark Shipton's office. When he arrived, he found Kelly scooting around with a vacuum cleaner. 'That bad, huh?'

'Tell me about it, Mick. No one can find Mrs Whatsit and Clarkie's reputation isn't helping us get a new cleaner.'

'That's what I came to see you about. We need to find her and get her out of the loop ASAP. Angela Carter's mob have tracked down Agnetha's dad, in Sweden, but she was too late, he's been arrested for murder after shooting a bloke who started asking too many questions about his daughter.'

'You think it's the work of Mrs Whatsit?'

'Well, everything started getting shaky soon after we discovered she was a mole. We still don't know how high or wide this trafficking goes, and I'm sure there'll be plenty of people who would like it to remain their closely guarded mystery.'

'I've managed to find an address for her…'

'I've been there. There's no one around it's like she's flown the coup.'

'Well anyway.' Kelly dropped a post-it-note on her desk while he was speaking.

'That isn't the address I visited,' Mickey said.

'It's the one she used when she was working for us.'

Mickey thanked her and almost ran for his car. Kelly had written down an address in Mount Claremont which seemed way beyond the reach of an aging cleaning lady. He found the house using his GPS and noted it was an imposing residence standing back off the road behind a well-kept garden.

Mickey parked his car where he could spend some time with an unobstructed view of the house. There was very little activity from what he could see but that seemed to be the norm for the other places within his view. Most of the folks who could afford places like these would no doubt be out and about spruiking the funds to operate their opulent lifestyles. His thoughts flew back to his dad's place in the bush. A white ant ridden shack that fell apart a few days after the old man died. The intensity of that memory distracted him for a moment and when he looked back, he saw someone pull the front door shut from within.

He called James Carter and told him where he was. 'I think I've found Karla Kosanovich. He read out the address.'

'Sounds a bit upmarket for a cleaning lady, Mick. How did you get on to that?'

'Kelly. It was the address she used when she was working for Clarkie.'

'What do you want to do?'

'Angela has found Agnetha's Father, a Mr Daniel Byquist. He's under arrest for murder in Sweden. Someone turned up asking questions about his daughter and he somehow managed to shoot the bugger.'

'Harsh.'

'We don't know what baggage Agnetha's father is carrying, and we don't know the nature of the questions. If I had kids and it was one of mine...'

'I'll see what I can find out. You haven't said what you want to do.'

'If I go in all policified we'll almost certainly tip off the leaders of the cabal and they'll probably sink down under the mud and out of sight. I learned as a kid, the only way you'll find things living in the mud is by digging with your fingers and toes. I'd like to get Karla on her own on a hard surface and isolate her from any connections she might have.'

'How do you plan to do that?'

'I don't have a plan yet. I've only just started working on it.'

'Has to be above board, Mick.'

'It will be…' he pressed end and turned his attention back to the house.

47

The time was two am and Kriminalinspektör Kristina Ahlström was speaking precisely, in perfect English, making James Carter feel embarrassed that he could not reciprocate in her language. At least there would be no misunderstanding about the meaning of their conversation. She was at first reluctant to discuss the Byquist case until James pressed her and mentioned Byquist's daughter.

'His daughter? Agnetha?'

'She is in a secure rehab centre in Western Australia, while she recovers from her induced heroin addiction.' He heard papers shuffling, as though Ahlström was flipping through a file.

'This girl is not yet sixteen, and you are saying she is a heroin addict, and in Australia?'

'Not by choice, Kriminalinspektör Ahlström, but at least she is safe, and we now have a name for her. I hope you will let Mr Byquist know she's been found.'

The paper shuffling continued for a few more moments before Ahlström spoke again. 'I may have to refer this to a senior officer, DCI Carter.'

'That's okay, Kriminalinspektör Ahlström, as long as you understand that Mr Byquist is in real danger. We believe the man who came to see him might be part of an international human trafficking cabal with connections to the Russian mafia. Mr Byquist's daughter was probably taken by them around her twelfth birthday and has since been put to work in a Bosnian brothel, from where she was rescued a little more than a week ago.'

'May I speak confidentially?'

'I hope, Kriminalinspektör Ahlström, everything we say to each other will remain confidential.'

'Of course. Firstly, please call me Kristina.'

'Only if you call me Jim.' He heard a soft giggle that was different to the super-efficiency of her earlier voice.

'Mr Byquist's statement claims he became involved in a struggle with his attacker, but he disarmed and shot the man with his own weapon. Does that make sense to you, Jim?'

'That would depend on his background, we know nothing of him only that he was married to an English woman who is believed to be Agnetha's mother. We still don't know her name, but if Agnetha was my daughter…'

'Yoh… May I call you back, when I have spoken to my superior?'

'Be cautious, Kristina. We believe our investigation has been infiltrated and for that reason it is proceeding, as far as possible, off grid.'

'Oh shit. Wait.' There was a long pause. 'You said, human trafficking?'

'That's a polite word for it.'

'Then there is someone, but it will need me to do as you say and go off grid.' There was another long pause. 'May I call you back… What time is it there?'

James glanced at the bedside alarm. 'Two-thirty am.'

'I will try to call you at a better hour, Jim. Is this number good for that?'

'I hope so, but we still have black holes in our telephone system so please leave a message or send a text and I promise you I'll follow up.'

'Then, goodnight, Jim. Sleep well.'

He heard the giggle again, as the call was ending.

***

It wasn't long before Mickey's worst fears permeated the interior of his car. A woman had just walked past. She stopped and turned to stare at him through the windscreen. He smiled and wound down his window.

The woman sucked in a loud breath, took out her phone and tapped on the screen.

'There's an indigenous man, in a car.'

…

'Yes, he's definitely acting suspiciously.'

…

'Well, he's an aboriginal, and he looks like he's casing properties in the locality.'

…

'How would I know.' She shoved her phone in her handbag and scurried away.

Mickey realised he now had a problem, and it wasn't the woman's racial attitude, he was accustomed to that. If he showed her his Police ID, it might satisfy her immediate fears, but the information would circulate within minutes. He started his engine and gave her a smile and a wave as he moved passed her.

She scowled at him, and he laughed inwardly, remembering the stories his dad used to tell him when they were out bush and alone.

As he was driving away, he saw a movement at the address of Karla Kosanovich. She had left the building, and it looked like she was about to get in her car. Mickey smiled, 'Gotya.' He pulled to the side of the road and waited.

Sure enough, Karla's car left the property and turned to head for the city.

Mickey allowed her to get well ahead and began following her at a distance. He called James.

'She's on the move, boss, and I have my eyes on her as we speak.' He memorised the rego and continued his cruise until she turned into a multi-storey car park. He followed her in, parked two rows away, still within sight of her, and waited.

Karla sat in her car for several minutes and Mickey could see that she was on her phone. When she finished her call, she disembarked and walked into the Cottesloe Central shopping centre. He scrambled to follow her but once she'd passed through the entrance, it seemed like she'd vanished into thin air.

Mickey had no choice but to find a place where he could wait relatively peacefully, in the hope he could catch her leaving wherever it was she had gone. He was confident she would be still in the centre, and he sensed the suspicious nature of the proprietor as he purchased a coffee-to-go at a small eatery before finding a place to wait.

The last time Mickey took a seat in a shopping centre he was moved on by their security personnel. At least this time he was clean, and he also had his police ID as insurance. He called James again.

'I could knock on doors and see if I can find her, but it might tip her off that we are onto her. I need to find out who she's seeing. It might be innocent… but.'

'How long can you hang out?'

'I got strange looks when I parked in Claremont. A woman even rang the police to complain there was an aboriginal checking out residences. I could have shown her my ID but that might have helped Karla more than me.'

'I'll check that out. If she rang our people, there should be a report.'

He was about to end the call when he saw her. 'Got her. She's just come out of a real estate office and looks to be heading for her car.' Mickey ended the call and texted the name of the real estate agent as he followed Karla into the carpark.

She went directly to her car, made another short telephone call and drove off.

Mickey followed her to the Claremont house and watched her park the car in the garage and close the door from the inside.

'She's at home, boss but I stick out like a bruised thumb in this suburb.'

'What's the address?'

He read it off the post-it-note, Kelly had given him.

'I'll check it out and see if I can get someone to take over the surveillance, meanwhile stay around as long as you can, and if it becomes too intense, do a runner.'

A few minutes after he ended the call with James, a patrol car pulled in behind him. He reached for his ID and waited, patiently, for the knock on the window. Instead of a knock on the window he heard the crash of his driver's side taillight breaking. *At what point do I draw the line at intensity, boss.*

Mickey opened his door, hauled himself up to his full height and pointed to his police ID with his rank of Detective Sergeant. 'You've got a problem Constable?'

The man seemed panicky. He turned to his partner in the car his lips mouthing WTF.

Mickey followed him to his car, climbed into the back seat and indicated that the man who broke his taillight should get in. When he had their full attention he said, 'So you think you're fucken smart. Names!' He snapped their pictures with his phone and pressed video record. 'Right, now we've got that out of the way, you need to know that you have probably compromised a delicate surveillance operation. Not only the physical damage to *my* car, but your damage to a major investigation will be heading for your records.'

The driver said, 'We'd had a report of someone matching your description sizing up houses for break-ins.'

'So, what was the matching description that so inflamed your egos?'

The passenger said, 'You know...'

'Yeah, I know alright, but it's gonna cost you two... unless.'

48

The family of Sachin Shukla were all waiting on the spacious veranda of their imposing colonial mansion and their genuine smiles lit up what could have easily been a traumatic experience for everyone.

'Welcome to my humble home gentlemen.' He gestured to a person, who seemed to be a servant, 'Please escort Mr Bub inside, while I speak with Mr Bib.'

The servant ushered them, and Shukla drew Bib aside. 'Come, walk with me,' he said and led Bib down a broad path into a meticulously tended garden.

'Bit of a gardener, then.'

'Alas, no, Mr Bib. This garden was my daughter's favourite place before...'

'Sorry, I...'

'No, please. She was so young when they took her, and we thought we'd never see her again.'

'You are aware of the circumstances, Sachin, if I may call you that?'

'Yes, Mr Bib and you may. My family is my main cause in life, my friend and as you can see, I have been able to look after them very well, thanks to my education at one of your most esteemed universities.' He paused for a moment. 'I am not a religious person, Mr Bib, but Anjali will, of course, be considered defiled by many and that might prevent her from marrying well in this country. I am hoping the world might become her oyster once you have returned her to us and she has recovered from this trauma.'

'It is heroin addiction and then there are psychological effects of being raped several times a day?'

Shukla's brow creased, his head bobbing sagely. 'There are places, and we have the wherewithal for what is needed.'

'You are aware that she's likely not in the original place,' he tried to avoid using the brothel word.

Shukla head wobbled again. 'I know that will make it more dangerous for you and I expect you will charge me accordingly. I want my daughter back, Mr Bib. I have learned of your history, and I trust you to do whatever it takes.'

Bib tensed at Shukla's comment about his history, but he said nothing.

'Come,' Shukla said and led him to a pair of French windows that opened on a room containing a large ornate desk surrounded by well stacked, carved timber bookshelves. He pointed to a pair of sumptuous, winged armchairs and said, 'Please sit.'

As soon as Bib had taken his place, Shukla dropped on one knee by a safe and began twiddling the combination. When he finished, he opened the safe, removed a file and handed it to Bib. On the cover were the initials, DIA.

Bib opened the file, saw his photograph and looked up. 'Been doing your homework.'

'I'm just a humble public servant, Mr Bib.' Shukla smiled. 'I think you would not hire a plumber if you did not think he was capable.'

Bib smirked. He was destined to be a tradesman before he scored highly and won a university scholarship. 'I think my qualifications are not in doubt, Sachin, but please don't ask me to fix your pipes.' He glanced at the set of bagpipes mounted on a small plinth inside the internal door.

Sachin laughed. 'Good then let us enjoy a meal together. I can't play the bagpipes, anyway. They're a hang up from the Raj.' He held out his hand and Bib shook it. Then they stood and he led him through to a wide hallway adorned with oil paintings that were either fakes or real old masters. 'Yes, my friend they are all real.' Shukla said as he led him to an even larger room where his family were seated around a long dining table. He then spoke in his own language to a servant who approached Bib.

The servant spoke in perfect English and said, 'What would you like to drink, sir?'

'I'll have a small scotch, neat, thank you.' The servant bobbed his head and left to collect Bibs drink, while he took his seat at the table and breathed in the opulence. 'The food smells wonderful,' he said, as servants served dishes around the table.

***

'That real estate agent, Mick. He's one of the big noises in the bizzo.'

'You wouldn't think it from his office front.'

'Pericles Dubois. He doesn't waste his time with anything under five-mil.'

'Nice work if you can get it,' Mickey said.

'He's also a mid-level name on Mandy's list,' James said.

'Shit! He might have something to lose then.'

'And also have a good reason to know our mole.'

'I can't just barge in on him.'

'No, but Clark Shipton has an axe to grind. Maybe he could be of some help. He owns a decent chunk of real estate in some of the posher suburbs.'

'You reckon he should hook him in from a real estate point of view? Mightn't his association cause speculation, given his ex-cleaner is our suspected mole.'

'Can you suggest anything better?'

'I'll need to think about it, boss. We know there is a connection, but we'll need more than that to put the screws on. I'd like some more surveillance on Karla. I'm convinced she's the mole but being an informant isn't exactly against the law, is it?'

'It will be difficult, but I'll try to get you some assistance, meanwhile let me know how you go.'

The call ended and Mickey decided to head for home. Anyone hanging around in a car in this suburb would surely draw interest, as he'd already discovered. He was about to start his car when he a thought crossed his mind. He called Mandy Stephenson on her personal phone, and she answered immediately.

'Hey, Mickey. What's new?'

'Pericles Dubois. He's on your list of suspects.'

'That's right, he was given breathing space because he was considered a low-level participant and had only a limited connection with one or two of the girls who were trafficked.'

'What if I were to tell that the person we believe to be our mole has visited his offices?'

'Interesting.'

'Are you able to do any digging?'

'Not officially and the risks are massive.'

'Okay, sorry I asked.'

'No worries, Mick. We'll get there, eventually.'

'And hopefully the girls, Bib and Bub rescued, will still be alive to tell their version of the tale.'

'Don't pressure me, Mick.'

The call ended.

'Shit.' *I've overstepped the mark.* He started his car and headed for home knowing his mind would be alive for the rest of the night.

***

It was ten am when James Carter's burner rang. The screen said International Call. He pressed accept and heard Kriminalinspektör Kristina Ahlström's voice.

'Hello, Jim. I hope I didn't wake you.'

'No, you're good, Kristina.'

'Good. Then I have some good news for you. The person I mentioned, who is off grid, has offered to help. He is an ex-colleague who blotted his copybook some time ago, when he became involved in the investigation of a trafficking scheme like the one you mentioned.'

'Sounds interesting.'

'When I told him what you said about Byquist, he knew exactly who I was talking about. Mr Byquist had a distinguished military career and was no doubt perfectly capable of looking after himself. Sadly, though, not his daughter. She apparently went a bit wild after the divorce, and then she disappeared.'

'And turned up in a Bosnian brothel specialising in underage girls.'

'That is so.'

'And?'

'My ex-colleague is, like you, concerned about the hierarchical links. These are what caused his own problems and subsequent dismissal from our police force. He asked if you are aware of Bratva, Jim.'

'I know it's another name for the Russian Mafia.'

'That is so.'

'Would it be possible to speak with him?'

'Better still. He tells me he is due for a holiday and the Australian weather sounds like it might just fit his bill.'

'He'll come to Australia on spec?'

'He leaves tonight, and I've given him your details.'

'He must be serious then.'

'I think so. His name is Lars Berglund, and I believe he might have some relatives in Sydney.'

'Byquist?'

'I think we will need to wait and see. Anything I say might trigger the kind of reaction we do not want. I have passed on a message to him, that his daughter has been found and that she is well.'

'Any response?'

'Not yet, I'm afraid.'

'Thank you for your help, Kristina. I'll look forward to meeting Mr Berglund when he gets here.'

'I will make this my calling time for Australia, is that good with you?'

'Perfect.' The call ended and James tapped Angela's number. There was no response.

49

On completion of the meal Shukla excused himself and requested that Bib once again accompany him to his study. He pointed to an armchair and arranged for more drinks.

'Now we are alone again, David. I see no point in not using your proper name. It will be between us only. I know you are aware of the nature of these evil creatures who steal our children.'

Bib nodded.

'Then you also understand that we are not dealing with amateurs in it for a quick buck.'

'What are you trying to tell me, Sachin.'

'Not long before my girl was taken, I was required to authorise a special event.' He raised his eyebrows.

'The DIA?'

'Like you, my friend, I am a loyal patriot of my country. When I see things that are done, not for the betterment of the people but for the betterment of certain individuals, my patriotism becomes stretched. In short, the event I authorised was expected to cause unease with certain officials who we knew had connections to Bratva and hopefully smoke them out.'

'Shit, you don't fuck about do you.'

Shukla smiled. 'You English have such a wonderful way with

words. My daughter and her friend attended the same school and they both disappeared on the same day. What I'm trying to say is. It was not a coincidence, David.'

'It makes a lot of sense though. The Russian Mafia specialises in trafficking. To them she'd be just another lump of meat for their grinder.'

Shukla frowned.

'Sorry, that's the way it is.'

Shukla's eyes wandered to a place behind Bib for a moment. 'Your friend the doctor, Amrita isn't it, she didn't come tonight. Is she not well?'

'She has a Migraine.'

'How sure of her, are you?'

Bib felt his gut cinch. He pulled himself together quickly. 'What do you mean?'

Shukla reached into his safe and removed another file.

Bib opened it and saw the face of the first woman he'd allowed to come close to him for years. It wasn't a good picture. She looked like she'd been through some strife before it was taken. He began to read the notes that accompanied it. The more he read, the angrier he became. 'How true is this?'

Shukla reached for the file, closed it and said, 'One hundred percent. That picture was taken shortly after her capture by my people. That event, I mentioned, fell apart after a mole infiltrated my department. That mole, we believe she now uses the name Amrita Devi, managed to escape and take refuge in the city. She had an accomplice. Strange chap, almost invisible.'

'Vishwananda?'

'Is that what he calls himself now?'

'He seemed harmless enough.'

'Bratva owned and paid for in full. Amrita does as she is told.

I am sorry, David.'

'What you are saying is that my mission to rescue your daughter is already compromised to the hilt.'

'How we get out of this mess is something that makes me glad that I asked you and your friend for help.' He reached for the bottle on the tray and offered it to recharge Bib's glass.

Bib shook his head. His mind was whirling and the last thing he needed was more grog. He stood. 'This remains between us?'

'Of course, David. I'll have a servant drive you and your friend to your hotel.' He pressed a small button on his desk and while they waited, he said. 'Name your price but please bring her home safe.'

Bib lay his proforma on the blotter.

Shukla's eyes registered no emotion as he scanned the fee and the details, then he shook Bib's hand and said, 'Agreed, my friend.' He reached for a pen and signed the paperwork. 'You will see the up-front payment in your bank account within twenty-four hours.'

***

'I've had a conversation with a Swedish cop who seems to think that the folks behind this trafficking are the Russian Mafia.'

'Far out, in little old WA. I wouldn't have thought we have the kind of infrastructure that would appeal to them, it's more a bikie hood.' Mickey said.

'Yeah well. There is a Swedish ex-cop arriving tomorrow. Apparently, he knows stuff.' James dropped a number of photographs onto his desk. 'Recognise anyone?'

'Pericles Dubois, Karla Kosanovich.'

'The bikies in the background?'

Mickey shook his head.

'Not surprising, the pics were taken at a music festival in

Sydney, about five years ago.'

Mickey said, 'Are you saying the Russian Maffia are hand in glove with local bikie gangs?'

'Looks like Mrs Kosanovich and Pericles might be. So why not?'

'But shouldn't this have come to light when we discovered George Gregory's involvement.'

'He was only small fry at the edge of the pond, Mick we slipped up badly by being too kind.'

'This is getting bigger than Uluru, boss. It's way above my paygrade.'

'Mine too, so when this Swedish bloke arrives, we'll have to see what we can wring out of him.'

Mickey left and headed back to his desk. If Karla and Dubois were connected to the Russians, things could turn dangerous very quickly.

James Carter tried his sister again. This time she picked up.

'I see you've been trying to call me. Sorry I've been a bit bogged down,' Angela said.

'How are the girls' treatments going?'

'It'll be a struggle for them in many ways.'

'I've been speaking to a Swedish detective. She's passed on information to Agnetha's dad, so he'll know she's safe.'

'That's nice. We're still trying to track down Bronwyn's family but no luck yet.'

'Perhaps she had her name changed, and we still don't know what those zombie drugs might cause to memories. Maybe talk to Siddhartha, perhaps he can work his magic.'

'I'll do my best.'

'While you are at it, warn him there might be a Bratva involvement. He'll know what you mean, and it will give him a heads up.'

'Bratva?' Angela said.

'Some call them the Russian Mafia.'

'The immigration people seem happy to let the temporary papers run out their time, given the circumstances, but we'll need to fix that as soon as we can.'

'Agnetha's papers should be an easy one. We now know at least one of her parents, and things should start moving relatively quickly.'

'This "Bratva" involvement. Should I be worried?'

'Mickey's looking into it and there is a man from Sweden, who is hopefully in the know, due here tomorrow. I'll keep you posted.'

***

It was two hours before Mickey could follow up on Mandy Stephenson's request for a meet. She'd said it was urgent, but everything seemed to have climbed on top of him at once.

When he eventually sat down with her, she said, 'Have you ever heard the term "Plausible Deniability", Sergeant?'

The formality made Mickey put down his coffee and stare vaguely at the serious face of the officer across the table from him. 'Sounds impressive, Sergeant Stephenson.'

'How much do you know about the British intelligence services.'

'If I said nothing?'

'You wouldn't be alone, but you asked me to do some rummaging, and I hereby deny doing anything that might link me to certain cyber activities in relation to a member of the real estate industry.'

'Who shall remain nameless?'

'Quite so. As you know, Australia is a part of the

Commonwealth but that doesn't mean other countries security services don't actively carry out unannounced activities.' She turned her screen towards him so he could see what was displayed.

'What is it?' he said, fixing the screen in his mind like the trails his father had taught him all those years ago.

'You might remember I had a teensy-weensy role in the war in Afghanistan. You wouldn't know that my group operated under a flag of plausible deniability. That meant if our actions accidentally affected troops on our own side, the government would say it was the enemy. If we were killed in an action or captured, it would be as if we never existed.'

'So, what does this have to do with a certain real estate agent?'

'He is not who you think he is.'

'Who is he, then?'

'I believe our real estate agent's real name is Pawel Kieslowski and I will deny that this conversation ever took place if I am asked.' She pressed a key on her computer, and the screen went blank. 'That's it, poof, all gone, shredded, wiped, and disinfected.'

'So?'

'So, Sergeant, think carefully. Whatever you do in respect to this person that could put us both in a no-win situation.'

'Mrs Kosanovich?'

'Your best bet is to either stay well clear or find something that will trip him or her up. I can't help you further.'

'I'll need to let the boss know.'

'Let him know what?'

Mickey looked over her shoulder, and said, 'Got it.'

'Anything else I can do?'

'Anything you can, Mands. You know better than anyone

what we're up against.'

'Then please give my regards to Bib and Bub, next time you are in touch, and if you get an opportunity to visit a certain real estate office, find a place to leave this. It will fix to most surfaces and is completely illegal, so don't get caught.' She handed him a small button-like object, which could easily be mistaken for a bumper from the bottom of an appliance. She demonstrated the removal of the paper from the adhesive. 'Once attached it becomes voice activated after about five minutes, and it remains completely inert unless someone starts speaking.'

Mickey raised his eyebrows.

'We're fighting organised crime here, Mick. They won't stop at a smidge of chicanery so why should we?'

Mickey stood and, with the button firmly clasped in his hand, the mental snapshot of Mandy's computer screen fixed in his mind's eye, he left to find some privacy that would allow him to transcribe all the words he could recall. When he finished, he folded the sheet of paper, tucked it in his pocket and with his brain racing, headed for his car.

50

Major David Ashton-O'Sullivan slid his card key into the slot on his hotel room door and once inside tapped on the adjoining door. It was open and he saw her laying fully clothed on her bed, seemingly asleep. Shukla's words and the evidence he'd presented had left him drained. *Why?* he thought and remembered the moment he'd first seen her on that first night. *I'd thought it was preordained. I'd thought she might be the one.* 'What a moron,' he mumbled as he opened the door to his ensuite.

When he'd finished his shower, he dried off, left his towel in the bathroom and as he returned to the room, he found Amrita stretched out on his bed. She had obviously let herself in via the adjoining door and was covered with a single sheet that left little to his imagination.

She looked up, her eyes wide at his exposure. 'Well, my darling, it seems we are both ready.'

Bib returned to the ensuite and dressed in the clothes he had been wearing. 'Sorry, Amrita, I need to take a walk first.'

'I'll come with you,' she said, hurriedly dressing in the clothes she had left on the floor beside the bed.

'No need. I have some thinking to do.'

'But I insist.'

'As you wish.' While she finished dressing, he glanced at his phone which was displaying the confirmation of their departure time for a connecting flight to Bosnia. He'd earlier mentioned it to Bub, who'd made the arrangements while Bib was showering. His intention was for them all to disappear, but that was before Amrita figured in his plan.

'Right?' he said, reaching out to take her hand.

Amrita responded, 'I must be saying that I had a different idea for this evening, but a leisurely walk before bed, with you, would surely be most pleasant.'

The Mithi River flowed not far from the hotel and Bib suggested they take a stroll along its bank.

Amrita's face stiffened with concern. 'But it is dark there and who knows what might be lying in wait for us? I'm not sure it is a good idea, David.'

'You'll have me, and I think I'll manage. Anyway, that's where I'm heading. Tag along if you wish, or not. Have you heard anything from Mr Vishwananda?' Bib said, as he pulled the door shut behind him.

'I sent him a text, but I have not yet received a reply.'

'That's understandable,' Bib said, as they descended in the lift to the lobby. When the lift doors opened, he reached out and took her hand again. 'I've so enjoyed your company, Amrita,' he said, and escorted her from the hotel.

The river's edge was no more than two hundred metres from the hotel, and she clung to his hand as though it might be the last thing she ever did.

'We could always hire a taxi and pop in on him.'

Amrita shook her head. 'Mr Vishu has his fixed rituals and the last time you met he was thrown into disarray. I am just hoping he found his way back from Myanmar.'

They arrived at the bridge, and he led her to the narrow walk path that followed the river's bank. Once on the embankment, he stopped and pointed to the Mumbai skyline. 'I remember the first time I visited this spot. It was back in the eighties, I was just a boy, and my father brought me here, so it has pleasant memories for me.'

'How lovely.' She turned towards him, and her face lifted to look into his eyes.

Bib leaned in as though to kiss her on the lips.

As she arched her neck to reciprocate, he held her body in a close embrace to frisk her for a phone or ID. There was nothing and he heard a clatter as he released her to slither, anonymously and almost silently, down the steep embankment, making only the quietest of plops, as the river drew her into *its* embrace. He looked down to see what she had dropped and recovered the fine-bladed knife she'd no doubt been about to fillet him with.

'I wish things could have been more amicable between us, my love. Regrettably, we were incompatible.' Ashton-O'Sullivan slipped the knife into his hip pocket and the garrotte into its usual stowage. He returned at a casual pace to the hotel, while shutting down the regrets that had begun piling into the part of his brain that he utilised as a conscience. He glanced at his watch. The flight to Bosnia would be leaving in three hours. He texted Bub to ensure he was alert and ready.

Moments later, his phone rang.

'Hey, Bib. I knocked on Amrita's door. There was no reply. I hope everything is okay.'

'She said she was trying to contact Vishwananda, and I haven't seen her since.'

'Okay. Might as well find our way to the airport. By the time we get there and check in, it'll be time to go. I'll send her another text nearer the time.'

'Good thinking. We can refine our plans on the plane and if Amrita doesn't make it, I now have enough Suboxone to treat a small army.'

'I thought you two were getting along so well.'

'Regrettably our business doesn't easily accommodate personal relationships.' Bib pressed *end*, pressed the *up,* call button at the lift, and stepped inside when it arrived. When he entered his room, he took another shower, dressed in fresh clothes, packed the old ones into his grip and made sure the adjoining door was locked, before tapping on Bub's door. 'No sound from her room. She must have left already.'

Bub hefted his bag, let the closer do its job, and the pair made their way to the check out.

As he was paying the bill, he said, 'I've tried to contact Dr Devi, but she isn't answering her phone. I know she was going to look in on an old friend and said she would return shortly, so I'm happy to clear her bill. When she returns would you please advise her that we have departed for the airport?'

The checkout clerk tapped a string of text on his keyboard, and Bib paid the entire outstanding bill with US greenbacks. If the hotel needed to charge more, only then would they discover that the card originally presented no longer existed.

At the airport club lounge, Bub sent another text advising Amrita that her ticket would be left at the check-in desk, should she decide to continue with them. He collected two coffees, joined Bib and said, 'Mr Shukla seems to know his way around.'

Bib's phone buzzed with a message. He stood just as their boarding call rang out through the PA and looked down at the screen on his phone.

***

James Carter stood beside his sister as they waited for the arrivals door to begin emitting passengers. Angela had made a small sign with the name Lars Berglund, and she was about to hold it up when the first passenger appeared. She held the sign against her chest and the large man barrelled towards her, causing her to flinch and step back.

'I am Lars.' He grinned and spoke in perfect English. 'I wasn't expecting a welcoming committee.'

James stood forward and held his hand out to have it crushed by Berglund. 'Welcome to Australia, Mr Berglund. I'm DCI James Carter. I have been speaking with Kristina.'

Lars grinned again. 'You may call me Lars,' and continued pushing his luggage trolley through the rows of waiting relatives and friends.

James said, 'I have some transport to take you to your hotel, then we can maybe meet up when you have recovered from your journey.'

'No need for recovery, Mr Carter. We can drop my things to the hotel and begin immediately. If there is truth in what Kristina is telling me, we have work on our hands and the people we are up against are dangerous.' He turned towards Angela. 'Forgive me?' he said and raised an eyebrow.

'Angela Carter. I'm his sister, acting as the lawyer for the girls, and my team is working on the discovery of their true identities. It was one of my people who discovered Agnetha's Swedish connection.'

As James hefted Berglund's bags into the boot of his car, he said, 'How did you get through immigration so quickly?'

'I never travel less than first class, my friend. Means I'm always first off the plane, and the diplomatic passport helps. Trust me, it is the only way to go.'

James disguised a sigh of relief, that Lars had made the decision to come to Australia at his own expense.

They did as he requested and dropped his bags at the hotel. There was no need to check in. Everything had been taken care of, and the concierge dispatched his baggage to his room. Next stop was the letdown of Angela's dingy office in the back streets of Northbridge.

Berglund didn't seem to notice the dodgy paintwork and threadbare furniture of the meeting room when Angela escorted him in. Gloria was on hand to provide coffees and as they settled into their chairs, Berglund said, 'How secure is this building?'

Angela said, 'We haven't had so much as a toilet roll stolen since we set up office, Lars. Now what are you going to tell us that we don't already know?'

James flinched at her tone, and his look said, perhaps this was not such a good idea.

Lars Berglund smiled at Angela, patted James on the shoulder, and said, 'They said you Aussies could be blunt.'

'So?' Angela said.

'So, my friend's daughter was kidnapped, and you did what I couldn't do. You found her in a brothel in Bosnia. This is not something new, and I was assigned to investigate her disappearance when I was a police officer. As soon as I began closing in on the subjects, the case was closed from above. I was angry and the things I said ensured I was no longer required.'

'Seems we have a similar problem. Just to let you know, I have been quietly assigned to this investigation by our commissioner of police. We have a list of suspects as long as your arm and they exist in our society at all levels. So, my involvement and those of my colleagues are effectively off the books.'

This time Lars said, 'This police commissioner...?'

'He is one-hundred percent behind us,' Angela said. 'But he must watch his step. This is a politically unpopular investigation that has the potential to touch many in government.'

'Bratva?' Berglund said.

'The Russian Mafia,' Angela said. 'We know who that represents, and we have our suspicions. Incidentally, it wasn't us who found her, but a small team of professionals who have since left the country on another project. We are simply dealing with the aftermath.'

Berglund reached into his briefcase and spread a number of papers across the table. 'This is a list of the Swedish girls who have gone missing with the dates they disappeared. The only one that has been found so far is Agnetha.' He pointed to her photograph.

Angela gasped. 'They all look so young.'

'Agnetha was almost thirteen years old when she was taken.'

51

As they took their seats on the plane Bib showed Bub the message he'd just received from Mickey Krakauer.

Bub noticed the name before anything else. 'Pawel Kieslowski? He's dead, isn't he?'

'Not according to Mickey. He's alive and well and working in a real estate agent's office in one of the posher suburbs of Perth. The person they suspect has been passing information about us, is in regular contact with him.' He scrolled down the message. 'Recognise this name?'

'Karla Kosanovich. Different spelling same sound.'

'Think she could be related to Uncle Draggy?'

'Makes sense.'

'Even more so given he says she was working for Clark Shipton as a cleaner. She's probably had access to everything about us through Shipton's slack set up.'

'So, what's next.'

'We hit the ground running in Sarajevo, find the girl, and then we beat it. If Uncle Draggy turns up he's fair game. No questions asked. If the girl wants us to bring her friends, we say no way and take her away, wrapped in a rolled-up carpet if necessary.'

Bub smirked, 'Yeah right.'

'We now have intel that infers they know we're coming. That means they'll be ready and waiting and I don't think I can ask Frank to look after us a second time. What we know is that all the trafficked girls are issued fake local papers which identify them as Bosnian. If we're picked up, in Bosnian eyes, we'll be the traffickers and, given their record in this respect, you can bet we'll be made an example of, so that those who come after us might be deterred.'

'But we have genuine papers for Shukla's kid.'

'In our eyes.' Bib accepted a flute of Champagne from the flight attendant, tapped in a text message and leaned back to enjoy what might be his last before dozing off, while trying to avoid thoughts of Amrita.

***

'Good morning, Mr Dubois. So sorry to bother you.'

Dubois offered Mickey a seat at his desk and politely asked, 'What can I do for you sir. Do you have a property that you wish to sell.'

Mickey leaned forward to show him his police ID and take the opportunity to stick the bug under his desk.

His action didn't seem to faze Dubois in any way.

'No, sir, but we've received some complaints, and as a courtesy, I'm asking all the businesses in the complex if they've witnessed any unusual activity in the last few days.'

Dubois shook his head. 'I'm rarely here, Sergeant. I spend most of my time with clients. You don't achieve success in this business unless you put in the hours. If that's it? I have things to do.' He raised his eyebrows in a symbol of summary dismissal. 'Thank you for your interest. I am pleased to note that the constabulary are on the ball, and I will pass on my regards to the commissioner. Goodbye, Sergeant.' He stood and showed

Mickey to the door.

As the door closed behind him, Mickey heard the lock swivel. He turned and saw the closed sign swing as though Dubois had flipped it over. He texted Mandy:

> Fixed.

She replied:

> I know

Dubois' office was now effectively bugged, and he expected that Mandy would be recording any conversations that took place until the next time he had it swept.

He'd headed back to the station to check in with James when he saw another text from Mandy:

> Pop in when you get a minute.

Instead of joining his boss he headed directly to Mandy's workstation. 'What gives?'

'Soon after you left, he had a visitor — Karla Kosanovich — and from the tone of his voice, he wasn't too pleased to see her.'

'Anything interesting?'

Mandy handed him a set of earphones.

He pulled them over his ears and waited.

> *'You had better pull your head in, Pawel.*
> *They are on to us, and my people believe it*
> *is your actions that have triggered the*
> *interest.'*

'I don't know what you are talking about, Karla.'

'Today's visit from the police?'

'That was nothing, there had been some complaints. He had been sent to investigate them. I told him I had no problems and had seen nothing unusual. He left and that is that.'

'The people in your past believe Pawel Kieslowski is dead. There is always a possibility they might have found out that is not the case.'

Mickey left the earphones on while Mandy switched the audio to real time.

Mandy said, 'There is some evidence that Pawel Kieslowski used to have a connection with MI6 until he was pronounced missing presumed dead. I believe the other voice is that of Mrs Kosanovich who obviously knows of his past.'

'But as Pericles Dubois, he has a good little business flogging palaces to the rich, so why would he be involved with trafficking?'

'He's on our list as a suspected kiddie fiddler and that makes him a prime target.'

'So, Mrs Kosanovich?'

'As a go between, her job as a lowly cleaner is a perfect cover. You might have noticed she was making veiled threats to the real estate agent, and I think he'll make a move to distance himself, very soon.'

'If I talk to the boss about this, he'll be instantly compromised by our illegal bug.'

'So, don't tell him and let's see what else pops out of the woodwork.'

Mickey slowly shook his head. 'You realise if any of this gets out, we're both done for.'

Mandy said, 'Meanwhile we might be getting closer to a result, Mick.'

'No wonder you were selected for the army bomb squad. One false move and, Boom!'

Mandy grinned. 'You only survive by keeping your cool.'

Mickey's eyebrows raised when he saw the text on his phone. 'Shit.'

'What's happened?'

'Federal cops are at Dubois' place. He's being taken into custody.'

'You still in touch with Bib and Bub?'

Mickey was uncertain of what she was fishing for.

'Send Bib a text. See how he reacts.'

Mickey looked down at his watch. It was late afternoon. 'They are heading to Bosnia for another extraction. Right now, might be too soon.'

***

Gloria arrived and interrupted them with a tray of tea and biscuits, 'If you need anything else give me a cooee.'

'So many,' Angela said.

'James' phone bleeped. 'Excuse me.' He read the message and groaned.

'Something wrong?' Angela asked. 'Sorry. Mr Berglund.'

'Dubois has been arrested by the feds.'

Berglund replied, 'Is he one of your people?'

'No, just someone of interest. Please continue.' Angela said.

Berglund responded. 'Everyone thinks the slave trade ended

in the eighteenth century, when in fact it is still in full swing. Then it was driven by the wealthiest in our society, and nothing much has changed, except now their slaves are recycled for reuse.' Lars paused and helped himself to a cup of tea. 'The only thing different about modern slavery is that it usually sits side by side with money laundering, spare parts surgery, and drug distribution.' He unzipped his travel bag and removed a stack of papers. 'These are my case notes. I managed to grab them before everything related to my investigation was shredded, including hard evidence of misbehaviour by certain people in our government.'

'May I make copies?'

Berglund grinned, 'As many as you like, my dear. Technically they no longer exist.'

Angela smiled and took the bundle out to Gloria. When she returned James and Lars were deep in a conversation that they abruptly ended on her arrival. 'Anyone might think you were talking about me behind my back.'

'I was telling Lars about Tom Gregory, so in fact we were.'

'I'm never going to live that down,' Angela said.

'You are not alone, Ms Carter. The insidious nature of these people is to use anyone and anything to get the result they desire.' Berglund shuffled through his papers until he found the item he was looking for. He handed it to Angela. 'Read this.'

She sat back in her chair and concentrated on the translated text. When she finished, she said, 'How come this is in English?'

'Because I was working with an English investigator who was also discredited. You see, we have all suffered at the hands of these people.'

'But I believed that Tom Gregory was innocent. I then spent a lot of time collecting evidence for his appeal and used the fact the officer in charge of the investigation was corrupt.'

'Is it possible to speak to that officer?'

'He was murdered by an unknown assailant the day before he was to be discharged from prison.' James looked at his sister. 'Around that time, we discovered the connection to human trafficking of Tom Gregory's father. We hoped to question him, but…'

'So, he too can no longer answer your questions. I put it to both of you. Whatever action you take that exposes one of theirs, that person will be dead within days. That is how deep this goes.'

'There are two men who offer their services to recover trafficked individuals at the cost of their families. What of them?'

'As far as I know the few men involved with this activity have experience and skill in the taking of life. They act first and talk later. This is the only language our traffickers fear.' Berglund sipped at his tea. 'Whereas we, as officers of the law, must follow the rules. This person of interest who has just been arrested?'

'Shit,' James said, reached for his phone and messaged Mickey.

'You are probably too late. Unless your person of interest has specialist skills, he is probably already sleeping with the fishes.' Berglund growled softly. 'I have terminal cancer and have nothing to lose, DCI Carter. Tell me what you need to know, and I will be of as much help to you as I can.'

52

The aircraft landed hard, and several passengers let out a gasp before feeling the G forces of reverse thrust, and it began its sedate taxi to the terminal.

'Geez, Bib, I've had softer landings under fire in Afghanistan.'

Bib laughed, 'At least we're on the ground and still alive.'

The call to first and business class passengers to depart the plane followed, and the pair grabbed their bags from the overheads. They'd brought no other luggage, intending their visit to be short and the first indication of a problem, was Bib spotting the gaunt figure of Dragomir Kosanović lurking around the immigration desks.

'See that, Bub?'

'Looks like we're done for, before we even get out of the airport.'

'Watch and learn, my friend.' Bib sidled up to a fellow passenger, rested his hand on the man's shoulder and said, 'Hello. Please excuse me, but do you know of any good restaurants in Sarajevo?'

The man stopped walking and became thoughtful. A moment later he collapsed to the deck of the Aero bridge.

Bib immediately dropped to one knee and appeared to

administer first aid, while the stunned disembarking passengers all milled about in shock. He saw Kosanović heading their way and signalled to Bub to keep his head down and blend with the flood from economy crowding down the bridge. As the mass of passengers enveloped them, they both moved smoothly and broke from the line only when Kosanović was well behind them and making his own attempts to look useful about the fallen passenger.

Bib signalled to Bub, who followed his partner into a public toilet facility. They each occupied a vacant trap and waited in silence. After about one hour Bib whispered, 'By now I hope Uncle Draggy will believe we were not on the plane.'

'How will we know?'

'Trust me. Dragomir is not that bright, but if he thinks we were not on the plane, despite the manifest, he will be trawling through the security videos and his computer systems looking for a reason.' He stood and opened the door of the trap. 'Put this on.' He handed Bub a lanyard that identified each of them as airport facility workers. 'I get these made up for every trip. They are by no means perfect but it's amazing what you can get away with a smattering of confidence.'

They stepped into the concourse, split up and made their way separately to a door labelled SAMO OSOBLJE (STAFF ONLY) in Croatian. Once through the door, they linked up again and followed the exit signs to leave the building.

'Now we clear the airport complex and start moving our arses,' Bib murmured.

A gate with a drop-down boom was an obvious choice, and they flipped their lanyards then walked through the pedestrian access alongside the boom.

The guard poked his head out of his cubby, shouted

something in Croat and Bib answered like a local. The guard laughed and went back to whatever he was looking at on his computer.

'First rule, Bub. Show nerves and they'll ping you in seconds.'

Bub knew exactly what he meant. Sometimes the only way to get through a checkpoint was to casually flash an ID of some kind and continue walking as if it was something you did every day. It had got him out of trouble many times.

They followed the signs to the staff car park and Bub found a nondescript vehicle they could use. Within seconds it was open, and once he'd jump started it, the petrol gauge showed more than enough for their needs.

***

'The body of well-known celebrity real estate agent, Pericles Dubois, was found by a worker, in a drainage pond on Great Eastern Highway, early this morning. Police are calling for witnesses or drivers with dash cams who may be able to shed some light on his death. Mr Pericles was last seen yesterday morning by federal police officers who had taken him into custody, in respect to ongoing enquiries into undisclosed matters.'

Mickey Krakauer killed the radio and headed to his boss's office. He knocked on the door.

'Come in Mick… I take it you've heard the news.'

'Didn't take long did it,' Mickey said.

'Did he seem nervous?'

'Nah, cool as. He did close his office and stayed inside with the door locked after I left, but I don't know how unusual that might be.'

'Think it might be connected with Karla Kosanovich?'

'I stuck out like a sore thumb in that hood, boss. It felt really creepy.'

'Think your visit might have triggered something?'

'Like what. All I asked him was if he had seen any unusual activity in the area.'

'Why?'

The last thing Mickey needed was to spill the beans over Mandy's illegal bug. That might happen anyway but by then they would be well clear of any investigation. 'Because I wanted to get up close and personal with him to try to find out what makes him tick.'

'Was it worth the effort?'

'Not really he's just big money, and he's on Mandy's list of low-level perpetrators, like many of the ratbags we let through the last time.'

'Think you can run Karla to ground and find out what her connection with him is?'

'I'll give it a go but all we have, so far, is that she's a cleaner who worked for Clarkie and the Rehab centre.'

'But she also knew Dubois and now he's dead.'

Mickey stood. 'I'll knock on her door, perhaps you might talk to the commish about a sneaky warrant?'

James smiled as Mickey pulled the door shut on leaving.

He went directly to Mandy's desk. She wasn't there and leaving a note would be a little over the top.

***

Clarke Shipton walked to the door of the temple and pressed the video entrance bell.

A voice responded 'Namaste, please state your business.'

'My daughter Kaitlin is here for rehab. I'd like to review her progress and speak to your head man.'

'One moment, sir.'

Shipton waited for several moments and his agitation when the door opened was obvious. He was about to blurt something rude, when the pretty young girl who opened the door smiled. 'Please follow me sir.'

He followed her to a small sparsely furnished room and took the seat she offered him. She then joined her hands together, said, 'Namaste,' and left him alone.

Shipton wasn't used to being left to his own devices and she hadn't even offered him a coffee while he waited. As it happened, he didn't have to wait long.

'Good morning, Mr Shipton. Siddhartha, we have met.'

Shipton stared at the tall skinny monk and said, 'Then you will remember my daughter?'

'She has come on very well. In fact, all three of the girls have improved considerably.' He indicated that Shipton should follow him and led him to a door with a viewing pane. He slid the cover aside, said, 'They cannot see you and I'd rather they had more time, but look.'

Shipton peered through the pane and saw Kaitlin sat on an old-fashioned bean bag with a book in her hands and her friends close by. He watched as she calmly flipped pages to continue her reading and felt his eyes moisten. 'How long?'

Siddhartha said, 'As long as it takes, there is no fixed limit.' A small bell rang; the three girls stood as one and moved to an area on the opposite side of the room.

There appeared to be no one supervising them when they dropped cross-legged onto a thin mat and placed the palms of their hands together. Their faces then took on a uniform look of peace and they began to chant.

'As you can see, they have taken to our ways easily. To disturb them at this stage of their recoverance might trigger dark thoughts in their minds. My intention is to clear away the bad they have experienced and allow them to become human again.'

Shipton could hardly believe his eyes, the girl he once knew had changed dramatically from a rebellious teenager to calm and assured. 'She will be able to function normally when your work is complete?'

Siddhartha said nothing but indicated he should follow him to another room like the one he was earlier left waiting in. 'One moment, sir.' He pulled the door shut and a few minutes later it reopened. The pretty girl who opened it was the one who had let Shipton in.

'My name is Marianne. I have been tutoring your daughter in our ways, and I understand you have some questions?'

'I was wondering how long my daughter will remain here?'

'Not long all three are quick to learn and that means perhaps two months might be enough.'

'You don't seem very confident, Marianne.'

'I too experienced addiction.' She held her arms out to show the scarring. 'I was an addict by choice, and I was brought here following a suspected overdose. I was reluctant to change my ways but Siddhartha's care, and that of the other monks, saved me from self-destruction. I owe them my life.' She joined her palms together and bowed.

'You are still here though. Will Kaitlin ever be free to leave?'

'I am here because I choose to return the blessings, and the purity of mind afforded to me. I now enjoy helping other addicts recover. Does that answer your question?'

Shipton asked if he could see his daughter again.

Marianne led him back to the door with the viewing pane and slid the panel open.

He peered through and saw the girls sitting side by side and not moving so much as an eyelash. 'How long do they do this for?'

'As long as it is necessary.'

'And then?'

Marianne pointed through a window to a group of tennis courts where several people of various ages were playing. 'If she wants. There are many other activities also available, but Kaitlin enjoys reading.'

Shipton's phone vibrated. He let the call go.

53

'Have you discovered the family of the third girl.' Lars Berglund asked.

'Not yet,' Angela Carter responded. 'She seems to be something of an enigma. No one with her name appears on any misper lists and we've made it known to police forces around the world. The rehab centre is keeping a tight rein on the girls and maybe she'll slip up and tell them something.'

'Any indication of accents or language traits that might point to her origin.'

'They were all forced to speak in Croatian so that is confusing the issue. Agnetha was easy she had a father who had reported her missing and your Swedish police had given it a go. Poor Bronwyn seems to have no one looking for her.'

'Where are the men who found her?'

'I can't answer that. They simply disappeared after the girls were brought to Perth.'

'Do you know their names?' Lars asked.

'All I have is Recoverance Inc. That is the name they operate under, and they are very secretive.'

'Pity. If I knew more, I have some connections who might be able to track them down.'

Angela picked up her phone and called Mickey Krakauer.

He answered brightly with, 'Hey Angela.'

'How much do you know of Recoverance Inc?'

'Nothing.'

'But you have been in contact with them, I know that.'

'Look, Ms Carter, I made a pledge that I would keep their information a secret. They can't do their job while everyone knows who they are. I think they travel on fake papers and only carry cash to avoid being traced.'

'I have you on speaker and have Lars Berglund with me. He is from Sweden and was involved with the investigation into the disappearance of Agnetha. He has been through the same difficulties with authority that have burdened you.'

'So?'

'So, he has asked me if I can tell him who Bib and Bub are. I've said I don't know. He wants to pick their brains about Bronwyn. No one seems to have reported her missing so she's in Limbo and you're our only hope.'

'Clarke Shipton might be your best bet. He signed papers with them and paid for their services.'

'Thank you, Mickey,' the voice was male with a European accent.

'Mr Berglund?'

'Yes?'

'I don't know who you are, but any security slip ups could put Bib and Bub in more danger than they already are on these recoverance operations. There is also a mole in the network who is tipping off the traffickers.'

'I fully understand Mickey. The last thing I want to do is make things more difficult, I have connections who might be able to track down Bronwyn's family, but to do that I would need information about Bib and Bub.'

'Tell you what, Mr Berglund. Contact Clarke Shipton, Angela has his details. If he can't help you, then neither can I.'

The line went dead. Angela dialled Shipton's number and was directed to his voicemail. 'We can go to his office it isn't far from here.'

Berglund stood. 'Let's go.'

The walk to Shipton's office was barely five minutes in duration and Kelly greeted Angela.

'Ms Carter, what can I do for you today?'

'Mr Shipton?'

'Clarkie's out at the moment. I can take a message and get him to call you.'

'Kelly, this is Lars Berglund from Sweden. We're in the process of establishing the identity of the girls. Obviously, Mr Shipton's daughter is confirmed, and Mr Berglund has confirmed Agnetha's parentage, but we are struggling with Bronwyn. Lars needs to contact the men who rescued them. He thinks they might be able to shed some light on her identity.'

'Haven't a clue about Bib and Bub. Clarkie might but I'll have to ask him when he gets back. They did sort of swear him to secrecy, so…'

'Thanks for your help, Kelly. If Mr Shipton can contact Ms Carter, then that will be good otherwise we will need to fall back on what we have.' Lars Berglund reached out and shook Kelly's hand. 'She is the only one we can't confirm. Such a pity if her family cannot be found.'

'Look, perhaps I'm being a bit overblown here. Wait.' Kelly entered Shipton's office and returned with a manilla folder. 'This is all we have.'

Berglund opened the file and saw the name Major Ashton-O'Sullivan pencilled into the margin of one of the papers it held. 'May I?' Kelly said and he snapped the words with his phone. 'I know this man. Thank you.'

They left while Kelly returned the file to Shipton's office.

On the way back to Angela's practice Berglund said. 'Well, well, David Ashton-O'Sullivan. Good man but lethal to be around.'

Angela turned her head sharply.

'If you are against him.' Berglund added.

'So, what now?'

'Knowing it's David's team won't help. He runs a tight ship, and we'll have no way of tracking them after Perth.'

'So, Bronwyn will have to come up with a memory of her own that we can use.'

'Not quite, you never know what my friends might turn up.'

***

Mickey thought long and hard about the conversation with Angela and Lars Berglund as he drove to his home.

Jackie was there to welcome him with a kiss and pulled back when she sensed tension. 'Something wrong?'

'Like you mean more wrong than usual?'

'You seem stressed out, it's not like you.'

'That third kid, Bronwyn. No one can find who she is. Unless she can come up with something of her own, she'll be alone for the rest of her life.'

'What can you do?'

'Break a promise and hope I don't wreck it for everyone.' He slumped onto the lounge and keyed a number into his phone. The call rang out, so he tried again with the same result. 'Three more times he said. Then wait an hour.' He set his phone time and said, 'What's for tucker, girl?'

Jacky grinned. 'What's your favourite?'

Mickey looked at the elapsed time and said, 'Think I can do you justice in under an hour.'

'I'll turn the oven down, then.'

Mickey's timer beeped and he kissed his wife-to-be on the lips. 'Have to make a call.'

'Don't take too long or dinner will be ruined.'

Mickey tapped in the number from the photo of the card Bib had given him.

'Sergeant Krakauer?'

'Mr Bib?'

'What can I do for you, Mickey.'

'We're trying to track down Bronwyn's parents, but no one's reported her missing. There's a Swedish bloke poking around who was asking about Bib and Bub.'

'Name?'

'Lars Berglund.'

'Ah Berglund, he got kicked out of the Swedish police for using muscle over mind. I'd regard him with caution.'

'Where are you now.'

'Sorry mate.'

'Okay, I guess that's it then.'

'Yup. Agnetha and Bronwyn were a collateral find that caused us some angst.'

'This Berglund bloke says he's working with Agnetha's dad.'

'That might be possible, but first. Could you get a photograph of Bronwyn and send it to the Consul General in Mumbai. He's Steven Colins and don't forget to put the AC after his name or you'll piss him off. Ask him if he recognises her. If that draws a blank, then I can't help you further.'

'Thanks, Bib. I'll get on to it now.'

***

'Interesting,' Bib said as he dropped the burner through the grating of a street drain and gave a satisfied smile when he heard it plop into the water below.

'Who was that.'

'That Aussie copper. Mickey Krakauer. He still had the burner number.'

Bub rocked his head and said, 'Ah.'

'No more though, and we have some work to do.' Bib pointed to a flashing neon sign a couple of hundred metres up the road. 'Home for a very short while my friend.'

'There are a few places that the junkies hang around, but you can bet they'll be harder to work with than the last batch.' He handed Bib a map of Sarajevo and pointed to the areas he'd shaded in colour. 'We'll need to downmarket a bit, boss.'

'I think we can manage that.' A few minutes later they arrived at a seamy hotel entrance and Bib banged on the counter bell.

The female receptionist appeared from behind a beaded curtain and said in Croatian, 'We don't cater to gays.'

Bib responded with a bundle of US dollars and said, 'Who said we were gay?'

'Two men together, they always are.'

'Is there enough there for two rooms?'

The woman counted the dollars and reached out for more.

Bib grabbed her hand and pulled her towards him. 'You have our reservation sort it.'

She glanced over his body as if to check if he was armed before saying, 'Name.'

With the registration out of the way she blushed and handed him the keys. 'I'm sorry but you know how it is. Reputation is everything.'

Bib glanced around the seedy lobby and responded, 'But not the occasional coat of paint, I guess.'

54

Mickey Krakauer was astounded how quickly the reply from the Mumbai consulate came. He'd always believed that civil servants generally took their time over everything.

Dear Sgt Krakauer,

Thank you so much for contacting me. The girl, Bronwyn, in the photograph you sent, might be an ex-colleague's daughter, Jessica Barnes. Even so, it would be difficult to be sure because she will have aged considerably. Where is she staying?

I will forward details of this message to my ex-colleague, Sam Barnes, who will make contact with you, to arrange a meeting with the girl for confirmation of her identity.

Yours sincerely
Steven Colins AC
Australian Consul General
Mumbai

He forwarded the email to Angela with the comment:

What do you think?

Angela rang him immediately it arrived, her response underwhelming. 'Lars is going to try to talk to her. He thinks she might open up with the right questions.'

'If the Mumbai consul's ex mate is here, I think he might carry more clout than a blow-in ex-cop.'

'I guess the more the merrier, but I gather Bib and Bub seemed to believe things at the consulate weren't crash hot. Frank, the pilot, mentioned some incriminating photos that seem to have mysteriously slithered from the public eye.'

'Incriminating who?'

'He didn't say.'

'So, you think the consul might be protecting someone?'

'Your guess is as good as mine.'

'Then, this colleague might also be sus. When are you planning to take Berglund to the rehab?'

'First thing in the morning. I'll call the monk and let him know we're coming. Do you want to join us, informally of course?'

'Done.'

***

Bib and Bub parked their kit in their rooms and met in the hotel bar.

'From the moment we leave this dump we speak only in Croatian.'

They walked out onto the street. 'I'll head that way,' Bub said.

Bib patted him on the shoulder, headed in the opposite direction and tapped his finger on the only number in his contacts list. The text message said "test." A moment later a thumb up emoji appeared. From now on they would be lone operators, and the only communication would be via text through their matched burners. Bib had already scoped out a few places where he knew addicts would be found and he was within fifteen minutes of the first.

Bub was taking a route past the brothel where they found the girls and decided to check if it was still operating. He stepped to the bottom of the small stair and pressed the doorbell.

A voice answered in Croatian. 'State your business.'

'Is this where I'll find Mary Božić?'

'Who?'

'Mary Božić?'

'Not one of our girls.'

'Sorry.'

The door lock buzzed. 'You come in and look. Maybe another takes your fancy.'

Bub couldn't believe his luck but immediately went on his guard. As far as he knew the two who were running the show before, were now out of circulation, but it paid to be alert. Nothing much had changed. The workers still looked and behaved like children and the groping hands of their bloated clients churned his stomach. He glanced around to see no faces he could recognise. 'Sorry my preference is for older women.'

The man laughed. 'If you wait long enough, they'll all be old.'

Bub thanked him and left. He knew that most would never make sixteen and a dog would sniff out their bones in a forest somewhere. He forced the thought from his mind and continued his walk with so many regrets that his present undertaking could be of no help to them.

Bib and he had divided the city into two areas, and they each agreed to work their way through the doss houses and dens. They'd allowed only twenty-four hours to complete their task, and they were confident that between them they would find Shukla's child quickly. She might be slightly darker skinned than most of those trafficked but by the time the drugs had done their work she'd probably be an old woman, anyway. He turned into an alleyway that was a known haunt and saw a group huddled around a glowing fire built of an old car tyre and other debris. As he approached one or two looked up. They seemed oblivious to his presence but when his phone buzzed, it was enough to galvanise them to action. Phones were valuable. A lanky individual stood.

'Why are you here?'

'I lost my way.' Bub checked the faces in the fire light, and none were Shukla's daughter. He'd turned to walk away when the lanky one made his move.

A hand tightening on his jacket was enough motivation, and the last thing the lanky one would have felt was the heat of the fire before his head burst inside the flaming tyre.

None of the junkies moved they just sat there open-mouthed as their colleague continued barbecuing and Bub backed away. He reached a gap in the alley and as he turned to step into it, he glanced back to see them ripping into the fallen hero's pockets.

Bub felt a vibration and reached for his phone. It was a message from Bib.

> Sorry, duty has called, you're on your own.
>
> 4B2

Bub recognised the code his friend had used and knew he was now truly alone. 'Thanks, Bib,' he murmured and cocked his head half listening for a helicopter disappearing into the night.

A moment later another text arrived it was GPS coordinates, and a hurriedly taken phone pic of what looked like a comatose young girl with an Indian appearance. She was surrounded by other addicts sleeping rough and the message ended with, "Don't leave it too long!!!"

Bub made his way back to the sleazy hotel and checked his kit. Bib had put an additional bag with his things. He grabbed it and then hurried in the direction of the GPS coordinates.

Without Bib he would be at greater risk, but he was sure that Dragomir Kosanović had never seen him. Kosanović was primarily an old adversary of Bib and providing he could raise the girl's awareness enough to board the aircraft, she'd be on her way home to her family within hours.

Anjali was alone and still slumped in her heroin coma when he arrived. It seemed that most of her cohort had left to find their next fix, and Bub dropped to one knee to check her vitals. He'd seen all of her symptoms before, via his own daughter's addiction, and that presented a major problem. He would be required to treat her with limited medical knowledge, and a hospital ED was not an option.

Thankfully Bib had provided him with everything he thought might be needed, including three naltrexone nasal spray containers. They were his only resort. He had no idea how much to administer but anything was better than nothing. He read the pack and used the directions to lay Anjali on her back before inserting the nozzle of a spray into one of her nostrils. Then he followed the remainder of the instructions.

Nothing. *How long should it take? I have two more single-use packs. Some notes might have helped Bib.*

He turned her into the recovery position and waited. Several minutes later he noticed her eyelashes flicker. The instructions recommended seeking emergency medical support but that had already been rejected as an option.

Anjali moaned.

'Shit or bust,' Bub said and gave her a second shot.

Her eyes opened and she looked around with a panicked expression. 'What the…?' she spoke in Croation.

He answered in Croation, 'You're going home to your dad, Anjali.'

'Who?'

'Can you stand, with help?' he offered his hand.

She took it.

'I have a hotel room, it's not much but you can get cleaned up before we head to the aircraft.'

There was virtually no response from Anjali, but she followed obediently. It was only then he realised she probably thought of him as a punter who might be offering to pay for her next fix.

There was no one in the hotel reception when they arrived, so he rushed the still dazed girl to his room and gave her a shot from the last nasal spray. That seemed to do the trick. He pointed her at the bathroom and handed her a pack of fresh clothes. The next phase of his rescue could come tumbling down if she decided he was in fact a punter and began making a fuss.

Bub heard the shower start and a few minutes later it stopped. He allowed her time to dry herself and dress in the new items, before knocking on the door.

She opened it and growled in Croation at the crappy clothes he'd provided.

'They'll have to do until we get you home at least you are somewhat presentable. Where's your old outfit?'

She pointed at the bundle on the floor, and he handed her a

plastic bag.

'Pack everything in here and we can dispose of it later.' He opened his bag and removed a chocolate bar.

Anjali snatched it and began stuffing her mouth.

'Hold on, take it easy. There'll be plenty more when we get moving.' He pulled a can of soft drink from the fridge. 'Get this down you. You need to rehydrate yourself.'

Anjali sat on the bed and then, to his surprise, spoke in perfect English. 'Where are the others?'

'Which others?'

'The ones you took before.'

'What were their names?'

'The bitch, Kaitlin, and Agnetha. Where is the one who called herself Bronwyn?'

'Safe in a rehab in Australia.'

Anjali replied with a wry smile. 'Bronwyn isn't her real name it is Jessica Barnes. She was my friend at school. They grabbed us brought us here and made us take the drugs. We thought we were going to die.'

'Who were *they*?'

She looked away and tears trickled from her eyes. 'I can't say they will kill my family.'

Bub handed her a box of tissues.

Eventually she calmed and sniffed, 'Samuel Barnes, an Australian, is Jessica's father. I knew he was in some kind of financial trouble, and he had arranged to sell her to clear his debts. We were together at the time, and they decided taking me would double they're earnings.'

It wasn't quite what her father had said, but Bub tapped a text into his burner, stood and hefted his bag. 'We have a plane to catch, and I have some special drugs to help you recover until we reach our destination.'

Anjali stood and pressed her head against his arm. 'Am I really going home, Mr Bub?'

'I hope so, but we have a few hurdles to get over first. You must do everything I say. Do you understand what heroin withdrawal is?'

'If the drugs were late, we'd feel really sick?'

'Were they often late?'

'Sometimes we waited days but if the place was busy, we'd get them quicker.'

'Okay, if you start feeling the sickness, do not hesitate to tell me.'

55

A meeting had been arranged with Siddhartha who had agreed to allow Bronwyn to answer some simple questions that might lead to the discovery of her parents.

She was looking much better, considering the ordeal she had been through, and sat quietly on the chair that Siddhartha offered. She nodded when he explained why the people had arrived to question her.

'Why are you trying to find my parents?' She spoke English but with a barely noticeable accent.

Angela replied, 'Do you have any memory of your parents?'

Bronwyn shrugged.

'Is your real name Jessica?' Mickey asked.

Berglund and Angela both reacted with shocked expressions.

'Sorry. I just thought it might be better to come to the point.'

Angela reached out and took the girl's hand. 'Does that name mean anything to you?'

'He doesn't want me?'

Angela shook her head. 'Who.'

'My mother died. I never want to see my father again.' Bronwyn's face stiffened. 'He was a pig.'

'A pig, Bronwyn?' Berglund said

'My name is Jessica.'

'And your father worked at the Australian consulate in Mumbai?' Mickey said.

She looked at Siddhartha, her eyes suddenly frantic with fear.

'That is the end of the meeting.' Siddhartha stood and took Jessica's hand. 'I think this person needs more time.' He ushered her from the room and returned a few moments later holding a mobile phone. Siddhartha tapped on the screen and showed the contents to the three.

The message was from Bub it said:

> Do not, under any circumstances, allow Bronwyn's father anywhere near his daughter. His name is Sam Barnes. She is Jessica Barnes. If he finds out where she is, she will be in great danger and so might the other girls.

Mickey felt a cold shiver run down his spine. 'Didn't expect that.' He tapped James' number on his phone and, when he answered, gave him the update.

'Shit. This is far worse than I expected. I'm calling Arty. Stand by.'

***

Anjali was fully compliant and alert during the taxi drive to the airport. She didn't say much but it seemed to Bub that she was stressed about meeting her family again. He handed her a package 'This is your Indian passport and ticket home. Your father and mother are looking forward to seeing you again.'

'When they know what I have been doing, they will throw me out onto the streets.'

'They know what you have been doing, and they have promised

to help you regain your self-respect. I've met your father, and he seems completely genuine.'

'You do not know Indian families. I am sullied and I no longer have a future.' She pointed to herself and blurted, 'What boy in his right mind will marry a filthy prostitute!'

Her outburst was the first sign that things might not go as smoothly as Bub had hoped. 'Marriage isn't everything. You can take that from me. My daughter is just out of prison and she want's nothing more to do with me.' He sensed Anjali's face turn towards him.

'Why? Did you rape her?'

Shocked at her use of words he shook his head and said, 'No. I only tried to help her get over her drug problem.'

'Was she taken like me?'

'No. She drifted into drugs because she was a bit of a rebel, and I wasn't there to be her father.'

'Your wife?'

'My job took me away for long periods…'

'And she found someone else?'

Bub flinched when he felt Anjali's hand rest on his.

She looked into his eyes and said, 'I think you are a good man, Mr Bub… but look, here is the airport.'

The touch of Anjali's hand had sent a shiver down his spine, and he pulled his away. She'd become practiced at entertaining men of his age and the thought of her coming on to him, even unintentionally, made him feel physically sick.

The taxi halted at the entrance to the terminal, Bub paid the driver in enthusiastically received US dollars, then he led Anjali to the check-in desk. 'Remember to use your proper name if anyone asks you.' The moment he stopped speaking he froze.

He felt Anjali's hand tighten around his. 'That man…'

They'd both seen Kosanović at the same time.

'Don't turn to face him,' Bub said. 'He doesn't know me, and with any luck we can be on the plane before he guesses who we are.'

Anjali kept her face down and shuffled towards the business-class check-in desk. Even though they were travelling at a prestige level, the queue seemed to be moving at an excruciatingly slow pace. At last, they passed through, and Bub escorted her to the lounge whilst keeping her face away from the line of sight of Kosanović.

'He is an evil man, Mr Bub. They all called him Uncle Draggy.'

'Did he…?'

Anjali made like she was going to vomit.

Bub rested his hand on her shoulder. 'Soon be over.' He led her into the business class lounge and escorted her to a place in the corner that seemed private. Although Bub knew that privacy was at a premium, he also knew there would be subtly placed cameras everywhere. 'Keep your head down and your face away from other passengers. We'll be called for boarding soon, and hopefully that will be it.'

Anjali followed his instructions to the letter and to anyone watching them she would seem like a timid introverted child travelling with an overbearing uncle.

They didn't see Kosanović again, and when boarding was called, they mingled with the other business class passengers heading to their allocated seats on the aircraft.

Bub breathed a sigh, and Anjali smiled sweetly as she accepted a glass of orange juice from the flight attendant. They'd done it. They were on their way. It had been almost too easy.

***

DCI James Carter ordered an immediate BOLO (be on the look-out) for anyone fitting the description of Sam Barnes. It was probably a hopeless order but sometimes, just sometimes. He also called

Siddhartha and advised that Bronwyn was believed to be Jessica Barnes who was taken by traffickers in Mumbai along with another school friend.

Siddhartha responded calmly. 'Her name is not important. We are committed to taking care of her DCI Carter. Please do not worry yourself.'

James couldn't help being concerned. He'd almost lost his own kids and now he was on the verge of closing down a cabal of what could only be considered devils. 'We believe her father is Sam Barnes. He may try to take her.'

'Thank you, DCI Carter. She will be safe in our custody.'

There was little more James could say, and he scanned the list that Mandy had given him. One name stood out. He had recently retired from politics and had left the country, apparently, to enable his family recover from the stresses and strains of his portfolio. He stood and headed to Mandy's workstation. When he arrived, she quickly killed her screen and turned to face him.

'DCI Carter. What can I do for you, sir.'

James held out the list and pointed to the recently retired attorney general's name. 'How deep?'

Mandy cleared her throat. 'I had him at light… No, a stern warning level…' She fired up her screen again. 'But…'

James canned the list of connections and the swathe of video thumbnails that Mandy had collected since the trafficking cabal had been discovered. He pointed to the first thumbnail.

Mandy clicked on it and a video commenced. The ex-AG was easily recognisable as he walked into what looked like a fancy bedroom, with a young woman. 'He likes them young. This one was only fourteen at the time, but you'd never guess from the makeup and couture.' The video continued with the ex-AG pulling the girl into an embrace. 'It gets worse. Wanna continue?'

James declined. 'I've seen enough. Maybe if it ever gets to court…'

'Well, that might be a problem. He's currently at an unknown destination. At least for the time being.'

'Also, it doesn't prove he is involved with the trafficking, does it?'

Mandy selected another thumbnail. This one depicted the ex-AG in the company of a gaunt-looking man in a dark suit. 'The Dracula type is believed to be Dragomir Kosanović. He is an official with the Bosnian security services. I believe one of the last people to see Pericles Dubois alive was Karla Kosanovich. Perhaps it's a coincidence but Mickey believes she's been passing information about the Bib and Bub extraction. They are not available to confirm that, but someone was.'

'We'll need to pull in Karla.'

'Can I do anything?'

'Right now, I'd like to keep you out of this as far as possible. I'll fix up a warrant to search the address Mickey found her at. If that doesn't turn anything up, I might need your help. A question of keeping something in our back pocket, just in case.'

'Just give me a hoy and I'll send what I can. Meanwhile I'll do some more pottering.'

James headed back to his office and prepared a warrant to check out Karla's address. He then contacted Mickey and asked if he'd like to be in on the raid.

'Bloody oath, Boss. When?'

'I've fixed up a warrant and we should be ready to go in a couple of hours.'

56

Halfway through the flight Anjali became restless and began to twitch and scratch at her arms.

Bub recognised her distress and reached into his cabin bag. He found the Suboxone films explained how to use them and gave her one. 'This should help with the withdrawal symptoms.' As a precaution he removed Amrita's prescription from the pack and inserted it in his travel wallet.

She accepted the film without question and her angst soon dissipated. 'Thank you, Mr Bub.'

After the other girls, Bub was feeling confused. Anjali seemed completely at one with her situation. She seemed to understand that she had been made into an addict, and she wanted to rid herself of its curse. 'Can I ask you something?' he said.

Anjali nodded.

'The other girls were difficult to deal with most of the time, but you seem to be coping well with your situation. Why are you so different?'

Anjali said nothing for a while then she turned and said, 'May I have a drink of water?'

Bub pressed the call button, and a young flight attendant appeared at his shoulder. 'Can I have some water for…' He didn't finish, because he recognised her as Fiona from the earlier flight.

'Certainly, Mr Clayton.' Fiona said before she headed towards the galley and returned with a small plastic bottle and a glass. She gave them to Anjali and dropped to Bub's side to smile excitedly. 'I didn't expect to see you again, but I'm so glad you're on this flight. I found our Beattie, told her about the conversation we had, and I got the impression it wasn't her intent to be rude to you.' Fiona frowned. 'She'd just left the jail and when she tried to call you… Need I say more?'

'What else did she say?'

Fiona stood. 'You'll have to ask her when you see her.' She scribbled something on serviette and handed it to him. 'This is her present address and phone number. She can't say how long she'll be there, so I wouldn't leave it too long. I've arranged to meet her when I'm next in Perth. Is there anything you'd like me to pass on?'

Bub felt a sudden surge of wellbeing. He thought he'd lost his daughter again, but it might still be exactly that. His first priority was to return Anjali to her family and there was still an obstacle course to negotiate before that happened.

'Thanks, Fiona. If you see her, before I get the chance, would you give her my love.'

Fiona left to attend to her other passengers and Bub rested his head back, to close his eyes and try to remember how things were in better times.

His reverie was shattered when Anjali said, 'Who is Beattie?'

'My daughter.' He smiled. 'It looks like everything is going to be fine.'

'I'm glad, Mr Bub. Why did she call you Mr Clayton.'

'Bub is a special name I use when I'm helping people like you.'

The answer seemed to satisfy Anjali, and she slumped into a

deep sleep.

Bub dozed a little too, and soon the descent was announced. He nudged Anjali but received no response. He now had a problem. She'd slipped into a coma-like state, and he had no choice but to call for help.

Fiona was first to arrive, but the plane was close to touching down and there nothing anyone could do. As soon as they were on the tarmac, he texted a message to Shukla.

> Anjali is home. Please provide urgent
> medical assistance at the airport.
> Recoverance Inc

He hoped Shukla would pull strings to speed things up and he wasn't wrong. Before the aircraft had reached the terminal, a small convoy with an ambulance was ready and waiting to whisk her away.

***

Mickey was in the lead vehicle that pulled into Karla Kosanovich's driveway. Despite several loud knocks, there was no sign of anyone being home and he instructed his team to break down the door.

They could smell Karla's fate before they found her mutilated body. There was no evidence of forced entry, but the house had been ransacked by someone presumably known to her.

Mickey called in the crime scene and requested urgent forensics. James Carter pulled out all the stops and arrived with a team within thirty minutes. 'Looks like someone didn't want us asking Karla and Dubois questions in case they inadvertently spilled the beans. Waddya reckon Mick?'

'I agree. Every time we start getting near to these people

deaths occur. Usually, the very people we need to speak to.'

DCI Carter ordered a complete CCTV search of all cameras in the area. 'If it upsets anyone, tellem to call the commissioner.'

As he scanned around the room where Karla's body was found, Mickey noticed a small brown button stuck to the bottom corner of a mirror. It was identical to the one he'd attached to Dubois' desk. He tapped Mandy's number and waited.

'Mickey, what can I do for you?'

'That little bug you gave me. Are there many around?' He heard a giggle.

'I've only ever had two and I gave you one.'

'Would you know if that one had been moved?'

'Why?'

'I think I've found one in Karla's house.' He heard a rustle followed by the clicking of fingers on a keyboard.

'Ha! Same one. Someone must have found it and moved it.'

'Is it working?'

'Something's happening, and I can hear you guys talking among yourselves.'

'Has it been recording?'

'Let me check. Wait, someone has just come in. Can I call you back?'

'No probs.' Mickey found James and showed him the bug. 'I know I was out of order, boss, but I stuck one like it under Dubois' desk. Mandy thinks its defo the same one and she's now checking her recordings.'

'Sergeant Stephenson might have a few questions to answer, and now you've let the cat out of the bag we'll need to be very careful how we handle anything else that she finds.'

'There was no intent to gather formal evidence, boss, but we were getting close to a stalemate.'

'And you know how these things are.'

Mickey's phone buzzed. He checked the message. It was from Mandy:

Call me, ASAP.

He showed the text to James. 'I think she might have found something.'

'Come with me.' James ordered the crew to continue their search and led Mickey through the door to his car. 'Get in.'

Neither spoke during the journey to the HQ and James said nothing as Mickey followed him to Mandy's desk.

'Shit!' she exclaimed when they both approached. She stood and glowered at Mickey.

'Sit down sergeant,' James said.

His voice carried an edge, and she obeyed his order without further response.

'Show me what you have.'

Mandy glared at Mickey before she tapped on her touch pad and an icon appeared on her screen. She then tapped on the icon, and an audio visualising program appeared. 'I know I was in the wrong but...' Mandy tapped again, and voices emerged from the computer's speakers.

All three listened to the contents before James said, 'Stop. Go back.'

Mandy moved the cursor along the visualisation and tapped start.

'Again.'

She repeated the action.

'Was it just me, or was there a name mentioned?'

Mickey shrugged.

Mandy handed James a set of headphones. 'Try these.' She stood and offered him her chair.

James put the headphones on, dropped onto the seat and played the audio back several times. 'Definitely a name. Does, Lars Berglund, mean anything to either of you?'

They both nodded.

'Ex-cop from Sweden. That was the name, and Karla seemed to be on friendly terms with him. Listen again. Can this be played back a bit slower?'

Mandy pressed a key. 'Twennie percent so the voices will sound a bit weird.'

This time the audio came from the speakers. The voices were that of Karla Kosanovich and someone else.

'They are on to us, Lars.'

'You maybe, but not me. You should have done what was expected of you, Karla.'

'Pawel is out of the way. What more could I do?'

'You should not have drawn attention to yourself. It is such a pity.'

The next sound was like a dog about to vomit followed by a sound like someone thrashing around.

'I think that sound at the end are the last words of Karla Kosanovich.' James called his sister's office and pressed the speaker option.

'She's out with Mr Berglund, DCI Carter. I don't know when she'll be back, she didn't say.'

'Did you get that Mick?'

'Thanks, Mands.'

His boss caught up to him as he pushed open the door. 'Look,

Mick. You might have been technically wrong, but we need to get to my sister before Berglund gets his way.' There were no more attempts at subtlety when the top lights and sirens started. 'Any ideas, Mick?'

'Maybe the Rehab. Berglund wanted to speak with Agnetha who he believes is the daughter of Byquist. Byquist was arrested by the Swedish police after he shot an assailant. We have a second suspect, Sam Barnes, who we believe is Bronwyn's father. He was employed at the Australian Consulate in Mumbai when Bronwyn—slash—Jessica went missing.'

'And Sam Barnes is also on our wanted list.'

57

Bub accompanied Anjali to the Hospital where Shukla was anxiously waiting, with his wife. Anjali was whisked into the ED and Shukla followed leaving Bub to provide support for Mrs Shukla. 'He is understandably fearful,' he said.

'Very, Mr Bub.'

'You can call me Robert.' He shook her hand and said, 'I don't think I'll be doing much more of this. My partner has been called away. Bob's the name I go by, and I now have my own family to look after.'

Mrs Shuklasaid, 'Thank you so much for safely bringing back Anjali, you may call me Anjala. Do you have children, Mr Robert?'

'A daughter, Beatrice. She's had a few dramas, and my next stop will be to help her get her life back to normal.'

'Shukla tells me Anjali was forced into taking the drug called heroin.'

'She was doing well but...'

He didn't get to finish when Shukla pushed through the doors of the waiting area. He was beaming and reached out for his wife. 'She is well, but she will need some time. Come my dear they say we can see her now.' He ignored Clayton and drew his wife by the hand, back through the door from whence he came.

Bob Clayton checked his passport and ticket and made his way to the exit. He hailed a taxi and said, 'Airport.' He'd done his job. Shukla had paid his bill, and his daughter was home with her family. His work as Mr Bub was now at an end, Beatrice was his now only priority, and he felt her tugging at him.

His ticket allowed flexibility, and he was soon sitting in the business class lounge awaiting an adjoining flight, via Singapore, to Perth, his current hometown. Bob Clayton was originally from Sydney, but he'd amassed many friends in Perth from his time in the SAS. He pondered how good it would be, to be able to walk along a street again without the need for eyes in the back of his head.

He'd helped himself to a large scotch in a glass of ice and was wondering how he might be received by his daughter, when a loud voice drew his attention.

It was Shukla and he was demanding to be allowed entry to see a friend.

Clayton walked over to the reception area where he was hauled into an embrace by the man who had given him the cold shoulder only a short while earlier.

'I am so sorry if I appeared rude, Mr Clayton.' He released the man he'd previously only known as Bub. 'I cannot thank you enough. Please give my kindest regards to Mr Bib and accept this as a small token of my utmost appreciation.' He handed bub a brown paper package.

'How is Anjali?'

'She is well, and the medical people tell me her strength of mind will help her more than anything. I understand that her friend has been found too. That girl will be in great danger. My intelligence tells me that she was sold into this evil slavery, by her father, to cover gambling debts. The people who pursue this trade lurk in the highest levels of governments, Mr Bub, and they must be brought to justice.'

'I'm not sure what I can do about that, Mr Shukla.'

Shukla smiled. 'I think you do my friend. Next time you are in my country please call me.' He gripped Bub's hand and shook it fiercely, before turning about and marching from the lounge reception.

Bub returned to his seat and saw a smiling face. It was Fiona. She was wearing a pair of jeans, a tee-shirt, and trainers, but little makeup and her hair was hanging loosely over her shoulders. He almost didn't recognise her. 'How come…?'

'I knew where you were going and, as a freelance contractor, I opted to return too.' She picked from a selection of hors d'oeuvres on the small plate on the table in front of her, popped one into her mouth and washed it down with a sip from her glass of chilled white wine. 'I've messaged Beattie. She's meeting us at Perth Airport.'

Bob Clayton shivered, suddenly he was feeling scared. He was close to meeting his daughter again, but worse, he was beginning to feel a growing affection for her friend, around twenty years younger than himself, and he wasn't sure of the righteousness of it.

'Don't look so worried, Bob. I'm not planning to jump your bones. Not yet anyway.' She blinked her eyes, and her face cracked into the cheeky smile that first drew his attention to her.

Pity, he thought, and as he took a sip of his whiskey, he wondered what had gone so wrong for Bib and Amrita.

***

There were two cars in the parking area of the Temple building. One was Angela's the other was a hire vehicle. 'She's here James said,' and stepped from the car while the others followed. He ran to the main entrance and almost collided with Siddhartha who was bleeding profusely from what appeared to be a bullet wound.

'They are all safe...' Siddhartha slumped to the ground and Mickey called an ambulance before dropping to one knee to check his vitals.

'I think he'll live boss,' Mickey called as he drew his Glock and tentatively eased in through the door. A trail of blood across the floor led to where the action had occurred and he yelled, 'We'll need armed response and forensics, boss.'

James called in the request for assistance while Mandy made Siddhartha comfortable with pain killers and a field dressing from the car first aid kit.

'Can you say what happened?' she asked.

'Two men...' he coughed up some blood. 'The first claimed he was Jessica's father. He demanded we let him see his daughter.' he coughed again, clearly struggling to speak. 'He threatened me and my staff but when he drew a gun, I dealt with him.'

'You killed him?'

'He will live. Then the next one arrived with your sister, DCI Carter, and I thought we were safe.'

'Lars Berglund?' James said.

Siddhartha winced.

'My sister?'

'She is fine and with the girls.'

'Berglund?'

'He is no longer with us.'

'Where is he?'

Siddhartha shook his head. 'He threatened Ms Carter, and I wasn't quick enough...' he coughed again.

A siren skirled through the trees and an ambulance stopped outside.

James Carter drew his police weapon and waved to the ambos to keep their heads down as he scanned the area. 'We have an unaccounted shooter,' he called, knowing the man could be anywhere and making cover difficult. He'd called for an armed response team but knew it might take a while to assemble. All they could do was attend to those in need and wait. He yelled to Mickey to help provide cover for the ambos so they could reach Siddhartha, and they did so without a shot being fired.

Having placed him on a stretcher they were about to return to their vehicle when a bullet narrowly missed and created a star in a window behind them. They dragged the stretcher back into the building and provided additional aid while they waited.

James Carter then tapped on Kriminalinspektör Kristina Ahlström's number and felt relieved when her dozy voice answered.

'DCI Carter?'

'I'm sorry if I awakened you.'

'No problem. Have you met with Lars yet?'

'How well do you know him?'

'Only from my time in the police. Why?'

'He is right at this moment, in the process of taking pot shots at me and my colleagues.'

'Please hold.'

The line fell silent along with the voice of Kriminalinspektör

Kristina Ahlström.

James almost threw his phone across the entrance foyer but stopped when he heard a tinny voice emanating from it.'

'This is my boss, DCI Carter. He would like to speak with you.'

James sucked in a frustrated breath and waited.

'I am Kriminalkommissarie Andersson, DCI Carter. There seems to have been a misunderstanding.'

'I'm inclined to think that might be an understatement, Andersson. We were led to believe Lars Berglund was collaborating with us on the behalf of the Swedish police, but it seems more like he has declared war on us.'

'Yes. This is very bad news, and you must do what you must. Regrettably this is now out of my hands.'

'I understand Daniel Byquist was arrested after shooting an assailant. His daughter was taken by a cabal of international traffickers sponsored by the Russian mafia. She has since been rescued with two other girls and brough to Australia, where we had her safely ensconced in a secure rehabilitation unit. That is until Berglund began shooting at people.'

There was a long silence with a faint background of whispering voices.

'Hello?'

'Hello, yes, we are still here DCI Carter. Kristina wishes to speak.'

A rustling occurred as the phone changed hands. 'I am so sorry DCI Carter. I was completely misinformed about Berglund. But I am pleased to inform you that Agnetha's father will be given the opportunity to speak with his daughter via Zoom. If he can identify her to the satisfaction of our legal system, then maybe we can make positive moves towards their reunion.'

The phone fell silent again before Kriminalkommissarie Andersson spoke. 'I have set the wheels in motion DCI Carter and Kriminalinspektör Ahlström will be your contact. I hope we can resolve this quickly and bring this unfortunate family together again soon.'

James listened open-mouthed. *Am I hearing this correctly.* 'When will this communication channel be available?'

Kristina answered. 'The boss has said he will put in a priority request when he arrives at the office. It should be actioned by the end of today, our time, and ready for a connection as soon as it can be arranged.'

58

For Bob Clayton, the flight to Perth was intensely enjoyable in the company of Fiona. Their conversation was easy, and they seemed to have much in common. While her aura and proximity triggered every emotion and sensation possible within Bob Clayton's body, she gave no indication of it being reciprocated by anything other than her desire to see her friend reunited with her father.

As the flight progressed, she talked of her dream to one day own a small property and keep some horses.

'That was Beatie's long-term goal, too. Then she got trapped in a bad scene, and… Well, you know the rest.'

'We always talked horses at school but then our lives moved on, and here we are… Thank you for the work you have done to free so many girls from those bastard traffickers, Bob.'

'Taking Anjali home will probably be the last. My associate has been called to other duties and the kind of work we did needs a team of more than one.'

'Does that mean you will be having more time for Beattie?'

'I hope so. I'm looking forward to being the dad I could never be before all this happened.'

'That'll take a bit of getting used to.'

'I'm prepared to give it a go.'

'I was thinking more about Beattie.'

'So was I.' The pilot announced the descent, and he felt Fiona's hand close over his. The feeling was different to that of Anjali and though this time he wanted to respond he was frightened of scaring her off.

'Nearly there, Bob. Are you ready for this?'

'I'm not sure. You're not going to run away and leave me with her, are you?'

She lifted her hand from his and placed it on his neck, just long enough to hold him still while she leaned over to plant a kiss on his lips. 'Not on your life.' The aircraft wheels hit the tarmac, and the rumble of reverse thrust cut in to slow it down. 'We're home.'

Bob Clayton swallowed hard. He could handle life-threatening danger with ease, but what was happening now had his nerves jangling as if he were a recruit on his first op.

Fiona felt his tension. 'She'll be right mate,' she said, as the aircraft rolled to a halt. Then the aero bridge moved into place, the doors opened and the announcement of first and business class passengers to disembark, cackled over the PA.

Clayton followed Fiona along the aisle to the exit where he sucked in a deep breath of clean air, in the hope of kicking off what might be a new life. Then, with immigration and customs out of the way, there was nothing more to do but step out into the inevitable. He reached into his right pocket and palmed his garrotte. He switched the weapon to his other hand and tentatively slipped his left arm around Fiona's waist.

She felt his move and turned with a smile on her face.

As she did Clayton flipped the weapon into the bin they were passing and breathed out, more with relief that the killing was over, than anything else.

Fiona reached down to cover his hand with her own. 'There she is. Oh, gosh,' she said pointing to the sallow black-eyed figure waving to them from the crowd.

***

The mood at the rehab grew tense as more random rounds were fired from the surrounding bush. James Carter puzzled over the pointlessness of their assailant's actions. He couldn't possibly have enough ammunition for a prolonged attack, and every shot was one less in his inventory. His ears pricked at the sound of distant sirens, and he relaxed a little. He'd found Angela, who was safe, and he showed his surprise at how cool she'd remained throughout the events.

'What's the worst that can happen, Jim. The girls are safe we've discovered their parents, and your armed squad will soon hand Mr Berglund his comeuppance. Mickey's taken care of Sam Barnes and has him in cuffs. He's refusing to talk to anyone about his actions, but we know his daughter will be capable of giving evidence. She's already informed me that he sold her to the traffickers for the relief of a gambling debt, some dad. Hey?'

James looked out of the window to see an armoured police vehicle rolling up the driveway, 'You'd better take cover, sis. Get down as low as you can and wait for the all-clear.' James gave a nod to Mickey, who left Barnes where he lay, and joined him.

Mandy had taken up a position with the three girls and was deep in conversation with them.

The siren stopped and a bunch of black clad individuals disembarked from the armoured vehicle. Their leader saw James and called, 'Where is he?'

'We don't know,' James said. 'He's in the bushland somewhere. He keeps letting us know by firing random shots in our general direction.'

The men surrounded the building and a few seconds after they deployed a shot was followed by a terse obscenity and several more shots.

'Got him!' A voice yelled.

Several minutes later two of the squad dragged what appeared to be a body from the bush and lay it on the ground. 'Is this him the leader said?'

James signalled his assent, and Berglund was bundled into the paddy wagon that followed the squad. 'Look after him he has a lot to answer for.'

Sam Barnes had the luxury of his own conveyance, and he too was transported to the delights of the lock up. It was beginning to look like the end of a perfect day when Mickey's phone rang.

'Sergeant Krakauer.'

'Bib left me your number. He wanted to thank you for all your help.'

'Who is this?'

'You know me as the other half of Recoverance Inc. Bob Clayton AKA Bub. Our partnership has served its purpose and has been dissolved amicably. That means I'm likely to be in Perth for the foreseeable future. So, if I can help you with anything, please call me on this number.'

Before Bub could hang up Mickey said. 'You couldn't have rung at a better time. We have two suspects in relation to the trafficking. Lars Berglund and Sam Barnes. They have just been taken into custody.'

'Thanks Mickey, like I said, I'm here if you need me but I have a couple of personal matters to attend to first. Let's keep in touch.'

***

Bob Clayton pressed end, tapped on his screen and turned back to the two women who'd been tightly embracing each other, while he'd made the call to Mickey. 'Well, Beats, do you have a home to go to, or…'

Fiona blurted, 'I have a small apartment, Bob. I'm sure I can squeeze Beatie in for a while until she finds her feet.'

'I've a better idea.' He held up his phone to show the picture of a rather splendid looking beachside residence. 'Air BNB. It's ours for at least six weeks, if we choose, but we'll need to decide now.' He held his finger above his phone screen and looked at the two faces smiling in his direction.

Fiona yelled, 'Yes!'

Beattie growled, 'No!'

Bob said, 'Shit!' and was about to swipe his screen when Beattie reached out and stayed his hand.

'I was only joking, Dad. Yes! Yes! Yes!'

'Thank dog for that, I've had enough of sleeping rough.' He tapped his screen, raised his hand, and the next cab in line stopped. 'Here please.' He showed the taxi driver the address on his phone, threw Fiona's bag, and his own, into the boot and opened the rear door before clambering into the front next to the driver.

Bob was expecting the shock of seeing his daughter for the first time in many months. He wasn't disappointed. She appeared gaunt and had aged considerably since he'd last seen her in the eastern states jail. He dropped the passenger visor and flicked open the vanity mirror so that he could watch them.

They were so obviously good friends and when Beattie smiled, she seemed to shed all the years and memories of her troubled times. He knew she wasn't out of the woods and that it would take a while but with Fiona's help, maybe, just maybe.

Fiona looked directly into his eyes, smiled tightly as though concerned but countered it with a thumb up signal.

'We'll need to sort Beattie out with some clothes as soon as poss,' he said.

'We'll go shopping tomorrow, Bob. While you kick up your heels and maybe do a bit of surfing. That okay with you, Beats?'

Beattie dabbed at her eyes with a tissue. 'I'm so sorry, Dad.'

Fiona drew her friend into a gentle hug and glanced back at the face in the mirror. 'She'll be right mate,' she mouthed.

59

Berglund and Barnes were checked over by the medical officer before being patched up and assigned their cells. The next few days would be tricky. So far, the entire operation had been a furtive off the books affair and now the time had come to formalise things. James Carter knocked on the door of Athur Bertram's office.

'Come.'

He found Arty sitting behind his desk, surrounded by a chatty group of police officers of various ranks who fell silent the moment he entered.

'Welcome DCI Carter. I am sure these chaps would like to hear what you have to say about your work over the last few weeks.'

James walked to an area to the side of the group, reached into his inside Jacket pocket, withdrew a standard police notebook and said, 'As you might understand, the very nature of my recent work has required the maximum secrecy.' From the rear of the book, he removed a number of sheets of folded paper and held them up for those present to see. 'These are the names of those who will be coming under close investigation in the next few days. Sadly, I can see some of them sitting right here within this group...'

Bertram stood to interrupt him. 'And this, gentlemen, is your opportunity to come clean before… I'll say no more for now. You all know why you are here and there is no hiding place.' He stood. 'Dismissed.'

The group shuffled in their seats. Some looking about shocked, others in wide-eyed protest, as they stood to leave.

None spoke but their faces froze when Arty added. 'Twenty-four-hours should be enough. Do you agree DCI Carter?'

'Written statements will be acceptable for starters and given our list of witnesses grows daily there is every possibility that any one of you might seek to redeem themself. Whatever, assisting in the closure of a major international criminal human trafficking cabal is our goal and twenty-four-hours should be more than enough.' He returned to the door and opened it for them to leave.

'You think the word redeem was a good idea, Jim.'

'I thought it was a better word than, snitch, but we'll know soon enough. Meanwhile we have three girls in recovery at the rehab and two directly connected suspects who have already attempted to take lethal action against them.'

'Are the girls ready to talk?'

'Siddhartha the monk who runs the show, had a connection with Recoverance Inc. He was injured in the recent attack but is highly protective of the girls. Mickey Krakauer has a direct connection with the one known as Bub, AKA former SAS sergeant Robert Clayton, who is now back in Perth and has offered his support.'

'How soon can we get started?'

'Mick says Clayton has some personal business to attend to, so I guess he is the sticking point.'

'Think you can get Mick to lean on him?'

'I can only try, sir.'

***

The taxi pulled into a neat driveway and a woman who looked to be in her fifties waved. Clayton left the women in the car while he discussed the brief tenancy, handed over some cash, and collected the keys. 'All sorted,' he said when he returned and opened the boot to collect their bags.

Fiona and Beattie followed him to the main entrance, and he pushed open the door to expose an immaculate entrance hall with a small ornate stand upon which rested a sheaf of papers. 'She said everything we need to know is in here.' He picked up the papers and headed for the similarly spotless kitchen.

Beattie's eyes goggled as she took in the opulence.

Fiona groaned. 'Might be a bit posh for us, what do you think, Beats?'

Clayton said, 'I think we give it a bash,' and laughed. 'Supposed to be five bedrooms so we should all get a good night's sleep, somewhere. Why don't you two have a poke around and make your selection, while I make us all a cuppa.'

Fiona picked up her bag and took Beattie by the hand. 'Yeah, come on, it'll be fun.'

Beattie's face suddenly crumpled with pain, and she began to sweat profusely.

'Shit, withdrawal still?'

'I'm so sorry. I...'

He reached into his bag, withdrew one of the Suboxone films and handed it to her. 'This seemed to work for some friends of mine.' He explained what she needed to do and said, 'As soon as we get settled, I'll get you on a program that will purge the crap out of your system for good.' He pulled his daughter into a hug and looked across at Fiona.

Fiona said, 'Perhaps I should leave you two alone. I *do* have my own place and...'

Beattie reached out and grabbed her. 'No way. I can't do this without you, Fi.' The Suboxone began to kick in and the two made their way up the staircase.

Bob Clayton filled the shiny chrome kettle with water and found some tea bags and cups. The fridge was stocked with fresh bread and milk, and the walk-in pantry held several packets of biscuits and breakfast cereals. He wished there were beers, *maybe tomorrow*.

While he waited for the kettle to boil, he glanced down at his phone and saw the text from Mickey Krakauer:

> Sorry to intrude Bob, any chance of a couple of hours
> of your time? I realise you have things to do but I can
> come to you if it helps.

Bob put his phone to one side, poured the boiling water over tea bags and called to the women upstairs. He waited with bated breath and relaxed when he heard their foot fall on the stairs.

'All sorted, Bob.' Fiona said. 'And we'll each have a nice view of the beach.'

Though Beattie had partially recovered from her withdrawal, she still seemed fatigued, and her dullness manifested itself in her voice when she said, 'Would anyone mind if I had an early night.' She picked up a cup, sipped on its contents and grabbed a couple of biscuits from the plate which she took to the small breakfast table.

'As it happens, I need to speak with someone. He reckons he'll need a couple of hours of my time. If that's okay with both of you?'

'My biological clock could do with a correction too,' Fiona said.

'That's it then. I'll text this bloke and set it up.' He tapped in a text to Mickey and pasted in the address of the property. 'Done.'

***

It was around seven pm when Mickey knocked on the door of the BnB. He was accompanied by Jackie who'd insisted that they took a bottle of wine for Bub and some flowers for his daughter.

She was a little disappointed when Bob Clayton escorted them into the lounge area and said that both women were totally buggered and had decided to get an early night.

'Well then, I'll put these in some water, and she can have them tomorrow.'

'Mick, good to see you again, thanks for the grog I was hanging out and there is not a drop in the place. I'll grab some glasses.' He followed Jackie into the kitchen and found something that might work as a vase. Then he said, 'You a cop too?'

'Ha! Fat chance of that. I was, but ten years in the slammer sort of puts the hierarchy off.'

'Prison?'

'I was framed, but I've just been pardoned. Mickey was my saviour and we're getting married as soon as this all blows over.'

'Then we'll need to move quickly.'

They returned to the lounge and Jackie curled up next to Mickey while Bob opened the wine and filled their glasses.

'Right, Mick, you have my full attention.'

'We have a problem in as much as we need to get the three girls to spill the beans on the traffickers. The crims obviously don't want that to happen and there has already been attempts on the girls' lives. First by three characters that turned up the day after they arrived. Then a guy from Sweden who claimed he had a connection to Agnetha's Father. And another, Sam Barnes, who claimed he was Bronwyn's dad.'

Bob Clayton took a sip of his wine and said, 'I didn't put my neck on the block to bring them home, only to have someone succeed with a hit on them.'

'I thought you might see it that way but as cops we're just a smidgeon hamstrung by the rules.'

Bob smirked. 'You reckon I'm above the law?'

'Not quite, Bob. This is a massive trafficking operation that has been protected by senior cops and certain people who make the laws. If we are to crack this, we'll need to gather evidence to knock at least one of them down to set off a domino run. Statements from the girls will help, but a confession from a trafficker complete with named names would really put the icing on the cake.'

'Sam Barnes is alleged to have sold his kid to save his neck over gambling debts.

Mickey said, 'He isn't talking, and neither is Lars Berglund. We have them both in custody…'

'And…?'

'I have an idea, but I'll need to clear it with my boss.'

'Go ahead.'

'As far as I know, Berglund and Barnes don't know you. Both people who were acting as moles were dealing with someone called Kosanović. They have been dealt with by unknown suspects, and we can't ask them any questions because they have been eliminated.'

'Okay,' Clayton said.

'I suspect that Berglund knows something which is why he was on a plane within hours of discovering Agnetha was safe. Barnes must have met someone in India in order to prove his worth as a father by flogging his only child to a criminal franchise, and he too suddenly appeared on the scene. My guess is that they are under pressure to keep their mouths shut.'

'You have them all nicely locked up Mickey so there's not much I can do as an ex-soldier turned civvy.'

Mickey grinned. 'Bit defeatist for a trafficker, mate. There aren't too many blokes who could do what you and Bib did, across international borders too. Little old Perth will seem like a doddle.'

Clayton nodded slowly as though he'd twigged what Mickey was thinking. 'What about my daughter and her friend? They'll need protection.'

'I'll still need to square that with the boss.' He stood. 'Robert Clayton, I'm arresting you on the charge of human trafficking, you have the right to remain silent…'

Jackie almost snorted her wine down her nose as he spoke.

When the spiel was finished, Clayton pushed his hands out in front, and smirked. 'Not too tight, Sergeant Krakauer I have delicate wrists.'

60

Eyes rolled when Mickey led Clayton into the lock up and within minutes his phone squawked. 'Boss?'

'What the fuck's going on, Mick. Is it true you've arrested Bob Clayton?'

'Um… I need to talk to you about that, boss. Have you got a minute?'

'My office… Now!'

Mickey pressed the lift call button and waited. By the time it arrived several people had gathered around him, and he was squashed to the rear of the car. The rise to James Carter's office would only take a few seconds but it was long enough to catch a furtive mumble.

'They've just arrested that SAS Bloke, Clayton. Trafficker apparently.'

'Shit.' Another voice muttered.

'He must know summat.'

The lift arrived at his floor and Mickey smirked as he ignored the speakers to push through the group and the door. Without looking back, he turned immediate right and knuckled the door that was once Birchmore's.

'Come in Mickey.'

Mickey opened the door with a grin on his face.

'Close it and sit.'

He did as he was instructed, and Jim Carter raised his eyebrows as if asking a question.

'That has to be the fastest bit of scuttlebutt ever, Boss.'

'Well, even I got the word within microseconds of your arrival, so what the hell is happening.'

Mickey placed his police ID on the desk and slid it towards his boss. 'Save you askin when you've heard what I have to say.'

'Go on.'

'Bob Clayton has been arrested on a charge of human trafficking, and he has agreed to use his particular skills to assist us.'

'But how will he do that if he's in our lock up?'

'Aren't Barnes and Berglund in there too?'

'Yes but...'

'And I heard a couple of voices in the lift. The word is already around that we've arrested an actual trafficker.'

'And?'

'Let them stew for twenty-four hours then withdraw the charges for want of evidence. Clayton will pretend to be Berglund and Barnes' friend and saviour, maybe even attract the attention of who knows who.'

'Shit, Mickey. You had no authority to create a sting of this nature.'

'Hey-ho, boss.' He pushed his ID closer to his boss. 'I'm getting married in a couple of weeks, and Jack and I are thinking of setting up with Clark Shipton. He's got some big ideas for funding indigenous projects, and it'll be nice to get back to country and do something useful for my folks.'

'Twenty-four hours?'

Mickey grinned. 'Make sure Clayton and the other two are close enough to speak and I need around the clock protection for Bob's daughter and her friend. Jack is with them at the moment.' He handed James a card with the address of the Air BnB.

'She isn't even a cop?'

'Yeah, but she was, and some of the folk we're after are. Jack can handle herself and I'll head up there when I've finished here.'

James picked up his desk phone, tapped in a number and said, 'I need a minute of your time, sir.'

Mickey waited until he'd put down the phone, stood and turned to leave.

'Have you forgotten something Sergeant Krakauer?'

Mickey looked down at his boss's hand, reached out, and took possession of his ID.

'The commissioner says to pass on his regards to Jack, he says he's looking forward to the wedding.'

***

Bob Clayton swore loudly as the cell door clanked shut. He'd been in this position before but then it was in an Afghan adobe building. He'd been rendered unconscious in an action and taken prisoner before he could be secured by his patrol.

The next two days were horrendous and punctuated with a vicious interrogation technique. Thankfully his patrol was able to free him but not before he'd learned the harsh realities of capture by a brutal enemy.

He slumped onto his bunk and began mumbling incoherently. He muttered the name, Barnes, and continued his drivel. Then he mumbled, 'The fucking Swede knows too.'

The man in the cell to his left whispered loudly. 'Who're you.'

Clayton responded, 'Fuck off, prick.'

'You'd better watch your mouth, matey.'

'There's an accent. Are you the Swedish prick?' Clayton slurred.

'Sam Barnes. My lawyers'll have me out of here in a couple of hours.'

Clayton laughed. 'Me too, and then… Pop! One less to worry about.' He laughed again. 'And the Swedish prick.' He heard a rustle from the cell on the right.

'I know who you are, and you'll not be hearing a pop, coz you'll be dead.'

'Mr Berglund, I presume?'

'Fuck off.'

'I'm not here for the good of my health, and I have my instructions. Of course… unless I get a better offer. I do nothing for nothing and you two are on borrowed time as it is.'

Both cells fell silent.

He'd given them something to think about with every word being recorded for posterity. 'Good night chaps. See you on the outside, eh.' He pulled up the threadbare blanket and allowed himself to drop into a tactical nap.

He was awakened by Berglund's voice. 'Maybe we can work together.'

'I already have my job. Talk money and maybe you can change that.'

There was no response.

About one hour later the left-hand cell spoke. 'How much?'

'Half a mil could keep one of you alive.'

'Fuck off!' the right-hand cell blurted.

'Suit yourself, now if you two don't mind, I need my beauty sleep. If you saw my lawyer's ass you'd understand why.' Clayton smirked. *We'll see*, he thought. *Nighty night, Beats*. The light in his cell went off and he settled in for an erratic sleep punctuated by the imagined sensations of Fiona's lips working their magic.

***

Angela Carter angrily tapped the end button on the screen of her

378

phone. 'How dare you!' she spat into the empty room. *Shit, it isn't fair, Jim. I could lose everything I've worked for if I do this.* She looked around at her shabby office and gave a cynical laugh, *you've already been from partner to pleb in one throw. You don't have anything Angie Baby.* She stood and walked through to Gloria's office. 'Hey, I'll be out for a while. Nothing you need to worry about, just keep things ticking along as usual.'

'Business or pleasure?'

'I wish I knew.' She returned to her office packed some files into her briefcase, walked out to her car and drove to the police lock up where Berglund, Clayton, and Barnes were languishing. When she arrived, she met two other lawyers who greeted her.

She said, 'I don't know what you are expecting but I'll be seeking the withdrawal of all charges against my client on the grounds of lack of evidence.'

Both solicitors nodded, probably grateful for a lead from someone who was once a junior partner in a city firm.

'Good to see you again Angela, I'm hearing good things about your, ahem, social practice.'

'Eric Kloster, well-well. The last time we met was when we graduated. I see *you've* come up in the world.'

The other lawyer said nothing. He looked like he was still wearing his first ever suit and she glanced over him to check if he still had the price label affixed.

A door opened and sergeant said, 'This way Ms Carter, your client awaits.'

She smirked at the other two and left to join Bob Clayton in the interview room.

He was sitting at a shabby table, with his wrists cuffed, and she took the adjacent seat. 'Shouldn't take a minute Bob. Leave everything to me.'

Clayton said nothing and waited passively for the interviewing officers to arrive.

They were a male and a young female who looked like they might be just out of the academy. The male took the lead and introduced himself and his colleague.

Angela said. 'Can you show me the evidence that was relied upon to arrest my client.'

The two officers looked blankly at each other. The female shook her head slightly just as Angela's phone vibrated.

She glanced at it, stood and said, 'Well thank you kindly but my client has better things to do. Please remove those shackles. My client had no case to answer.'

The male did as he was ordered, and Clayton followed Angela from the room, smirking at the other two who were being escorted for their interviews.

'Told ya,' he said, laughing, as he followed Angela to collect his bits and pieces.

They didn't speak again until she escorted him out of the building and into the car parking area.

'Thanks, Bob,' she said quietly, handing him her card before she left him while she found her car to return to her office.

He hadn't waited long before the doors opened, and Berglund and Barnes appeared. 'Ah, I see you heard the magic words too.' Clayton made a shuffling sign with his fingers then made the shape of a gun with his hand, pointed it at each of them and said POP!

'Wait!' Berglund said. 'I have money. We should talk.'

Clayton looked at Barnes, who said, 'Me too.'

61

Jackie Morton had slept fitfully on the couch in the lounge room of the beachside mansion. Her mind was alert to the possibility of someone following Mickey and waiting until he had left, to cause mischief. She needn't have worried, and she dozed lightly as she waited for the two sleeping women to come to life.

'Who are you?'

Jackie's doze was shattered by an attractive woman in a pink towelling bath robe, who she didn't recognise.

'Where's Bob?' The woman in the pink robe said before Jackie could answer.

'Jaqueline Morton. I was asked to stay and keep an eye on things while…'

'Where is he?'

Jackie pointed to an armchair. 'Grab a seat while I make us a cuppa, then I'll bring you up to date.'

'Coffee, splash of milk and two sugars, please.' The woman in the pink robe slumped into the chair, a look of confusion on her face.

A few minutes later Jackie returned with a mug of tea and another of coffee. 'I checked earlier. Beatrice was sleeping well so the drug Bob gave her must be doing its job. Are you Fiona.'

Fiona winced as she sipped on her coffee.

'Sorry I don't usually do coffee... Anyway, Mr Clayton has been arrested on a charge of international human trafficking. He has a lawyer appointed and hopefully it should all come good.'

'But Bob was helping those girls, why has he been arrested?'

Fiona's felt her phone buzz in the pocket of her robe. 'Bob... What the hell is going on?' ... 'What?' She smashed her finger against the phone screen, looked up at Jackie and said, 'He says he might be some time. He'll call when he can.' She looked around at the room. 'I knew I was expecting too much.'

'Well, at least you have a nice place to stay while you wait.'

Another woman appeared in the doorway, 'Who are you? *Who is this, Fi?*'

Jackie was about to introduce herself when Fiona said, 'Your dad's been arrested on trafficking charges, Beats.'

'But...' Beatie slumped into another chair. 'I've only just got him back.'

For a while, no one spoke, and Jackie was beginning to feel she was a serious intrusion in the lives of the two women she'd only just met. She called Mickey.

'I'm on my way over. I'm nearly there so give me five.'

True to his word a loud knocking made them all look up.

'That'll be Mickey, now.' Jackie went to the front door and opened it. 'Explanations needed Mr Krakauer.'

Mickey followed her into the lounge and said, 'Bob sends his greetings. He is well and what I am to tell you must remain strictly between us.'

'You're a cop you arrested him. Why should we keep your secrets?' Fiona said.

'Because Bob Clayton's life depends on your confidentiality.' He looked each of the women directly in the eye and said, 'He's agreed to help us close down a major international crime group and has been positioned in a temporary undercover role.' He'd barely finished speaking when someone else knocked on the front door.

Jackie led a man in a suit to the room.

He introduced himself, 'Doctor Karolis, I'm here to attend to Ms Beatrice Clayton at her father's request.'

Beattie raised her hands from her lap and shrugged.

'May we have some privacy,' Karolis said.

'It's okay Beatrice,' Mickey said. 'I think he has something that might help make you feel better.'

'I feel fine.'

Mickey shepherded Fiona and Jackie from the room and closed the door. He then led them to the kitchen and said, 'Karolis is a rehab specialist. He's only here to help.'

'What would help, is if we knew what was going on,' Fiona snapped, her cool façade showing signs of heating.

'What is going on, is human trafficking on a large scale that is linked with a stratum of society that is protected from prosecution by those within its group.'

'Shit. I've heard of this, but I thought Bob was only in the recovery business not actively seeking those responsible.' Fiona pulled out a chair from the breakfast table. 'I first met him on a flight to Mumbai. I've known Beattie since school. We talked. I like him. He wants nothing more than his daughter's health and that's why we're here in this beach place.'

'I believe Bob's experience will help us draw out the ringleaders. At least those in Australia. Once that's done, he's all yours,' Mickey grinned. 'If it's any help, he told me enough to make me understand that he too wants it over quickly.'

***

The bar of the Grosvenor Hotel was almost deserted when Bob Clayton ordered a cold middy for himself and the same for Berglund and Barnes. He picked up his drink and walked to a corner table that might provide the degree of privacy needed for their conversation.

Berglund plonked down his beer and said, 'This is too pat.'

'Pat,' Clayton said.

'You know what I mean.'

'Do I?'

'You turn up out of the blue and start demanding money for our safety.'

'Safety from who, Lars.' Clayton picked up his mobile phone and tapped on its screen.

'Who're you calling?' Barnes said.

'No one just checking something. Who are you scared of? I know who I'm being paid by, and I made you an offer. I don't do this shit out of the goodness of my heart, boys.' He handed them each a drink mat and said, 'Each of you write down the name of your handler and where I can find him. Then, when you pay me the money, I'll see that they no longer bother you. We all know what we're dealing with here so don't fuck me around or I'll take my current deal, and you'll cease to be a bother for me. Capisce?'

Barnes shot a glance at Berglund who wrote a name on his mat.

'He is in Sweden. How will you get to him?'

Clayton tapped the side of his nose with his finger.

Barnes followed suit.

Bob Clayton sculled his drink, picked up the mats, and stood. 'Meet here same place tomorrow around noon. Bringa da money, I don't take credit cards or cheques.'

'How do we know we can trust you?'

'How long do you want to live?' Clayton walked out, hailed a taxi, gave the driver the address, and phoned Mickey as it moved off.

'How'd it go?'

'Meeting them again tomorrow, at the Grosvenor. They'll either bring a bag of cash each, or something will go down that might just give us an in.' He read out the two names. 'Recognise them?'

'Partly. One's a freakin billionaire who lives in Perth, the Swedish name means nothing. I'll ask Jim Carter to follow that up, he has a contact in Sweden. The last thing we need is to tip them off that we're onto them and that we have potential witnesses to their crimes.'

'Okay, so I'm heading off to see my daughter and her friend. I trust you have no problems with that.'

'Karolis has seen Beatrice and will be providing support with her habit. They were a bit miffed when I told them we'd hijacked your services.'

Clayton laughed. 'Hardly surprising, but I'll sort things out.'

'My mobile number.' Mickey spelled it out. 'Call me if you sense anything might be kicking off.'

'If I need to.' Clayton pressed end.

***

There seemed little point in dealing with Kristina given her boss, Kommissarie Andersson, was fully aware of the situation. He looked at his watch, it was two am. He tapped in the number Andersson had given him and pressed record.

'Kriminalkommissarie Andersson.'

'DCI James Carter, we spoke recently about Lars Berglund…'

'Yoh, that is correct. What can I help you with.'

James paused.

'Carter?'

'I have a name for you, but...'

'You do not trust me, yah?'

'Berglund went gaga with a gun and was arrested. We thought he was on our side. So... Maybe you might agree with us in respect to our level of trust.'

'We had a big turnover in policing two years ago, DCI Carter. Several members of the force left under what you might call a cloud. We know of at least two members of the Riksdag, who also came under suspicion at that time but there has never been any evidence to take it further. If you have a name and we can confirm some details, then...'

'The name I have is Ulf Engblom. Does that ring any bells?'

'Oh yah, but not in connection with any trafficking investigations.'

'So?'

'So yah, Mr Engblom *is* a member of our Riksdag who has come to our attention in respect to a number of matters. The Riksdag is our parliament, and, like most democratic law-making establishments, it has certain rules. Mr Engblom seems to sail close to the wind but there has never been enough to take the matters beyond speculation.'

'He must have connections perhaps, if you are already looking into his affairs, there might be a list of connections, and we might compare notes.'

'I will look into it, DCI Carter. If there is anything at all, I will let you know. Thank you for calling.'

The call was ended at the other end and James began doubting his wisdom. He rang Kristina who answered immediately.

'James, hello.'

'I've just spoken to Kommissarie Andersson.'

'Okay.'

'I gave him a name, and now I'm having doubts.'

'I understand, but he is a good man who will respect your confidence.'

'It is critical that the named person is not tipped off that we know of him.'

'Of course. You needn't worry. He's just asked me to get a specific list of names for you, and they will be on the way shortly. Have a nice day, James.'

62

With an agonising wait for the list to arrive and two nutters on the loose with access to firearms. Carter called Clayton.

Fiona answered the mobile and said, 'He's just taking a shower. Shouldn't be long.' She put the phone down and he heard her shout, 'Phone for you, Bob.'

It seemed like an eternity, but Clayton eventually picked up.

'At last. James Carter, Bob. Mickey tells me you're meeting up with Berglund and Barnes today.'

'Yep, about noon.'

'Expecting any trouble?'

'I'm expecting two bags filled with unmarked notes. If not, I've promised them they won't see the night out.'

'Shit.'

'Don't worry, Jim, no one is going to get hurt in public. Have you checked out those names?'

'In progress. I'm expecting a contact list from Sweden any time, and if that connects with anyone on our list here, we'll start making moves. What if they don't turn up?'

'I cloned their phones while we were in the pub, so I know exactly where they are… Right now, they are together. Probably plotting my demise.'

'Doesn't that worry you?'

Clayton laughed. 'If they were pros, it might. I'm about to get in a car. Can we talk later.' The call ended.

***

'G'day Bob.' Mickey switched his phone to loud, so Jackie could hear what was going on while she drove him to work.

'I've just had DCI Carter on the phone. It's not the way I work, Mick. Too many people on the team and… well, you know.'

'I needed to update him so we could get some surveillance on the money man. That's now in place so we'll know if either of our friends call him or pay him a visit. The target is a major player in state politics who provides high-level funding for political parties, so he expects a return on his investment.'

'Yeah, mate, I know who the money man is, but it will only take one of your people to slip up and it's my neck on the block. Until I have moved to the next phase, I'll be incommunicado.'

The call ended and Mickey turned to Jackie.

'No good lookin at me, lover boy.'

'Shit. So close.'

'I reckon Bob Clayton'll come good, Mick. He got those girls home, didn't he. He's used to operating alone or in a small team. Chill and give the bloke some space. Jackie grinned. 'I remember a certain bloke, not a million miles from here, who put a bullet through another bloke's knee then calmly changed the barrel of his gun to confuse the evidence. If that bloke hadn't done what he did back then, we might be pushing up spinifex in a shallow bush grave.' She reached out and rested her hand on his thigh. 'Chill,' she said again. 'Trust Bob, he has an especially good reason to make this work.'

'I hope you're right.'

Jackie drove into the car park and stopped to allow him out.

'Plannin anythin today?' he said as he opened his door.

'Nah, just a bit of this and a bit of that, you know. See yas.'

Mickey made directly for the lift and pressed the number for James Carter's floor. This time the lift was unoccupied and when he knocked on his door, there was no reply. Mickey nudged it open and peeked inside. The room was empty, so he headed in the direction of the Cyber division.

Except for a couple of heads bobbing behind their cube farm walls, it too was deserted. He approached one of the heads and said, 'What's going on? Where is everyone?'

The operator said, 'Dunno bit of a stink, someone said. Then they came in and escorted a whole load of people away. I just kept my head down.'

'Mandy Stephenson?'

'She wasn't in today, dunno why.'

Mickey found Mandy's station. Her desk was tidy, and her computer was missing. *I hope that's a good thing*, he thought, and he was heading to the carpark before he remembered that Jackie had his car for the day. 'Shit, Bob,' He murmured, and headed to his own desk.

He'd no sooner sat when his phone buzzed. It was a text from an unknown number.

> Keep out of this or you might as
> well cancel your wedding plans.

His first thought was, whoever Clayton was after, had Jack. He tried Bob Clayton's number and received a message saying it was unavailable. Mickey ran to the main road and flagged down a taxi. He showed him his police ID and gave his address.

'Things happening, mate?' the driver said.

'Why do you ask?' Mickey replied.

He pointed to the car radio. 'Your mob's pulled in Crommelin

Bolin for questioning.'

'*The* Crommelin Bolin?' Mickey said.

'How many are there? It's been all over the news. He's spittin dummies everywhere and y'can bet the tills will be ringin, in all the silks' chambers.'

Crommelin Bolin must have been the name Bob Clayton alluded to. *Jim Carter wouldn't have moved if he had no evidence. Where the fuck are you, Bob?'*

The driver pulled over at the end of Mickey's short driveway. 'Twennie bucks, mate. Wanna receipt?'

Mickey shook his head and paid the man. There was no car on the drive, so he walked cautiously to the door and remembered the time that Angela Carter was saved from the worst of a bomb blast by the heavy-duty door on her house. He skirted the front and pushed open the small gate to the rear. The back door was locked, and the telltale was still intact. He breathed a sigh of relief and pushed in the key. The door opened easily, and a quick check told him nothing was out of place. He remembered Jacky rolling her eyes when he suggested the thin strip of clear tape over the back door lock. '*We* never come in that way,' he'd said, 'and we only ever lock it from the inside.'

'Where are you, Jack?' He tried James Carter's mobile. There was no answer. He rang his land line and Stacey answered. 'Have you heard from Jim?'

'I wasn't expecting to. Is something wrong?'

'No everything is fine, but his mobile isn't answering.'

'Big news about that billionaire. It's all over the news.'

'Bolin?'

'That's what they said.'

'Maybe that's why he's gone offline. Ask him to call me if he contacts you.'

'No worries, Mickey. How's Jackie doing with the wedding plans?'

'She's getting there. Thanks, Stace.' He pressed end knowing the text message he'd received might be coming to fruition and he had to find her before it did. He found Jackie's old bike, jammed her helmet on his head, and began pedalling in the direction of Clark Shipton's office. If anyone could help him find her, Clarkie would be the one.

'It's all happening, Mick.' Kelly Coulson said as he burst in through the door.

'If you mean, it's gotten out of control, Kell, yeah. Is Clarkie in?'

She picked up her phone and pressed a key. 'Mickey Krakauer's here.'

Shipton's door opened. 'Come in Mick. Your mob have started kicking arse at last. Well-done.'

'I think they've got Jack again. She's not answering her phone, and I've had a threat.' He showed Shipton the text message.'

'I know that number.' Shipton pulled out his phone and flipped through his contact list. 'Here we go. It's a burner but I know whose burner it is.' He wrote a name and an address on a sticky note. 'That's where she'll be, mate. Need any help?'

'I want her back in one piece.'

'Then we'd better get going.' Shipton pulled a jacket from a hook on the back of his door. 'We'll be out for a while Kell.' He stopped as if an afterthought had struck him, reached into the bottom drawer of his desk and pulled out an ancient automatic. 'Might not be fancy but it's loaded, and it shoots.'

'That a Colt 45?'

'Don't ask, Mick.' He shoved the weapon in the back of his waistband. 'We might not need it. It's just insurance.'

'Looks more like a random 45 to me, just like the one that probably sorted Birchmore.'

'Look…'

'I'm lookin Clarkie. If I'm thinkin what you're thinkin. It'd be better if you left that behind, you know…'

Shipton said, 'Maybe you're right.' He dropped the pistol back in the drawer.

'Right about what, Clarkie?'

'Fuck, you're a good bloke for a black fella, Mickey Krakauer. Anyone ever tell you that.'

Mickey raised his eyebrows and pointed to the drawer. 'I don't ever want to see that again.'

'New leaf, eh?'

'Let's go.'

63

Bob Clayton parked his vehicle two streets away from where he was heading. He'd scanned the google map of the area and scoped a route through the buildings. He slipped in through the front door of a shop and out the other end. He stood to one side and faced the wall, reached out and tapped a random number on a keypad on the apartment building opposite. His luck held and the door buzzed open. *Anyone watching CCTV will need to work much harder to catch Bob Clayton.* He checked his phone and noticed an alleyway that would take him on a convoluted tour to the underground car park of the address he was heading. Then he scooted through the building he was in, to leave by a service entrance at its rear.

He'd picked up the vibe about Bolin and it had set him back in his planning. Jim Carter should have waited, now his target was hypersensitive and that could make things messy.

Every bay in the car park was taken which made it relatively easy to move through without being seen but he kept a low profile and a subtle eye on the location of cameras. Ahead of him were the glass doors of an elevator lobby containing a row of stainless-steel doors awaiting their travellers. Clayton scanned the area for cameras again and was about to make his move when a low-slung Lamborghini stopped between him and the door. He waited for the vehicle to disgorge its occupants and froze.

Clark Shipton was struggling to his feet from the driver's side and Mickey Krakauer grunted and groaned as he clambered out of the passenger door and rushed around to give him a hand. 'You need to get a more practical vehicle, Clarkie. It might be fast, but it takes forever to get out when you get to where you're goin.''

What the hell's going on? Clayton thought as he waited until they called a lift and positioned himself to see which floor showed up on the telltale when it arrived at its destination. It was no guarantee, but it gave him a good idea. He was right, the floor the lift stopped at was number fifteen. The legal chambers that occupied the floor had an anecdotal connection with human trafficking. Though nothing substantial had ever come to light. They were also a part of Bolin's legal kit.

Clayton had called ahead to make an appointment with one of the partners. He'd met him when overseas on a previous op and the man remembered him. They knew of his financial status and had almost bent over backwards to see him about representing him in a potential action involving Beatrice. Now his own fishing trip had been compromised by the arrival of Mickey and Shipton.

Clayton found the fire stairs and easily jogged up the fifteen floors. Doing it the hard way would provide the disconnect with Shipton and Mickey, while giving him the opportunity to observe from a relatively sheltered position.

***

'Clark Shipton, to see Roger Ambrose. He'll know what it's about.'

Mr Ambrose is in a meeting at the moment, sir, I'll take a message and get him to call you.'

Mickey pulled out his police ID and leaned across the desk. 'Sergeant Krakauer. Tell Mr Ambrose he can either meet us now, here in his office, or I will formally arrest him, and we can continue under caution at the station. That should impress your clients. Shouldn't it?'

'One moment, sir.' She pressed a number on her console, gave the appearance of listening, and then said, 'I'm so sorry, Mr Ambrose has left for the day.'

'Where will we find him?'

'I'm sorry, sir, I'm not permitted to share private information...'

Mickey cut her off. 'Your name?'

The woman froze. 'I... I...'

'Think carefully, Ms...' He looked at her name tag, 'M Bergen. You may be aiding and abetting a serious crime with your reluctance to answer my questions.

'It's Molly, Molly Bergen, and I know nothing of Mr Ambrose's business affairs I'm only a receptionist...'

'Who just happened to know he was out of the office but said he was in a meeting.'

'I... I... That's what I'm told to say.'

Mickey felt a degree of sympathy with the woman but according to Clarkie, the text message about Jackie was sent from Ambrose's phone. 'His personal address will do for starters Ms Bergen.'

She rummaged through a notebook she withdrew from the top drawer of her desk. When she found the page, she was looking for, she handed the open book to Mickey.

Mickey smiled inwardly and took a photo of the visible pages. 'Thank you, Ms Bergen, don't leave the state, we're likely to be in touch.'

She cringed as his words penetrated.

***

Molly Bergen felt relieved when the cop and his mate left and she smiled sweetly at the handsome stranger who arrived a few moments later.

'What can I do for you sir?' she beamed.

'Ambrose. I have an appointment with Roger Ambrose.'

'One moment, sir.' This time she was prepared, and she went through the same procedure as with Mickey and Shipton but said, 'I'm sorry, sir. He had an urgent call and needed to leave early.'

'Not good enough. I've come a long way for this meeting. Does he have a secretary or PA?'

'One moment, sir.' She pressed a button on her panel and then sat back in her chair, with a smug smile on her face. Molly Bergen's lips then curled into a smile and her eyebrows rose when the black uniformed team of three arrived behind Clayton.

The tallest of the three said, 'Kindly leave the building sir.'

Bob Clayton turned to see who was speaking. 'You are?'

'We're the practice security team and I won't ask you again.'

'You're right, there, old chap.' He turned back to Molly read her name tag and said, 'Just get Ambrose, Ms Bergen, let's not make a fuss, hey.' He felt a strong hand grip his wrist. 'I see.'

The tallest of the three security men had a name tag that said he was D Colbert, but it was no longer visible when he was face down on the floor and semi-comatose. His companions, named F Burke and J Wills took a step back and adopted a stance they'd probably learned back in the days of their childhood Taekwondo classes.

Clayton smirked. He turned back to Molly and said, 'Please.'

'It's like I told the people earlier He's left for the day.' She glanced across at Burke and Wills in a vain hope they might begin earning their wages.

'They'll be no good to you, Ms Bergen.'

Molly handed Clayton the notebook opened at the page Mickey had photographed and said, 'I gave them this.'

'Thank you, I know that address.' He picked up the notebook, instructed Burke and Wills to handcuff themselves to Colbert and hand him the keys. Then he left the building the same way he came in.

The walk to his car was uneventful but he still took the precaution of a quick check underneath using his iPhone on a long selfie stick. The bad news was the place being used by Ambrose was the building next door to the air BnB currently housing Fiona and Beatie. *I hope they're not connected.*

Clayton didn't waste much time returning to the BnB and when he arrived, he saw the ostentatious Lamborghini parked across their next-door neighbour's driveway.

There was no sign of Mickey or Shipton and that was a worry.

64

The gate to the BnB Driveway was open so Clayton drove directly to the garage and used the remote to open the door. Almost the moment he switched off the engine his phone bleated. It was a text message from Mickey's phone:

> I recognised the place when we arrived
>
> and we're in your lounge room drinking
>
> tea

Clayton smiled and made his way through to the lounge. 'What's happening, Mickey?'

'Nothing. Are you okay? They said you'd gone off grid.'

'I've just been to the place you visited earlier. I think we might have been looking for the same person.'

'Roger Ambrose? He sent a threatening text message.' Mickey showed him the text.

Bob Clayton turned his head in the direction of the neighbouring property. 'You think she might be there?'

Mickey shrugged.

'Okay, Mickey, now I know you are here, I think it's time to play it down. Keep a discrete eye on the place next door. If they think we've pulled back, they will probably do nothing to Jackie. They'll assume she's serving her purpose as a hostage, while they spend their time working out how to permanently stop us.'

'I don't think I like the sound of that, Bob.'

'Mr Shipton. I'd like you to move your car away from the end of the next-door driveway. Park it somewhere safe and then head back to assist Mickey. Meanwhile I have a meeting in Perth that I think might stir things up.' He leaned over and kissed his daughter then the same with Fiona. 'I might be some time,' he said. 'Take care of her for me.'

Beatie looked shocked and Fiona grabbed her hand. 'He'll be right, I know it.'

***

Bob Clayton found his way back to the garage, checked the contents of a small backpack and then headed to the Grosvenor Hotel where he was hoping to find Berglund and Barnes. He did and they were deep in conversation in the car park.

'Sorry, chaps, circumstances have caused me to be running a bit late.' He slipped his hand into his pocket and felt the comfort of a garrotte, in readiness for use, if needed.

As expected, neither man was carrying a bag of cash.

Berglund said, 'There's been a change of plan.'

'Perhaps you will enlighten me,' Clayton said.

Berglund reached into his jacket and withdrew a semi-automatic pistol from somewhere behind his back. He immediately jammed it into the pocket his jacket, presumably to hide it from view, then he pointed its muzzle in Clayton's direction.

'Very melodramatic, Lars. You see that at the movies?'

Barnes used the distraction to take a swing at Clayton who parried his attack swinging the man hard against Berglund. Whose gun fired to send a chunk of Barnes' flesh ripping through his shirt.

'Oops,' Clayton said, before disarming Berglund and pistol whipping him into unconsciousness with the butt of the weapon.

Barnes fell to the ground, whimpering, while Clayton tightened the unconscious Berglund's belt, as a temporary tie around their ankles, as if they were entering the three-legged race in a school carnival. When he'd finished, he called Mickey and told him there were two suspects in the Grosvenor's carpark. 'Tell your people they might not want to leave it too long, one has a serious bullet wound, the other's out cold. I'm outta here for the moment, I'll catch you later.'

His next stop would be his new next-door neighbour's house, but he would be dealing with that aspect alone. He headed back to the BnB, parked two hundred metres away and made his way to the front of the mansion via the dunes, where he could get cover for himself in the rugged bush land that separated the houses from the actual beach. Once he sighted his target destination, he unhitched his pack, extracted a pocket-sized, camouflaged monocular, and hunkered down to wait. He could see movements through the windows, but the time wasn't quite right.

He checked his silenced phone. A text from Mickey confirmed that Berglund and Barnes had been taken into custody again. Both men's injuries were serious enough for hospitalisation and they were being held under guard.

There was no point telling Mickey that Jackie was probably next door. He already knew but was sensible enough to realise that any police operation would almost certainly see Ambrose eliminating the need for a hostage. Clayton's next move would see Jackie freed and Ambrose secured for an arrest by Mickey. Mickey would then make his move, obtaining the necessary warrants for the next stage of the operation.

I'd like to be at Ambrose's office when they're raided, and they find the connections needed to finish Bolin. He unzipped his backpack and checked out the semi he'd used to silence Berglund. It was the same weapon he'd earlier used to shoot up the rehab and the magazine had only five remaining rounds, including the one up the spout. He'd have preferred more, but as he had no intention of getting involved in a shootout, the need was moot. *Suburban gunshots attract all the wrong people and the last thing I need is a bunch of panicking kids, and mums and dads.*

He checked the building through his binoculars. Ambrose was talking on his mobile phone and making aggressive gestures with his free hand, but there was no sign of anyone else. Clayton jacked an earbud into his ear linked the binocular via the Bluetooth app on his phone and aligned the cross hairs with Ambrose's head.

The audio was at best scratchy, but clear enough to confirm the man was under serious duress and making demands, "Your support, Mr Bolin," came over clearly. His phone app would smooth out the audio and record further conversations, while he watched and relaxed until the sun went down. While he waited, he flipped through the pages of the receptionist's notebook.

***

Mickey sighed with frustration when his call to James Carter ended. James had been pleased to be tipped off about Berglund and Barnes but the vagueness of the tip off had left him wanting information that Mickey was unable to release. He'd known James for years and despite the disparity of rank they had remained friends, but their friendship was being sorely tested. Right now, his faith was firmly behind Bob Clayton, a freelancer with no police authority. On top of that, Mandy Stephenson had disappeared from the scene and not even her wife knew where she was.

He tried calling her police issue mobile, but there was no answer. Her personal number also came up a blank. He knew her computer was missing from her desk but that was normal, she did much of her work away from prying eyes. As a last resort he sent a text to both her private and police numbers:

PCM

If she could get to her phone, and didn't understand what he meant, it was just bad luck. Clarkie, Fiona and Beatie were watching a movie. They seemed relaxed enough and he didn't want to disturb them, so he went to hide and stew, in the kitchen. He's no sooner sat when his phone buzzed. It was a text from Mandy's private number:

Can't talk now. I'm Okay, trust me.

It told him nothing he wanted to know except that she was okay. He put the kettle on and yelled, 'Anyone wanna cuppa?'

The ayes had it. Mickey brewed a whole pot and found an unopened carton of Monte Carlos in the pantry. They were Jack's favourite, and it made him feel uncomfortable. He was relying on Bob Clayton, and he hadn't heard anything to say he was on top of things. He pushed open the front door and peered at the house next door but there was nothing happening to confirm she was there or not. There was no sign of Clayton either. The pressure to take a personal involvement was mounting and he texted Bob.

Anything happening, Bob?

He received an almost immediate reply.

I have the place under surveillance and am biding my

time. Stay cool, Mick, there is no indication that she might be in any danger, but you'll be the first to know.

While he felt a degree of relief, Mickey still felt uncomfortable with his lack of control. He sucked in a deep breath and decided to give Clayton one hour.

65

Mandy Stephenson closed the lid of her laptop reclined her seat and closed her eyes. She'd advised her partner, Jean, that she might be away for one or two days on police business and felt bad about the lie. Jean assumed she would be staying in some swanky hotel and had grizzled that she was never allowed to go with her, when in fact she'd be hiding far from prying eyes, working and living in her car.

She'd found the high speed 5G hotspot a few weeks earlier and it enabled her to work, free from police restrictions. Her hacking skills had been put to full use, and she was now directly hooked into the corporate computer networks of Crommelin Bolin's various business enterprises. She knew that everything she did would fail the rules of evidence, but then the people she was up against didn't care about conventions, and they were well and truly compromised in every way.

She closed her eyes briefly and allowed her mind to loosen into the right-brain thinking mode that released her creative juices. She was close to cracking the coded access of Bolin's heavily encrypted private files, but she would only get a tiny window for success before warnings would be triggered, and she'd lose everything she'd gained.

Fifteen minutes later her eyes popped open, and her face cracked with a smile. 'Gottya.' Her fingers began dancing over her keyboard. She copied and pasted her code into a field and pressed Enter.

Syntax error!

'Shit!' She reviewed her copy and sighed, made a minor change and pasted her new attempt.

Enter Password!

That was the easy part. She'd already found an encrypted document that listed all of Bolin's passwords, and it was a simple matter to decrypt it then copy and paste the most likely one. Mandy copied the word "TяafFicLïghT101" and pasted it directly into the field. She smirked when she moved through to the next stage. *Prick. You couldn't resist using a touch of Cyrillic, could you,* she thought as she slipped in a USB Memory stick. Time was of the essence, and she knew that the longer she was in his private world the quicker he would learn of the breach.

What she was about to learn, was that Crommelin Bolin's sticky fingers went far beyond the trafficking of young girls and boys for the pleasure of the world's sexual deviants. There were lists of willing participants and spreadsheets detailing the subsequent blackmail rewards he had gained and that were available for future exploitation.

Major government projects had fallen the way of his companies despite the weakness of the tenders they submitted. The hubris contained in some of the writing made her scalp tingle, but she persevered until she found a file "Dangers.docx".

She opened it and found a list of names with links. Even her own name was present and what frightened her the most was the detail displayed when she clicked on the link. Bolin knew everything about her, from her war experience to her present address and the name of her partner and child.

Mandy was tempted to close the link and go home to protect her family. Then she saw Mickey Krakauer's name. She followed the link and found an even larger dossier, at the end of which was in effect an order to eliminate him at the earliest opportunity. "Suggest Roger Ambrose looks into using a hostage as a lure."

The next line was a note that Ambrose had taken Krakauer's partner and was holding her at his beach side home. It listed the address and continued… "It is a secluded venue in a premier suburb and, should an indigenous person show his face, there would be excellent reasons for a protective response."

The names of a number of police officers who might be relied upon for such a response, followed.

Mandy decided enough was enough. She downloaded the remainder of the files for future reference and saved them into a dark web cloud as a backup, closed the connection, and rang Mickey.

***

'Yes!'

'Mick? Is everything okay?'

'Mandy? What happened, you vanished without trace.'

'Sorry. I had my reasons. That's why I am calling you. Have you seen Jack recently?'

'Some bastard's holding her hostage.'

'I know where.'

'So do I. I'm in the house next door and I'm scared that a major police presence might…'

'You're right mate. She's being held by a puppet lawyer of

Crommelin Bolin, Roger Ambrose. Know him?'

'You're way behind the eight ball, Mands. I have a bloke called Bob Clayton surveilling the place until he feels safe to make a move.'

'The Bob Clayton, of Recoverance Inc?'

'That's him.'

'Well, I have confirmation that Ambrose is holding her as a lure to attract you. Whatever you do stay away and leave it to Bob.'

'Easier said than done. I don't even know what he is doing to her, and she's already been through far too much.' He looked out of the window. 'It's getting dark. If Bob is planning anything, you can bet it won't be until four-am.'

'Yep, the old rules of war, attack your enemy when he's in his deepest sleep.' She paused… 'I can tell you, Mick. Nothing will happen to her while you stay away. Bolin has issued a memo to his minders inferring that if anyone with your skin colour approaches lethal fire is approved. He's listed some friendly cops, and a couple of judges who can be influenced.'

'Shit.'

'Top of the town, Mick, and we're just the bunch of plebs expected to do their bidding.'

'Shit, Mand's there's someone banging on the back door. Back in a tick.' Mickey kept the line alive and rushed to the rear entrance of the property. He peered through the window but could see no one. He scratched his head and tentatively opened the door.

***

'Grab her Mickey. I'm going back…' Bob Clayton shoved the limp body of Jackie through the door. 'She's been drugged. Dunno what it is but you'll need a medic ASAP.' Clayton turned and ran back in the direction of next door. It might have been harder to rescue Jackie if there had been a more secure method of fencing. As it was, he was able to kick out several wooden palings and make a big enough gap to lift her through.

He returned through the gap and made his way to the unlocked back door. The exercise had been made much easier because of Ambrose's sedentary lifestyle. When Clayton sneaked into the house, he'd found him away with the fairies in front of a large TV displaying a poor-quality porno movie. On the table beside him were a box of tissues, a pump action bottle of COVID hand sanitiser and a three-quarter empty red wine bottle.

Clayton had fingered his garrotte—the easy way out—but he decided there would be more to gain by keeping Ambrose alive. He was deeply unconscious and didn't notice him taking a series of photos with his phone.

Instead of the easy way out, Clayton removed a roll of gaffer tape from his backpack and taped Ambrose to the chair he was reclining on. By the time he'd finished the man's feet, Ambrose was awake.

He shouted, 'Siri, call Bolin.' The tape around his mouth silenced him.

Clayton ended the call and then used the same phone to snap more photographs, as potential evidence in the abduction of Jackie, and to call James Carter.

He gave the address and advised there was a man restrained by gaffer tape and perhaps the police might like to attend. He followed it with a text, and the photos as an attachment.

'Who is this?' James replied.

'Roger Ambrose. I'm a lawyer and I'm a bit tied up at the moment.' Bob Clayton ended the call and wiped the phone over with a tissue soaked in the COVID sanitiser. He returned to the BnB, let himself in via the rear door and found his daughter, Beatrice. 'Where's, Mickey?'

'He couldn't wait. Fi's driving them to hospital. Sorry again, dad.'

Clayton drew her into a hug. 'Been a bit of a pressure cooker for you, girl. What with trying to get clean and having all this action going on around you.'

She gave him a squeeze then pushed him away. 'It's okay, Dad. I'm just glad you're here, and I am doing my best, I promise. You got those girls away from them. That's the most important thing. Now you need to finish the job.'

66

She'd done all she could and now she needed to get home to her family. With all the relevant data stored in her cloud drive, an intuitive IT pro might be able to detect her access, but she felt comfortable that no one would know about it until after the hammer fell.

Mandy Stephenson was a careful driver, and she took it steady until she reached her home. The lights were off, which was not unexpected but when she reached up to put her key in the lock, the door opened at her touch.

The instant panic infused her blood stream with adrenalin. She rushed in to find the TV volume turned down and her partner and child asleep on the settee. She touched her on the shoulder, 'Jeanie, I'm home and the front door was open.'

Jean awoke confused and bleary-eyed. 'Sorry, I locked myself out yesterday. I felt such a fool, so I put it on the latch while I did some gardening. I must have forgotten. How did your trip go? You look like you've been sleeping in your clothes.'

'All good and it feels like that to me, too. I'm just going to grab a shower, and I'll see you in bed.' She lumbered into the bathroom and turned on the shower.

A few seconds later Jean heard Mandy's terrified scream. She rushed into the bathroom to find her partner naked, the shower running and a large partially beheaded rodent getting cleaner by the minute. She reached down, picked up the creature by its tail, 'How did that get in here?'

Mandy shook her head. 'Don't look at me, I've had more than enough ratus-ratus for one day.' Mandy wrapped herself in a towel, returned to the bedroom, and removed her Glock from its holster. 'Shit is about to happen, Jeanie, and I'm thinking it might be better if you head down to Margs and stay with your mum for a while.'

'You think…' she looked down at the rat and grimaced. 'You think *this* might be to do with your work?'

'Something big is about to break and when it does, it'll get worse than random rats in the bathroom.'

'Are you involved?'

'I'll be the one breaking it. Get the bub, get into bed and stay there.'

Jean tossed the rat into the bin and washed her hands before picking up their child. 'What will you be doing?'

'Making sure you are safe. Now go to bed.'

***

Mickey left Fiona in the car with Jackie, while he headed for the ED. As expected, it was packed with the kind of late-night revellers who preferred their revelry chemically enhanced. He queued at the triage desk, getting more frustrated by the minute. Eventually he strode to the front of the queue and flashed his police ID.

'You'll have to wait like everyone else,' the harassed nurse said.

'She is in my car, is the victim of a crime and is suffering from some kind of drug. If you won't get me some help, I'll carry her in here in full view of your CCTV.' He blurted. 'That'll look good on my report when you find yourself failing to assist.'

The nurse's face froze into a look of shock. She turned and spoke to an ambulance paramedic from another case who was standing behind her.

He made his way around to the public side. 'Where is this "victim"?'

Mickey replied, 'You'll need a gurney, she aint walkin.'

The man left and returned with a hospital trolley. 'They're full on at the moment. So…'

Mickey led him to the car park and Fiona stepped out of the car. 'No change,' she said.

'Have you any idea what she's on,' The paramedic said.'

Mickey tapped on the screen of his phone and two strings of Cyrillic characters appeared. 'Try this. The first one translates as *walking dead* the second, *back to life.*'

'Never heard of them.'

'Well, one thing is for sure, unless she receives treatment, and soon, she may never recover.' He scrolled down to the name of a doctor. 'This man was responsible for treating several young women who had been subdued with a similar drug in readiness for being trafficked to an eastern European brothel. It is possible he might still have some of the antidote.' He helped lift Jackie onto the trolley and followed the Paramedic back into the ED.

The man parked the trolley in an examination space and said, 'Wait here, I'll see what I can do.' Before he disappeared into the melee.

***

James Carter had finished speaking with the officers who'd brought Roger Ambrose in following Bob Clayton's call. He'd been charged with hostage taking and placed in a cell while his

413

lawyers were contacted. At last, he could sit down at his desk and scroll through his abundant emails. Nothing looked too urgent, but a note with several docx attachments, from Mandy Stephenson, caught his eye. He opened one that was a letter purporting to be from Crommelin Bolin to Roger Ambrose. The text of the supporting email included an apology, explained how she came by the documents and how her actions would probably prevent them from being used as evidence. She went on to say, "However, they should be enough to initiate a warrant, based upon reasonable suspicion, to search his various premises and computer files."

Most people turned white at the mere mention of Crommelin Bolin and James Carter was no different. The very concept of searching Bolin's various outstations sent spasms of horror through his body. He picked up his phone and said, 'We'll need to meet.'

'Were and when?' Mandy Stephenson said.

'Preferably away from here.'

'I'll call you back.'

While he waited for Mandy to call, he began scrolling through the various other documents she'd attached to the email. On their own, each was enough to make life difficult for Bolin. Together they would represent a ticket to a long stretch in jail, but as Mandy had mentioned in her email, the way she recovered them would likely render them inadmissible. He needed to think carefully. He needed to act responsibly and most of all he needed to be within the law because one false move could flip the guilt back on him and his team.

It was believed that Bolin had most of the judges in his pocket and politicians had been known to go as far as changing laws to prevent action being taken against him. He reflected on the last breakthrough that led to traffickers being slowed down and how they'd agreed that to minimise the clogging of the legal systems they'd only prosecute those who could be categorically proven to be in deep. They'd let a lot of prominent but "minor" perpetrators off the hook. The documents Mandy had retrieved showed that to have been a mistake, and they were now leading the charge for the new wave.

He called Arthur Bertram and explained his predicament.

'Ambrose is as shifty as buggery, Jim, and he's close to you know who. Let me know where and when Sergeant Stephenson wants to meet, and I'll join you. The walls in here have eyes and ears. Well-done, Jim.'

The tone and brevity of Arty's response confirmed his concerns. One false move and everything they had done might be jeopardised.

His phone beeped it was a text from Mandy. She'd sent him the GPS coordinates for the meet, and a time. He texted Arty with the details and headed for his car.

Mandy's car was parked in isolation. There was no sign of Arthur Bertram's, and he decided to park further up the road and walk back. When he arrived, he found Arty in the passenger seat, engrossed in the information held within Mandy's computer. He knocked on the window, opened the rear door and squeezed onto the rear bench. 'Waddya reckon, sir?'

'I reckon she's done well, Jim, but now we must make it stick. Think you can get Ambrose to talk?'

'As you said, he's a slippery customer and he'll have all the financial backing of his client, who has the most to lose.'

'And all we have to lose is our careers.'

Mandy said, 'Maybe I could slip a couple of the docs to the press via an encrypted address. There'd be an uproar if any of them decide to use it, but it might just…'

'Let's try Ambrose first, Sergeant Stephenson. If DCI Carter can get Ambrose to admit to something, that might be the better shot. We can fall back on your suggestion if all else fails.

'I think DCI Carter has enough information to pressurise Ambrose, if not Bolin. The sooner we can get warrants, sir, the sooner I can get on with doing my job.'

67

Bob Clayton had left his daughter confident she was capable of looking after herself, for the moment at least. His next stop would be the rehab in the hills. The three girls would be prime targets with the momentum gathering, and while he knew Siddhartha's previous career had set him up for most situations, a bit of extra help might be needed. He hoped, welcomed.

He drove up the wildflower drive and stopped outside the main entrance. He didn't even get the chance to step out of his vehicle before a man in saffron robes descended the short set of steps. It wasn't Siddhartha but he looked as toned.

'I'm here to see Siddhartha.'

'I know. We were expecting you. Please follow me.'

Clayton was a little stunned by the comment, and his guard was up when he stepped out of his car and followed the monk into the deserted temple building.

'Please wait here, sir. Someone will be with you in a moment or two.' The monk floated off silently, to somewhere in the building.

Clayton knew Siddhartha's background was similar to his own and there was a feeling of doom permeating the place. He didn't need to wait long before a tall blonde woman appeared.

She wasn't dressed as a monk, but in business suit more like a senior executive of a large company.

'Mr Clayton. Thank you for coming. This establishment is a Crommelin Bolin Corporation's staff rest and recouperation facility. Is there anyone you particularly wished to see?'

'Siddhartha?'

'Ah yes, Mr Siddhartha. He is no longer with us. Is there anyone else?'

'What about the three girls that were admitted a few days ago?'

'Yes. They are here, but they are being cared for under the direct supervision of Mr Bolin who has instructed me that they must not meet with anyone without his prior permission. Will that be all?'

Clayton weighed up his options. He knew Siddhartha wouldn't have given up without a fight and there was a fair chance that The Bolin Group would have made sure any corporate transfer paperwork was watertight enough for one of their legal hacks to wave it about in a court. 'Thank you, Ms?'

'Granger, Malone Granger. May I see you out?' She sidestepped him and walked to the entrance.

Clayton felt the tug of the garrotte in his pocket and suppressed the urge. He followed her to the door and stepped out into the fresh air. There was now an eeriness about the place that concerned him, and he had no intention of going far until he figured out what was causing it. He started his car and headed down the drive, noting in his rear-view mirror that Ms Granger, *is that really her name*, remained watching him from the main door.

Once on the main road, he checked his GPS and found a number of places where he could park his car in relative privacy.

Once that was taken care of, he would return using maximum stealth. Now convinced that Bolin had beaten him, and everyone else, to the draw it was time to take off the gloves and start fighting dirty. He called Angela Carter and told her of the takeover.

'You can bet they'll have that tied up as tight as a drum, Bob, I'll look into the details and see if I can find out who handled it, and what else I can come up with.'

He thanked her and pressed end. *Whatever she comes up with will need a serious fallback position.*

A rough gravel road led off the main and the GPS showed a turning circle about two hundred metres into the bush from the junction. It also placed him relatively close to the rehab boundary. He parked hard over so that anyone else, who happened this way, would be able to pass easily. He then unpacked the contents of his pack and lifted the false floor to remove the holstered pistol that he would prefer not to use. He slipped his belt through the holster, then checked its magazine and the two spares in the stowage.

As expected, they were both fully loaded and gave him thirty-six shots, *if I can't do the job on one mag, I'll be in trouble.* A silencer lay in a slot next to the spare magazines, but he elected to ignore it in favour of the six throwing knives on the opposite side of the case. If a shootout was to start, the sound of his shots would more likely indicate that he'd have failed.

He hoped there was a fair chance that Siddhartha was being held somewhere within. disposing of bodies, even for Crommelin Bolin, presented problems. He figured their plan was probably to stone wall and keep the girls from view until all legal avenues had been taken care of. After that they might accidentally fall from a bridge, or a tall building, in the dead of night. Problem solved.

Finding Siddhartha might give him a head start.

***

The doctor assisting with the recovery of the kids, who'd fallen under the spell of George Gregory, was no longer available. He'd moved over east and was now working in a hospital in New South Wales. Mickey held his head in his hands and struggled to comprehend how this had happened. One minute she was his bright-eyed wife-to-be. Now she was little more than a locked in mute with no control of her bodily functions.

Without the back to life antidote that is the way she might stay. It was unacceptable to him and all attempts to contact the doctor led him into a mire of red tape and professional privacy twaddle.

It was Jackie who had discovered the drugs in Gregory's Peppermint Grove mansion, and it was Jackie who jammed a needle of the stuff into Angela Carter's arm to prove it worked. Now she was unable to take advantage of her discovery. He stared at the lifeless body on the bed and remembered how James Carter had communicated with his sister.

Jackie was staring directly ahead only the occasional blink indicating she was alive. He raised himself from the visitor chair and looked directly into her eyes. 'Can you hear me, Jack?'

Her eyes blinked.

'Can you remember how Jim Carter communicated with his sister.

Her eyes blinked.

'Left for yes, right for no?'

Jackie's eyes flicked left.

'They've used that drug on you.'

Her eyes flicked right.

'The doc who treated the girls has moved and there is no way of getting access to any of the antidote he might have kept.'

Jackie's eyes blinked rapidly.

'What's wrong?'

Her eyes flicked right several times.

'Are you trying to tell me something?'

Her eyes flicked left.

'Do you know where there is some?'

Her eyes flicked left'

'Where?'

She blinked several times.

'At home?'

Her eyes flicked right.

'Angela's?'

Her eyes flicked right.

'With Stacey?'

Her eyes flicked left, and she blinked several times.

Mickey grabbed his phone and punched in Stacey's number with his finger.

'Mickey? How's things.'

'Do you remember when your daughter was drugged by Gregory's mob...'

'How could I forget?'

'Jackie left some of the antidote with you?'

'I can't remember it was so long ago, and I was a bit uptight if you remember.'

'If she did where would you keep it?'

'We have a locked cupboard for drugs. You can't be too certain when you have kids around.'

'Would you check and see if there is anything with what looks like Cyrillic text on it?'

'Can I call you back?'

'Soon please. I have a major problem that it might help with.' He heard the line go silent and turned to Jackie. 'Let's hope she stashed it rather than tossing it.'

Jackie's eyes flicked left.

***

Bob Clayton silently made his way to the rehab boundary fence. It looked new and appeared to have cables entwined through its fencing wire.

'Shit… They've rigged alarms.' He'd found himself in this situation before. *Tampering usually unleashes an attack from those who set the alarms, you'll need to work with extreme caution, Bobby.* He looked around to see if there were any options immediately noticeable.

The area either side of the fence had been cleared back to bare earth by the contractor, and he couldn't visually detect sensing paraphernalia other than the wires interlaced through the fencing. That didn't mean it wasn't there. He stayed bush side of the cleared land and made his way along the fence line. Then he grinned. The contractor had placed a sign on the wire that declared who had proudly constructed the fence. He tapped in the number on the sign.

The number went to voicemail and requested his information to receive a return call.

That's not going to work. He called Mickey, explained his predicament, gave him the number, and asked him if he could make contact with the contractor.

While he was on the phone to Mickey, he saw a tall thin barefoot man in a straw-hat, shorts and a tee-shirt. He was calmly tending a vegetable garden and while he had never met Siddhartha, he guessed who he might be from the descriptions of others.

422

He took his binoculars from his pack, hooked up his phone and homed in on the man's face. The resulting close-up picture was forwarded to Mickey with a text.

Mickey responded almost immediately, confirming Clayton's guess. *Now all I need to do, is get his attention without drawing the wrong attention to myself. I can't shout.* He remembered that Siddhartha was ex-special forces, like himself. He took out his torch and flashed it in Siddhartha's face. It seemed to do the trick because he turned his head.

Clayton then tapped SOS on the torch flash button.

Siddhartha stood and looked about before picking up his spade and a bucket and heading in the direction of the light. He stopped about five metres short of the wire and said softly. 'Mr Clayton. So good to see you, sir.'

Clayton tossed a burner phone over the wire. It landed within half a metre of the monk, who bent over, picked it up, and dropped it into his bucket before heading back to his vege patch.

68

It seemed like forever before Stacey responded, meanwhile it appeared that Bob Clayton had made himself known to the rehab people. Mickey Krakauer was torn between leaving Jackie alone, at the mercy of the hospital staff, or contacting the fencing contractor. The second message he received told him that Clayton was in proximity to Siddhartha. He had a gut feeling that Clayton might now be on top of things and decided that Jack was more important, so he waited for Stacey's call.

He took Jackie's hand in his, rested his head against her flaccid body and allowed his aching fatigue to win. He could not estimate how long he'd been out when he felt a tap on his shoulder.

'Hey, Mick. Stace found this. She asked me to bring it to the Hospital.'

Mickey focussed his bleary eyes on the intruder and saw that it was DCI James Carter. 'Shit sorry, boss. I must have dozed off.'

'Well, Stacey said that this is the only bottle with Cyrillic text in our drug cupboard. Is it the right one?'

Mickey grabbed the bottle and turned it around to check the label. He tapped on his phone and found the picture. 'Yep. Now all we need to do is get it into her.' He looked into Jackies's eyes and said, 'Stacey's come good. wanna give it a go?'

Her eyes flicked left, and she blinked rapidly.

He pressed the call button, and a nurse arrived.

Holding up the phial, he said, 'This is an antidote to the drug she was given. It's Russian and there are no instructions.'

The nurse stood her ground. 'I can't.'

'Well find someone who can, or I'll do it myself.'

She scurried from the room and Mickey searched around for a syringe. There was nothing in the room.

***

It was almost dark when Bob Clayton's phone buzzed. The number was that of the burner he'd thrown to Siddhartha.

'I've heard of you, Mr Clayton. David Ashton-O'Sullivan mentioned you in one of his texts.'

'Then you'll know I'm here to help Mr Castle.'

'That is no longer my name, but I am in a difficult position, Mr Clayton. My charges have all been secured in a locked storage room and I am unable to make contact with them. I have been warned that any communication with the outside world will place them in danger of losing their lives. These people regard them as their enemy and have hinted they will be silenced, anyway.'

'What do you know about the perimeter fence, Geoff?'

'Nothing. Despite my best efforts, I was overpowered and have limited freedom.'

'I need to get in there.'

There was no response.

'Geoff, Siddhartha. Think, mate, we have to work this out and you might need to briefly shove aside your vocational aspirations.'

The line was still silent.

Clayton heard a rustle in the bushes beside him. He turned to see a bony face peering at him through the scrub. 'Sid?'

'Geoff Castle, Bob.'

'If you got here, I can get there, right?'

A hand gestured and Bob Clayton followed soundlessly to a small gate that was almost invisibly inserted in the fence.

'Shit.' Clayton whispered.

'They do not know about this. I knew the contractor and I was able to negotiate.'

Clayton smiled.

'He believes in karma.'

'Could we get the patients out?'

'Sadly no. They are all securely imprisoned.'

'How could we achieve their release?'

'Not without a fight.' Siddhartha turned his phone screen towards Clayton and showed him a photograph.

'Virtual SWAT squad.'

'Nothing virtual about it. They are all heavily armed and if they find that I am missing, the balloon will go up big-time.'

'Then we need to move quickly.'

Geoff Castle pulled a nunchaku from the back pocket of his shorts. 'Like you, I have martial arts skills but to use them I will need to be up close and personal with our enemy. Now you will understand the problem.'

Bob Clayton patted his holster. 'I've about thirty-six rounds, plus this.' He removed the garrotte from his pocket.

'Dyneema twine?'

'A metal detector won't register it, and it's about as silent as they come.'

'There is a common room. They have guards posted around the perimeter and specific buildings. Think you can use your choker on a few?'

Clayton grinned.

'Follow me.' Siddhartha moved silently through the gate and

Clayton followed him to his first victim.

The man was leaning against a wall, half dozing his way through his cigarette. 'Real pros,' Siddhartha whispered.

The only sound that followed was a low-level gagging and the zip of a ratchet before he lowered his target to the ground and moved on.

'That was easy. Somehow, I think it will get harder.' Siddhartha glided over the ground to another sentry and Clayton dispatched him with similar ease. He pointed to a larger building. 'That is where the patients are being held in a cellared storage room.' He pointed to the guards at each door and whispered, 'They are not very attentive, but I believe they will fly into action if we make a mistake.'

'Think we could get the patients out and through that gate?'

'It's a big ask, Bob.'

'You up for it?'

'I am certain there are only guards on the outside of the buildings, but there may be others hidden from view.'

'Where are the keys held?'

'Each guard has a full set.' He looked at the sky's fading light. 'There'll be a change while they have their meals.'

'Perfect. Keep that nunchaku handy. You're my backup.'

***

Jackie blinked her eyes rapidly and flicked right.

Mickey was puzzled, she'd said yes to the drug now she was saying a forceful No. 'Why have you changed your mind?'

She flicked her eyes right several times and then held them in that position.

Mickey shook his head then he noticed the small cabinet beside the bed. He pulled open the drawer and saw an open pack of syringes.

Jackies eyes flicked left.

'Fuck, babe, you're a genius.' It took Mickey less than a second to grab one and draw in some of the antidote. He swallowed hard, inserted the syringe into the piggyback connector and hoped he hadn't killed the woman he loved.

Nothing happened.

'Shit, Jack, I'm sorry. I...' He felt her fingers squeeze his hand. Then her head turned towards him.

'I want out of here, Krakauer... Now if you don't mind.'

James Carter patted his friend on his shoulder and said, 'What she said.'

The nurse returned with a young doctor.

'She's awake.' The doctor said.

'Right first time, where are her clothes? We're going home.' Mickey Krakauer had become accustomed to argy-bargy when it came to his freedoms and when the young medic shook his head, he almost lost it.

It was a combination of Jackie and DCI Carter's input that reduced the heat of the moment to a mere warmth. 'I'll take full responsibility for Ms Morton's safety,' He showed his ID to the doctor. 'She's a significant witness in a major investigation. And we require her availability immediately.'

'Her clothes should be in that locker.' The nurse pointed to the cabinet that held the syringes.

Mickey told everyone to get out while she dressed, and he remained to help her. 'Never thought I'd be putting your clothes *on*, girl.'

She murmured, 'Thanks, Krakauer, you're such a gentleman.'

They both laughed loudly causing the medical staff to peer around the door.

The nurse presented a self-discharge form for signature and looked relieved when Jackie signed it.

69

Just had a text from Angela Carter. They've closed the rehab down. It's now a staff R&R for the Crommelin Bolin Corporation.'

'What!?' Clark Shipton spluttered. What about Kaitlin?'

Kelly Coulson shook her head. 'As far as I know they are being looked after but...' She hurried from the office and closed her eyes.

Shipton picked up his desk phone and hammered in Mickey Krakauer's number.

There was no reply, so he left a voicemail. 'What the fuck's going on with the rehab, Mick. I thought all this was sorted.' He slammed the phone down and poured himself a large whiskey. 'Kelly. Get back in here.'

Kelly returned and sat in the chair opposite her fuming boss. 'Angela also said that Bob Clayton was on to it, so...'

'He was the Bub in Recoverance Inc?'

Kelly nodded.

'There's some hope then, I guess. What can *I* do Kel?'

'You have some influence. Even the premier was droning on about the special philanthropic assistance you've given to remote communities. Maybe a word in his ear. Would you like me to get him on the phone?'

Shipton shivered. 'I've never liked begging, Kel.'

'This wouldn't be begging, boss. You might simply ask him how the new takeover of the rehab might affect the girls you helped save from sex slavery and see what he comes up with. You can bet your life he's close in with Bolin, even if it is only from a position of political necessity.'

'Good thinking, Kel. Get him on the blower, invite the bastard for dinner. Anything, anything that will get his immediate attention.'

Kelly smiled. 'Onto it. Oh, and Mickey called, Jackie's looking good. She's out of hospital and firing on all cylinders.'

***

They continued their progress around the compound until Siddhartha stopped Clayton with a light touch to his arm. He pointed to a large building that was shrouded in darkness, and whispered, 'That is where they are holding the patients. It also has a concealed cellar that is used for storage purposes. We hold important drugs that, if it became known, might attract the wrong visitors. They have no conscience and there is every possibility they might have incarcerated the girls in that space.'

Clayton held his binoculars to his eyes and indicated the positions of sentries. 'Three of the buggers, would that be right?'

Siddhartha's silent nod told him all he needed.

'I can get at least one with this.' He held up the garrotte and gestured to the furthest man. 'That leaves one each and silence will be of the essence.'

The light had almost entirely given over to darkness and the bright stripe of the Milky Way overhead provided enough of a glow for their adjusted eyes to see by.

Siddhartha held up his hands as if clutching a soccer ball. He made a twisting motion and whispered, 'Nunchaku for fighting. Other ways kill a cat, Bob.' He waved Clayton on with a finger, pointed to himself, then to a man whose face was lit by a mobile phone, and moved silently towards his quarry to wait for a signal from Clayton.

Clayton dispatched one dozing sentry with the garrotte and moved silently towards the other.

The man must have noticed something and became immediately alert. Clayton heard the familiar sound of a charging handle and stepped for cover. It *had* been too easy. He looked around and saw Siddhartha grappling with a man on the ground. 'Shit.' He heard a crack that sounded bony and focussed his attention on his immediate problem. All the sentries seemed addicted to their phone screens, so their night vision was already impaired, and Clayton took advantage of his relative invisibility to confront the man face to face. He grabbed the rifle and shoved it aside while he lunged with one of the throwing knives and lacerated the guard's belly.

The brief burst of automatic gunfire would have set the entire hills area on edge, had it continued. Instead, it alerted the backup crew who began emerging from a building on the opposite side of the compound.

Clayton turned to focus on Siddhartha. The sentry and Siddhartha were locked in a frozen embrace on the ground. Neither moved. A flood light lit up the compound and he could see why.

He raised his hands and faced the group of men who were approaching him.

'On the ground face down!'

Clayton complied and waited. A glimmer of blue light caught his eye. The sound of heavy vehicles deafened him to everything that was happening, and he looked up to see an armoured police vehicle surrounded by armed men who were ordering the residents of the compound to drop their weapons. He felt a hand on the neck of his shirt. He was hauled to his feet and dragged into what he assumed was a paddy wagon. The door was slammed shut and he was alone.

***

'I've done the best I can Jim. Bolin's businesses are being turned over as we speak, and a swat team is.' He looked at his watch. 'About now, at the rehab centre. Can't promise they'll save anyone but there'll be a few arrests, and Bolin is surrounded by lawyers awaiting the start of your interview with him.' Arty grinned. 'The Premier's pissed off, Bolin's his golfing mate, apparently.'

'Any news of the rehab patients?'

Arthur Bertram shook his head slowly. 'Sorry Jim, they're all in the lap of the gods right now.'

'Thanks, sir, let's hope we can make things stick.' Clayton stood and texted Mandy Stephenson as he made his way down through the building to a reception area that was teaming with masculine and feminine suits. 'Good evening, ladies and gentlemen, so glad you could make it. Which of you is representing the accused?'

Several hands rose, simultaneously.

'Sorry, you will need to decide among yourselves, which one of you will attend the interview.' James Carter raised his eyes to see if a solitary hand rose. None did. 'Very well. I will ask the accused who he wants, and the rest of you can pick the bones of what is left.'

'Sir?' Mandy Stephenson smirked as she entered and saw the array.

'We have an interview to conduct, Sergeant Stephenson.' James opened the door and gestured that she should lead in. He then shut out the growing hubbub and took a seat next to her, across the table from the glowering persona of one of Australia's wealthiest men.

Mandy introduced herself and her boss, noted the date and time pressed the button on the recorder and cautioned Crommelin Bolin. She then said, 'Like everyone else you are entitled to have a lawyer present. There are several waiting outside perhaps you would advise which of those waiting you wish to represent you.'

Bolin said, 'No comment.'

'For the tape,' James said. 'Mr Bolin has refused a solicitor.'

Mandy opened a file and spread the contents across the desk. 'Recognise anything, Mr Bolin?'

'No comment.'

'You realise that the charges against you are serious and human trafficking, along with not only the supply of narcotics but the use of drugs to incapacitate human beings, carry serious penalties.'

'No comment.'

'Very well, sir.' Mandy stood, opened the door and drew the attention of two uniformed officers who were standing by. 'Take Mr Bolin to the custody suite please.' She turned to face Bolin. 'Perhaps you will have something to say tomorrow.'

'You can't hold me. You know who I am.'

'Custody suite, chaps.' She closed the door and grimaced. 'Epitome of fucking evil, boss. Sorry about the F word.'

'Call for you, sir.'

'Who is it?' James Carter asked.

'Says her name is Malone Granger. She says she's the manager of the Crommelin Bolin Rest and Recuperation Centre. Isn't that the place we just raided?'

'Thanks.' James made his way to his office and picked up the phone. 'Ms Granger. What can I do for you?'

'You can tell me why your armed thugs have just turned up at the establishment I run.'

'Oh, I see. You are exactly the person I would like to speak to. If you give me your address, I'll have someone pick you up and bring you to the station.'

'I beg your pardon.'

'It's okay Ms Granger I can find your address if you won't give it to me.' He heard the pips of another call waiting. 'One moment please.' He switched to the new caller.

'DCI Carter, it's Clark Shipton. My daughter is currently at the…'

'Yes Mr Shipton. We know, and a police raid has just been completed. I have no word about the patients yet but as soon as I do, I'll make sure you are one of the first to know. Is there anything else?'

'I've waited a long time to get her back, and if anything has happened to her, I'm not sure what action I might find myself taking.'

'I understand your concern, sir, and you can be sure we are doing everything in our power to bring this to a successful conclusion.' He switched back to Malone Granger. 'Three young girls were brought into your establishment for drug rehabilitation. What is the position regarding these children?'

'I have no knowledge of any children. Our establishment was acquired for the R&R of the employees of the Bolin Corporation.'

Another call began pipping in the background. 'First thing in the morning make yourself available for interview at nine fifteen, at the police headquarters Your failure to do so may result in a warrant being issued for your arrest. I have another call.' He switched lines.

'Sergeant Black, sir. Our task has been completed. Four bodies have been found one of which belongs to a Buddhist monk known as Siddhartha. We found no children in any of the buildings. Mr Robert Clayton is on his way for questioning, and a full report will be on your desk in the morning.'

'Shit. Sorry, thanks, sergeant.' He ended the call and phoned Mandy.

'No kids? Where would they have taken them?'

'If indeed they took them anywhere. The warrants are still open so I want that place turned over for anything that might link it to Bolin or those girls. Their new boss is coming in tomorrow morning for a chat. I'd like you to be there.'

'I'll contact Mickey and get a team together. See you tomorrow, boss.'

***

Bob Clayton had seen little during his brief confinement in the paddy wagon. He was fully expecting to be cuffed and charged with the unlawful killing of the rehab guards. He wasn't even cuffed when he arrived at the Police HQ and was escorted directly to the office of the commissioner.

'Mr Clayton. Good to meet with you at last. Please take a seat.'

Clayton obliged but said nothing.

'You probably weren't aware of the police raid that stumbled on your attempt to free the girls you had once rescued.'

'Bit of an understatement, Commissioner.'

'We have been gathering evidence that points to Crommelin Bolin as a key figure in the trafficking trade. We were hoping to find some corroboration, subsequent to the raid, but there were no signs of the girls. These children are of course prime witnesses.'

'They'll be there. We just need to find them. Siddhartha. He was the man who set the place up as a drug rehab facility. He told me the building they were being kept in.'

'We found no one.'

The building has a concealed cellar that they used for the storage of some of the specialised drugs they used in their rehab process.'

The commissioner pressed a button on his desk.

'Sir?'

'Escort Mr Clayton to the rehab centre, immediately.'

'Sir.'

70

It was the early hours of the following morning when Mickey and Mandy arrived with their team. The sun peeping above the escarpment gave an eerie light to the now deserted establishment.

'Where do we begin Mick?' Mandy said.

Mickey scratched his head. 'The last time I was here it was all sweetness and light. Then Siddhartha got dead helping Bob Clayton do his thing, and the police raid cleared the place out.' He pointed to the lawn area. 'That was where they were brought on the first day. I can remember Clarkie getting all tearful, but where they took the girls after that? Who knows?'

'I guess we should go through each building until something turns up.' She stopped talking when a car entered the gate at speed.

It screeched to halt, and Bob Clayton stepped out. 'That building, Mickey. It has a concealed cellar entrance.' He began a fast jog to the veranda and flung the doors open. 'Kaitlin! Agnetha! Bronwyn!' He stopped to listen and shook his head. 'Let's hope we're not too late. Rip it apart Mick. They'll be in here somewhere.'

Mickey summoned his men, and they began methodically

dismantling the walls and flooring. The area was divided into small rooms that might have been used for meditation purposes and there was little in the way of furniture other than incense burners, large beanbag cushions and yoga style mats.

'How would Jackie do this,' he said aloud. He remembered how she let herself fall into a relaxed trance and very soon found the antidote phials in an unassuming plain wooden box in full view of anyone who might have entered the room.

He plonked himself on a bean bag and tried to emulate Jackie's way of things.

'Sleeping on the job, Sergeant?' Mandy Stephenson said.

'We're looking for something hiding in plain sight, Mands, and we can look till we're blue in the face, but we'll never see it.'

'Over here!' Bob Clayton's voice echoed through the emptiness of the rooms. 'I think I've found something.'

When they arrived, he was peeling a yoga mat from the floor. It seemed to be held down with Velcro and made a sound like someone's pants tearing. Inside the Velcro on the floor was the almost invisible line of a possible trapdoor.

'I can't imagine this would be difficult they would be up and down all the time if it was a drug store.'

Mickey tapped the area. It didn't sound hollow. 'Maybe this is a fake.' He turned to the members of his team who were nearest. 'Rip up every one of these mats.'

Soon the sound of tearing filled the air, and another voice yelled, 'Got something sarge.'

This time the outline of the trap door was clear and there was a small, recessed, clasp at one end. Mickey jammed his finger into the indentation and pulled.

***

As the morning progressed, Crommelin Bolin was, once again,

escorted to an interview room. This time Mandy was replaced by a constable who went through the same procedure as the night before.

James said, 'Have you changed your mind about a solicitor?'

Bolin said nothing.

'Very well, your silence tells me you are refusing legal advice. Is that so?'

Bolin said nothing.

'No worries, I have allocated the entire morning. Would you like a cup of tea, a glass of water?'

Crommelin said nothing.

The constable in attendance began asking questions from a list he had been handed.

Each time he asked a question Bolin said, 'No comment.'

The interview was well into one hour of no comments when the door opened. 'DCI Carter. Phone.'

Bolin's face was a picture of smugness when his inquisitor left the room. The recording device had been switched off and he felt confident enough to inform the constable that the police had no evidence. 'And I'll be out of here within the hour.'

Five minutes later the door opened, and James returned. 'Good news. The rehab patients have all been found alive, and though not entirely well, they're all singing like canaries, and you, Mr Bolin, are charged with several accounts of abduction with the intent to harm. Read him his rights and take him down to the cells Constable. We'll deal with him later.'

Bolin smirked and then stood to follow the police officer as if he were her pet dog.

***

Mickey called Shipton to tell him his daughter was fine. Kelly took the call.

'Thanks, Mick, I'll let him know.' As an afterthought she asked about Jackie.

'She's good, Kel, and she's looking forward to the big day.

'I'll give her a call. She might feel like doing a bit of shopping.'

'Good idea, she hasn't had much of a chance lately.' Mickey let the line go and returned to the bus that was being used to transport the various patients to an alternate rehab unit. It seemed that the work Siddhartha had done had worked wonders and even though they were strung out for a fix, they were all thinking positively.

'When can I see my dad?' Kaitlin asked Bob Clayton. 'And what about Bron? She has no one.'

Mickey chipped in his four penneth. 'Clarkie said he might consider adoption. The silly old fool is a reformed character these days.'

Bronwyn grinned and hugged Kaitlin, while Agnetha looked downcast.

'We'll still be mates, Aggs and once you get set up with your dad again, everything'll be great.' Kaitlin drew her friends into a group hug. 'You'll see.'

Mandy struggled from the hatch holding a large box. 'This'll make interesting reading for someone.' She pulled out a swag of files and lay them on the table. 'It's all in here.' She returned to the cellar and returned with a ten-litre jerry of petrol. 'Reckon this wasn't scheduled for the filling of a vehicle any time soon.'

'You guys seem to have this all in hand, so I hope you won't mind if I head home to my daughter. I've neglected her for too long.' Clayton patted Mickey on the shoulder. 'Thanks Mick. You've been a great help.' With that he turned and headed towards the perimeter fence and its special gate.

'Think that'll be the last we see of Bob, Mick?' Mandy said

'He deserves a break, and you seem to have everything in hand, so I need to get home to Jack. She needs a break too.'

***

'It's about Agnetha, Kristina. Is anything happening in respect to her father?'

'How are you, James?' She didn't wait for his reply. 'Yoh, there is some good news, but it might take a little while. I am so sorry about Lars Berglund, James. I thought he was one of the good guys. Just shows how wrong we can be.'

'And the good news?'

'Daniel Byquist's case has come up for review. It seems that Mr Berglund was very much involved with his arrest for murder, and as you know…'

'What about Agnetha, she should be reunited with her father.'

'This is what we are working on. As I said, it might take some time.'

'Has anyone tried to track down her mother?'

'She has disappeared off the face of the earth, I'm afraid.'

'You realise that Agnetha has a temporary visa that could easily be revoked. Some more positive move in respect to her father's release would be helpful. Can she at least have telephone access? We can arrange for her to be available at a suitable time.'

'I will speak with my superior, James. He has more inflytande than me…' She paused. 'I think it's what you call clout.'

James ended the call with a feeling of despair for the kid, stranded in Australia, with one parent missing and the other in jail on what might be trumped-up charges. He called Athur Bertram and left a message. If anyone had enough clout to kick arse in Sweden, it was Arty.

71

Clark Shipton had been doing his own undercover work and he had arranged to do a bit of shopping before his scheduled meeting with the state premier. They had become close since his dramatic switch to the philanthropic side of the law, and he was patiently twiddling his thumbs, in the anteroom adjacent to the premier's office.

At last, the door opened, and a sharply dressed woman spoke. 'He'll see you now, Mr Shipton.'

Shipton hustled to his feet and followed her into a spacious office.

She pointed to a chair at a meeting table. 'Take a seat, sir, he won't be long.'

Shipton had been through a similar process several times in the past. It was a tactic used by people with power. Five minutes passed before another door opened and George Wakely entered. He was accompanied by the sharply dressed woman and a Harry Potter lookalike in horn-rimmed spectacles.

'Clark, so good to see you again. All I'm hearing, is the good work you're doing with our disadvantaged folk.'

'That's not the reason I'm here, Mr Premier.'

'Oh, you can call me George when we're alone, Clarkie.' His

smile as charming as ever.

Shipton moved his head to acknowledge that others that were now sitting at the table. 'Maybe you will think differently after I say what I have to say.'

George Wakely's eyebrows rose, and his forehead creased with a frown. He nodded towards the others. 'Leave us please.'

The woman and man left, pulling the door shut behind them and the premier frowned. 'Say what you have to say.'

'You have a close friendship with Crommelin Bolin, I understand?'

The Premier gave a strange sort of crooked shrug in response.

'Not that close then.'

'Mr Bolin *is* a major sponsor of my party, I can't deny that, but whether that makes us close friends…'

'Are you aware he is right now, in custody over links to child slavery and human trafficking?'

One of George Wakely's eyes twitched. 'That is the sort of thing a man in my position must seek to distance himself from. I hear you got your daughter back from a place worse than hell. How is she?'

'Much better but the rehab facility she was placed with, was crushed on the orders of Bolin. My daughter was imprisoned along with other patients of the facility, and I'm hearing that arson might have been considered, to close off any possibility of her or her friends, giving evidence of their abduction.'

The premier's face stiffened.

'They found the accelerants close to the place they were being kept. It was only a matter of time, but he was interrupted by the heroic actions of certain people.' He handed the premier a clear plastic folder. 'This is a list of the Bolin connections, suspected to be in league with him.' He handed the premier a copy of the list

Mickey had given to him.

The blood drained from the premier's face. 'You realise what this would do if it became public?'

'Reads a bit like a who's who, doesn't it.'

'Is that likely to happen?'

'I think so, and I believe it would be in your best interest to pre-empt its release. Don't you agree?'

'There are people in my government who are listed, and some are highly respected.' He shook his head. 'If I were to pre-empt the release of this information, I would almost certainly lose government.'

'If you don't pre-empt its release, you will almost certainly lose government anyway because they'll all be locked up. Thing is, there are plenty of members of your opposition who are also implicated...'

Wakely pursed his lips. 'I need to think.'

'May I respectfully suggest that you think fast, because this will hit the news outlets very soon. No one can keep Crommelin Bolin in a police cell for long, without the word finding its way to the media grapevine.' Shipton stood. 'I hope that one day we can be friends, George. There is so much to be done, and I need you to be there for me.' He stood and left, pulling the door closed behind him. *It's up to you now, George*, he thought as he made his way to the ground floor. He *was* planning to walk back to Northbridge, but he saw a taxi slow, and he lifted his hand.

Kelly Coulson seemed surprised when he arrived back so quickly, 'That was a short meeting, boss.'

'He has the information, and he's been given the opportunity to kick some arse, Kel. It's up to him now. Hey, I am close to having my family together at last. We've always got along so well and... You know... Katie needs a mother figure in her life more than ever now.

'What are you leading up to Clarkie?'

Shipton reached into his briefcase, removed a small velvet covered box and handed it to Kelly.

Her face drained of blood when she looked down at the thing in her hand.

'Open it.'

The moment she saw what the box contained her eyes filled with tears. 'Oh, Clarkie, it's beautiful.'

He lifted the ring from its slot and slipped it over her finger before she could respond further. 'I'm not that fancy but…'

'Of course I will… You dope.'

***

Mickey's return to his home was met with a hug and a wide grin from Jackie. 'What's the big deal?' he said.

She showed him her phone with the text from Kelly. 'He's been and gone an done it and she's accepted.'

'Ha! Who'd a thought it.'

'And I'd never have thought I'd be about to tie the knot with you, Krakauer…'

'Well, you've only got a couple of weeks to back out. What's for tea.'

'Takeaway and you're getting it.'

He looked down at his watch and then hit the uber eats app. 'Might as well watch the news while we wait.'

Jackie curled up beside him on the settee and rested her head on his shoulder. 'Guess what? There's compo coming with my pardon. They called today.'

'How much?'

'Dunno, but I don't care anymore. I just want it behind me.'

The news started up with a bright red "BREAKING NEWS"

followed by the premier standing before cameras and announcing an election date.

'Several members of my government have decided they will not be standing for re-election so there will be an opportunity to bring in some new and forward-thinking younger blood, and room for the promotion of deserving back benchers.' He went on to broadly thank those who were leaving followed with a word salad relating to policies.

The news reader then made passing reference to a police incident at a drug rehab facility situated in the Eastern Hills of Perth before continuing with other news.

'No mention of Bolin then?'

Mickey smirked and said, 'It's good that Clarkie and Kelly have got together. There's always been a bit of a spark between them. I suppose we'll get an invite to their do.'

'What about Bolin?'

'Something tells me that Clarkie's been pulling a few strings. I guess it'll all come out in the next few days.'

The news reader said, 'In news just to hand, it appears that the offices of one of the country's most successful businessmen have been simultaneously raided around Australia, by the federal police and the WA Serious Crimes Division. We understand that a yet to be named person is being held in custody and we'll keep you posted as more details emerge.'

'I think you just got your answer, Jack.' The doorbell rang. 'That'll be dinner. Hope you're hungry.'

72

The following day the news bulletins led with bevy of politicians, Both State and Federal, spouting sob stories about their families coming first and how it was time to step aside from the intensity of the political life. A flurry of speculation surrounded the person in custody, and it wasn't until later in the day that the Arthur Bertram, the WA Police Commissioner made the statement that shut down all speculation.

'I'll be brief. In order to quell the continuing rumours, I am confirming that we are holding Mr Crommelin Bolin on a range of charges. As these matters involve potential future trials, I will be saying no more. Thank you.' He stepped away from the microphone and left through a door to his rear.

'Well done Arty,' James said. 'Now let's get on with eradicating this filth from our society.'

'Bit profound for you, darling,' Stacey said.

'And the work is only just beginning, Stace. Sorry, I'm gonna be flat out like a lizard drinkin.'

'Will that be any different to usual?'

'Well, there is a wedding to attend, and Mick sent me a text saying that Clark Shipton and Kelly Coulson have declared themselves to be an item, so there might be another.'

'How are those girls?'

'They're doing well, and they've handled their traumas better than anyone could have expected. The trouble is the poor kids will soon be subjected to interrogation as witnesses. Hopefully they might remember something that can be used in a court. I'd never have thought it, but Clarkie has applied to adopt Bronwyn, or Jessica, whatever her name is.'

'Well, that *is* good news.'

***

'Hey, Mick. I guess you've heard the latest?'

'We're both very pleased for you Clarkie, I knew Kel always had a soft spot for you though I couldn't for the life of me guess why.'

'Cheeky Bugger. Look mate. Tell me to fuck off if you like, but it's Kelly's suggestion.'

Mickey said. 'What, now?' He flicked the phone to loud so Jackie could listen in.

'Kel said I was to offer to pick up the full costs of your wedding as long as we can do ours on the same day at the same venue…'

Jackie was taking a sip of her wine when she heard what Shipton said, and she snorted wine everywhere. 'No way. It's our day Mick.'

'Hear that, Clarkie?'

'Pretty much what I said she would say, but we'll be inviting the same mob, more or less. Anyway, give it some thought and let me know.'

Mickey pressed end and stared into Jackie's eyes.

'Suppose he has a point, Mick, but I'm not into doin one of those double wedding thingoes. I've waited too long for this.'

'Has Kelly contacted you about a shopping trip?'

'Yeah, I said in a couple of days' time.'

Before he could say anymore his phone squawked.

'Yeah!'

'DCI Carter, Mick. I'm using a burner. Things are moving fast, and we'll be all-hands-on-deck for a while.'

'Why the burner?'

'Sergeant Stephenson has discovered some intelligence that leads her to believe the Police HQ communications are deeply compromised. We can't afford to take any risks. Arthur Bertram has approved the provision of secure comms for the whole task force. If we let go of Bolin, we're done.'

'Shit.'

'We'll be setting up at the rehab place with a specially prepared coms van, so don't come in here tomorrow. Let only those you can trust know and I'll meet you there.'

'Okay, boss.'

'Bring Jack. I don't want her left alone and I'm sure we can find something useful for her to do.'

Mickey pressed end and turned to Jackie. 'I've just been given permission to bring you to work with me tomorrow. I hope you'll behave yourself.'

Jackie said nothing.

***

The next few weeks raced by, punctuated by news reports of suicidal politicians, wailing wives yelling, "police corruption" at every opportunity, and Crommelin Bolin's day in court for a preliminary hearing. Everyone was relieved when he was remanded in custody to await trial in six months' time, but his legal team clicked into overdrive, and he was bailed within two days.

Clarkie and Mickey's relatively informal barbeque cum

wedding day went off without a hitch, their brides seeming completely at ease with everything including each other. Some described it as the love-in of the century, and it even made prime time news.

While the politicians continued the metaphor of throwing themselves on rusty swords, almost in total secrecy, Arty Bertram and Angela Carter tied their knot in front of a minimal number of guests. James Carter acted as best man, and Jackie Morton looked splendid in the role of matron of honour.

After six months of utter turmoil things settled down, Mickey and Jackie transferred to Warakurna. Mickey, as officer in charge of the local station, and Jackie, along with the financial assistance of Clark Shipton, took on the role of establishing a state-of-the-art medical facility.

The political vacuum and the shake up in the local business world had caused rumbles in the stock exchange but it soon recovered. The premier was re-elected on an improved majority and the only person left without a prominent future role was Kelly Coulson. As it happened, she wasn't too worried. She joked, I still have Clarkie to look after and that's a big enough job for anyone.'

Crommelin Bolin's arraignment was classic. The court filled with a multitude of silk garbed lawyers, and he walked away free, if a little poorer, at the end of the trial.

Despite becoming a pariah in business circles—few would wish to be tarred with his brush—Crommelin Bolin's wealth and influence soon returned and the disappointment throughout the newly restructured police force was manifest. Under the orders of Arthur Bertram, Mandy Stephenson was promoted to DI and put in charge of cyber investigations. Crommelin Bolin was placed under an officially approved covert data surveillance program. One misstep would almost certainly draw him back into the court.

Then one day, twelve months later, almost out of the blue, Jackie Morton received a cheque for two-point-five-million dollars in compensation for her wrongful imprisonment. She read the accompanying letter and sat for a long time staring at the strange piece of paper with a monetary sum that was calculated by some nameless person to be the gross worth of ten years of her life. Then she burst into tears and called her husband. 'Mick they've given me a measly two-point-five-mil for ten years in the slammer while that arsehole, Crommelin Bolin has walked free.'

'I'll speak to the ALS, but I think that might be about the going rate. But, hey, at least you're fully exonerated.

73

While the shakeout in government and the business world occurred, Bob Clayton melted into the crowd. He bought a suburban home close to medical facilities, his primary concern being his daughter's recovery. She had, so far, done well and with encouragement from Fiona had rapidly progressed through her recovery.

Clayton had attempted to keep his distance from Fi — as he called her — she seemed to want so much more than he felt he could realistically give, and that was despite encouragement from Beattie.

'Fiona likes you a lot, dad. I reckon the pair of you would get on like a house of fire.'

'Might be a bad choice of metaphor, Beats.'

'You know what I mean. You should really make an effort, she's lovely, she loves you to bits and she's my best ever friend. Without Fiona I'd probably have been straight back to the nick. You know that don't you?'

Clayton had already been through the anxiety of separation caused primarily by his job. 'It wouldn't be fair to her, Beats. The sort of business I'm in doesn't work well for relationships.'

Beattie turned and glared at him. 'But you've retired… You have, haven't you?'

He didn't dare tell her of the burner-to-burner text message he'd recently received from Major David Ashton-O'Sullivan, MI6 — supposedly — retired. If he accepted the challenge, he knew he could not predict the outcome or whether he would even return at all. This wouldn't be a simple extraction job involving kids and the criminals who trafficked them. Those ops had a fixed time frame and relatively incompetent opponents.

If what David was hinting was true, it would mean crossing the lines into a serious enemy territory. The Russian mafia were small fry by comparison, and he looked directly into the eyes of his daughter.

'Shit, dad. You haven't retired, have you?'

Bob Clayton said nothing.

Beattie's face erupted like a blacksmith's embers on the bellows. 'Ha!' she stood and stormed to her room, slamming the door fiercely behind her.

'If you like I'll talk to Fi. See what she thinks,' he called after her. *Well, that didn't go down too well*, he thought. He'd already arranged a meeting with Ashton-O'Sullivan. After that he'd know exactly what he was in for. This time he would be working under the auspices of the British government and MI6. His life had become charged with excitement and excruciating danger ever since the day he qualified for the SAS. He'd survived everything the regiment and the enemy had thrown at him, and he could feel his blood fizz with the thought of an even greater challenge.

Bob Clayton knocked on his daughter's bedroom door. 'Hey, Beats, let's not get all wound up about this. Nothing has been decided, why not invite Fi over for dinner and we can all chew over our future.'

'You invite her, you don't need me. Then maybe…'

'Maybe what?'

'If you don't know I'm not spelling it out for you.'

'I have a few photos that I'd like to show you, if you'll indulge me for a few minutes.' He heard a movement from within and then the door opened to a teary faced Beatrice.

'Okay. But it changes nothing.'

Clayton led his daughter back to the settee and said, 'I'll be a couple of minutes. Don't go away.'

She dabbed at her eyes and thought about the trauma she'd been put through by her parents. How her mother had dumped them both when she first started out on her adventure with drugs. Her father wasn't much better, never home when he was needed. Then one night he turned up and dragged her away from the people she'd thought of as friends. They didn't care they were just as addicted as she was. Beatrice looked up when he entered the room carrying what looked like a distressed shoe box.

'I thought you said a few.'

Clayton smiled, sat down beside her and opened the box. Most of the photos had a look of age about them but there was no way of knowing who the subjects were. Someone had gone to a lot of trouble to sort them chronologically, with separators, and the first one he removed was a picture of his ex-wife. 'Your mum. She didn't leave you, she was killed in a hit-and-run. You were too far out of things at the time, so I just said she'd gone away.'

Beatrice looked hard at the photo of the attractive woman she remembered as her mother. 'Dead?' She turned to her father and noticed a wetness in his eyes that she'd never seen before.

While she was contemplating the first, he began flipping through the stack, then he pulled another from the pile. It was the same woman, but this time she was holding a child.

'Me?'

Clayton quickly showed her another.

'Ha! I remember that day. We had such fun... What happened to me, dad?'

'Nothing for a while, but when you go through these pictures, the one thing you might notice, there are none that feature me. I was barely a part of your life, except for these that came in letters from your mother, and I lived for the moment we were all together again.' He dabbed at a wayward tear. 'Your mum was the one who cared for you while I was away. She could never know when I'd return... or even if I'd return.'

'But you were divorced.'

'No, we never got the chance to try that approach. One day I received a notification that she'd been killed...' This time he couldn't dab a wayward tear way, there were too many. After a while he recovered his composure. 'I was sent home on compassionate leave, but it was too late for you, and I've never held it against you that you didn't attend her funeral.'

'I didn't know she was dead. I thought she'd just buggered off... Shit, dad.

'It happens every day to some poor sucker. I never stopped loving her, Beats, and as things were, I could do nothing for you. I made the decision to step away from the army and the rest is history. Now here we are. You're on your way to a full recovery and you have a friend a million times better than any I've ever had...

'Fiona?'

'The day I met her on a plane... I thought... well, you know.' He dropped the photo of Beatrice's mother on the table. 'But *she* won't go away.' He felt his daughter's arm curl around his shoulders, and he felt a huge surge of grief of the kind, he'd thought he'd never experience.

'I'm going to call her. This is no way to live, dad.'

The meeting with David Ashton-O'Sullivan took place on a park bench in a deserted riverside picnic area in Guildford. O'Sullivan had grown his beard long and he looked more like a refugee from a Ned Kelly movie set, than a top MI6 Operative.

'You'll have heard the term "plausible deniability" Bob?'

He'd lived with it for a long time until one day a press release dragged many of his colleagues into a war crimes debacle that should never have become public knowledge. 'Didn't help some, Dave.'

'The Bond movies call it, a licence to kill. At times that is our only job, and we do it cleanly, if it's possible to use that word in this context. However, in this op we will be plausibly deniable. Though we will have access to arms as needed and we'll be prepared for the worst that can happen. If the worst does happen it will be every man for himself, and we will be issued with capsules. You know what that means?'

Clayton knew what his friend had referenced. The secrets he'd become privy to must never be leaked in a smart arsed press release. If necessary, a cyanide capsule would be there to relieve him from the worst depravities the evilest of torturers could apply, and in the event of his death, his involvement or existence would never be acknowledged.

'Heard of the Weddle Sea?'

'Part of the British Antarctic Territory?'

'We'll be inserted into a Russian operations group who are planning to conduct drilling right there in the Weddle. They are desperate to find covert reserves that will help propel them to victory in Ukraine and their next adventure.'

'Wouldn't the Royal Navy be on to that?'

'They'd like to be, but for the Antarctic Treaty, and the risks of a ship-to-ship confrontation would be too high. They are watching from afar and our job will be to provide intelligence that might ratify any future actions. You speak Russian, don't you?'

'Un peu. I can get around in it, but I wouldn't say I'm fluent.'

'Perfect. Your persona will be that of a defecting, disgruntled, English ratbag who'd prefer the Russian style political system.'

'And you?'

'Similar but I will regard myself as far superior to you, and I have fluent Russian. I might be an obnoxious bastard, and we might even get into a punch up or two.'

'What will they do if they find a viable source of oil?'

'They've developed a new way of submarine drilling, and they won't be too concerned about environmental concerns.' O'Sullivan paused, then he said, 'Your uncanny photographic memory will be needed because there will be a long haul and there will be nothing to reference if this goes ahead.

'I'll need to think about it, David. Beatrice is doing well, and she must be my primary concern. I have your number.' He stood and walked one way while O'Sullivan walked the other.

***

'Hey, Jack, at least with your compo, you'll be able to afford something spiffo to wear for the inauguration.'

'Inauguration?'

'You haven't heard then.'

'Am I ever likely to?'

'Clarkie. It hasn't been publicly announced yet, but he's dead cert for the next WA Governor.'

'Clarkie!? With his background? Surely not.'

'He's never been charged with a crime and there've been rogues in the role, in the past.'

'Wow! Have you spoken to Kelly?'

'Not yet, if you call her, try to remember it's not yet official.'

'That'll sorta make her royalty, won't it?'

'In a sort of in-loco-kingies way, I suppose.'

'Now you're being stupid, and I'll need to get down to Perth, quick-smart.'

'Thought you might… Say hello to their excellencies for me.'

The End

Author's Note

After the discovery of a human trafficking ring the news attracts, a pair guns for hire who turn up out of the blue with a proposal to rescue the daughter of a well-known Perth rogue who seems to have seen the ight. It is not intended as a work of fact more of a what-might-be in certain circumstances.

All names used in the novel are selected at random and have no intended relationship to any actual business or person, whether living or dead. Some of the places might exist, some don't. I include all places for the benefit of the story only, and there is no intent to malign or otherwise the honesty and efficiency of employees or their operational status.

Dan Cotton

About the Author

Dan Cotton spent the first fifteen years of his working life travelling the world with the Grey Funnel Line (Royal Navy). He then joined the world of commerce and pretty much carried on travelling as before. In the eighties, he started a business that eventually listed on the Stock Exchange and delisted in 1989 after the crash of 1987. He didn't make much money, but he learned the hard way, about the underbelly of high-end business operations and decided there were better ways to earn a crust.

Twelve years in the IT world kept him going until he decided to do his own thing and start an art gallery with a picture framing service. They are all in the past and in the event that he doesn't make squillions from his writing, he'll still be scratching away until he carks it.

*

Who is Dan Cotton? Sometimes, even he's not sure. He's one of those folks who, no matter where they are in the world, will always be mistaken for someone else.

*

Having written nothing more than business proposals and letters, he started on his first manuscript and soon realised he badly needed help. That's when he joined the Katharine Susannah Prichard Writing Centre (WA) and, with encouragement and critique from KSP's Thursday Night Group, he has been able to complete three trilogies comprising, "Triptych", "Toxic Trade" and "Terrorist". "WTF," "Quarry" and "Bird of Prey," then "Full Circle," "End Game," and "Spore". "Recoverance Inc" is the second novel of a fourth trilogy which includes "Traffic" and "Plausible Deniability".

He has also written a number of short stories, poems, and drabbles which are published in various anthologies. In addition, he has completed another full-length work, "The Second Meridian," in the speculative fiction genre.

Also, by Dan Cotton

Global warming has reached a tipping point, and The President of the United States believes the world will be a better place if split, north and south, by an imaginary border that protects the wealth of his powerful friends from a resource hungry world. Imported goods will have massive tariffs, technology exports overpriced, and all immigration will be banned.

The imaginary border, known as The Second Meridian, is only one part of his plan. Another is to send hundreds of handpicked elites into space to orbit, in pods, for the duration of the impending nuclear war, before returning to rebuild.

One pod escapes orbit, and with nowhere to go, the crew, five males and five females, must ponder their fate as they are drawn closer to the sun.

A retired special forces soldier is set to expose the corruption and decadence of the upper levels of Australian society. The day arrives to present his evidence but there is a glitch, and he is ordered to flee to Western Australia, where he finds himself in the frame for the murder of a 14-year-old boy.

The killer's intended victim, a lawyer about to start a new job with her old boss, a QC known for his success in prosecuting political corruption trials.

When the counter-terrorism laws are used against her current business partner, she suspects someone other than the elected government is controlling the strings of power, and her past comes back to haunt her

Only a man who had become a freak of nature saw the stealthy preparations for the invasion of our world by the strange inhabitants of a distant planet.

Before Magnus Campbell was killed by a terrorist bomb, he had implanted his psych into the quantum code he had developed.

While realisation was dawning on the world's scientists, that interstellar travel would be impossible without a break in the light barrier, his avatar had discovered a way.

For Magnus, a trip to Alpha Centauri is no more challenging than the flick of a light switch.

Acknowledgements

Thanks to my friends at the **Thursday Night Group** (attached to the Katherine Susannah Prichard Writing Centre WA) who are my major source of ongoing encouragement and inspiration. Without them, I might have given it all away (Some might say I probably should have). Thanks to Tim Nelson for quietly easing me through any matters relating to law and plot, and Victoria Mizen, Sue Carameli, and Kath Evans, for listening and providing their varied, fearless, and much appreciated female views on my blokey style. TNG is the one place where I know I can get that much-needed, wider audience viewpoint, delivered raw and unselfconsciously, and with sometimes hilarious results.

*

My greatest thanks are for my staunchest ally, Deborah. For being my life and business partner and managing to suffer through my angst and frustrations over the last 44 years without poisoning my coffee.

*

Last, but not least our Border Collies, Echo and Tika, and all the other departed dogs who have faithfully warmed my feet during the loneliness of the writing hours and who now lay at rest on our property.

1

Bob Clayton looked down at his phone, saw the text from his daughter and realised it was too late to back out. It was supposed to be dinner with the three of them. Beatrice, her friend Fiona and him. Now he'd been forced into sharing an intimate dinner with a woman twenty-plus years his junior, who he'd been trying to avoid. Not because he didn't like her. In fact, it was more because he'd been inexplicably drawn to her.

Clayton had lost his first wife, Beatrice's mother, to a hit-and-run driver, and he had since struggled to move on from her loss. Then he saw Fiona enter the restaurant and felt a rush of goose pimples the moment she smiled in his direction.

He stood, pulled her chair out from the table, and she brushed lightly against him as she moved past him to take her seat.

'The bitch called off,' she said with a smirk. 'I promise I had nothing to do with it, Bob.'

'Better make the most of it then, I guess.'

Her smirk turned to a smile. 'I can do that,' she said as a waiter handed them each a menu, popped a champagne cork and filled their glasses before beginning his specials-of-the-day mantra.

Clayton watched her face as she studied the fare. She had changed almost magically from a sophisticate to a little girl attempting to choose from a box of candies.

She frowned, then smiled and her tongue brushed her lips before she said, 'We are going Dutch, aren't we?'

'Sorry Fi, I'm an old-fashioned old stiff, maybe next time. Choose whatever you like.'

Fiona frowned again, and said, 'Okay.' She turned the menu towards him and pointed to her selections.

'Well then, we'll need a special drop of wine too.' He flipped his menu closed, raised his hand to attract the waiter, and felt another tingle of excitement as he made his choice and ordered for her.

What had started out as a frightening excursion into a relationship he'd been trying to avoid suddenly became an adventure not to be missed.

Her eyes sparkled as she sipped on her champagne and said, 'I wasn't expecting this.'

The evening progressed as easily as if they had known each other for years rather than brief interludes on planes, enroute to and from ops. Fiona laughed easily at his stupid jokes, and he hooted with delight when she enthralled him with stories of in-flight disasters.

He even told her of his secret ambition to one day buy a boat and sail around the world.

'Wow, I'd love to do something like that, one day,' she said. 'My dad liked to sail. He took us everywhere. I tried to get Beats interested, but it wasn't her thing.'

Clayton smiled, wistfully, 'I have a mate, Zac Merriweather, he's doing it right now and I sometimes call him on his sat phone. I'm as jealous as hell. He's having a ball and it's not like those non-stop publicity thingoes. He's just doing a world tour for his own pleasure and the last I heard he was somewhere in California.'

'If you ever decide to give it a go, I hope you'll ask me.' Fiona sucked in a deep breath and, hoping she hadn't been too presumptive, took a sip of her wine.

'I'll remember that.' His face took on a look of sullenness. 'Beats will have to be right, though, before I could even think of giving it a go.'

He was soon smiling again, and, by the end of the evening, they'd become a couple, cemented together by more than just the bond of his daughter. 'I'm so glad Beats is over it, Bob. I've seen people fall into massive holes once they go down the drugs path.' She reached out, rested her hand on his, and frowned when he flinched.

Instead of pulling away, which was his initial intent, he interlaced his fingers with hers. 'Coffee?'

'Yes, please, and thank you for such a special evening. I was worried that…'

'Me too. Maybe we should do this more often.'

Fiona bit her lip. 'Do you think Beats tweaked us into this assignation?'

'She's been on about you and me for months.'

'She told me you were still raw from the loss of her mother.'

'Time I grew up, hey.' He sipped at the coffee that had arrived before him and grimaced.

Fiona grinned. 'I'll make you a decent one at my place.'

The die was cast. His pulse raced as he paid the bill, and he felt a shivery thrill when her arm brushed against his as they walked into the cool night air. He hailed a taxi. She gave the driver her address and sealed his destiny.

***

He awakened in a bed scented with the body of the first woman he'd slept with since Beatie's mother. Guilt washed over him and he almost panicked, but Fiona wasn't there. 'Hey,' he called. The

3

apartment was as silent as a grave. 'Fi?' No response.

Clayton clambered out of bed, found the bathroom and started the shower running while he gathered up his things, which were left still strewn around the room where they'd fallen as they enthusiastically disrobed each other. He smiled. *Some night, Fi.* Then he noticed there were none of her things to be seen. He stepped into the shower, and as he soaped his body, it reminded him of the pleasures of the night. Embarrassed, he tried with difficulty to push the memory into a cupboard somewhere, in the hope his engorgement might… Too late. He felt her lips brush his shoulder when her hands reached around to sample what he had on offer. 'I called.'

'I'd run out of milk…'

Her lips found his and he lifted her up to him.

She moaned.

'Mmmm,' he responded from somewhere deep inside his chest.

***

After last night, his meeting later that morning, with David Ashton O'Sullivan, seemed to have paled into significance. He took his place on the park bench in the same riverside picnic area in Guildford as the last time they had met.

'Are you sure you haven't been followed?'

'Getting twitchy, David. It's not like you.'

'The bastards are watching everywhere, Bob. Are you on?'

Suddenly, the night before and the early morning delights took on a new meaning. 'Tell me what I have to do, and I'll tell you if I'm on.'

'Good man.' David Ashton O'Sullivan spoke softly and explained the nature of their mission in a little more detail than their last meeting. 'As I said, once before, this is deep cover stuff and if you're not up to it, then we should go our separate ways.'

'I'll need more details.'

'For obvious reasons, you'll not get *them* until you're fully committed.'

'When do we start?'

Ashton O'Sullivan glance down at his watch. 'As of noon today.'

Clayton glanced at his own watch it said twelve noon.

'There's a flight leaving Perth airport for London at 1430.' He handed him a pack of papers. 'A ticket and your new identity are in there. Don't go home. Tell no one. Contact will be made after you arrive.'

'What about you?'

'You'll know when I know.' O'Sullivan stood and walked away.

Clayton glanced at the ticket. He had only two hours before he'd be joining the cattle for a crammed economy flight to the other side of the world. 'Thanks Bib.' The thrill of another adventure began to seize his enthusiasm, and he did as he always did. He took a deep breath and expelled the excitement along with it. By the time the aircraft touched the tarmac in the UK, he would be Abraham Wilkes, a dreary incel with the scent of rank Ruskie body odour. He smirked. *I'm looking forward to our first clash, David. It might even make this stinking trip worthwhile.*

***

Beatrice felt smug. Her father hadn't returned to his bed after her creative manipulations and she didn't want to imagine what went on, but she couldn't help herself. She knew Fiona had the hots for him and she was glad that he'd at last found someone. Her phone rang at about one pm. 'Fi… Sorry I couldn't make it last night. I hope…' she heard a choke at the other end. 'What's up?'

'A meeting he said. I thought he'd be back. Has he contacted you?'

Beatrice shook her head and said, 'I didn't expect him to. I thought…'

'Well. you obviously thought wrong. I've tried to call him, but his phone is not answering.'

'Oh gosh. I hoped you'd hit it off and…'

'I thought we hit it off fine. I love that man to bits, but he could have at least dumped me to my face.'

'He's dumped you?'

'He's not answering his phone.'

'I'll try him and call you back.'

Beatrice dialled her father's number, and his cheery voicemail answered, asking her to leave a message. 'Shit.' She called her friend. 'Same, straight to voicemail. I hope he hasn't had an accident.'

'Can't have. If he had, the cops would be on to you as his next of kin.'

Beatrice remembered a night from her childhood. He'd kissed them both goodbye and turned up twelve months later as though the time in between had simply evaporated. He never discussed what had happened in the between time. 'Fi, I'm getting a feeling he might have a different reason than you think. Just to be sure, I'll call that copper mate of his. He might be able to do some checking around.' She could hear her friend's stifled sobs. 'Don't worry. It'll be nothing you'll have done. That I promise.'

Beatrice ended the call, tapped the mobile number of Mickey Krakauer and introduced herself when he answered.

'Hey, long time no…'

'It's my dad. He's not come home, and his phone isn't answering.'

'Oh, I'm sure he's just been delayed for some reason that isn't clear right now. There isn't much I can do, anyway, I'm at the

Tjukayirla Roadhouse and at least two day's solid driving from you.'

'Thanks anyway.' She ended the call and phoned Angela Carter.

'There isn't much the police can do until it's been a few days. If you haven't heard by the weekend, call my brother and tell him *I* said.'

'Thanks.' She pressed end and called Fiona again. 'Dead end, we'll need to wait a few days before the cops will take us seriously.'

'I had a lovely evening with your dad, Beats. I thought everything was good between us. Now I'm thinking I must have done something terrible to upset him.'

'He's not that easily upset. It'll be fine. He's probably got a bee in his bonnet over something, and he'll work it out. It was a big thing for him, and he might need some time to come to terms with his feelings for mum.'

www.ingramcontent.com/pod-product-compliance
Lightning Source LLC
Chambersburg PA
CBHW050602170726
48283CB00001B/72